ECHOES
OF THE
TIDE

Emma Hamm

ALSO BY EMMA HAMM

Deep Waters
Whispers of the Deep
Song of the Abyss
Echoes of the Tide

Seven Deadly Demons
The Demon Court
The Demon Crown
The Demon Prince

Dragon of Umbra
Fire Heart
Bright Heart
Brave Heart
Torn Heart
Taloned Heart

and many more...

Emma Hamm

Visit author online at www.emmahamm.com

Cover Design by Giulia Soeima
Interior Artwork by Seductighoul

As with every book in this series, lemme get up on a podium here and scream -

NONE OF THIS IS SCIENTIFICALLY ACCURATE.

Should you attempt to touch wild animals under the ocean? No ladies and gents. Leave the wild animals alone. Don't put your hand near a shark's mouth and certainly do not tempt fate without a certified guide.

The bends? Doesn't exist in this world. Water pressure was the only thing I really couldn't come up with a "Oh it works out this way" without completely changing the story line.

Yes, I know it's a monster fucker book that makes you think, and it's slow burn, and all of these are reasons why maybe I could have figured out a scientific way to fix these things. But the reality is, humans are very very soft little flesh bags and we're barely surviving on the land as it is.

So.

shrugs

I wish we were more sturdy creatures, but we ain't.

Chapter 1

You know you're worthless, don't you?" The voice haunted her in moments of silence.

It was the same voice that always interrupted her moments of peace. The sound of her father hissing right before she'd been arrested. Of course, Ace had been arrested a lot of times. But those words were from the first time her father had realized that his daughter was beyond saving.

It wasn't like Beta gave them a lot of opportunities. He'd been a man of few words and fewer talents, which meant he ended up working the odd jobs that literally anyone could do. Jobs that didn't pay well. Her mother had been out of the picture for years, which left just Ace and her sister to pick up the pieces.

Laura. The prettiest girl in all of Beta, who never had to worry for a single moment because her bulldog of a sister had always been right behind her.

Sighing, she shook her head and tried to dislodge the old memories. They didn't serve her now. She had to focus on the droid in her hands that needed repairing.

And still, the words came.

"Did you see Laura's sister today? Looking more and more like a man every day."

"A man? Hilarious. Those broad shoulders are there, but she's got an ass on her. Some thick thighs, too."

"That mug don't ruin it for you?"

"Turn her around and it won't be an issue!"

Snippets of conversations she'd overheard nearly every day walking with Laura, and that hadn't mattered in the slightest. Until it had been her own father saying it. And then, all of a sudden, it had mattered.

She took off her glasses and rubbed her eyes, before hissing out an angry breath when they slicked over her skin and left a burning sensation in their wake. Grease. She had grease on her fingers because she was working on the damn droids, like always. It was so easy to forget. But that was part of the problem, wasn't it?

Grease monkey. That had been her nickname before she'd been arrested that last time, and now it still was. Grease monkey in the city of Gamma, where they sent all the miscreants to rot.

A light tap on the glass in front of her brought her back to the moment. She wasn't in Beta with everyone laughing at her. She was right here, in the clockwork tower of one pillar in Gamma. And she had a job to do. Because her job was the one thing that defined her.

Her room was filled with bits and pieces of droids. Metal bobbins, wires, panels of droid pieces, all scattered around the floor haphazardly around her. A small cot in the corner was the only homey thing in the entire room, but then again, how was she supposed to make this homey? It used to be an attic. Empty, with a dented metal floor and heavy beams making up the walls and ceiling.

She'd chosen it for the giant circular window, though. Back when Gamma had first been made, this place had been a testament to the immaculate talent of artists. But then it flooded, and after it was turned into a sort of prison city. More like an experiment to see if they could throw people away without the guilt of murder.

The circular window had large bars through it, like the face of a clock. Hence the clockwork tower name that she'd given this place. Outside of that window was a small floating droid.

It had a cylindrical body, nearly a foot in length, with large flippers on either side that flapped in the water where it hovered. It wasn't much of a droid, but she'd put it together for one reason and one reason alone.

Hurrying over to that wall, she hit a button for an arm to grab the droid. Rigging that thing had been a lesson in patience—Ace was no engineer—but soon enough, it grabbed onto the droid. Drawing the whole thing in through the pressurized chamber outside, she eventually got her hands on the droid itself.

"There you are," she muttered, carrying the dripping metal to the back corner where her workstation was set up. "I haven't seen you in weeks."

Plopping it down on the table, she ignored all the water spilling onto the floor. All she cared about was the chip in the base of this droid that would give her the small details she needed to stay alive in here.

Grabbing the chip with stiff fingers, she inserted it into another box-like droid and greedily stared into the grainy screen.

Her sister stood in the same room where she usually was. Laura had become a gardener in the time since Ace had last seen her. The projection showed so many plants surrounding her sister, and she looked so happy. There was always a smile on her face these days. The room was decorated in art nouveau styles, with golden carvings of people surrounding her as she sat down on a bench and grinned at her plants.

This was the life that Ace had traded everything for. A chance for her sister to be something other than a grease monkey like her.

Touching a finger to the image on the screen, she blew a kiss to the only person who had stuck around after all her fuck ups. "Love you, Laura. See you soon."

She said the words every time the droid came back with new footage of her sister. Maybe because she was surprised the droid hadn't been blasted out of the ocean yet. No one in Gamma was supposed to have any kind of interaction with people outside of the city.

But she had already broken the law more times than she could count. Why not break it a few more times?

Replacing the droid before anyone realized it was missing, she returned to the job she was supposed to be focusing on. "Right," she muttered, sitting down and staring at the smashed droid. "You're supposed to be in one piece by the end of the afternoon."

Which she couldn't do by herself. Reaching into her pocket, she pulled out a string of magnetic beads that were anything but that. All the criminals here thought she kept a necklace with her. But Ace was significantly sneakier than that.

"You up, Tera?"

There were five beads in total. At the sound of the droid's name, they all rolled to look up at her. When Tera was actually awake, she looked like a handful of eyeballs.

Grinning, Ace asked, "You wanna fix a bolt drone?"

That woke the droid up pretty quickly. The beads all rolled in her hands, detaching magnets so individual ones could zip around the room. It was the most genius droid she'd ever created. Tera was essentially multiple individual droids in each of those beads. Magnets and hard drives in each one made it so that it could latch onto anything metal, roll freely, and still drag whatever it was attached to. In a matter of seconds, she had all the parts she would need to put the bolt drone back together.

"Droids make everything so easy." And that was why she loved them so much.

Then Ace got lost in her work, putting the drone together with hammer and screws until it was nearly as good as it had been before. The sounds of the workshop drowned out the memories that threatened her too still mind. No one could think when all they could hear was metallic bangs and zipping screws.

"Nasty little sucker," she muttered, making sure it was off before she placed it on the ground.

A bolt drone fired electrical bolts at anyone that moved in front of it. The weapon was a necessary part of living in Gamma. Too many people with too much violence in their bones lived here to be without protection.

She stood, cracking her back and trying to get feeling back into her numb ass as she stood in front of her window and looked through the water at all the other towers that made up this city. She'd heard once they looked like old skyscrapers, whatever that meant, with glass bridges that connected them. But each bridge was protected by another gang or segment of a gang that ran that particular tower.

Making friends with a gang was the best way to survive, and it was certainly what she had done. Fixing up drones so they could shoot anyone that tried to cross their bridge? Sure, she could do that. Make the bolts with higher electricity? Easy work. Whatever it took to stay alive in this place, even if that meant killing folks.

No one was innocent in these cities. Not even herself.

The trap door that opened into her room banged open. A dark, greasy-haired head stuck through it, and the man grinned at her. He was missing teeth, quite a few of them, but that grin somehow still made her smile back.

"You got it done?"

"Just in time."

"Good, the boss wants to see you again." He hauled himself up through the trapdoor and sat on the edge while letting his legs dangle. "So you really got it done? With the upgraded bolts?"

"The bolts I did awhile ago, Gregor." Ace wrapped everything up together, each in its own package, so the bolts didn't accidentally activate and then kill them all in a chain reaction. "What's he want with it, anyway?"

"Boss didn't say. I got a feeling it's something to do with those undine coming to see us." Again that gap-toothed grin. "You wouldn't happen to know anything about that, would you?"

Was that today?

Fuck. She hadn't realized it was today, and she wasn't prepared at all. The undine were coming here to make a deal, and she'd been part of that conversation. Ace had been talking to them for a while now and that... well, it had made everything a little complicated.

Talking to one in the same way she'd talked with Anya had spun her head for a bit of a loop. She wasn't entirely sure how she was feeling about it still. The undine had been capable of using technology. He had talked to her like a real person, and asked questions about things that she hadn't even realized they understood, let alone knew about. And then she'd worked with him to bring Alpha to the ground, which, on top of everything else, was the most surprising.

She had her own reasons for wanting to destroy Alpha. So did Anya, most likely. But the undine were an entirely uncontrollable part in the plan.

"Right," she muttered, looking around for Tera before gathering up all the steel pearls and sliding them into her pocket. "I know enough about it to be nervous. They're coming right now?"

"You're the one who set up the meeting."

"I know I did, I just... I lost track of time."

She looked out her window, and every thought in her mind trickled away.

The undine weren't just coming, they were already here. She could see their dark shadows sliding through the murk. Their undulating movements were so graceful and mimicked how she'd seen whales swimming in the depths. And these creatures were huge. Massive beasts with the torsos of men and women. Their tails moved up and down, flicking a silhouette of a massive paddle shape that propelled them through the water with ease. Each one of them had long hair that flowed behind them. Even at this distance, she could see the webs of their hands that slashed through the water and helped them swim even faster.

"Wow," she whispered, and Gregor stood behind her.

He whistled low under his breath. "Those are some big beasts."

"I heard they can get up to twenty feet long."

"Never seen one this close before. I've only seen them from far away, when they're lurking in the depths looking at our city." He pushed air through his teeth, then shook his head. "Never thought I'd be this close to one, either. Aren't they supposed to be real dangerous?"

"You've seen what they can do." All of them had. One of their own had been mad enough to swim out there on his own. He'd thought it was a good idea until the undine had caught up to him. She'd never forget how quickly four of them had grabbed onto each of his limbs and just... pulled.

He'd come apart like they were pulling on cotton candy. So easy that it seemed like there wasn't muscle, sinew, and bone holding him together.

"Come on," she said, her mind already fraying at the edges with that memory. "We've got to go see what the boss wants, right?"

"You're supposed to be managing the meeting, I guess."

"I don't know all that much about the undine. I just had a contact who knew them." But she went down the ladder after him, shutting the trap door above her head before heading into the main section of their tower.

They had one of the smaller towers, but that didn't make them the weakest. There were enough supplies here to last them several generations. Of course, this was a prison city. So what had once been a rather utilitarian area of Gamma was now in ruins. Store signs had fallen on the floor, some of the neon still blinking as they walked past. Barbershop. Butcher. Nail salon. She'd walked past them so many times that she hardly noticed them anymore. The stores were now empty, lights hanging loose from the ceiling and wires already torn from the walls. They were useful, these stores, but not for anything other than their parts.

Most people here lived in the ruins of old stores and homes that had once been beautiful. Some people lived in the alleyways or made the old dumpsters a bed. But everyone used the streets for fire and food. As they walked past small groups of people all clustered around burning trashcans, she filled her lungs with the scent of cooking meat.

Rats, mostly. Everyone here loved rat. They were easy to grow fat and strong, and they were quick to cook. She'd been so afraid to eat it when she'd first gotten here, but time had worn her down. A couple years in Gamma, and her stomach didn't turn as much when she smelled it. Rat just smelled like food, now.

She hated every second of living here, but it was necessary. Her sister needed her to do everything she could to ensure the safety of her last remaining family. Her father? He could rot in hell for all she cared.

Sighing, she skirted around another large group who had built their fire on the ground. They were all dirty and greasy, like the man beside her. Fresh water was hard to come by, and if they had any, it was for drinking. Cleanliness in this place was rubbing a dirty towel over her head and hoping she didn't look like a freshly drowned creature who had just come out of the bowels of the sea.

"Boss man said you know this undine?" Gregor asked, snagging a skewered rat from a fire that no one was tending.

"Sort of. I have talked with him a few times."

"They talk?" He ripped a chunk of the rat's back off and chewed loudly.

She'd never get used to that. "Seems like."

"Can't imagine what they have to say to us. Nothing good, I'd wager a guess."

She wasn't sure either, but she could only hope it was good. Because as she approached the large glass windows that had once been a dining area four stories high, the massive shadows of the undines chased her across the floor.

Chapter 2

Maketes surged forward through the water, ensuring the small bag he carried was still closed and everything inside was water tight. Mira had made it very clear that any water would have disastrous effects on their plan. He was not about to let any water into the bag. The translation device he'd been given needed to stay dry until it was implanted.

There was only one. None of his kind trusted the creatures who had summoned them, and he knew all too well that most achromos were bloodthirsty creatures. They could be dangerous, and he wouldn't take any unnecessary risks. His blood had heated at the thought then, and it did now.

But it was a beautiful day. The sea was bright with sunlight that sent beams through the water, and the silver schools of fish scattered as he blasted through them.

"Maketes!" One of the others in the pod called out. "Slow down!"

Those words had never been in his vocabulary. Slow down? Why would he ever want to slow down when the sea called for him to move faster?

With a laugh already bubbling free, he swam in a huge circle around the others. With his back arched and his tail rippling behind him, he was faster than the most darting fish. Nothing could evade him. Nothing could even catch him.

At least until a massive hand caught the back of his tail and yanked him back toward the others. He stared up into the disapproving expression on Agalma's face and tried not to anger her any further. She was the one running this whole mission, after all. Maketes was just here to talk with Ace and then get out. He wasn't supposed to do anything other than that.

He was definitely going to do a lot more than that.

As if she could hear the thought pass through his mind, Agalma's hand tightened around his fin. "Stop it, quick one. Your mind wanders too far from this mission and you're going to ruin it."

"My mind is firmly on the mission. Get in, implant the chip, see what answers we can get. It's not a hard mission."

Other than his interest in Ace. They'd been talking quite a bit since the end of Alpha, and he'd gotten the sense that Anya's contact had a lot more information than he was providing. Every question Maketes had, Ace had an answer for. Which could only mean that the man was involved deeper in Gamma than any of the others realized.

Maketes didn't trust anyone who was in a prison city like this. The moment Mira had told him what the city was used for, with Anya replying that it was even worse than what Mira knew, he had been the one who wanted this mission.

Not because he wanted to hunt the achromos. Not because he wanted to hurt anyone at all.

Simply because Ace hadn't seemed like a criminal, and he couldn't get that out of his head. Answers. That's all Maketes sought.

Agalma gave him another shake before releasing him. "Stay with the rest of us."

Right. Stay with the rest of them. Narrowing his eyes, he looked for the first opportunity to head out and explore this city. He'd go to the meeting first, of course. He knew how important it was. But if he zipped around the back of that tall building and then darted into the murky waters that were kicked up from the filtration systems of the city, no one would be able to find him. The other People of Water wouldn't stay looking for him for long. They didn't like this haunted city that always seemed like a gravesite more than a home for the achromos.

Then he'd be all on his own here, and he could explore.

"Maketes!"

Right, he was falling behind.

Zipping along with the rest, he made his way to the building the achromo had noted. Ace had given them the directions, and he had to admit, it had been easy to find. What he didn't understand was how Ace knew what the building looked like from the outside. Had the man gone out into the sea? Had he swum around the city even though the threat of Maketes's people was always there?

It was curious for any achromo to do that. They weren't a naturally intelligent or brave group of people, and he counted those who did go out into the sea as an altogether different kind of creature. The bravery it took to do that was far beyond the normal achromos he had seen.

Such were the reasons he respected Mira and Anya far more than the others. They didn't stay hidden in their stone and metal homes. No, those two women had gone out into the wilds so that they could explore. That was the mark of a true warrior.

They approached the building Ace had indicated and dove beneath it. As promised, one of the floors had been peeled up in preparation for the People of Water's arrival. Each one of those panels would eventually be replaced so his people couldn't get back inside. But for now, they were open because the achromo were open to talking with them.

The others hesitated. They stared up at the light above them and the slight tang of fear tinged the water. How were they supposed to talk to these creatures? The People of Water mostly had translation chips, so they would understand every word the achromos said. But the achromo in this building could not understand them. Nor did they really wish to.

He was the first to emerge from the water, making sure his entire head was visible as Arges had explained made them more comfortable. Apparently, only predators stayed low with just their eyes showing. He'd replied that the achromos should know by now that the People of Water were their natural predators.

High arched walls surrounded him on all three sides, each one made of glass covered in algae. The last wall disappeared into darkness, which he could only assume led to the rest of the tower. Black bars held the glass up and cast shadows on the groups of people all huddled around cylindrical cans full of fire. The people here were grimy. They were covered in dirt and oils from their own skin. He'd seen achromos before. They were not usually like this.

One of the groups peeled off from the others. A man at the front, dirty and dusty like the rest of them, swaggered with the confidence of a leader. He was surprisingly strong. The others were lean, but this man was almost puffy with muscles. His shoulders bulged, his arms nearly split the shirt he wore. It was an impressive amount of strength. Coupled with the pale blonde hair on his head and strangely light blue eyes, he was an intimidating creature, to say the least.

Maketes was big. But this achromo? He was almost half the length that Maketes was.

The others were less impressive. Three males with bald heads, almost identical to each other. They were large as well, but not nearly as large as their leader. Strangely enough, there was a leaner male and a female with them. He didn't let his eyes linger too long on what could very well be one of the male's mate, and instead focused on the man who walked up to them like he had no fear of the People of Water.

"Welcome," the male said, his arms spreading at his sides as if to show he had no weapons. "I have been informed you can understand us. Is this true?"

Maketes nodded, his gaze narrowing on the male. He watched the leader's expression as more of his people appeared above the water beside him. There were quite a few warriors who had traveled with him. An impressive show of power.

But this male didn't even flinch. He barely reacted to the others except to acknowledge their existence.

"Good, all of you are here, I presume? We called you here to make a deal. It's come to my attention that the undine have been looking to get a little more… involved in the human world. You took down an entire city piece by piece, and we want some of those pieces. Beta has a few objects of my desire as well, but that will come later when you have more need of us."

No, that wouldn't be at all what they did. Maketes didn't trust this achromo already.

"Why can't you get these objects on your own?" he asked, knowing full well that no one here could understand him. "Is it because you are so much weaker than us? Or perhaps it is because your stick-like little legs can't swim fast enough to get you there?"

A few of his people chuckled behind him. That was all it took for the male to guess that Maketes was making fun of him. The leader glared.

"I do not ask you to do this without offering my own form of payment. After all, this is a partnership I wish to continue." He gestured behind him and the thin male strode forward.

He was greasy and smelled like something dying, but there was a weapon in his hands. Something that looked similar to Byte and Bitsy. But it couldn't be a droid, because it didn't have a screen for a face or eyes. He was surprised that the achromos would offer them a weapon, and even more surprised when the thin male set it right by the edge of the water.

"Go ahead," the leader cajoled. "Take it. I want you to see what weapons we can offer you. This is a deal you won't want to deny."

Agalma moved first. She lifted the weapon quickly and darted back to the others, showing it to all the people. Maketes could already see how it worked. There was a slot in the front for something to be inserted, and then he'd seen Mira's ability to fire things like that with other weapons. It could shoot. That much, he was certain.

He looked at the male again, trying to see through his thin skin to the soul beneath. Why would he offer them weapons? The People of Water had no need of achromo weapons.

The leader was watching him. He didn't watch the other sea folk who were trying to figure out the contraption, no. He looked at Maketes as though he knew the real person he had to convince to take the deal.

"The bolts we have created are electric. They work underwater, in case you were wondering. One bolt, one weapon, and whatever you shoot will be electrified until you take the bolt out."

The female made a noise in the back of her throat. If he didn't know any better, he would think it was a sound of rage. But she was silenced immediately by a look from the male who led them. Even more strange behavior from the achromos.

He'd had enough of this. There was only one person he wished to speak with, only one discovery that meant anything at all in this strange meeting of two peoples. Maketes swam to the edge of the water where it met the floor and lifted his bag up.

Mira had been very specific. Take the device out of the bag and then hit the button on the top. Not something he could easily mess up.

Once he tapped the button, he braced himself on the edge of the floor next to it, listening to Anya's voice suddenly speak loud and clear.

"We've sent these undines here to barter with you. But we will only speak to the one who calls themselves Ace. That is the only person in your group we will trust, and no one else will get any answers out of us. The undine delivering this message has a translator. That translator will only be given to Ace."

The male snorted. "I'm not giving a translator to Ace. Clearly I'm the one in charge here. I'm the one you need to talk to."

Maketes lifted himself out of the water. Just to his hips, but then he was nearly the same height as the male. His tail lashed in the water behind him, lazily stirring up sea foam as he held the male's gaze. His black eyes had unnerved many an achromo before, and this male was no different.

When faced with dark eyes that reflected only the achromo's own terrified look, it was hard to remain so brave. The leader cleared his throat and took a step back.

"If it's Ace you want, then it's Ace you will get." He gestured with a waving hand behind him. "Come on forward then, Ace. Get your translator and we'll get this deal finalized."

Maketes would promise nothing. Ace was the only one who had a tie to Anya, and the only one who might cave if they told him what was at stake. Maketes didn't want to risk any of his people if he didn't have to.

Himself? Oh, he'd risk his own life every day. That was part of the fun. But the other People of Water who were here with him didn't deserve that.

The female stepped forward, and he waited for Ace to arrive. Then he realized she stopped right in front of him and he really looked at her.

She was unremarkable. A female who blended easily into the background. Plain brown hair covered her head, lank and limp like the rest of the people here. She had a pair of round glass objects on each eye that made her gaze seem a little larger. He could see the faintest dusting of freckles on her cheeks, but the rest of her was just as plain. Drab clothing hung off her form, giving her a rather boxy shape that seemed too large for her body. The boots on her feet had to be too big, because they clomped when she walked toward him.

A strange creature. Mira and Anya both stood out in their own way. Mira for her flaming hair and loud voice, Anya because of her gold locks and her soft smiles that drew people in. This female was neither of those things. She was secretive. Hidden in plain sight.

"You are Ace?" he said, his voice low with wonderment. "You're female?"

She didn't understand a word he said, of course. Both he and Anya had thought that Ace had to be a man. Only a man would be so foolish as to risk all that Ace risked. And yet... This was a female before him. A female with soft, brown eyes that stared up at him like he was looking into the depths of the sea.

He'd never seen a gaze that deep before. And in those depths, he saw a secret that was hidden from everyone else.

How he wanted to peel back every layer she'd built around herself to hide whatever that treasure was, just so he could plunder it.

Without a word, he reached into the bag and held the translator chip out to her. If she wished to understand him, then he would let her make that choice. But he found he desperately wanted her to choose... *him.*

Chapter 3

Ace really should have paid attention to what was being said, but she couldn't pull her attention away from the undine in front of her. She'd always heard they were big. She'd seen them outside the glass and knew they were big, but to see them right here? Right in front of her?

This was an entirely different circumstance than seeing them from beyond the safety of glass and sea.

The male who spoke, the one that pulled out the box as well, was massive. His hair had been slicked back from his head, revealing twin gills that abutted the sharp edge of his jaw. Yellow and lined with black details, they were so thin she could see his hair through them from where they were flat against his head. His webbed, clawed hands were massive where they rested against the floor. But her eyes were drawn to his pale chest, where more golden color streaked down in rivers from his shoulders to the scales that started at his waist and then disappeared under the water.

And then there was his tail. It was huge, like a giant eel

undulating underneath the water, but she couldn't stop staring at it. It was so big! Thick and powerful, the massive fluke at the end churned up the water into foam that soon gathered around his waist.

He was an ocean god before them, and every part of her seized in fear. What would he ask of them? She knew the undine wouldn't help humans without getting something in return.

She'd been more than a little furious when fucking Jacob handed over her newest weapon and then lied right to their faces. That bolt drone wouldn't fire underwater. Maybe a couple of times, but the electricity wouldn't work underwater. She'd never tested it, and frankly, she had a feeling it would electrocute everyone within a fair distance.

Gregor nudged her hard, then nodded at the boss. Right, she had been gestured forward. She was the one who was supposed to get the translation chip. Already she could see the rage on her boss's face. Jacob didn't like anyone being more important than him. He used his fists to make that point very clear for all who worked for him, and she was certain she'd be hearing about this the moment the undine swam away from the room.

But for now, she let herself feel a little thrill. She hadn't expected to get access to their language. Even as the yellow undine before her spoke, all she could hear was a loud, whale-like sound. The low, rumbling tones were captivating.

Breathing out, she made her way to stand before him and saw surprise in his eyes. Maybe he hadn't expected a woman to be here. Maybe he hadn't realized that she'd been a woman this whole time.

A lot of people didn't. Any of their contacts considered her genderless, as she sometimes wanted to be. The world didn't need to know what was between her legs to respect her.

The undine held up a chip for her, and she knew it was going to hurt. She'd only gotten one before when someone had moved in next door to her and spoke a different language. The screaming pain had been more than enough to convince her to never get another one of these again. Of course, she didn't have a choice this time. It was either one of those electric bolts to the head, or she was going to get this translation chip.

Not really much of a difference, if she was being honest.

She took the chip and then sank it behind her ear before she could second guess herself. Gritting her teeth through the pain, she stood there and stared into Maketes's eyes. All the others were talking around them. Jacob was saying something about a deal that would benefit both of them. The undine were murmuring behind Maketes, even the chattering of other people seemed so loud as the translation chip did its job.

But she was stuck staring into Maketes's eyes. The dark orbs reflected her own pained expression, the lank hair that clung to her face, because she was already sweating. When had she become this monstrous creature who stood before him? She'd never been pretty, but she'd never thought of herself as particularly ugly either.

What she wouldn't give for a bath. Or even just dunking herself in the ocean, so she didn't have to suffer with the grime on her skin anymore. And then the pain stopped, flipped like a switch, and she could breathe again.

Ace pressed her hands to her stomach, willing the meager bile to stay in her belly. She wanted to eat today, and she definitely didn't want to vomit up the rest of her stomach contents.

The yellow undine in front of her reached out his hand. The webs were more than just black, she realized. They glimmered in the light, like an oil slick. Countless colors all caught between his fingers and surrounded by deadly claws.

A trap, just like the angler fish she'd seen once before. A pretty thing caught in the midst of all those deadly claws.

"You are Ace?" he asked, and she understood him. It was a slow conversation, but it was there. Words.

"And you are Maketes."

Right here in front of her. It was the undine she'd been talking to for so many weeks now. Over a month, perhaps. She knew this monster in front of her, and it was hard to envision him like... this. Everything in her said he was just a man. She'd talked with him before, she knew who he was. He had a shrewd mind that saw a significant amount of details when he was planning quite literally anything. He had a funny sense of humor that never ceased to entertain her. He'd even told her about his life outside of destroying Alpha. But in her head, even though she knew what he was, she'd always imagined him as a human.

So seeing that he was right here in front of her, finally, but he wasn't the man she had imagined?

It was messing with her head.

Jacob stood behind her, a wall of muscle and angry energy. "What did he say?"

"He was just confirming I am who I say I am."

Jacob sighed. "I need you to give me an answer, undine. Weapons for your help."

She could see the mistrust in the undine's eyes. All of them. None of them believed the humans would stay true to their word. And she supposed that was fair enough. They'd been fighting with each other for a long time.

"He's telling the truth," she interjected, worrying only slightly that

Jacob would consider her to be stepping out of line. "He's not lying. I'm sure there are some humans who would lie to you, and they would try to do anything they could to get you to work for them. But the weapons are real. I helped make them myself."

She omitted that the weapons wouldn't work exactly as Jacob had said, but she could clarify that later. Right now, she needed this deal to go through. Because if it didn't? She was the person who would be beaten.

Jacob clapped a hand on her shoulder. "That's right. And it's a good thing you already talked with Ace, because she'll be helping you get what I want."

Wait, what?

She wasn't supposed to go anywhere. Ace had her spot in this tower, and that was fixing the droids and making weapons whenever those were necessary. She didn't go on missions. She didn't risk her life or do any of the other stupid things that everyone else did. Ace stayed home. Safe, sound, and useful. That was her job.

Until, she realized, Jacob decided it wasn't any longer. She never should have trusted this lint licker.

Maketes eyed her and then looked back at Jacob. "You will not wish to repeat this to him. This man is lying. We can smell it in the air, and whatever he wants, it's not worth the risk. I would prefer that you risked your life with me, because I can keep you safe in this sea. However, you need to know that this man does not mean well. He feeds you to the sea, knowing that you may not return."

She knew Jacob expected her to say something. She had to repeat and translate. "He asks what kind of mission you're going to send them on."

"Seemed like an awful lot of words for so little meaning." Jacob's hand on her shoulder tightened. "You telling me everything, Ace?"

"They speak very slowly." It was a shit excuse, but it was the only one she had.

Maketes shifted in front of her, his gills flaring at her lie. "Good. Now you're going to tell him that I will agree to nothing without more answers from him."

A significantly larger undine swam up behind Maketes. This one had vague breasts on her chest, although they were not the same color or shape as humans. They were much more flat, like swollen pectorals. Almost as though she merely had more fat there for some warming reason, rather than just for feeding their children.

"You do not make the decisions here, Maketes," the new undine spat.

"I do when it comes to matters of these achromos."

Achromo. She'd read the word he'd sent her before, but she hadn't realized what it meant. Achromo must mean human.

They were already bickering again, both of them sending jabs at each other until she interjected, "Jacob, why don't you tell them what you want?"

Both of the undine stopped talking and glared. They were intimidating when they did that. Otherworldly and monstrous in a way she hadn't realized could exist outside of story books. One of the undine behind the other two bared its teeth, and she stared into the razor sharp maw with dread. If Jacob made one mistake, just one, then everything really was going to shit.

Jacob cleared his throat, obviously a little uncomfortable. "There is a key in another tower that I need you to get. The problem is that we can't get into the other towers, and we aren't sure which tower it's in to begin with. But that key is vital to us being safe and living where we are. It holds a great amount of power in Gamma, and I want it."

She hadn't ever heard about a key. A key to what?

"All we need from you is transportation. You will bring Ace to the main tower where I believe the key was last seen, and then you will pick her back up and bring her here. We even have a dive suit that will suffice for travel, so the only thing you have to worry about is getting her in and out of a building." Jacob spread his hands wide with a grin that was far too smarmy for comfort. "It's an easy job to do, and in return, I'll give you the best weapons you'll ever have."

That was a stretch. She didn't have to say it though, because Maketes was quick to reply, "The best weapons are my own hands, achromo. I could rip your head off and toss it into the crowd of your people before you take your next breath. Let's not pretend you can create any weapon more deadly than me."

She felt faint. She knew her face had turned white at the same time she felt dizzy because Jacob immediately snarled, "What did he say?"

She didn't know how to lie about that one. All she could envision were these undine crawling out of the water and starting to tear limbs off. She'd seen them do it the one time, and she didn't want to see them do it again. She couldn't protect herself. Not from that amount of power and speed. They would kill her so quickly—

Jacob shook her. "Ace, what did he say?"

Before she could try to make up something that wouldn't cause Jacob to tell everyone to open fire, Maketes spoke again. This time, he scratched his claws down the metal floor as well, making a horrible sound that all the humans winced at.

"We will accept this deal of his. We will take you to the tower you speak of, and we will provide you with whatever else you need."

The other, larger undine hissed, "We need to talk about this."

"Tell him now, Ace."

She respected that the bigger undine might have a little more say in this situation, but she wasn't going to risk ignoring a direct order. She looked at Jacob and said, "They accept."

"Unwillingly, it seems."

"There's some back and forth between them, but it seems like the overall consensus is that they accept." Which was a lie. But she knew it was the only decision she could make, considering the threat of death right in front of her.

"Good achromo," Maketes said with a grin, all of his sharp teeth on display. "I will be back for you soon."

"When?"

The undine were already sinking back underneath the water, one by one. Her yellow finned devil was the last one to go. His dark eyes watched her every second that he moved away. "Tomorrow. Be ready in the same place. I will not wait long."

And then he disappeared, too. Just sinking into the black water and then... gone. Like they were never here. Like everyone in this room had shared a fever dream that would leave them forever changed.

"The fuck was that?" Gregor muttered. "I don't like it, boss. I don't like having them so close to our home."

"It's the best chance we've got," Jacob said. Then his hand clamped down on her shoulder again, squeezing so tightly she swore she could feel her bones creaking. "Come on, Ace. You and me need to have a chat about what you're going to do."

No one stopped him. No one even offered to help. They all just watched the two of them walk out of the room with worried expressions on their faces and pitying glances that told her everything she needed to know.

This wouldn't be a good meeting. Nor would it be an easy one.

She held her breath until they made it out into the semi private hall. Jacob threw her against the nearest wall the moment no one could see. Dust rained down on her head, and the sign above her rattled against the metal wall with an ominous threat. He didn't care, though. If it fell on his big ass head, then he would just shake it off like an enraged bull.

"Listen to me, you little lying sneak. I know your kind. You got here because you snuck through the shadows, fucking around with whatever you wanted until you got caught. You think you're smarter than everyone else, but let me tell you, you're not smarter than me. I get even a hint that you're out of line, I have a direct way to kill your sister. You hear me, Ace?"

Her blood ran cold. But her sister was in Beta, not here. Her sister was safe. Her sister was untouchable by anyone in this horrible place.

"I can see those thoughts going through your head. But you've been sending a droid to go check on her, and I've known about that since the first day you built it a year ago. I know where she is. I have friends in low places, and I will not hesitate to kill her. Now nod your head to say you understand."

She nodded. He had her by the throat and he knew it. She would never let anyone take her sister away from her. Never.

"Good. Now that key unlocks a vault in the main tower. The one where all the security is. We can get to that tower if we want to, but the key still stands in our way. According to the logs in the maintenance area of our tower, there is a key that unlocks it. The last known person to have it was in the medical pavilion. That's where you're going. His name was Doctor Kraus. Get in, get the key from his office, and then come back here. Got it?"

"Doctor Kraus's office in the medical pavilion, look for a key. Got it."

"It's not..." Jacob hissed out an angry breath and then seemed to pull himself back together. "It won't be a door key, you idiot. It'll be something like a chip or a card. They didn't live like we do. So figure out what the key is, get it, and your sister stays alive."

She nodded again, her mind fraying at the edges. He was too close. Too big. Too angry.

And then he lunged even closer, pressing his forehead against hers and grinding the back of her skull into the wall. Rusted metal bit through her hair, and she could feel the thin skin shredding open with the movement.

"I need you to understand the risk, Ace. You fuck up one time, and your pretty little sister is mine. Let's just say that. I'll kill her, but I'll make her wish she was dead long before I hand her a knife."

She felt her entire body go numb as he leaned away from her. Fear made her knees weak, but she remained standing. Because there was nothing else for her to live for other than her sister.

31

Chapter 4

That could have gone worse. It could have gone better as well, but Maketes preferred to think on the bright side. They had gotten somewhere with the achromos. He knew what they wanted now, and he was able to at the very least make a deal to spend more time with them to get answers out of that... female.

Ace was a female.

It was still hard to reconcile the voice in his head with what she looked like. He'd been so certain he'd been talking to a male, and to realize that it was a rather odd looking female? His mind simply couldn't match the words with the person.

Agalma stayed back as some of the others returned to their home. She watched them all swim away, and he had the feeling that he was about to get scolded.

Maybe if he just swam slightly to the right, he could sneak past her. All he had to do was move his hip fin a little more, and then he was facing the correct direction to dart forward before she would even notice.

"Stay right where you are, Maketes," she snarled under her breath.

Right. Staying where he was. Because he knew that tone and it said she would not handle any of his shit even if he rushed forward and darted away from her.

"You always take things so seriously," he muttered.

"Yes. I do. Because everything is rather serious right now, Maketes. You don't seem to understand that we threatened one of the achromos' cities, and then we destroyed another. We are on the brink of war if we are not careful and here you are, antagonizing them. Making deals without getting approval from the person who is supposed to be in charge."

"Oh, so you're mad I took your job?"

She glared at him. Her hands flexed at her sides, and he wondered if she wanted to throttle him for saying those words. "That is not what I'm angry about."

"I can handle this. I've been talking to Ace for quite a while now. I know what she's like."

"You thought she was a man!"

He shrugged, a motion he'd picked up from Mira. "I was wrong."

"You do not know this person. Therefore, you cannot trust this person." Agalma slapped his back with her fluke. "Stay the night, if you must. But get this over with soon, Maketes. I fear you may not realize just how much danger you're putting yourself in."

Well, when she said it like that, it sounded bad. He watched her swim away and felt the wriggling of doubt in his mind. Had he underestimated Ace? If he was swimming into a trap because he'd thought she was more of a friend than she really was, that wouldn't be ideal. But he'd learned a long time ago that worrying only wasted energy.

So he threw the emotions out for the sea to take care of, and every other worrying thought that might follow. He wasn't interested in the anxiety, and he sure wasn't interested in the headache of feeling.

There. That was better. Life was so much easier when he just didn't care.

Floating on his back, he wrapped a long strand of kelp around his waist and tried to get some rest before the trip with Ace. But his mind was still racing with all the possibilities. He'd never explored the achromo homes much outside of Beta. He'd been born in deeper waters than the others who were now his family. There were few people in his pod at all, and those that did exist didn't travel far. Other than him.

He'd always traveled.

Halfway through the night, a clawed hand grabbed his tail and yanked hard. He'd just about fallen asleep, so when he turned with a growl, he was ready to rise to whatever fight this other of his kind wanted. He wasn't big, and his claws were smaller than the others, but he could still do some damage to whatever beast thought they could chase him away.

But even Maketes wasn't dumb enough to fight the depthstrider in front of him. Let alone two of them.

Fortis was the largest of the People of Water that he'd ever seen in his life. So big that his tail sometimes just hung limp beneath him, as though dragging it was just too much effort. It was why he was suited for deeper waters than the ones they were in now. Yellow tips of glowing fins cast light from below on his severe expression, just enough to illuminate the deep violet hues that made up his tail and the rest of his body.

His son floated behind him, smaller but no less intimidating. All depthstriders were, though. Maketes had always heard they could see into the future with just a touch, and he didn't want to know anything about his future. Not even the barest hint of what might happen.

Fortis withdrew his hand that was always a little too rough. Maybe the big beast couldn't help himself. His hand was, after all, twice the size of Maketes's head.

"You are here," Fortis said, his black eyes already swirling with colors. "This is where you are supposed to be."

"Eh!" He waved his hand in front of Fortis's face, breaking him out of the trance. "Don't do that. I don't want to know anything about that."

"But it is exactly where you should be, Maketes. You have been fighting against fate your entire life."

"I sure have, and I plan to continue doing so." He used his tail this time to blast water into the depthstrider's face and also propel himself away from him. "Don't say a word about it. I don't want to know."

"What if it would help you?"

"It's not going to help me, though. It's going to put thoughts in my head that aren't my own. I make my own way in life. I don't listen to prophecy or whatever it is your kind do."

He didn't want to know. He feared what the other male would say because he knew he wasn't the same as all the others. He was smaller, prettier to the females, but useless to them. Maketes had all of his walls built up and all the coping mechanisms he needed. A depthstrider would not mess with all the carefully constructed walls he'd purposefully kept in place.

"We're here for a reason," Fortis snarled.

"What do you want, then? I know you love to stare into my future, but aren't you just wasting the present? You're obsessed with me, Fortis. It's flattering."

Fortis sighed, and even his son seemed to have a small amount of reaction. Maketes wasn't used to the younger—yet somehow an exact copy of Fortis—reacting at all. The young version always seemed to be stoic and unmoving. But this time, Fortis's son smiled, almost as though he was amused by what Maketes was saying.

He pointed at the son. "I see that expression."

As soon as the words were said, the small grin disappeared.

"Doesn't matter if you hide it. I saw it."

Fortis slapped him with his tail and then turned to his son. "Go home. If you can't keep it together, I will do this myself."

"Father." The son disappeared without argument, which could only mean that Maketes was, in fact, as funny as he thought he was. Or maybe the boy was just laughing at him, rather than with him. Both were acceptable. He just enjoyed making people laugh.

There was a small moment of silence until Fortis turned back to him again. Those eyes were already swirling with colors, a bad sign for sure. Maketes took a deep breath and then let it filter out of his rib gills. A billowing wave of air bubbles obscured him from Fortis's gaze for the few moments it took to pull himself back together.

"What do you want?" Maketes finally asked. "I don't want to know my future, and I don't want you helping me find my future, or whatever other nonsense you're here for."

"I will not tell you your future if you do not wish to know it, but there are things about this place you need to know." Fortis's voice was low, quiet, and sounded more like a prophecy than it did words. "This city hides many secrets."

"Gamma is a prison city. From what my brother's mates have said, they aren't hiding anything here other than what people brought with them. And I highly doubt they were allowed to bring anything important." At least, he didn't think the achromos were that stupid. Maybe they were.

"This city was not always a prison. It was more than that. And it has valuable information that we all need." Fortis's gaze did that odd thing again. Colors swirled in his eyes, similar to what Mitera could do, before he shook his head and the colors cleared. "I cannot see what it is, though. There are too many decisions between now and then for that future to be clear."

"Sounds like your power is useless. This place is dangerous. There are things we need to know about it. But I don't know what those things are or how to find them. Are you sure you can actually see the future, or do you just pretend?"

Fortis narrowed his gaze. "Would you like me to read your future and you can decide for yourself?"

The threat hovered between them before Maketes held up his hands in surrender. "Not really, big guy."

"I have seen that there is something here that could help us just as much, if not more, than the achromos. You need to find out what it is and bring it to us before the achromos get their hands on it."

"Do you know what it looks like?"

"No."

A laugh burst out of him. "Right, so you really are useless then! Fortis, you have us all tricked. Of that, I am certain. Do you ask for payment for these fortunes? Because I wouldn't mind doing them on the side for myself. Perhaps then I could get a better nesting site in the pod."

The bigger male seemed to get even larger. His fins flared around his head and sides, and his tail suddenly started moving again. He was a vision of their people. Huge enough to be intimidating and even bigger than before. Nineteen feet of massive creature and Maketes could tell he'd made a mistake.

Swimming backward, he held up his hands again. "Cool it down, big guy. I meant nothing by it, just that it sure seems like you're a little useless."

"Would you like me to show you how useless I am?" The spines all along the back of Fortis's arms rose, and then the ones on his back too.

"No. No, I think I'm good. Perhaps I was wrong."

"Perhaps you were," Fortis snarled, before seemingly pulling himself together. "I do not know how you always get under my scales."

"It's a gift."

"More like an annoyance."

"Some might even call it a blessing from the sea herself."

Fortis took a deep, steadying breath. "I am leaving before I kill you myself."

"Yourself?" Maketes frowned. "Did you just tell me my future?"

"You will never know." The sly grin on his face was his only warning before Fortis darted away.

"Wow," he muttered. "That big guy can really move when he wants to."

Those were ominous words for him to even consider, so Maketes also tossed those fears out. He wouldn't dwell on what someone like that said. Depthstriders were notoriously difficult to understand, not to mention that they manipulated the world however they wanted. Fortis might have seen nothing in his visions. He might have just decided that he wanted to be bothersome.

Maketes stilled his mind and worked on getting all of those thoughts out of his head entirely until he could see the slightest rays of sunlight above his head. Or rather, the faintest light blue of the water. Gamma was so deep that the rays didn't penetrate this far down.

But the lighter water meant it was tomorrow. Or rather, that tomorrow was today. And all he could think was that now he would go and get Ace. He could gather her up and together they would start a new adventure.

How odd it would be to have a human pressed against him, as he'd seen his brothers do. They always seemed to enjoy the act, although he couldn't tell if that was because they were in love, or if it was simply just enjoyable to hold an achromo female like that. He was excited to learn, though.

Even if Ace looked like she'd rather set herself on fire than have him touch her. Soon enough, she would know he posed little danger to her.

He returned to the same meeting spot on his own this time, and there was the fleeting worry that someone might have laid a trap. But they didn't, and thus he let the thought drift away. Because they were all standing in the exact same spots they had been in before. The same males. The same people. The same strange barrels full of fire that made his eyes hurt just to stare at.

And she was there too. Ace. The strange and curious achromo who had made him wonder just exactly what she had hidden. They'd dressed her in a ridiculous suit. It was nearly twice her size, bulging around her like she was some strange puffer fish. There was a massive dome on her head as well, a strange looking device that resembled a bubble. From his vantage point, he could just barely see the heavy metal tank she had strapped to her back.

Was that how they expected her to breathe? With that tank?

Perhaps she saw him staring, because she spun so he could see it, then turned back around to say, "It's oxygen. It helps me breathe underwater."

They were going to do away with that immediately. Once he got her in the water, he was going to make sure she never had to put that stupid thing on ever again. But he couldn't do that here. Not with everyone else looking.

She strode toward him, but paused when the leader of the group spoke.

"Hey, undine."

Maketes bared his teeth and stared the other man down.

But the man just grinned, like he'd expected Maketes to not want to listen to him. "Remember our deal. If we don't get that key, you don't get the weapons."

"I couldn't care less about your weapons," he replied, knowing full well that only Ace could understand him. "I do this as a favor for her, not for you."

He thought he was the only one who heard her tiny gasp echo inside the chamber of her bubble. And it would probably be dangerous for anyone else to have heard it. These people didn't seem trustworthy to him, and he'd rather have Ace in his arms now rather than theirs.

He reached for her, his hands wide and his claws already curled. Ready to protect her. But unfortunately, she only saw it as a threat. He knew how scary he must look, but he'd forgotten that he was large in comparison to her. No one was frightened of him. Not usually, at least.

But she hesitated before putting her hands on his shoulders, and then he scooped her up and dove perhaps a little too quickly. But he would take no risks when it came to this strange achromo. She would be safer with him than with them.

Chapter 5

She told herself not to scream in the bubble of her diving suit, and she didn't. But she definitely might have let out an embarrassing whimper. There was something horrible about the sensation of going underneath the water. The old dive suit wasn't exactly as warm as it should have been. There was too much space between her skin and the insulated fabric of the suit, so she felt it suction to her and then they were off.

She had the momentary terror that the oxygen tank wouldn't work. It was old, after all. They'd had someone look at it to make sure that she wouldn't drown, but there was always the chance. Or that they hadn't sealed it right and soon enough she would feel water creep in underneath the helmet. A thousand things could go wrong, and that was all she could focus on for a long time.

The dark water covered her head and once she had time to calm her nerves about the ancient suit that was supposed to keep her alive, all she could feel was the muscular arm around her waist.

There was so much strength in that band of forearm that held her back pressed against his chest. He glided through the water with ease, holding onto her like she weighed absolutely nothing when she knew that damn well wasn't true. The faintest pricks of claws brushed along her stomach, and her belly tensed at the sensation.

No light penetrated this deep into the ocean. All she could see was the darkness surrounding them. And with that, came the realization that there were other sensations. She could feel every individual claw as it brushed along her suit. The flexing of his muscles as he darted away from her home and dragged her into the deep. The sound of her own breath, coming too rapid and too shallow because she couldn't focus on anything other than the terror that raced throughout her mind.

She could die. He could drop her and she'd sink like a stone. The ocean could claim her just as it had so many other bodies. She'd never realized until right now how much she hated the ocean.

"Where are we going?" he asked, his deep voice somehow even louder in the water than it had been out of it.

She flinched, but he only drew her back into his chest, even firmer. It was like he wanted her to get closer to him, because his arm tightened even more, drawing her so close that her legs brushed against his tail as they fairly flew through the water.

"Um..." Where were they going? Her mind had frayed with fear and now she wasn't... Jacob had said something... He'd made it very clear that she had to go somewhere to get... shit.

His other arm joined the first, wrapping her up in him. Then, suddenly, she was flipped mid swim. Turned again like she weighed nothing, so she was facing him with her helmet mashed against his strong chest. She tried to still herself, wondering if he was just going to snap her neck or if this was his apology hug before he dropped her into the abyss.

But nothing happened. He just held her. Quietly. Calmly. Then he slowed his speed until they weren't darting through the water like a missile, they were just floating. Letting the sea hold them up together as though this was the most normal thing in the world.

Maybe it was. Maybe it was entirely normal for him, but it was so strange for her.

She took in a deep, rattling breath. Then another. She had to get herself under control because if she didn't, then she wouldn't remember a damn thing of what she was supposed to do.

A steady thud caught her attention. Not quite a beat of a drum, more of a bump-thud sound that was so unusual. She couldn't think of anything else. She listened to that sound, wondering what in the world it was, until she realized it was his heartbeat.

He'd stopped swimming so she could be wrapped in his arms, listening to his heart. What kind of monster did that? Not a monster at all. Just someone who saw another person in distress and wanted to help.

Taking a deep breath, she let her own fears float away. Taking one deep breath after another, she slowed her heart rate down until she nodded against his chest. "Right. We're going to the medical pavilion."

"And where is that?"

"It's so weird talking to an undine," she muttered under her breath, before trying to rotate in his arms. "I need to look around."

"Why is it strange to talk to me?"

"Because you're..." Ace tried to find the right words. "Massive? The only kind of sea creature capable of speech?"

"Not true." He let her turn, even helping her by holding her under the armpits like she was a child. And then he just... held her out in front of him. Arms straight, hands under her arms. "Dolphins and whales speak."

This was a distraction she didn't need. Ace's vision had finally adjusted to the darkness of the sea and she could see there were pinpricks of light ahead of her. The medical pavilion should be blue if she remembered right. She wasn't sure if it would have a neon blue exterior, however. It would make sense that all the signs would have some kind of color coded legend, but... Well. It wasn't like everything here was consistent.

Apparently, she didn't respond fast enough, because he swayed her side to side. Swishing her legs through the water in the slowest kind of shake. "Did you hear me?"

"I heard you."

"Why did you not reply?"

She recognized this behavior. He'd done something very similar when they had been talking through their devices. He wasn't very patient when it came to responses. He wanted an answer, acknowledgement, all the things that sometimes she just didn't have time to give him.

Sighing, she replied, "Because I'm looking for where we need to go. The medical pavilion is where the last known owner of the key was. It should be blue, and have something that looks like a cross outside of it."

"A cross?"

It took some effort to hold her hands up, but she bent the gloves on her hands and overlapped her pointer fingers. "Like this."

"Oh!" He slammed her back against his chest with such force that she let out a little disgruntled sound. "Sorry. I know where that is, though."

They were off again. Blasting through the water with so much speed that she had a hard time holding onto him. All she could do was hope that he had a hold of her before they were suddenly rounding a corner in between towers and then...

The entire sea burst into light.

Neon surrounded them. Signs on every single building, though pieces of them had fallen off, but she could see their names flashing as they passed. FOOD HERE, with a giant red arrow. STOP FOR ENTERTAINMENT, marked with flowers around it. A giant naked woman that blinked on and off, one of her heeled feet pointing in the direction to go. So much color and light surrounded by tiny schools of silver fish.

A manta ray swam in front of them, larger than she was tall. It arced over their heads, black and white spots so close she could have touched it if she reached out her hand. It was like the sight of that manta ray gave her the ability to see every single other creature here.

While the city of Gamma might be a dying ruin of neon lights and blinking, boring existence, the outside of the city roared with life. Fish swam in every single direction, everywhere the eye could see. The manta ray dove, drawing her attention to jellyfish that were coasting by them. She'd never seen a jellyfish in her life.

Maketes rolled them, suddenly turning her onto her back so she looked up and stare into all the darkness that surrounded them. And then there was movement in that dark, a slight shudder revealing the outline of something massive. The silhouette of a whale blocked out her view, but it must have been some distance away, because it almost looked small.

Ace lifted a hand, comparing the size of it to the whale before they rolled again.

"There?" he asked, his deep voice rumbling through her entire body until she followed where he was pointing.

The medical pavilion was right in front of them. The big blue cross wasn't blinking like the other signs. She wondered if maybe it had a different generator attached to it, just in case the power went out and people couldn't find the one place they needed most.

Her stomach twisted with worry. She had no idea what gang was in the medical pavilion these days. Ace had kept her nose out of everyone else's business. It was a skill she'd perfected over the years. Just in case another group came into her tower, then she could say she wasn't really attached to anyone. Her loyalties could be bought, and she was useful.

But now she was heading into their territory with the intent to take something that wasn't hers. It was going to be a lot harder to convince anyone to help her. Perhaps it was best if she stayed hidden.

"Yeah," she whispered. "That's it."

He must have sensed her subdued mood, because he didn't talk as he swam them toward the building. There wasn't a lot to say, anyway. She wasn't going to tell him much about the why or how of what she was doing. And he probably didn't care all that much to ask. Human business was human business.

"Looks like there's an opening," she shouted, trying to make sure he could hear her through the diving helmet. For good measure, she pointed to a small tear at the bottom level of the building.

It didn't bode well. A lot of these towers were in rough shape. Engineers were rare in these parts, apparently they either were do gooders or they were too valuable to send to Gamma. Whatever it was, if a building was damaged, the people who lived there patched it the best they could and hoped the tower didn't flood.

Large drainage tubes ran up and down the sides of this building. She'd seen them on a few others as well. Drainage systems that should pump any water out of the building. If they were working, then flooding the tower would be next to impossible.

The tear was on a lower level, and large enough for them to slip through. Maketes handed her through the hole first. Then he guided her rather than swim through the sharp shards of metal with her in his arms. She was almost insulted until she knocked the diving helmet against a jagged edge of rebar and realized he was letting her pick her own way to make sure the suit didn't rip.

After that, she was a lot more careful. Using her gloves to grab onto stone and metal, yanking herself through the twisting labyrinths of old rooms and floating tables until she saw a light at the surface.

"Finally," she wheezed before breaking free into fresh air.

She was heavier here, though. Way heavier than she remembered ever feeling. Grabbing onto the first ledge she could, she tried to pull herself out, but the water in her suit made her feel like she was carrying another person on her back. A hand palmed her ass and heaved.

Like a wet seal, she plopped out of the water and slammed onto the floor.

Ace rolled onto her back and fiddled with the ties that kept the dive helmet on her body. If she could just wiggle it off, she knew she could breathe here. There was always air in the medical pavilion. And she needed to take a few seconds to actually rest, because that had been the most terrifying experience of her entire life.

A big body loomed over hers, reaching for her helmet and pulling it off her head. Maketes frowned down at her, the expression on his face was one so clearly of confusion that it almost made her laugh.

"You are still breathing?" he asked.

"Yes."

"Not very well."

A laugh did burst out of her then. "No, not very well. But I'll be fine here."

He withdrew slightly, giving her room to sit up and start wriggling out of the suit. All she had to do now was find the office of doctor whatever his name was—she'd remember it in time—and then loot the whole place. She'd done that before. Ace was good at stealing things.

But the undine in front of her gave her pause. He was leaning against the open floor, nothing behind him but a blank wall that might have once had artwork on it, considering the holes. But he was halfway out of the water. His tail was long and coiled beneath him, not unlike a snake. He drew it nearly completely out of the water until just his thin fluke was still hidden from her sight.

Ace looked over her shoulder and realized they were in a little waiting room. There were still teal covered leather chairs where people would sit and wait for their appointments. An eye chart was on the wall in the back corner, right behind a desk that still had an honest-to-god phone sitting on top of the counter.

She'd never seen so many pristine things. Everything in the tower she lived in had long ago been destroyed, but all of this was perfect. Still here, like it had only been a few moments ago that the receptionist had walked out of the room.

Halogen lights blinked off above them before humming back on. The wooden door even had a sign on its window. She could read it backwards.

Opthamologist.

"An eye doctor," she mused, before shrugging her way out of the dive suit. She quickly stood and hung it over the back of one of the chairs. "Hard to forget where this is."

"You're leaving me here?"

"I don't think it would be all that easy for you to come with me. Thanks for the ride, though. Come back in... I don't know, a day or so? Then I'll definitely have what I need."

There was a sudden silence. Not even the sound of dripping water.

She turned to look at him, and he reached out his hand for her to take. "Ace?"

Some stupid part of her reached out for him, too. It whispered "Just take his hand", so she did. "What? What is it?"

Did he sense some danger? Was there something here that she hadn't realized?

"You stink." And with that, he yanked her hard and tossed her into the open water.

Chapter 6

Maketes watched her hit the water with a harsh slap. Perhaps he'd thrown her a little too hard. Poor thing clearly wasn't used to being graceful in the water, because she struck face first and then seemed to sink like a stone.

Had he knocked her out with the sheer force of his throw? Unlikely. She must not know how to swim.

Without another thought, he dove into the water after her. Everything was vaguely lit by the lights above them. The room that she had entered was so bright it had made his eye ache. But that brightness gave him the unique opportunity to be able to see everything under the surface.

And to see the shocked expression on her face. Not at what he had done, but at what she was seeing.

"You've already swum through this portion," he reminded her, slowly circling her still form.

He wondered for a moment why she didn't respond, only to remember she was holding her breath. Was now the time to connect with her? Did he draw the tentacle out of his hair and give her the air she so desperately needed?

He waited too long. Already Ace was heading back to the surface of the water. She kicked her feet, those strange pants seeming to slow her down only for a few moments. But then she was treading water at the top and he had a momentary flare of pride. For a second, he feared she couldn't swim. Mira and Anya had both warned him that not all humans could. In fact, many of them couldn't swim at all.

He had never been so afraid in his life than when he heard such a thing. All the humans were surrounded by water. What if their homes flooded? What if they had to go out into the sea? Not being able to swim seemed almost impossible to him.

With a flick of his tail, Maketes joined her at the surface. She still had her glasses on somehow, and had a glare on her face that threatened his life without a single word being said.

Grinning, he said, "Now you do not stink."

"The fuck was that, undine?"

"If you were to come across any enemies, they would have smelled you long before they would see you."

Her face somehow turned red, even though he could see she was starting to shiver. "Are you insane? I can't get wet! If I'm freezing cold, I could die of hypothermia or never dry out. Besides, it's far more likely someone would hear the water dripping off my body before they would smell me!"

Maketes considered her words and then wrinkled his nose. "Unlikely. You really smelled quite pungent."

She stared at him. Just stared. Didn't stop staring until all of a sudden he felt a little uncomfortable. It was like she was looking into his soul and he didn't want her looking there.

Words bubbled up in his throat. He'd never been very good at sitting in silence. It pressed down upon his shoulders, made it feel a little hard to breathe. He wanted her to say something. Anything. Just fill the silence with something other than this.

Finally, he cleared his throat and asked, "Would you like some soap?"

Again, she stared. Until finally, blissfully, there were a few words. "How do you know what soap is?"

"We have a few humans in our pod. They are female like you, and they've both pressed on the necessity of soap." He started sinking underneath the water for a moment before pointing out at the floor. "You should find different clothes. Like you said, they're going to hear you coming."

"And whose fault is that?" He heard her mutter before she moved off and pulled herself out of the water.

Her wet clothes clung to her body, and he found himself curious about the differences he could already see. Mira was strong, her body flexed with muscles even when she was sitting. Anya was a delicate little thing who looked like she could break at any moment. But Ace had tantalizing curves that she'd hidden from sight. She was soft, plush, and she looked so much more tempting than the other two.

Or perhaps that was just his own loneliness talking. Of all things, he just wanted someone to look at him the way Mira and Anya looked at their mates. It seemed... nice. More than nice to have someone who cared about their partner. Perhaps he wouldn't be quite so solitary, then.

But he couldn't think like that. Those thoughts were a little too serious for him, so he tossed them away and swam out of the building to find the seed pods that foamed up. When he'd brought them back to Mira for the first time, she'd squeezed his face hard and kissed his cheek. Arges had nearly beaten the scales off him, but it was worth it to see both of the women squealing with excitement.

He'd do the same for this achromo.

It didn't take him long to find the little pods. They were abundant in the deeper waters of the ocean, because they grew best on the sea floor. To an untrained eye, they looked like large mussels. Their shells were dark in color and frequently had little white scars made by barnacles. Once he cracked it open, there was a soft spongy interior that foamed up when it was rubbed between hands. Apparently, it was perfect for cleaning hair.

He quickly made his way back to the achromo he'd left alone. Ace could have gotten into trouble while he wasn't there. But as he rushed past broken pieces of furniture, he was quick to find that she was right where he had left her.

The dirty, ancient clothing she'd worn was gone. Instead, now she was snuggled up in a blanket that had seen better days. Her feet were bare for his gaze, their shape still odd. Even to him. He'd seen Mira and Anya's feet many times before, but the sight of new ones was never easy to get used to.

Her toes were smaller than either of the other two. Itty bitty toes with the tiniest claws he'd ever seen on the tips of them.

She drew her feet underneath the blanket, those brown eyes watching him yet again.

"What?" he asked.

"You were staring at my feet."

"I know."

"It's rude to stare at people's feet."

"Why?" He tilted his head to the side, genuinely confused why that would ever be considered rude. "They are very unusual appendages for my people to see. I have only seen two pairs before yours. Some of my people have seen more, but I never watched your kind very often."

Ace's face screwed up in a strange expression. Her mouth pressed thin, her brows drew down, and her eyes squinted at him. Was she trying not to laugh? Or perhaps she was simply constipated.

"What?" he asked again.

"They're just feet."

"They are so tiny, though." He moved a little closer and then placed the pod down on the floor beside her feet. "I did not know that they came in such a small size."

"Well, I didn't pick them and then affix them onto myself." Grumbling, she grabbed the pod and turned it over in her hands. "How's this work, then?"

He grabbed it from her hands, an idea forming in his mind. Instead of explaining anything to her, he backed away into the water. "You have to come in to get clean."

"I am clean."

"You are covered in saltwater and I can still smell you." He gestured with a clawed hand, hoping the sight of those deadly weapons wouldn't scare her off. "Come here, Ace."

She jolted at the sound of her name. He wasn't sure why it was so startling to her, only that it was. And in just a moment, she brushed the blanket from her shoulders and slipped into the water.

He sank underneath the surface for a brief moment, if only to look at her better. She wore very little now. Just a small scrap of fabric hiding what was between her legs and twin cups that were formed around her breasts. But he could see her so easily, so perfectly. The soft curves of her body, the way her stomach was slightly rounded. Though she was so small compared to him, there was much of her to grasp.

Perfection, he thought as he cracked the pod open. Just as he'd thought she would be.

He moved back to the surface with two halves of the pod already open. "The innards of this plant foam. One of our females said that it cleans the hair very nicely."

She reached for it, huffing out an angry sound when he held it back from her. "Can I have that?" she growled.

"No."

A muscle in her jaw jumped as she clenched her teeth. Somehow she still ground out, "Why not?"

Because he wanted to touch her. Because he wanted to see how soft she was and if she felt the way he thought she might. But saying all of that would scare her off, and he had no interest in ending this adventure. So instead, he reached for her.

His hand slid around her waist, fingers curling around the cooled flesh even as he felt the strange sensation of her shivering. She shuddered against his touch and he thought for the briefest of moments it was because she might enjoy his touch. Even if that was only a dream, it surely was a wondrous one.

Maketes drew her through the water, turning her body so her back was pressed against his chest. At this angle, his tail was just long enough to wedge against the wall. It gave him a steady brace for her spine, with his tail lifting between her legs. She could sit on him, which she seemed to fight for a moment before giving in. Then her legs straddled his tail, the sudden heat of her core nearly burning through his scales, and he had to remind himself he wasn't doing this for that sensation.

Cleaning her. That's what he was doing. Helping her find what she needed to find. Getting weapons for his people.

He wasn't here to seduce the female he'd been talking to for weeks on end. And he certainly wasn't here to find himself an achromo mate of his own.

But what if he was?

To distract himself from the thoughts that were entirely beyond reality, he scooped some of the spongy substance out of the pod and lathered it between his hands. "Why were you in Gamma?"

The question blurted out of his mouth before he realized just how awful it was to say. It was like asking Daios why he was missing an arm, or Mira why she was so abrasive sometimes. These weren't things a male asked when a female was straddling his tail and stiff as a board beside him.

She somehow became even stiffer. "Why do you want to know?"

"Because no one is in Gamma without good reason, and I suppose I wish to know if I'm helping a murderer..." He paused, tilting his head slightly even as he lifted his hands to her hair. "Murderess?"

"Murderess might be correct. I failed English class, but..." She froze as his claws skated through her hair. There wasn't much of it. She'd shorn it off at her shoulders and the ends were particularly uneven. But she seemed to lean a little into his touch as he started to work the foam into her hair.

"You were saying?"

"I'm not a murderess," she murmured, and he had the distinct pleasure of feeling all the tension leak out of her body. It started in her shoulders, as the tight muscles there loosened and her arms dropped. Then it went down her spine like liquid dripping down her entire body. Her legs fell limp against his tail, and she even leaned further back into his touch.

What a joy. What a pleasure to know that she trusted him not to hurt her. He knew it must have been a shock to see him, but he had thought they had a friendship brewing between the two of them. Now, he was certain of it.

"Not a murderess," he murmured, slowly moving through the strands of her hair knot by knot until his claws slipped through them smoothly. "Then what did you do to end up in Gamma?"

"Oh, nothing terrible. I'm a thief, is all."

Now that was interesting. "A thief? What did you steal, Ace?"

"Just a few things here and there. It started with food to eat, then it was clothing my sister wanted, but we couldn't afford. And then I started being more interested in money and... well. It all went downhill from there."

"You stole... money? I have heard humans need this, but I do not know what it means."

"You don't have currency?"

He tried to think of the word that might even match what she was saying. But there wasn't anything that was the same, not really. Not in his language. "In a way, I suppose. We trade what others might need for things we do. We take care of each other in our pods, although I cannot say that we are particularly kind to other groups. It is merely who we are. We take care of our own, perhaps not so much of others."

She nodded. "That makes sense. Well, anyway. I went too far. I stole from a bank that apparently kept accounts of a lot of very rich people, and the people I took from weren't thrilled that I did so."

"Did you wish to hurt them by taking the money?" Intent meant everything. The Ace he knew was not someone who wished to harm others, only to help. But if she was here because she did want to hurt others...

"No," she whispered, moving away from him and using her own

hands to scrub her scalp a little harder. "I just wanted to see if I could do it. And I could. I did. One glorious heist that no one had seen the likes of in years, and now look at where I am? A broken city, surrounded by criminals, taking a risk I never should have taken."

He watched her dunk under the water and vigorously slide her hands through her hair. When she came back up, he was looking at a different woman. Her expression was hard. Her features said she was no longer an open book, and she would talk to him no more. But he wasn't done peeling back her secrets, not even remotely.

She hauled herself out of the water, dripping on the floor as she rushed back to the blanket and rubbed her skin until it was bright red. "I have to get going. I don't know where this man's office is, but I can only assume it is in the upper levels of this place. Who knows what I'll have to deal with between here and there?"

"Right," he muttered, watching her body as she dried herself. She even bent over and ran that blanket over her short hair, rubbing so hard he thought she'd rip strands right out. And when she righted herself, pushing those strange round glass pieces up her nose, he felt something inside him click.

This was Ace, he'd known that from the start. But now he felt like he was looking at the real Ace.

A person who was not only capable and confident. This woman was so much more than that.

He just didn't know what words were right to describe the woman who had been through so much, and somehow continued forward. She hadn't given up yet. She was still fighting.

And that was impressive.

Five silver balls rolled out of the bundle of her clothing. They clicked together, making strange metallic noises until she scooped them up in her hand and held them out for him to see.

"This is Tera," she said quickly, before dropping them back onto the floor.

They all scattered, running in different directions like fish fleeing a predator. But one stayed, and he could see his own reflection in the shiny metal. Almost as though the ball wanted him to know that it was looking at him.

"Tera," he repeated, before giving it a slight nod. "It's lovely to meet you."

The ball did a slow circle on the floor before zipping off to join the others. When he looked back up, Ace had changed back into clothing. Her skin was no longer a mottled dark gray streak and appeared to be more olive toned now. Her brown hair, brown eyes, all of it was so much better when she was clean.

"Stop looking at me," she muttered. "I have things to do."

"Hard not to look, Ace." He leaned his elbow against the floor and propped his head up. "I wonder what color your hair will be when it's dry?"

"Shut up." But he swore there was a tiny smile on her lips when she said it.

Echoes of the Tide

Chapter 7

Ace spent the better part of what felt like a day trying to figure out how the fuck to get out of the opthamologist's office. There was a lot of useful shit in here, though. Medical supplies, antiseptics, things that probably no one assumed an eye doctor would have. But then she looked at the doors to exit, she found that unfortunately she was completely barricaded in.

Someone had known this was an entrance into the rest of the medical pavilion. They must have seen the part of the pavilion that had broken, and known eventually, someone would use the opening to get in. Why would these people not cover all their bases? Stupidly, she'd assumed they were more like the gang who ran her tower, who didn't really care if there was an opening. Someone would have to be insane to even attempt to swim between towers.

Ace tried for at least an hour to work the nails out of the hammered wood pieces that barred her way out. There were too many of them though, and her droid might have a powerful magnet, but it wasn't capable of wriggling nails out of wood.

"Ridiculous," she muttered as she stared at the very last exit she could find. There was a staff entrance and exit that had taken her too long to figure out. She'd needed to find a set of keys to unlock certain doors, and even then, the doors were stuck by salt and rust. Hammering through that had exhausted her.

But, once through, she found the staff door was also barricaded. This time by water.

"Who floods part of their own city willingly?" she asked Tera. The little droid made a circle in her hands before dropping down onto the floor and zipping away. Likely to triple check that they'd found every single door that might get them out of here.

She stood there for a few moments, staring into the darkness of the flooded room as a scalpel floated past the small window on the door. There really was nothing on the other side of it. Absolutely nothing. Just a blank space of darkness where anything could be lurking.

For a while, she stared directly into the eyes of the abyss. She wanted to look at that darkness. She wanted to feel the hopeless sensation of loss that even though she had tried her hardest, she could not get out of this room.

For some reason, it grounded her. It always had. Looking into the water and realizing how weak and how small she was, even if everyone else seemed to think she was neither of those things.

Then she turned away from the door and made her way back to the waiting room. At least those windows showed a little more of the sea.

She staggered into the room and sat down on one of those plastic chairs. It wasn't comfortable. She didn't imagine it ever had been. But she sat there, her elbows braced on her knees, staring out at the water beyond. There were some neon lights still blinking that she could see. This office didn't have much of a view, though.

The waiting room faced the back of a wall and an alleyway. At the very end of the alleyway was the smallest glimpse of those neon lights. She could just make out the letters OMNI, and that was about it. But there was a figure of what looked like a film camera, and a few other objects that made her wonder if that was an entertainment building. Must be nice to live there.

Trickling water echoed in the room, which was her only warning that there was an undine looking at her. Then again, she'd always been able to feel his eyes on her. Since the very first moment they met.

She wasn't sure why he was back so soon. Maybe he'd never left. That sounded like something Maketes would do. Just linger in the water until she returned. Maybe he already knew there wasn't an exit from this place.

"Can't get anywhere from here," she sighed. "All the doors out of these rooms are barricaded. I can't get to the upper levels."

"That's a shame."

"Did you know I was going to be stuck here?"

"No. There aren't any windows on that side. I couldn't see anything more than you could. This was the first crack in the pavilion we saw, but it won't be the last."

That didn't settle well with her. Already she could feel the ticking time bomb going off that was her sister's life. She didn't have time to just sit here and wait for things to get better.

"All right, well... That's not ideal, but we'll figure it out. The diving suit is still wet, but that's okay. I don't mind being cold." She stood and turned to see him in the water where she'd expected him. But then he gave her a little frown that made her freeze. "What?"

"We can't go anywhere right now."

"That's stupid, because we are going somewhere right now." She wouldn't take no for an answer. "You're swimming me to the top of this tower to see if maybe there's another entrance. Or we can bust through a window and make a crack of our own, if we have to."

"We can't, Ace."

How could he sit there all calm and looking at her like there wasn't any rush at all? Even though he didn't know about her sister or Ace's reasoning for being here, he had to know that there was a time limit on him working with Jacob and his gang. This wasn't a game. They couldn't wait here and chat, or get to know each other, or whatever it was he was expecting.

"I don't care what your excuses are for staying here, we have to go." She'd just tell him. What pride did she have left, anyway? "If I don't come back with that key, and I mean like tomorrow, Jacob knows where my sister is. He threatened to kill her. He said he was going to bring her to Gamma and 'make use' of her before he killed her. I think you can understand what that means."

His expression darkened the more she spoke. She was used to Maketes's face looking rather roguish and handsome. He always had a grin on his face, that much she had learned since meeting him. Even while he was speaking with Jacob, he'd been grinning like a lunatic.

But now? Now she understood why he was so terrifying. Now she saw only the intimidating expression of a monster who lurked in the deep and hunted beasts much larger than she was. He looked like he wanted to tear apart the world and she almost didn't hesitate to think that he could.

His hands clenched on the metal edge of the floor and she swore there was black blood on his palms. "This is the kind of person you keep company with?"

"I didn't exactly have a choice, now did I?" She shook her head, then slashed a hand through the air. "None of this matters at all. I need to go to the top of this tower. Right now."

Ace reached for her diving suit, ready to yank the wet material on over her clothing—who cared what it felt like—only to freeze as Maketes grabbed her hand.

There was something visceral about his touch. All she could focus on were the claws that wrapped around her wrist and how massive his hand was compared to hers. He could palm her entire face in one of those giant mitts. He could easily squeeze and break every bone in her hand while she writhed on the floor in pain, but he was so gentle holding onto her.

"We can't go anywhere," he said, gently this time. Almost as though he didn't want her to think he was joking. And then he pointed at the glass.

She'd just been looking out of those windows and there was nothing there. He was trying to distract her, to get her to focus on something other than the churning fear in her belly. But she still looked, and then she saw them.

The creatures on the other side of the glass weren't like any of the undines she'd seen before. Maketes and his people were the blueprint for what she knew an undine to look like, but these creatures were monsters. They were almost twice Maketes's length and so dark she hadn't noticed them the first time. Their skin was nearly black, deep purple lining their much more eel-like tails. Bright yellow bits tipped their thin fins, but they weren't like Maketes's in shape. These fins had globes at the end, like an angler fish. And those yellow lights flickered now and then, clearly trying to call something to their sides.

One swam so close to the window that she could see a flashing of sharp edged teeth filling its mouth and then it turned those black eyes to her and for a moment, she swore she saw something in her own mind. A vision. A flash of blood on the floor and searing pain in her wrists. A moment from her past when she had tried to…

"No," she whispered, yanking her gaze away from that monster who had seen too much.

But in whirling away from one monster, now she stared at another. A bright yellow and orange creature, who watched her with pity in his gaze. "Sorry. I should have warned you they do that."

"Do what?" she gasped.

"See into the future, sometimes the past. Anything that can happen, will happen, or might have happened." His gaze flicked to the window and his welcoming expression changed to one of disgust. "We call them depthstriders. And you, dear Ace, happen to live right in the middle of a nest of them."

"A nest?" She tried to clear her mind of the memory that she hadn't wanted to relive. "I thought you said you came from a pod? That's what a group of you are called?"

"Yes and no. My kind of the People of Water live in a pod. We tend to be more similar to what you would consider whales and dolphins. The depthstriders are unusual and different from all of our kind. They live in a nest. A grouping of them that all twist and churn in between each other. It's as remarkable as it is disgusting." His black gaze flicked to hers. "Unfortunately, that means we are stuck here. These are their hunting grounds, and they come out at night to feed."

"What? For how long?"

"As long as they decide to eat." With a few ushering movements, he made her back up and then hoisted himself out of the water.

Ace was momentarily distracted by the massive tail that he flipped out of the sea and into the waiting room. It was surreal to see a creature like him in a room like this.

She'd been in a waiting room identical to this one when she was little. She remembered her dad bringing her in and arguing with the receptionist about the price of her glasses. In that moment in time, there was no way she ever would have guessed she'd be back here with a massive fish man flopping onto the floor and then dragging himself toward the glass.

He made some gurgling noise and then water rushed out of his gills. She side stepped the mess. Her eyes widened in shock as he did it again, almost as though he was vomiting before he settled and then took a deep breath in. His gills didn't move this time, only his chest.

Like a human breathed.

"What are you doing?" she asked, trying very hard not to notice that his fluke was flat on the ground and reflecting the light in tiny rainbows of color.

"Joining you to watch the show. I don't want to be in the water when they're hunting. Someone might take a nibble on my tail." He must have seen her looking at it, because suddenly his tail bunched like a snake, coiling closer to him so he could grab that massive fluke and hold it up for her to see. "Did you want to take a closer look?"

Yes.

No.

She definitely didn't want to take a closer look, even though this might be the only time she'd be near an undine. It seemed so paper thin that it was odd it could propel him through the water. The sight of it was almost mesmerizing, and she took a single step forward.

Before she could say a word, Tera came careening out of a corner and rushing right at him. With a few echoing plinks, it stacked each ball on top of itself as though it too wanted a closer look at the tail that was offered for them to peer at.

"Right, that answers your question, then." She scooped the droid up, all the pearls in her hand flattening so they could all look at the tail at once. She could almost hear the ooing and ahing noises it might have made if she'd ever given it a voice.

Maketes reached his hand out for the droids. "If I may? It would be a fair trade for me to see your droids while you look at my tail."

"Just don't crush them."

"I have some experience with droids."

She found that hard to believe, but when had he ever lied to her? Especially when he then handed her his fluke, like it was a giant leaf rather than attached to his body. Ace grabbed it, grunting at the weight that suddenly dragged her arms down. Though it was nearly translucent, it was very thick. Like silicone rubber, particularly strong. It was cool and soft beneath her touch, pliable when she pressed her fingers against it, and such a lovely shade of yellow that faded into purple.

As she ran her fingers and palm down the flat surface, he let out a little chuckle.

"What?" she asked.

"I should have asked to see your feet in return." Maketes held up his hand, one little silver ball balanced between the space of each finger, although there were two between his thumb and pointer finger. It appeared they were using their own magnetic force to hold themselves staggered on either side of his webs. "I think your droid likes me."

"It's just curious. It likes to learn new things."

"So do I." He held Tera up to look at them, and she was struck by the vision in front of her.

Somehow, this massive undine was holding her droid with such care. He didn't even seem uncomfortable by the technology. The halogen lights cast him in terrible shadows, making him appear like the monster everyone claimed his species was. But he wasn't that at all. In all her experience knowing Maketes, she'd only known him to be gentle and kind.

His gaze flicked down to hers. "What are you thinking?"

"Nothing important."

"Looks important."

"You're a lot more tolerable with your mouth shut." She could feel her cheeks flaming bright hot. Damn man kept doing this to her. She didn't want to blush in front of him, but he pushed so hard. Every time she thought she had control over the situation, he flipped it back to his favor.

He grinned, as though he knew her frustrations. "A lot of people have said that to me. But you know what I always say?"

"No, I honestly don't care to hear it, either."

He leaned a little closer, so close that she could see there were faint purple freckles on his cheeks. Just barely visible, like little lavender paint flecks. "You'd miss me if I shut up."

"I really don't think I would."

"You want me to disappear and leave you here alone?"

Immediately panic flared. She didn't want to be alone in this unknown tower, and she didn't want him out with those depthstriders. "Didn't you say it was a hunting night? And you wouldn't even stay in the water because they might bite you?"

"Maybe I just didn't want you to be alone." Her droid clinked in his fingers, a slight whirring sound coming from them as though they were humming. "It's awfully scary in here, don't you think?"

"It's a doctor's office."

"But you don't know who's on the other side of that door, or on the other side of that window." His hand came down on his chest, smoothing down the rippling muscles there and drawing her gaze to the movement. "Perhaps you need a big, strong male to keep you safe."

That's exactly what she needed. One with abs that flexed under her gaze and biceps that made her want to bite them.

What? No!

She let out a disgusted sound and stalked away from him before she did something stupid. "Shut up, you big oaf!"

"Whatever you say, kefi."

Ace refused to let him goad her. She would not turn around and ask what the hell that meant. Even if she wanted to.

75

Chapter 8

Maketes watched her sleep. She probably didn't think he could see her, especially not when he slid back into the water. But the much smaller room she'd chosen to sleep in had a window as well. It was easy for him to swim out into the dark waters and situate himself where he could watch her. Just in case anything went wrong.

And maybe just because he liked looking at her. He'd been right about her hair drying into a pretty color. There were streaks of lighter brown in it, and it was darker underneath, giving layers that made her hair shine now that it was clean.

He had half a mind to ask how it had gotten that greasy and unclean. Was there nowhere to bathe in Gamma? That couldn't be right. There were so many places for her to bathe, considering they lived surrounded by the ocean. But everyone there had been dirty. Even the men that had been surrounding her had been grimy, just like her.

With his tail anchoring him to kelp, Maketes watched her. Sure, it had been a slight lie about traveling in the middle of the night. The depthstriders were a risk to swim through with a human, and one he wasn't going to take. But the risk to himself? Nonexistent. None of the depthstriders attacked their own, although the other pods were fair game.

A human, though? He wasn't sure they wouldn't want to battle him for the right to rip her apart.

The moment she stirred, he quickly headed back to the opening. He was right where he should be the moment she staggered into the main room, yawning and rubbing her eyes. She had her glasses in her hand, and he marveled at the roundness of her features.

He was so used to his kind's angular faces. The sharp edges and hard jawlines were strong and proud, and he was certain she must find him attractive in a way. But she had a face like the shape of the moon. Her cheeks were so soft looking, with a smattering of freckles and the rosy hues of a blush. And when she slid those glasses back in place, focusing on him where he waited for her to look at him, he felt like all the breath in his lungs was stolen.

An achromo that was all his own. Maybe that was all he'd been waiting for.

"Good morning," he said, feeling his gills already standing straight out as he waited for her to notice him.

Her brows furrowed, and she winced. "Is it a good morning?"

"You seemed to sleep well."

"What about this—" she waved up and down her body "—makes you think I slept well?"

He pillowed his chin on his fist, looking her up and down before saying, "You drool in your sleep."

Immediately she wiped at her chin, but there wasn't anything there for her to wipe. Her expression changed to one of confusion before she glared. "Were you watching me sleep?"

"Someone had to keep watch."

"The door is barricaded, and I would hear anyone trying to get in. That's so weird that you watched me sleep!"

He shrugged. "Anyway, we have a busy day together. You wanted to get to the top of the tower, right?"

As expected, his swift change in subject threw her. She stood there, staring at him in obvious confusion, and almost as though her body had stopped working. He had to hide a grin, because he knew it would only make things worse. But really, she was adorable, floundering to find something to say to him.

Maketes couldn't help but prod just a little more. "You did want to go, right?"

"Yes," she blurted out before muttering under her breath about meddlesome men.

He did grin then, watching as she yanked that ugly diving suit off a chair and started pulling it onto her legs. One by one. He watched her movements avidly, wondering if she'd let him touch them. She'd let him touch her hair, and that had been very enjoyable. Maybe if he asked really nicely, she wouldn't mind if he explored that interesting bend in her back.

Really, he just wanted to touch her. It seemed like it would be pleasant.

"Would you stop staring?" she grumbled. "It is way too early to be dealing with your nonsense."

"Unfortunately, I am the only undine who made the deal to work with you, so you do have to deal with me no matter how little you want to." He smiled at her when she looked. "But I think you want to spend time with me."

"What would ever give you that impression?"

He shrugged before pointing at her legs. "You put it on backwards."

Ace looked down at herself before letting out a little growl that was impressively intimidating before pulling the whole thing off again. She made quick work of getting the entire suit on and then yanking the helmet down over her head. She fiddled with it a few times, again making those little grumbling noises that were adorable, before she huffed and held her hands out at her sides.

"Fine, I'm ready." Those arms flopped up and down at her sides.

Did she want him to pick her up? How adorable. And he would gladly use any excuse to touch her, if only to feel how soft she was again.

Maketes surged out of the water, ignoring the splashing wave that rolled over the floor and soaked the chairs that were once pristine. He placed his hands on either side of her waist, waiting for her to relax and not be quite so tense before he lifted her up and then drew her into the water with him.

She made a long, sustained hissing noise the moment she touched the water. Likely because of the cold. He knew the achromos were a lot more sensitive than his people were. Of course, Mira and Anya were in a much higher area of the sea. The water there was warmer, and still they complained about the cold when they got into the water without their suits on.

"Are you cold?" he asked as they sank underneath the surface. A floating picture moved between them, sticking onto her helmet. It was once the image of a man's face, and he couldn't read what it said. But there were only four letters, bright red over his head as the man seemed to point at him.

She dashed the paper off the helmet while spluttering, "Of course

I'm cold! It's the ocean!"

He was coming to realize that his achromo was not a morning person. Which, unfortunately for her, he was. Maketes loved the morning and the adventure of a day left unplanned. It seemed Ace was not the same. Perhaps he had known that already, though. She never messaged him early in the day, but he had assumed that was because she had been busy.

Releasing her, Maketes held out a hand to guide her through the labyrinth of this building and out into the open sea. She was smart, though. His achromo knew not to shoot out into the sea blindly. She braced her hands above her head on the very edge of the cracked opening and stared out into the abyss.

He'd thought perhaps she would feel some sense of fear in it. But he didn't taste that in the water at all. Instead, all he sensed from her was a determination as she watched the waters for any threat. If he were a depthstrider, he might not want to attack her. She was a fiercesome creature, and capable of biting back.

What a wondrous discovery.

Swimming up behind her, he smoothed his hand all the way up her spine until he could palm the back of her helmet. Gently, he nudged her out and used his grip to show her the upper levels of the building above them.

"We go up there. I believe there are other structural issues with this tower. We should be able to get inside."

"There's an office up there that I need to focus our efforts on."

"Understood." Although, he wasn't all that certain what an office was. Mira had a few rooms that she kept for herself in the larger floating home they had built for the humans. Perhaps that was what Ace referred to.

Gathering her up in his arms, he pressed her tightly against his chest and started off. It was a slow journey, one he didn't quite like. But if they were to get inside, he needed them to be far enough away from the building so that anyone inside couldn't see them, but also so that they could see any rips or tears in the metal and glass.

It only impeded what they were able to see. Still, she clutched onto his shoulders and every inch of her was pressed against him. That was a good enough reason for him to take his time.

Her legs were tight around his waist, tucked up against his rib gills and making it a little difficult to breathe. But he didn't mind so much, because all he could smell was the faintest hint of her scent. It filtered through his gills, giving him the sensation of bright places above the surface. She'd never been, but he was certain her scent was what it was to smell sunshine. Those tiny hands were pressed against his chest, and he could easily feel the strength of her thighs against him.

Already he could feel his gills starting to shake. Which was foolish. He knew he was here on a job, and she hadn't shown any inclination that she was interested in him at all. In fact, he would suggest that she was anything but interested. Ace had made it very clear that she wanted to stay far away from him and just get this over with.

Unfortunately for them both, his gills that had never moved in his life were starting to wake up.

Clearing his throat, he tried very hard to distract himself. "Why did they send you, of all people?"

She looked up at him, her nose wrinkled in confusion. "What?"

"Why did they send you? There were plenty of other people."

She shrugged. "I assume because I was the only one who was offered the translation device."

He doubted that. There was a calculating look in her leader's eyes that clearly stated the man had more of a plan than just to send off the only person who the People of Water had picked.

"No," he murmured. "I don't think it was just that."

Perhaps it was the serious tone in his voice that made her tense up. Or maybe it was just the sea itself. Everything was rather quiet in the ocean today, a detail he hadn't noticed until Ace started climbing his body like she was terrified.

And then the scent of her fear stank up the water. There was a balloon of it covering him, cloying and awful in its need to assert there was something terribly, dreadfully wrong.

"Swim!" she shouted, though her voice was muffled by the helmet. "Please, for the love of god, swim!"

He had no idea what god she was talking about, and likely would need clarification on that soon enough. But first, he wanted to understand why she was so frightened.

"What is happening?" he asked, wrapping his arms around her and flaring his gills wide so he looked bigger to any other of his kind that might try to attack them.

"Shark!"

Shark? He hadn't seen any... oh. There it was. The massive female was longer than he was. A great white of her size likely had traveled the seas for sixty years, and she was a beauty. Her massive belly was stuffed full already, suggesting she'd had a meal around here recently. Although, the closer he looked, the more he thought perhaps she was pregnant. Shark pups took a long time to grow in their bellies.

Black eyes looked back at him as the great white started toward them. He could read the curiosity in her movements, and that there was no intent in her to harm them. She just wanted to see what the fuss was about.

"You're scared of sharks?" he murmured, moving his hands up and down her back reassuringly.

"Maketes, now is not the time for questions. Why aren't you swimming?"

"Because a shark loves to chase, and no one is going to beat her in a race. They are some of the best hunters in the sea." With some difficulty, he turned her in his arms. She had her back against his chest now, facing the giant shark that meandered toward them.

The beauty wasn't moving fast. She was just gliding toward them. Ace shook in his arms, shrinking back into him as though she might melt into his skin.

"I don't like this, Maketes." The poor achromo was shaking. But he knew he could challenge her fear in this moment. Why should she fear anything in the ocean when she was with him?

"Watch," he murmured, leaning down so his words were soft against the side of her helmet. "There is nothing to fear from the creatures of the deep."

As soon as the shark got close enough, he reached out his hand. He gently palmed her nose and turned her in the other direction. As the great white passed them, she looked them over with those dark eyes and then flicked her tail. He held Ace in his arms as the shark brushed against both of their sides, and then he turned with her.

"She wants to show us something," he said as Ace protested.

"Following her will only provoke her to attack!"

"No, it won't." He placed his hand along the shark's side, flicking his tail until they were almost even with her mouth.

And she didn't. The beauty guided them through the sea, side by side. She didn't seem nervous about the smaller fish who swam beside her, nor was she all that interested in the strange creature he held in his arms. She just moved gracefully and with purpose, flicking her tail every now and then but maintaining a slow pace.

The shark was letting Ace get used to her, he realized. Neither of the females were pushing the other. But after a long moment, Ace reached out her hand as well.

"You want to touch her?" he asked.

"Well I—" A soft chuckle interrupted her words. "I guess when else would I have another chance like this?"

"Never." He reached down and pulled the glove off her hand. Ace gasped, likely with cold water rushing into her suit, but they were going to be inside again soon.

He cupped her hand in his and then drew both of their palms to the shark's side. Together they stroked the smooth flesh, feeling her gills flare beneath their fingers and the steady beat of her massive heart. And in that instant, he felt all the fear in Ace drift away.

"There," he said quietly. "You can feel her, now."

"She's so soft and strong."

"Like you." He hadn't meant to say that. It revealed far too much about his thoughts and how he was feeling. In a distraction, he looked up at the building and pointed at where the shark had brought them. "Ah, she brought us to the next hole in the wall."

"What?" Craning her neck, Ace looked where he had pointed. "Well, would you look at that?"

"I'm looking." He patted the shark's side one more time and then turned them to head up toward the crack in the tower, hoping she didn't think too much about what he'd said.

Chapter 9

Had she really just swum with a shark? Fuck, she had. She'd seen it with her own eyes. The dark shadow that moved with menacing intent and she'd been so certain it was going to attack them. She'd imagined the terrifying moment when there was nothing but flashing teeth and darkness as she was stuck in the mouth of a massive creature who only thought with its stomach.

Then she'd swum beside the shark that was larger than Maketes, and somehow, she hadn't been so scared. It had only taken a few moments and then all that fear had loosened. And then she'd touched it. The rough skin was something she would never forget in her life. How could anyone? The shark had looked her in the eyes with that black gaze and she'd felt so seen.

Not that the beast had looked at her and recognized only that Ace existed. But like the shark had looked into her soul and measured the weight of her worth.

The undine still held her with her back against his chest. The power in his body was something to marvel at if she had the time to do so. And maybe she did. Maybe she could take a moment to sink into the reality that while this man should despise her and her people for everything they had stolen from the undine, he had protected her. He'd given her the gift of releasing her fear, and that was humbling. She'd only ever been able to do that for herself. And here he was, swimming into her life with the intent to just help her.

Maketes's arm tightened around her waist as they moved closer to the top of the building. "You are sure this is where you need to be?"

"No, I don't know where we're supposed to go. I have a name for an office to go into, because that guy was the last one to have the key. But that's all I know."

She felt something shifting against her back. Looking over her shoulder at him, she realized that must have been his gills fluttering against her spine.

Then a muttering grumble echoed behind her, "That man had no plan whatsoever."

"I'm starting to believe the same thing."

"He wants you to fail."

Maybe he did. Maybe Jacob had a larger plan than just this, and it was that he wanted to kill her sister. She had no way of knowing. He had always kept her out of the loop, only using her when he thought he absolutely had to, and she knew that wasn't from the kindness of his own heart.

As Maketes spun in the water, whirling them closer to the opening, she found the words spilling out of her lips. "I don't think Jacob cares about anyone but himself. He was imprisoned after killing a lot of people. So many people that I don't think he even knows how many he killed. He walked into a group of women, children, and men, set a bomb, and then left. Right in the middle of a busy shopping center."

Maketes twitched around her, his entire body flinching and then hardening as though he had turned to stone. "He killed innocents?"

"No one in Gamma is without fault," she whispered. "Even me. I took from people who didn't deserve to be taken from." But she hadn't, not really. Those people were wealthy, capable, and wouldn't have noticed that she'd taken that much if their financial advisors hadn't caught her. She'd stolen from people who could lose money and not even notice.

She might have given it back if she hadn't been caught. The guilt had been eating her alive. Now? Now she just wanted her own revenge against the people who had put her in Gamma. The people who had taken her away from her sister.

"When I first started talking to Anya," she started, pressing herself back against him for warmth and strength. "All I could think about was punishing the people who had locked me up. I wasn't like everyone else in Gamma. I wasn't a hardened criminal, and it was an offense that should have been forgivable. I just stole some things."

"My people do not throw away our own, not even the ones who have made mistakes." Then a low growl rumbled through him. "But people like your... Jacob? We cut the poison from our bloodlines quickly."

"As you should. We do the same, in a way. But I didn't think I belonged with all the others, so I was very quick to judge. I wanted to tear Alpha down and all the people who had made it seem like I was less than they were for doing what I had to do to survive." She shook her head, focusing on the looming building in front of them. "And I did it. I took them all down, scattered them to the seven seas, to an unused tower in Gamma, and back to Beta, where they will be forced to work. I succeeded, and I punished them all."

Some angry part of her was happy about that. She shouldn't be. She'd ruined more lives, all for the sake of revenge. There were likely innocents caught in the mix and some people had died. Ace should feel bad about it.

But she didn't.

"A true warrior knows when to let go of the losses and celebrate the victories," Maketes said as he paused in front of the glass. "You won. You did what you said you would do. This is a good thing. You deserved to have your needs met."

She was glad he didn't turn her around. As it was, she could see the image of them in the glass. She looked awful in his arms. A strange bubble of a human being who had no right to be here, with a monster surrounding her as though he were hunting her. But his words went right through her heart and deep into her soul. When had anyone else ever told her she deserved anything?

"Now I don't know what to do with myself," she whispered, her gaze locked on the image of them in the glass. "I am floundering on who I want to be now that I have done what I fought to do for so many years. So I'm still here. Still working with Jacob. Still trying to figure out who I am now that everything is over."

She could see his arm tightening. Felt him draw her closer to his body, and how there was barely restrained power in his touch that suggested he wanted to hold her even harder. "Then we will figure it out together, Ace. We're friends, aren't we?"

Why did that hurt so much to hear him say? Why did she want him to turn her around and rip this stupid helmet off?

"Friends," she repeated. "Of course we are."

Even though that felt so wrong to say. He hadn't been her friend when he was helping her destroy Alpha. He hadn't been her friend when they'd stayed in touch, learning more about each other's cultures while it was still easy for her to pretend he was just another human. She hadn't wanted to be friends then and admitting it to herself now was hard enough.

She'd never say these words out loud. Because he wanted to be friends. Just like everyone else always wanted to be friends with her. The think he desired more? That was an impossible dream that neither he nor she could entertain.

Swallowing her emotions down, she pointed to the tear in the building. "Do you think that's big enough for us to get through?"

"I think I can make it bigger if we have to."

"No, we can't. If we make it any bigger, then the pump system might not be able to drain the water. We'll flood the whole place."

His hands were so delicate on her as he pushed her toward the tear. The water held her for a few moments before she started to drop like a stone. And even then, he was there to help. He grabbed onto her hips, holding her against the opening so she could yank herself in. And then he was right there with her. Moving her limbs so no metal touched her, making sure her suit was intact even as he swam in the tight space behind her.

All the while, she schooled herself to remember this wasn't what she thought it was. Sure, they'd talked for a long time. She knew a bit more about his life than the average person, but nowhere near what Anya knew. They'd only exchanged a few messages every day, and that did not mean they'd made any more of a connection than a complicated friendship.

She needed to get out of her own head. This was an undine. A monster. A deep sea creature who likely was going to continue killing people and saw no issues with her having been the cause of an entire human city being destroyed.

It was silly for her to even think he wanted anything more. His careful hands were merely because he thought she was weak. He wasn't guiding her through the water because he didn't want her to get hurt anymore than a normal friend would. Their banter back and forth was just because he liked to talk.

Forcing herself to remember what all the other people in Gamma had said about Mira and Anya, she reminded herself of the hatred that others felt for those who sided with undines. She wasn't a monster fucker. She wasn't one of those women who fell to the evil attentions of creatures that were never meant to mate with humans.

She was not an animal. And it was wrong to look at him as anything more than that.

The twisted metal surrounding them soon gave way to an opening. Ace moved closer to the light a little too quickly, because she expected him to grab her when the current did. Unfortunately, he didn't. With a sudden sharp tug, she was ripped through the metal shards and bits of glass before spilling out into the room beyond with all the water that had created a tiny waterfall.

She tumbled so fast that she cracked her head against the floor. Or rather, her helmet. And with that hard strike, all she could see was the crack that formed all the way across it.

"Shit," she hissed, sliding to a stop as the water seemed to hit a smaller drain system and disappear. The entire room was wet, though. At least she knew it was unlikely anyone else was in the room. No one wanted to be this close to an area of the pavilion that was literally draining sea water into it.

But damn it. Damn it. She needed that helmet and now it was cracked. She couldn't go out into the ocean with the helmet, now. Even if it could withstand the pressure, there was still the risk that it would fill with water and that she'd drown. If she wasn't careful, then she would die even with Maketes holding onto her.

Ripping the helmet off the suit, she tossed the useless thing across the room with a sharp scream of rage before she realized where she was standing.

The center of the medical pavilion. The Heart, as it used to be known. This was where all the rich people would have gone to get their treatments, while everyone else waited downstairs for hours to be seen. This was luxury, and what she had seen before was just plain.

There weren't hard plastic seats here. Thick, plush couches had sunk into themselves with water damage. But they were still a beautiful beige color. The ceilings weren't so short, instead, they were cathedral ceilings at least sixteen feet tall with glass skylights that revealed more glowing neon signs above her head. The few flickering lights that still remained showed the floor was once perfectly white, although now it was cracked in multiple places.

Opulence lived on, though. The chandelier was hanging by a thread above her head, but it was so beautiful, with chains of glass hanging and reflecting rainbow light. The lobby all surrounded a massive stone fireplace. Real stone, with irregular circles and gray mortar that lasted to this day. The desk at the front was white stone as well, rising out of the floor like it was all one singular piece.

Standing there amongst all of it, she felt a bit like an alien. This wasn't her world. It wasn't the world she'd ever been apart of long before she was sent to Gamma. In reality, she hadn't even realized this existed. No one should live this comfortably when people in Beta had little coffin-like pods to sleep in.

Taking a step farther into the room, she looked over the crack in the wall. It was right through the heart of what had likely been a beautiful mural. But now, all she could tell was that it had once depicted an under the sea scene. Like they didn't get enough of that.

Walking away from the section of spraying water that cast a cold chill into the air, she approached the main wall of windows. Placing her hand on it, she found herself bathed in a glowing blue light. The nearest neon sign had an arrow pointing farther down the tower with twin turtles on either side. ARCADE, it said.

But that glowing neon light wasn't the only one she could see. There were countless others. So many of them that she could hardly guess at their numbers as they disappeared into the distance. The entire sea was lit up before her eyes. Her view of Gamma had always been rather limited to what she could see from her clock tower. But this? This was a sprawling metropolis of a city and she hadn't even realized it was there. She'd been here for almost two years, and she hadn't known there was so much more to this place than she'd thought.

Two levels below her, she could see the glass bridge that connected this tower to the next. There were people down there, about the size of her thumb, they were so far away. Soon enough, those people would realize that someone else was in their home. Someone they needed to get out of here. But for now, all she could do was stare at them.

Until she realized that she was staring and that at any point, they could look up. That was all it would take for her to be in the worst position possible.

Gasping, she reeled away from the window and started stripping out of her diving suit. Water sprayed all over the white floor, speckles of dirty sea water and dirty silt tinging the droplets dark. Her boots came off next, and she padded barefoot across the floor to the front desk.

"There has to be a registry," she muttered, walking around and reaching for the top drawer.

Nothing of use. Just a few remaining pieces of an eraser and what looked like old chewing gum.

She tried the next side drawer, but that had nothing in it either. The other side drawer? That one was locked.

Hissing out a breath between her teeth, she grabbed onto the handle and anchored herself with her foot braced against the desk. She'd use her entire weight to open the damn thing if she had to. If it was locked, that meant there might be something useful inside.

She didn't even hear the groaning from the wall she'd entered from. Nor did she think to pause at the grinding sound of metal and the rushing blast of water that seemed stronger by the moment.

Chapter 10

"Why are women like this?" he muttered as he ripped yet another piece of metal free from the wall. "They're always rushing off into danger. I don't want to save them, but here I am, rushing to save yet another achromo."

That was his experience, at least. Both Mira and Anya had been gravely injured in the first few months that he'd known them. In his experience, female achromos were crazy. They had no sense of self preservation, nor did they care that they were risking their lives. They sought out dangerous situations. That was all he could surmise. They sought them out, they wanted to be in danger, and that must be because they all were insane.

"Ridiculous achromos," he said again, tearing at another loose metallic piece. "This is why I haven't been involved with any of them. Achromos are worse than the People of Water. Stupid, fragile little monsters with absolutely no way to protect themselves."

Finally, the wall gave. There was enough room for him to ride the waterfall into the area where she was helpless. He'd watched her move. She wasn't a fighter, that much he was certain of. Those blunt little nails and shortened teeth could do nothing against an attacker. He doubted she even had a weapon on her.

He dove face first through the waterfall, riding it down onto the floor with a wet slap that echoed through the room. Immediately, he looked around. His eyes noted the strange stone sculpture, the rotting furniture, the view that was just as pretty even though he was outside of this achromo home. But then his eyes found her. Her leg was awkwardly raised, but he watched with rapt attention as that leg flexed.

Had any other of his people realized how strong the achromos were? Her legs strained with the effort she put on whatever she was holding. He could see the tension in her body and how swiftly her back arched into the movement. Veins popped out on her forehead and it was the most impressive act he'd ever seen in his life. For someone so small, so delicate, and so out of her element, she was capable of such strength.

Then the metal groaned. Whatever she was holding made a noise like a shriek and suddenly she dropped to the ground. A giant clanging accompanied her fall.

He'd never moved so fast in his life.

Using his arms and tail, he shoved himself across the room. Far beyond the water where he was safe. All the way to her side, where he loomed over her, looking down into her red features.

Her eyes were a little unfocused when she looked up at him and wheezed, "Ow."

"Where are you hurt?" He ran his hands up and down her sides, trying to find the wound that pained her. He skimmed his fingers down her sides, finding more of that softness that was so intriguing, but right now, he had to focus on the injuries that she'd thrust upon herself. Foolish female. Foolish achromo taking risks like that.

"I'm fine!" she insisted, slapping at his hands.

But she was still making that awful wheezing sound. It didn't sound like it was coming from her throat, but he didn't know what else would make that noise. She made a few coughing sounds, and he wondered if she'd broken her ribs. He could feel them when he squeezed her hard, so he knew she had them just like he did.

Leaning down, he pressed his head against her sternum. Right between the rather full, interesting breasts that he definitely wasn't looking at because he needed to listen to her heart beat. Perhaps it was her heart that was struggling.

The moment he pressed his head down, he knew what the problem was. She had seriously injured herself because there was only one beat in her chest. One thud. Steady and even, but it was still only the one.

He left his head against her skin, not wanting her to see his expression as he realized she was dying. "Oh, Ace. This is grave indeed."

"I knocked the wind out of myself, you moron! Get off of me."

He leaned into her harder, ignoring how she put her hands on his head to push him away. "No, kefi. You only have one heartbeat. It will not be long now. I will hold you until the end."

Why did it hurt so badly to think he had lost her this early? She had said they were friends. That is what she wanted from him, and therefore, that was what he would be. He'd never wanted to be someone's friend so badly. Perhaps more, of course. He would have been very happy with more, but he would take what he could get.

And if that meant holding her until the end, guiding her soul into the deep where the sea mother would watch over her, then that was exactly what he would do.

"Maketes—"

"Shh, kefi. I am sorry I failed you. I should have kept you safer."

If he had been here, prepared to enter the room with her, perhaps she wouldn't have made such a mistake. Perhaps she wouldn't have risked her life. This was his fault. This was all his fault, and how was he going to live with this guilt? He was usually so good at thrusting aside his emotions, but right now, it was almost impossible to do.

Then her fingers carded through his hair. Those talented, thin fingers brushed through the coiled tangles on his head and gently rubbed at his scalp. The same way he'd done to her.

He waited. Listening to her heart beat while her grip made its way down to the back of his neck, massaging tense muscles that couldn't release. No matter how hard she worked at them. No matter how wonderful it felt for her to touch him.

It set in that her heart wasn't slowing. She was still here. Touching him. Breathing. And her heart was still beating.

Slowly, he lifted his head from the comfortable pillows of her breasts and looked at her.

She gave him the smallest smile, and it was the first time he'd seen any expression on her face other than sullen seriousness. "Humans only have one heart."

"One heart?" he repeated.

"One heart."

Well. He felt silly.

And then he realized he was pressed against every inch of her. His tail had somehow looped around her ankles, holding her legs together while he was still on top of her. While he did that, her hips were pressed into his belly. His arms were on either side of her body and he'd had his head nestled between her breasts.

He was screaming the word "friends" in his mind and somehow, that wasn't helping. He was still here. Still leaning against her. Still staring down at her as he realized just how close he was to her.

"You have small flecks of gold in your eyes," he mumbled. The gills on the sides of his neck stood up, fluttering slowly for her.

It wasn't much of a display. But he'd never been one for big displays of affection. He'd tried before, he'd just never been able to do it. And yet right now, with this little achromo, he wanted to make those gills shake so hard she'd feel the wind of them on her face.

"Do I?" she asked, her tone amused and her gaze never moving from his. "Yours are entirely black."

"I know."

"I thought there would be some color in them."

What was he supposed to say to that? He already felt like an idiot talking about her eyes. But then he leaned forward and he could smell her. The soft scent of her, like the warmth of the sun after a storm. Electric and heated.

"You smell so good," he muttered, his eyes drifting shut as he told himself not to put his head back down. "I'm sorry I touched your breasts."

She made a choked sound, and when he looked back at her, she was bright red. Even the tips of her ears seemed to burn with some emotion he couldn't name. But he was quite certain it was his favorite color on her.

"Get up." She struggled underneath him, and he released her. "The cabinet I just pulled out should have a directory in it, and then I can get to the office and find that damned key."

"I said I was sorry."

"I heard you," she muttered, those ears somehow turning even deeper red. "Just... Help me find the key."

He might have teased her further. He wanted to see if he could make her ears so red they turned purple, but then he heard a sound from the door. Frowning, he looked in that direction, only to see a group of people standing there. At least five of them, one with a weapon already raised and pointed at Ace's head.

Maketes didn't think. He just moved.

In one moment, he was staring at the achromos he knew he could kill in an instant. And the next, he chose her. He lunged in front of her. His body became a shield, because he was faster than the weapon that struck his shoulder.

He grunted, feeling the sharp edge of what seemed like a harpoon sinking deep into his flesh. The barest hint of the tip came out of the front, hovering right in front of her eyes. A bead of blood welled and then dripped down his chest.

A soft sound came out of her mouth, and he pretended there was no one here but them. Slowly, ignoring the shouts from behind him, he lifted his hand and tucked a strand of her short hair behind her ear. Then he nudged her glasses up her nose.

"Get underneath the desk," he said calmly.

"Maketes—"

"I don't want you to see what I'm going to do."

She stared up at him with big brown eyes, swallowed hard, and then nodded. He waited until she ducked beneath the stone that would keep her safe, and then he turned upon the men. Slowly. He controlled every movement so he could glare at them with all the hatred he harbored in his heart.

Achromos were not the women he knew in his life. These were the achromos he knew. The men and women with weapons that bit and tore at all those they did not understand. These were the creatures that were a plague upon his ocean.

Crouching, all the gills on his body flared wide and stiff as he hissed at them. The sound of his rage echoed in the room, filling it until there was nowhere these creatures could run without hearing him.

The shouts turned into anger. A few of the men raced into the room, weapons in their hands that looked like sticks with shards of glass coming out of them. Did they really think that would hurt him?

Maketes might not be as big as his siblings, but he was faster. Even on land, he was not some massive elephant seal who struggled to move on land. No, he was stronger than that. He easily lunged forward and grabbed the arms of the first man, who raised a weapon to him.

Maketes dragged the man forward, staring into his terrified gaze as he snapped the man's arms backwards. The scream of pain that echoed throughout the room was music to his ears. This was what he was good at. No matter how much he was the funny sibling, the brother who always found humor in every situation, he was also one of the deadliest warriors in his pod.

Coiling his tail, he used it to leap forward onto the next man. He hit the floor hard with the other man in his arms, chewing through his throat as he rolled them both. Another he caught with his tail, wrapping the woman tightly in his scales as blood poured down his throat. She shrieked in pain as he tightened, gripping her harder and harder until her bones cracked through her flesh.

Another bolt when through him. This time, he raised his arm as a shield and it sliced through his forearm, sticking halfway through the skin.

"Ow," he snarled at the man who couldn't understand him. "You're going to pay for that. You'll be the last to die. Now watch your companions writhe in agony."

There were only two left, so it would be a brief battle. He let the woman's limp body drop onto the floor. He released the man in his grip who gurgled as he fell, frantically pressing his hands against a neck so mangled there was no healing it.

Dragging himself through the blood that only made it easier for him to slide toward the last two men, he dodged another bolt and casually lashed out with a claw. The second to last man fell onto his knees, grabbing at his stomach where ropes of innards spilled out. He hadn't even realized he was hurt until the weight dragged him forward.

And then it was just him and the man with the bolts. Maketes knew their kind. He could see the man was shaking so badly he wouldn't even be able to pull that trigger on the weapon.

So, as he loomed up to his great height above the man, he reached for the weapon and aimed it between his own jaws. Biting the end of the strange weapon, he stared the man down as he grasped either side of the achromo's head and twisted hard.

The man's body fell to the floor. Maketes stared at the head in his grasp for a few moments before tossing it to the side.

Breathing hard, he waited to get himself under control for a few moments. Bloodlust ran through him hard. He'd always had an edge of it from his father and his father's father. All of them loved the taste of blood a little too much.

Shaking himself, he didn't look back at the desk where he knew a little achromo hid. Instead, he dropped onto his forearms and crawled over to the waterfall that was hitting the drainage system. Quietly, he moved his body into the water, ripping the bolts out of his body, and cleaning the blood off himself. He even opened his mouth, letting the hard spray of water clear the blood from his teeth so she wouldn't have to see that either.

Only then did he turn his attention to the desk, sending a prayer to the gods of the sea that she'd remained underneath. But she stood beside the desk with a piece of paper in her hand. That hard expression was back on her face, which was paler than he'd ever seen it.

"You're hurt," she said, parroting his words from only a few moments ago.

"Flesh wounds." But they ached.

She waved the piece of paper at him. "We're in the medical pavilion. I know where we can get you some help. Follow me?"

He nodded and watched as she reached into her pocket and pulled out her droid. The little silver balls all clicked together a few times before racing out ahead of them, as though they knew where to go.

He had a moment where he wondered if he was really going deeper into the home of the achromos, far from the water where he was safe. But as she walked away from him, not even sparing a glance for the remains of mangled bodies, he knew he would follow her anywhere.

Chapter 11

Her hands were shaking. Ace wrapped them in the hem of her shirt, trying to tell herself that it was normal for them to shake after watching a friend crazily murder a bunch of people. It was normal that she was nervous after all that. It was normal for her to think that maybe she was losing her mind a little.

He'd torn that man's head off so easily. Twisted it in those massive hands and the body had dropped before the man could even scream out in fear. It had just been attached one minute and then... not. Dropped onto the floor like it wasn't even that big of a deal that he'd wrenched it off.

She knew now why he'd told her not to watch. Maketes hadn't wanted her to see the spray of blood that would soon fountain from his hands. Who wanted anyone else to know that they were so capable of terrible, awful things?

And yet there was some part of her that recognized he'd done what he had to do. Before he'd told her to come out, he'd washed the blood clean from his body. He'd taken the time to make sure that she wouldn't see the violence that had occurred.

Even if she'd already watched. Even though he'd told her to not look because he hadn't wanted her to be terrified of him.

She was, now. But that was her own fault.

Ace was still brave enough to look at him, though. The wounds that decorated his chest and forearm were from keeping her safe. The one on his shoulder was quite literally meant for her. She'd looked down the barrel of that gun and she had known she was about to die. Until he moved in front of her, taking the wound that should have been hers.

All she could do was get them to a safe place. This was the medical pavilion, after all. She knew where she was going now that she'd found the map. She tried to keep her mind occupied with lefts and rights and turns that weren't all that complicated. Instead, all she could focus on was the quiet sound of his scales sliding along the smooth floor. The sound of his palms slapping against the cold tile because he couldn't walk like a normal person. It should have sent disgust rolling down between her shoulder blades, and in some small sense, it did.

But every time she looked over her shoulder, all she could see was the blood that was dripping from his wounds. He'd left a slick black streak across the floor, which was then parted by the long length of his tail, like a child had gotten into ink and ran their fingers through it.

Her heart squeezed and finally she found the room she was looking for. "This used to be a surgical suite. It should still have a lot of the items we're looking for, but also shouldn't have too many entrances and exits."

He only watched her with an amused expression on his face. "You know better than I do. I've only been in a human city one other time."

One other...

She held the door open for him and stared as he squeezed past her. They were so close she could feel the chill of his skin and the strange electrical sensation that brushed over her when he got close enough to touch. She wasn't sure if that was him or just... her. Wanting to touch. Wanting to put her hand on that wound that was meant for her.

"You've been in a human city before?" she asked, both for curiosity's sake and to distract herself.

"I was there when we attacked Beta."

"Oh." Right. She'd so easily forgotten that the undines had gotten into the other city and nearly tore it apart from the inside out. They'd even heard about it in Gamma, and they didn't hear about any recent events.

Maketes didn't wait around for her to figure out what to say next. Instead, he coiled his tail around himself and slumped against the surgical table. Even like that, he was the same height as her. She'd be looking him in the eye if she stood right in front of him.

And then he just stared at her. Kept looking. No matter how long she stayed quiet, and that was unusual for him. Usually he was the first one to start talking when she...

There it was.

"You're afraid of me now," he said, that deep voice rumbling through the room and raising every hair on her body.

She rubbed her arms to get rid of the feeling. "No, I'm not."

"You watched when I told you not to."

"I did."

Ace needed her hands to be busy. She wandered through the room, gathering up the supplies she needed. Needle, thread, antiseptic, a bandage that she realized would fall off the moment he got into the water, but it would make her feel better for now.

He watched her every movement, clearly frustrated with this turn of events. "I told you not to."

"You already said that."

"Why are you feeling so uncomfortable with me now, then? I told you not to look. You were the one who decided to do so." His stare nearly burned a hole between her shoulder blades. "You knew what I was."

"I did." She kept her back to him for a second, taking in a deep, steadying breath. Then she turned around and marched toward him with determination. "I don't know why I'm feeling this way. I think it was easier when I knew what you were, but I could only send you words through a droid. You weren't right in front of me, reminding me of what you were every second of the day."

The fins around his face flared wide, and even that made her uncomfortable. Just the slightest show of surprise and she was so close to bolting it made her ashamed of herself.

With an angry exhale, she stacked everything next to him and tried her best to get control over the feelings. "It's hard to remember that I know who you are when you're so... so..."

He reached up between them and grabbed one of her flailing hands. "What about me scares you?"

She swallowed. "Maketes, I don't want to—"

"Tell me exactly. Tell me what pieces of me scare you so that I can ease your fears."

She shouldn't be doing this. This was stupid, anyway. There were so many parts of him that scared her. It would take them hours for her to list them all and they were on a timeline. She barely had time to stitch him closed, which was the other thing they should both be focused on right now.

Instead, she found her lips moving. "Your claws."

"My claws?" He lifted their hands up so she had to look at them, seeing her fingers coiled together with his. "These would never cause pain. They were made to protect, not to harm."

"But they ripped through that man's stomach so easily."

"I don't want you to think of that, kefi. I want you to know that they are gentle with you and that if you need someone to save you, that they are the first weapon you should look for."

Slowly, ever so slowly, he released her hand and lifted his. She could see it coming toward her face, and she let out a slow, stuttering breath so she remained in place.

The smooth back of his claw touched the highest peak of her cheekbone. Feather light, she almost couldn't feel it as he swept it along the curve of her cheek and down to the edge of her jaw. Gentle, always gentle. He wasn't even touching her at some points, but she swore he was.

Ace's eyes fluttered shut. Something was happening inside of her that she couldn't explain. Just that single touch eased the fear so quickly, when it shouldn't have. He was still the problem. He had murdered so many people in front of her. She should only see their dead bodies when her eyes were closed like this.

Instead, what she saw were all the pieces of him that she wished she could ignore.

"Your gills," she whispered. "They're very different from what I expected."

"How so?"

"They're larger than I thought they would be."

The faintest hint of a laugh made her imagine him smiling. Behind her closed eyes, everything was so much safer. She could imagine the grin on his face and ignore the thought that there were gills there. Instead, all she saw was the way his face wrinkled with happiness. How his eyes crinkled at the corners and deep smile lines on his cheeks were revealed. That expression was so familiar to her already, and they'd only been around each other for a couple of days.

Then his hand cupped hers, drawing her fingers to his neck. The softest velvet bumped against her fingers, gently fluttered the moment she touched them.

"My gills?" he repeated, his voice deeper than before.

She took a deep breath, squeezed her eyes shut a little harder, and explored. Just like with the shark, he gave her an opportunity to face something that made her feel uncomfortable, and she was going to take that opportunity.

From afar, his gills looked like they were similar to a lionfish. All spines and spikes and likely full of poisonous liquid that would make her writhe in agony. But they weren't like that at all. They were soft. They slid through her fingers and seemed to touch her back with the slightest of movements. She could feel him exhaling. The warm air that escaped through his gills was so much warmer than the air of the surgical room.

"This doesn't hurt you?" she asked.

"If you yanked on them, yes, it would hurt." His tone was twisted, like he was holding himself back from something. "But it feels nice when you touch them."

"Oh." Did she want it to feel nice?

Yes. Yes, she did. Because it was nice to know that he was safe. That he wasn't going to lunge at her in pain or bite at her.

"Your teeth," she blurted. There was a reason she was touching him, and it was so she wasn't afraid of him anymore. So she wouldn't be scared to lean on him, to use him to keep her safe.

"Open your eyes, kefi. If you are afraid of my teeth, then you need to look at them."

She didn't want to open her eyes. Ace wanted to stay in this world where nothing existed but darkness and touch.

But then he leaned closer, hesitating where the heat of his breath brushed against the junction of her shoulder and neck. She heard the ragged breath he sucked in before his lips were suddenly pressed to the soft skin there. She could feel the imprint of his teeth through his lips. The sharp edges of them were dulled by warm heat that spread throughout her body like a wildfire.

Then those lips parted. She could feel the sharp tips of his teeth pressing against her flesh before he leaned back once more. Just the barest hint of them, and she was ashamed to admit she wanted more.

So she opened her eyes, blinking in the glaring white overhead lights before meeting his dark gaze. He parted his lips, baring those teeth for her eyes. Maketes even let her look her fill before he spoke.

"I am made like a weapon. But many of my kind are more terrifying than me. I promise you, with every part of who I am and every part of who I will be, I would never hurt you. You have made every part of me shine with light, sweet achromo. You are brave and wild and free, and I would be a fool to try and dampen that light."

The same hand that held her fingers to his gills took her touch to his lips. Then he released her, never pushing her to do anything she didn't want to do. Because of that, Ace found she wanted to touch.

She gently ran her finger along his plush lower lip, tracing the outline of the cushion of it. She could see where he had been biting the soft flesh, as though he was as nervous about her touching him as she had been. Again, those lips parted. He even opened his mouth slightly so she could run that same finger over the sharp points of his teeth.

They weren't as razor sharp as she'd thought. Perhaps there would have to be more force to a bite to tear flesh like he had with the others.

It should have frightened her. Instead, a heat bloomed deep in her body. A heat she almost didn't recognize because it had been so long since she'd felt it.

This time, her finger traced his lips with a little more intent. If he was human, she would have maybe tried to kiss him. He would have pushed her away, a man as attractive as him would never kiss a girl like her, but she still would have tried. It was just the two of them here, after all.

Those big hands came down on her hips, holding her in place. "Are you still afraid of me?"

"You killed all those people with your bare hands," she whispered, her gaze still locked on his lips. "You ripped a man's throat out with those teeth. And you are everything so many have described a monster to be."

"And yet?"

She smiled. A real, true smile that made her cheeks ache. She was so rusty with smiling, Ace wasn't even sure if it looked like a genuine smile or if it was all wrong. "I know these hands will not hurt me. I know that your teeth will never rip at my flesh. And I suppose I can admit that I trust you. Even if you have the hands of a murderer."

His hands flexed on her sides, and then he let out a low, grumbling sound. It rumbled in his chest like the sound of a motor before he suddenly pushed down on her hips.

She went from standing to sitting. There was no fighting that grip. She thought she was going to tumble to the ground, but instead, she landed on his coiled up tail. The scales pressed between her legs, rubbing against the ache that had built while she touched him, and she was suddenly struck by their position.

She had one hand still on his gills, one hand tracing his lips. Her legs were wrapped around him, and his hands were on her hips. If she rocked even slightly, she'd be grinding herself against the ridges of his scales. Seeking out that friction that she desperately needed but that he likely didn't even understand.

Maketes must know very little about her kind. There was no reason for him to learn anatomy, and she'd never even asked him if he was interested in humans or what he thought about her people.

Cheeks flaming bright red, she drew her hands back to herself. Planting them on her thighs so she didn't touch him anymore, she cleared her throat. "Would you like me to stitch you up?"

He blinked, the movement so smooth and alien-like it almost threw her right back into the discomfort and fear. But then those enormous hands clenched on her hips again, and she had a hard time focusing on anything other than wishing he would tilt her hips for her and tumble them into a reality where they weren't friends at all.

"You may tend to my wounds if you stay where you are."

She blinked at him, her eyes wide. "Why would you want me to stay where I am?"

He looked back at her with those pitch black eyes, and she thought for a second she saw something in the depths. His gills were still flared wide, undulating in a slow movement that was almost impossible to see. Perhaps from being overstimulated, she could only imagine he wasn't touched very often either.

Maketes cleared his throat and looked away from her. "You're flighty and fickle. I don't want you to be afraid of me again because I chased when you ran. Just stitch me closed, Ace, and stay where you are."

She shouldn't, but she did. And with every loop of the thread through his skin, she had to admit, she noticed their differences less and less.

Chapter 12

Maketes kept himself together throughout the stitching process. He didn't care about the tiny spots of pain as she threaded through his flesh with that tiny piece of metal. Clearly, she thought it was hurting him, but he barely even feel it.

All he felt was the weight of her on his lap. The sensation of her legs on either side of his tail, knowing that she was right where he wanted her. And if she moved, even the slightest, he would likely extrude both of his cocks and terrify her to no end.

She was afraid of his gills. Let alone all the other physical differences he had to keep himself from blurting out. And he had thought about it. Maketes's first reaction to her saying that they were different was for him to think about his twin cocks that he knew for certain human men didn't have.

He'd seen an achromo man naked before. The tiny, floppy piece of meat between the man's legs had looked utterly useless upon first sight. And then he'd confirmed by talking with both Arges and Daios that their size differences were great between their females and themselves.

But they were much larger than Maketes. He was more manageable for an achromo female. He wasn't sixteen feet long and made of solid muscle. He was only thirteen feet, a perfect mate for both his own kind and achromos... If it weren't for a few key features that had always made him lesser to the females of his own kind.

Maybe they would make him lesser to her, as well. Maybe Ace wouldn't like that he couldn't flutter very fast. Maybe she would think less of him for... for...

No, he couldn't think of that.

Maketes adjusted himself where he now leaned against the door to the room, trying to keep his mind on the now instead of going down dark paths. He didn't want to think about what made him a poor mate when she was right here. So close he could touch her if he wanted.

They'd turned off all the lights, so the only illumination in the room came from the neon lights just barely visible through the single pane of glass that revealed the sea beyond. She refused to sleep on the surgical bed, even though he'd thought it looked rather comfortable and it was silly of her to not make use of it. Instead, she'd yanked all the blankets and fabric she could find in the room to pile them against the base. She'd curled up, telling him to mind his own business when he'd said it was a bad idea, and then tried to fall asleep.

He didn't think she was very successful at doing so, though. Every time he looked at her, she was moving. Rolling from one side to the other, drawing her knees up to her chest and then stretching them back out.

Obviously, she wasn't getting any rest. He'd seen the other two achromos sleeping in their rooms, he'd never seen them move this much. Achromos were eerie when they slept. They had almost no movement, no visible breath. They just laid there as though they'd died.

Sighing, he crossed his arms over his chest and looked over the room again. They'd barricaded the only other door. He was faster than the achromos were, anyway. If they tried to get into the room, he'd be on them before they could even set foot near Ace. Leaning against the only other door into the room, he knew they were as safe as they were going to get in this cursed city.

So why was he on edge?

Ace rolled over in her sleep again, this time adding in a cracking noise that repeated constantly until he realized it was her teeth chattering together. Her teeth! The woman was cold, and he was an idiot who hadn't realized that she was rolling back and forth seeking some kind of warmth.

To him, the room wasn't all that bad. Brisk, perhaps, but warmer than the ocean beyond. But to her, without her wet suit or anything else to keep her warm, this room and the cold floor must have been near to torture. Even the blankets she'd found were thin with holes in them.

Idiot, he thought to himself, before running his hands down his chest to make sure he was finally warmed up. It took his body a long time to react to being out of the water, but once he was somewhat dry, his body started to put off a lot more heat.

Once he'd finished patting himself down and was certain he wouldn't make her any colder than she already was, he moved quickly. Maketes used his fluke to wedge underneath her and rolled her into the base of his tail. She let out a little squeaking sound of annoyance, but by then she had already rolled to the muscular part of his tail. He wrapped the thicker base around her and then dragged her into him.

It all took a few seconds before she was in his arms. By then, she was struggling but incapable of much movement because the entire weight of his tail had her trapped against him. It took so little effort for him to bundle her up and press her against his chest. And then even less difficulty to drape his fluke over her back like a blanket and tuck it in around her body.

"Stop fighting, kefi," he muttered, getting a little more comfortable around her. "You're cold."

"I am cold, but what is this doing other than raising my blood pressure?" She was still struggling, although he had a feeling she would quickly realize she couldn't move any more than he let her. His tail was wrapped around her, after all.

A massive loop of it pressed her against his chest. But then he realized maybe she wasn't comfortable that way, so he shifted her to his side. Then she was cushioned in his arm, held to his ribs where his lower gills could taste her, and she had one thick thigh slung over his tail.

"Maketes," she hissed. "I was fine where I was."

"You weren't. You weren't sleeping, which means I can't sleep, and I would like to get some rest tonight if possible. I do have to return to the ocean at some point, which means you need to be in the water with me. Get some sleep."

But she was tense against his side. Even as he relaxed, hoping that she would follow suit, she didn't. Maketes stared up at the ceiling and prayed for silence, but there was no rest for either of them tonight, apparently.

Because her hand pressed against his chest and he knew that even if she had fallen asleep, he wouldn't have been able to. She was touching him. Her fingers stroking his skin as though she was mindlessly stroking something comforting, and that made it hard to breathe.

All he wanted was her. And damn it, that was a hard thought to have when she was pressed up against him. He wanted to roll over onto her. He wanted to kiss her like he'd seen his brothers do with their mates, even though he'd never thought about putting his mouth on another. But what did she taste like? Was her taste the same as her scent? All sunshine and sweet things?

Sighing, he tightened his arm around her and tried to distract them both. "What is going through your mind?"

"What do you mean?"

"I can hear your thoughts as though you are saying them. You are a loud thinker, Ace."

"I do not think loud." She almost sounded insulted before she sighed. "I'm just wondering about your life outside of all this. You're here with me, but you must have something or someone to go back to."

Did he tell her the truth? That he'd been wasting away with nothing for so long, and that he'd leapt at the opportunity for adventure with her? Or did he try to play this off as though he had another life?

Maketes was an honest man. He had no interest in lying to her.

"I have nothing to get back to, kefi. Don't worry about me so much." He shifted, his hand coming down on her hip because he couldn't resist the roundness there that called to him. "I have nothing and no one waiting on me."

"That's hard to believe. You're so..." Her words trailed off.

A glimmer of pride glowed inside of his chest. "Handsome?"

"Well, I wasn't going to say it like that."

"Like what?"

Her hand slapped down on his chest, and he grinned up at the ceiling. She hated it when he goaded her, but he loved these moments between them. He enjoyed nothing more than antagonizing her.

"My people believe me to be very handsome as well. You can say it if you wish. It's not the first time someone has told me that I would make a good mate."

She made a garbled sound in the back of her throat. "I said nothing about being a mate!"

"You didn't have to. All the females in our pod are very interested in me. I have even had strangers approach me and ask if I would be interested in being the father of their children. Mates are hard to come by, especially ones who look like me." With his free hand, he grabbed hers on his chest and rubbed her palm up and down his chest. "This coloring is rare, you know."

Her breath stuttered, and he wondered if touching him was affecting her just as much as it affected him. He wanted her hand to keep rubbing his chest and stomach. His skin was soft there, not quite so covered in scales. He could feel the heat of her palm as if she were made of fire.

Then she spoke, and he felt every muscle in his body tense.

"Why are you not with someone, then? If you wanted a mate, you could have had one by now."

"I suppose I could have." Did he tell her? Did he bare his soul in a way that he had been afraid to do since he was nothing but a small fry?

Her leg shifted, that hand moving over his chest all on her own. He couldn't think. Couldn't breathe. She was touching him willingly, and all he wanted was for more of that touch. But then he froze as she continued to speak into the darkness where secrets were easier to breathe into life.

"I can tell you that no one wanted me." Her words were haunting in the room where they slept, neither of them looking at each other in the dark. "My sister is gorgeous. She's got this long dark hair that's never frizzy, and a smile that lights up an entire room. So many people wanted her. I was just her ugly sister. Growing up, I was always a little overweight. I wore glasses, my hair never had pretty curls. And I was loud. So loud. Opinionated, with a mouth on me that would send even the most hardened of engineers reeling."

He could see it now. This brash, unaware young woman who had walked into a room and demanded that everyone give her attention. Because she was right. Because her words had meaning and no one ever listened to her. How he wished he could see her do that right now. He'd watch her with rapt attention and tear into anyone who didn't give her the recognition she deserved.

The click of her throat suggested she'd swallowed. "I'll be honest, I think I just settled into that. People thought of me as the ugly sister, and it was safe that way. I didn't have to hope that boys would like me, or find me pretty. I took that persona on, and it served me well. Look at Gamma? Do you know what usually happens to women when they end up in that city? Not good things. Not at all."

Which only served to make him angry. Because she'd been alone. No one had been there to protect her, and he'd been talking to her through a stupid little droid when he should have been here. For her. Making sure that, of all things, she was safe.

He hadn't known that she wasn't safe, though. Now, all he could do was make up for that which he had not known.

He tightened his hold on her and decided he, too, would bare his soul. "Our people perform to prove that we are interested in someone. We call it fluttering. The gills on our neck, our sides, they all move when we see someone that we like. It is an essential part of who we are and what mates we find. Unfortunately for me, I cannot flutter very well. The display that I create is… lackluster. To say the least."

Her fingers had paused, as though she realized that he'd fluttered for her before. And then those fingers moved again, slowly trailing down his stomach to the ab muscles that flexed at her touch. "I don't see why that would affect whether or not you would find a mate."

"Well, and then there is the uh..." He coughed. Even now, the words stuck in his throat as though there was something wrong with even admitting this. "Some colorings of our people are a prediction of what they can do. Blue generally shows an ability for reason. Red colorings are always more aggressive and have a harder time controlling their anger. But me? I... Well, yellows are usually where the line stops. A golden child, as my mother used to say, a sign that the ancients are pleased with our family line and that we have done enough to end it. I am a mate for fun, and that is all. But if anyone wants something serious or a future with children? I am not the one for that."

And it still hurt. A lot.

He didn't enjoy thinking about these difficult things, because then he didn't have to admit how much it hurt. He wanted children. He wanted a mate who would look at him with affection while playing with yellow bellied children that laughed as he chased them through the waves.

Her hand had frozen on his belly. "I'm sorry to hear that, Maketes. I can only imagine it's been very hard for you to deal with."

"It comes with the coloring, I guess. Us yellow finned bastards sure are pretty, but most of us cannot pass that color on to anyone else." And it killed him every single day to admit it. He hated knowing that he wasn't what females wanted, other than for his looks. He wasn't worthy enough for a long term relationship. They looked at him as funny, hilarious to be around, but not worth more than that.

Sometimes, he didn't want to be the fun one. Sometimes, he wanted to be the person who someone else looked at as if he were their forever.

Her hand slid again, this time far too close to his cocks. He grabbed onto her wrist just as her fingers brushed against the slit between his scales. It took every single ounce of his power to keep his cocks where they were supposed to be. He would not scare her. Not after coming this far through her fear and disgust.

"Sleep now, Ace."

"What did I just touch?"

He glanced down to see her looking at her fingers. They were glistening with the natural lubrication that existed where his cocks were kept. Normally, no one would ever see the substance. It only existed so his cocks didn't get irritated by the salt water. But to see it on her fingers? After this conversation?

He'd never been more embarrassed in his life.

Maketes let his head thud back against the wall and drew her hand up his chest, letting the movement wipe the fluid from her fingers. It would dry against his scales, a reminder that he shouldn't let her touch whatever she wanted.

"Sleep," he repeated. "Time for talking is over."

As if he would get any sleep tonight.

Chapter 13

Ace had such sweet dreams when she usually had nightmares. She was used to watching her sister die, or being chased through the empty hallways of a city that had died long ago. The worst ones were the people of Gamma hunting her down, all the while knowing that she had to stay hidden to keep her sister safe. It was hard for her to sleep at all these days.

But as she slowly woke from a dreamless sleep, she felt better than she had in years. It was so hard for her to even wake. She wanted to snuggle deeper into the warmth that held her. Listen to the repeating thuds of twin hearts that lulled her back into that dreamless state.

She couldn't entertain this any more than she already had. Her cheeks burned with the memory of what she'd touched. How her fingers had slipped down the grooves between his abs so mindlessly. Like she was touching someone she had every right to touch.

Then that slickness had covered her fingers. It had been so intriguing. She wanted to run her fingers over that faint slit in his scales, just to see what would happen if she maybe pushed through it.

To know what would happen if her fingers delved into those hidden shadows. Would he moan? What would that even sound like? She wanted to hear him when he was lost in the throes of passion. She wanted to know what he sounded like when he was completely unhinged.

And these were not thoughts for an early morning. Already she could feel herself growing wet between her thighs, that foreign need growing so powerful that it was hard to ignore. She wanted to sneak her fingers beneath the waistband of her pants and take care of the issue herself. But he was right here.

That would be decidedly wicked. What if she did? What would happen if she just ignored every part of herself that said she wasn't a sexual creature and just... allowed it to happen?

Would he wake up? Would he find her touching herself and decide to finish the job?

He shifted underneath her, those tiny scales brushing against her thighs and making a sharper rasping sound than they had before. One moment he'd been like a pillow she rested against, and the next, he was all movement. Every muscle in his body flared and tensed, rippling with life as though he had to use every single one of them to suddenly be alive again.

A deep breath flexed through his ribs and she could even feel the faintest flutter of his gills as though they were also striving for air even though he'd been using his lungs for hours now. Then his hand came back down on her hip as he had last night, cupping her flesh as though the roundness there didn't bother him in the slightest.

"Good morning," he mumbled, his voice still raspy with sleep. "You're up early."

It wasn't early at all. She could see the faint sunlight coming in through the window and that only reminded her that she was on a deadline. She was supposed to figure out how to save her sister, and if they didn't get moving quickly, then she was fucked.

Sitting bolt upright, she scrambled out of his arms and then struggled to her feet. She was a little uncoordinated. And why the fuck couldn't she see anything? The entire world was a blurry mess. She'd been sleeping so soundly, maybe she'd done something to her head. Or someone might have clocked her in the fight and she'd just forgotten because she'd gotten the world's worst concussion.

"Ace," Maketes said, a laugh hiding in that word. He grabbed her hand and placed her glasses into it.

She blew out a long, awkward breath and slid them up over her nose. The world came back into clarity and she looked down at the massive undine spread out on the floor at her feet.

Damn, he was pretty.

All those rippling muscles, like a banquet at her feet. He was just a solid wall of strength and power. He lifted one arm lazily over his head, those ab muscles flexing like they could feel her gaze on them. His biceps were the size of her head. Those clawed hands were draped near his hair, which was tangled in long coils over his chest as though they were fighting to get her attention. Even his damn hair made her want to touch him.

An image burst in front of her eyes. She could get down on her knees, straddle him like she had before, and then lick her way down those abs. She wondered if his skin would taste salty, like hers. Or if he would have some other flavor that would ruin humans forever for her. Where was his cock, anyway? Surely he had one.

They had to procreate somehow. Maybe they were like fish, though. Maybe he was the one who carried the babies, like the little seahorses her little sister used to have as pets.

Maybe he would expect sex to be something boring and transactional. Maybe they didn't even like sex.

He suddenly moved, flexing all those muscles and all of a sudden his face was right in front of hers. One of those long, dark nails curled underneath her chin, forcing her to stay looking into his gaze. "You're thinking too much, kefi."

"What do you mean?"

"I can see all those thoughts racing through your mind, but you're distracting yourself from what you have to do. The key, remember?"

"Right, the key." She remembered. It was the only thing she had to focus on.

Her sister. The death of her only family. She had to stay as focused as she possibly could so that she didn't lose this one opportunity to keep her sister safe. And then, maybe if she did a good job, Jacob would let her fade into the background.

He'd never let her go. Gamma was her home now, even if she could get out of it. No other city would take in a criminal like her. She was stuck there, and keeping Jacob happy was the only way to make sure that her family remained safe.

"Okay," she whispered. "I know where to go."

"Good." He stretched his arms over his head, and suddenly all she had was a wall of chest muscles in front of her. Then abs, as he stretched higher, then scales that were so bright yellow they looked like maybe they were made of gold.

She had the odd thought that she could sell those scales and make a good amount of money before he was coiled again like a snake.

"I have to go back into the sea," he reminded her. "My scales will start peeling up if I stay out here any longer. Do you remember where you left your wetsuit?"

"We don't have time for that. Go back into the ocean and keep an eye on me from out there. I'll be fine."

He gave her a rather unimpressed stare. "I'm not leaving you."

"A bodyguard wasn't the deal. You were supposed to bring me here, but then the rest of it was up to me." She took a step back from him, crossing her arms over her chest. "No one even knew you could get inside this tower, let alone that you could be out of the water for long periods of time."

"Well, achromos don't need to know everything about us." He sighed. "I do not believe it is safe for you to be alone in this tower."

"I'm sure it's not, but I can take care of myself. I'm used to being surrounded by criminals, remember?"

She needed him to leave. She needed to get her head screwed back on straight because it wasn't normal to look at an undine and want to lick him. It wasn't normal to look at her friend like that, and that's all they were. Friends.

He must have seen that panic in her expression, because he finally gave her a curt nod. "All right. I'll be just outside, though. And if you think I can't break one of these glass windows, you are very wrong."

They both knew it was a lie. The undine couldn't break the glass, because they'd tried countless times. That was part of the problem. They couldn't get into the cities to destroy the humans, and the humans couldn't stay in the water all that easily to fight them.

She watched him open the door and slither out into the hallway, all without even looking around. Like he wasn't afraid of her people. He didn't care if someone was lurking out there, because he would kill them if they tried to attack him and... well, she supposed that was accurate. He would kill them. He had already.

Ace took a few seconds to breathe and then pulled out the little bead droids from her pocket. "All right, Tera. What do you think? Can you get me there without being seen?"

Her droid clicked together multiple times before she let it down onto the floor. They all zinged in separate directions, and then out the door in a line as she opened it. They all disappeared, half in one direction, half in the other. And while she waited, she took some time to steady her emotions. She had a job to do. She had to search for that key and Doctor Faust's office.

That was it. There was nothing else in her brain. No thoughts of handsome undine, no dreams of friends who might become something more. Nothing at all. Just silence.

By the time Tera returned, she was back to herself. Her droid seemed pretty confident it knew where to go, especially since all of its pieces were back together.

"I'm as prepared as I'll ever be," she muttered, then turned to grab one of the remaining scalpels from the table. Just in case.

With that in her pocket, she headed down the brightly lit halls. Tera guided her, clicking and clacking in front of each split in the hallways before quickly choosing a direction. It was easy to get lost in this place. There were no markers. She could see the shadows on the walls where there used to be signs or paintings, but someone had taken them all down. So now, the only way to get through the labyrinth of the medical pavilion was to know where one was going. Thankfully, she still had the map. But it was easy to get turned around.

Then they reached their first obstacle.

Tera was so confident, it careened around a corner and then froze. She could see the little gears working quickly to pause it, even using some of the magnetic force to pause itself. Which could only mean there were people in the hall now.

She pressed her back against the wall, listening for any hint of a conversation. And there it was. Voices. Both men and women, talking about nothing all that important. But they were talking, and that was enough for her to change direction. Tera zipped back the way it had come, and Ace was forced to nearly run after it before she lost the droid.

They did that a few more times, each time finding more and more people coming out into the halls. Apparently, she should have tried this earlier in the day. Or perhaps in the dead of night.

Ace cursed her own bad luck. Every single time she tried to get somewhere, there were people. She was getting farther and farther away from her goal, no matter how many times she tried to go down the same halls in the hopes that people had moved on.

Until she had to stop and catch her breath, so she happened to hear what some of them were talking about.

"An undine?" came a woman's voice, filled with surprise. "What do you mean there's an undine hanging around?"

"I saw him against the glass. Gave me the stink eye and then swam away. Some other people have seen the same one. Damn bright bastard. Seems to be circling the building and watching all of us."

"Should we get the guns?"

"And what? Shoot it through the glass? We can't do that, you idiot."

They wandered away, but she had the sudden realization of why she was having such an issue getting to the office. She had a bodyguard who was looming over her shoulder and unknowingly drawing every single person in this damned pavilion right in front of her. The idiot had no clue what he was doing.

"Tera," she whispered, getting her droid's attention. "New plan. Where's the closest room with no one in it with big windows? I need to talk to this stupid undine."

Her droid clacked together twice, its usual answer for a yes. Which meant it also had made the connection that the undine was the problem.

She followed the glowing beads into another room and closed the door behind her. Ace winced at the slight click, knowing that if anyone was nearby, they would hear it. But that didn't matter, because she was in some poor soul's old office, which happened to have an empty bed in the corner, and a large window that looked out to the sea.

There he was. Already. A giant idiot in yellow, with his arms crossed as he glared through the window at her. Like she was the one doing something wrong. Like he was the one who was angry with her.

Stomping up to the window, she pointed at him and then pointed away. "You need to go!"

He pointed at his ear like he couldn't hear her.

"I know you can hear me, you stupid ugly… Ugh!" Ace dragged her hands through her hair to calm herself. "Get away from the windows if you're going to watch me. You're drawing a crowd."

Once again, the infuriating man pointed to his ears and then shrugged. He even had the audacity to follow that movement with pointing up, like he was asking her to keep going.

Even Tera clacked at the sight before them. This undine was going to get them caught, and he didn't even care. To him, it was more important that he be involved rather than her actually getting this shit done.

Grumbling under her breath, she yanked the map out from the back of her pants and slapped it against the glass. She jabbed the paper where she was going, hoping he was at least smart enough to read a map.

"This is where I'm going. This office. It's on the twenty-second floor, and I wouldn't be surprised if there was an entrance into the pavilion near it, considering there is a partial drainage system nearby. Get there, and then you can watch me all you want. But let me fucking get there without you looming over my head. Got it?"

He frowned and shook his head.

"Maketes, you have to trust me to do this. You have to let me find the office. Otherwise, people are going to find me here. If you don't leave, they will continue trying to look at you because they think you're going to attack the city. You're following me, and they're following you. This won't work."

He seemed to waver. She could see it in the way his gills froze for a second before they started breathing for him again.

Ace planted her hand against the glass. "Please," she said. "Please trust me to do this."

He gave her a nod before flicking his tail and disappearing out of sight. He'd headed to the higher levels, and that was good enough for her. Now, she just had to figure out how to get there herself.

Chapter 14

He didn't like that he wasn't with her. Maketes was the only thing standing between her and injury, if not death. He'd seen how she reacted to those people who were going to attack her. She'd hidden. If he hadn't been there, she would have died. There was no question in his mind about that. She would have been shot in the head and no one would have known she was even dead.

Then she'd slept on him. He could still smell her on his scales, and it was driving him mad. He needed to be in there with her.

But she'd asked him not to be. She'd asked him not to watch over her while she was so far from his reach, and he hated every second of it. She'd pressed that etched example of where she wanted him to go up to the glass and he wasn't an idiot. He knew when to say yes to a woman and when to say no.

She needed to do this. Hadn't he been working on her fear? He'd gotten her to pet a shark. He'd gotten her to pet him.

That memory was seared into his mind. All he could think about was her tiny hands rubbing his chest, the way her thick thighs had straddled him, and how badly he'd wanted to squeeze it. He wanted to grip every part of her just to see his hand against her bare skin. Her lovely, freckled skin would dent around his strong grip.

He wanted her all the time. And that was quickly becoming a problem, because he couldn't focus on anything else.

Sighing, he swam in a circle around the building one more time, trying to figure out what that map had meant. It was pretty clear there were markings on it, but he had always been terrible at following directions. Maps were more guidelines, anyway. He trusted the ocean to get him to where he needed to go, and usually she was kind enough to kick him in the right direction when he forgot what he was doing.

Today, the goddess of the ocean had abandoned him. Even the sea had a flavor of disappointment, as though she was reminding him that it was important to pay attention. Especially in times like these.

Frustrated, he flicked his tail and swam even faster. But then he was just circling the damn building, and he wasn't actually looking at the inside. His frustration had a way of getting the better of him, which meant he unfortunately was lost now. If he could get ahold of that temper, he could figure out where he had first met with her, and then backtrack from there.

Obviously, the achromos inside of the building were now all on high alert. They watched him through almost every window he could see. Which was likely good for her, because she could sneak right past them. But he didn't see her anywhere.

She'd made it sound like the office she had to go into would have a window. That he didn't have to worry about losing her in that window because he should be able to see her.

He was so angry he was starting to glow. The lights all up and down his tail flickered on and off, which was even worse. Now the humans could really see him. And if he didn't get control of himself, he'd end up lighting up the entire ocean.

The neon lights behind him cast his shadow on the building as he passed. In his gaze, it made him look ten times larger. A massive beast whose shadow enveloped the entire tower. His tail moved slowly, like the shark they had seen, his claws were visible on that shadow. It swallowed up the entire city, surrounded by a halo of red.

Another dark shadow joined his, this one significantly larger. He knew who it was long before he looked, but how could he not? He could smell the scent of sulfuric depthstrider from miles away.

"Couldn't stay away from me?" he muttered, casting his gaze along the building and hoping to catch a glimpse of a curvy figure with a scowl on her face.

"You looked like you needed some help. I am here to offer my assistance."

"I don't need help from the likes of you." Ace's words burned in his mind, and he turned to glower at the other undine. "You're too big. The humans are already looking at you. You draw too much attention."

Fortis just stared at him. The massive depthstrider didn't have to do much to look intimidating. Unlike many of his people, he was such a pale lavender at his chest that he glowed in the darkness. It was almost hard to look at him without squinting his eyes. Those yellow bulbs at the end of his tentacles sparked with emotion and then disappeared again. But it was his gaze that made Maketes uneasy. Those dark orbs were already swirling with colors, barely dark at all. Instead, they were a rainbow of the future that Maketes didn't have time to deal with.

All that bulk was eye catching, though, so perhaps Ace had a point. But then Fortis's expression registered. Not one of disapproval, as Maketes was very used to. This expression was one of... pity?

"Achromos," Fortis said.

"What about them?"

"You called them humans."

Had he? Maketes barely even remembered his rant. He'd just been angry, and he wanted Fortis to shut up for a few seconds and he'd wanted Fortis to feel like the bad guy. Not him. He wasn't too large so that he wasn't useful anymore. That was the other undine. That was all the others who had... had...

Shit. He had called them humans. He wasn't even using his own people's language anymore.

He growled low, the sound escaping through his gills even as his tail lit up with all the tiny specks of yellow that he had learned to hate so much. "What of it, Fortis?"

"You've been spending too much time with their species."

"I understand that, friend. What would you have me do? Ignore them? Mira and Anya would be so disappointed, considering I'm the only one of our kind who knows how to act less like a monster and more like a man."

He'd always prided himself on that detail. He was the one the women could go to when they needed to talk. No one else. They went to him, because they knew he would listen to them. That he wouldn't try to talk over them or try to solve their problems. Maketes was the one who always listened, even if he made jokes and took nothing seriously.

Fortis flicked his side fins, keeping him still in the water where he hovered like some monolithic beast from the deep. He shouldn't even be here. The depthstriders were supposed to stay where they were happiest. In the deepest parts of the ocean where no one would ever have to look at them again. Namely, Maketes.

"Part of who you are is the one who sees," Fortis replied, his voice low and raspy. "You are meant to know them as they are, not as we see them. You are destined to call them into the darkness with us."

"What the fuck is that supposed to mean?" Maketes wanted to slap him with his tail so bad. "I don't want more soothsaying or future telling. Can you please, for the love of all things in the sea, stop talking to me like I'm begging for the future and instead, try to be a real person for once?"

Fortis blinked. All the shimmering lights in his eyes disappeared as well. And suddenly, Maketes was looking at the real man behind the power.

Had he ever seen this side of Fortis before? He wasn't all that certain.

Fortis took a deep breath, his gills shuddering at his sides before they stilled, as though it took a great deal of concentration to not be the terrifying asshole who told people their future when they didn't want to know it.

"If you wish to deal with the man, then so be it." And that was it. That was all he said. He just floated there, looking like one of the People of Water for once, and not the depthstrider who looked into people's minds without permission.

Maketes didn't know what to say. This man had tormented him most of his life, trying to tell him bits and pieces of his future when Maketes just wanted to live it. And now here he was. No longer a creature. Just a man.

Clearing his throat, he tried to find words. "Well. That's good."

"You will be the one to determine if it is or not."

"Right." Maketes tried to find the humor in this. "You could have turned it off since day one?"

Fortis lifted his shoulder in a half shrug. "I suppose I could have. But why should I?"

"So people weren't scared of you?"

The big male spread his lips wide, showing all those sharp teeth that were far worse than the shark. Speaking of, the big beauty was still around the city. She coasted past them, her black eyes taking Fortis in and Maketes realized the depthstrider was bigger than the shark. He was beyond massive. He was larger than any male he'd ever seen.

"How did you ever have a son?" he muttered, shaking his head as he turned his attention back to the city.

"Much the same way as the rest of our people."

"But you're so big."

"And she was very brave." There was another flash, as if Fortis had grinned again. "I might have let her win a few times, but she never held it against me. She gave me a son that I am infinitely proud of, and I have raised him as she wished."

It didn't escape Maketes's notice that Fortis spoke of the female in the past tense. He knew very little about depthstriders, but he knew the dangers of pregnancies and their people. Females of their kind weren't exactly made for procreation. That was why they chose smaller mates. It made the birth easier.

Their numbers had dwindled in the recent years. Hard lives, seas that weren't as healthy as they used to be. All pieces of a puzzle that had drawn their kind to warmer waters and ever closer to the humans.

Achromos, he corrected himself. Even thinking of them as anything other than the colorless creatures they were was a dangerous path to go down.

Fortis pointed higher up the building. "Your little one is up there, if you are seeking her."

"What do you mean, she's up there?" He glanced up, which was far higher than she'd indicated. "She said she was in this area."

"You are not very good at following her or at hunting, little brother. She is on the higher levels. I believe she told you she was going in that direction." Fortis moved in a wave like motion, heading up the building without waiting for Maketes to join him. But his words trailed behind him as though they were right next to each other. "Perhaps you should listen to her when she speaks."

"I do listen!" He was the best listener there was! The women loved him because of it. He listened to everyone that spoke to him.

He just... wasn't exactly good at letting it all settle before his mind moved onto the next thing.

Flicking his tail to keep up with the much larger male who was already far ahead of him, they both traveled upward. And there, just past another crack in the building, he could see his little kefi. She was rummaging through drawers of a room. There were papers strewn all around her. Obviously not the right place for her to be, though.

There was no key in her hand, and that wasn't a good sign. She'd already had plenty of time to find it.

He could see her mouth moving. Somehow, she was talking. Not to him, though. But then he saw the little beads of her droid zipping back and forth in the room, as though even the droid was upset.

"Now what?" he muttered. There always seemed to be something wrong with these two. They were terrible at planning anything that worked.

"You were inside the pavilion with her?" Fortis asked.

"How did you—"

Fortis tapped his gills on his ribs, still not looking at Maketes as his gaze tracked Ace's movements. "I can smell it on you, little brother.

You are coated in blood."

"I killed some achromos who attacked her."

"Oh, now they're achromos?"

"They are when they think they can lay a finger on what is mine." The snarled words ripped out of him, rage hanging from every single sound. He still wanted to rip into them again. He wanted to tear their flesh from their bones with his teeth, listening to their screams of fear. He'd do it all a hundred times over if they thought he would leave her to their grip any longer than he had to.

"On what is yours?"

Shit. He shouldn't have said that. Fortis took words far too literally, and everyone else would hear that Maketes was interested in an achromo of his own.

"This is my mission." He tried to save himself by saying that, but he knew it was a losing battle. "I will not fail it because some simple achromos with tiny weapons attack us."

Fortis's lips quirked, just a hint of a smile, before he was back to the stoic rock that he usually was. "Interesting choice of words. Happy hunting, brother. It is good that you killed them. I can ignore the other future you might have swum down."

"I thought we weren't talking about that," Maketes replied in a sing song voice. "Now just help me find the crack in the wall so I can get back in and make sure no other achromos get ideas around my own."

"That will be a problem."

"Is that so? Did you see that in a vision, or did you use your worthless eyeballs?"

Fortis just pointed. And that was when Maketes realized there was, actually, a crack near her. She'd been right. There was a small area of filtration that was likely used for drainage. It just wasn't wider than his arm.

Groaning, he slapped his forehead with his hand. "You've got to be kidding me! How small does she think I am?"

A fish might swim up that. Or a crab. But a full-grown male of his size wasn't going to get through. He might be able to fit an arm, but that was it. The filtration system wasn't what Alpha's had been, but then again, Gamma was individual towers. These weren't at all what he needed to get to her side.

Swimming up to the glass, he slapped at it hard. "Ace!"

She whipped around, that glare on her face sending a tingle all the way down to the tip of his tail.

"What?" she hissed, stomping up to the window in that adorable way she always did and slapping it in response. "I'm busy!"

"I can't get in."

"I don't care! I'll meet you back where we first came in."

"What if you need me?"

She bared her teeth in a little snarl that might have been terrifying if he didn't see how blunted they were. "Maketes, I am trying very hard to be polite to you. But I do not need you. No one knows I'm here. I have not been attacked. Stay out in your giant ocean with all your wide open space and let me work."

"You said I could join you." Did she not want him with her? That thought stung a bit.

"I know I said that, but plans change. You're just going to have to roll with it. I'm this close to getting the key. This doctor kept a journal, so-" She pinched her fingers together and moved them over her lips. "Zip it, fish man."

He had no idea what that meant, but she'd already moved away from the window and back to the desk. He had a mind to slap the glass again and again until she was annoyed enough to come back, but Fortis cleared his throat behind him.

So Maketes would wait. Even if it was killing him to be out here while she was in there.

Chapter 15

There weren't any obvious clues, and that was annoying her. This key was supposed to be easy to find. Jacob had made it seem like it would be right here in the doctor's office. Considering what he said, she had a feeling other people might even want to find the key, or know where the key was. If this Doctor Faust was the one who had it, then surely he would have some record of having it.

Right?

But she'd torn his office apart. From the front to the back, every piece of paper that still existed in this room, she had read it. She'd torn up the pages that she'd already read, knowing there wasn't much use for them anyway. It wasn't like any other doctor was going to read this man's boring notes on what it took to repair vein ruptures. No one in Gamma had those kinds of skills.

And then, of course, Maketes had to come and distract her. He didn't understand how hard it was for her to focus when she knew his eyes were on her. Because she didn't want to do this. He made her want to be a better person.

He made her want to go back to Jacob and tell him to go fuck himself. She had an undine on her side and he wouldn't let anything terrible happen to her or her sister. Some part of her wanted to swim off with him into the sunset and just trust that he would take care of her.

In contrast, reality was a real slap in the face. There wasn't a chance on the face of this earth that she could do any of that. Her reality was a hard one. Her sister wasn't safe, she wasn't safe, and she was surrounded by criminals. If they wanted to hurt her or her family, they would. Jacob likely had already. She knew he'd killed that one massive crowd of people, but he'd probably done it before as well.

People in Gamma didn't talk about body counts, and not in the fun way. If she had asked, though, it wouldn't have surprised her to hear that any of the people she dealt with on a day-to-day basis had killed more people than they had fingers and toes.

So she returned her focus to the task at hand. She ignored the feeling that she'd been lied to, that the key wasn't here at all. Jacob clearly wanted the key. He wouldn't have created this elaborate plan just to have a reason to kill her sister. He wasn't that good.

Ripping the last drawer out of the desk, she tossed it onto the ground a little too hard. Tera rolled in circles at her feet, trying to get her attention, likely because the sound had been far too loud. Someone would come to investigate if she kept throwing drawers around, but at this point, her anger had gotten the best of her.

Because for fuck's sake, this was a waste of time. Obviously, the key was gone. Someone had taken it with them when they were evacuated or, likely, Doctor Faust had been caught in the flooding when Gamma was first destroyed.

She could see the hints of it now, and she slumped in the desk chair as she looked around. "Tera?" she asked, letting her head rest against the back of the chair. "Did you notice there are barnacles growing above our head?"

Tera rolled in a circle again, cracking the beads together and then rolling in the opposite direction. It drew her attention to the back of the room, where she could see there were even hints of dead coral growing in the back. This whole room had likely been underwater for a very long time for all of those things to grow, which meant anything that was useful was gone.

No one as smart as a doctor would let an important key just... linger. Not without knowing exactly where it was going. At least, if it was as important as Jacob thought, that is.

Tera clacked again, trying to get her attention as she wallowed in self pity. Or maybe that was a tap on the window. She didn't know. The undine might be trying to get her attention, too.

At least, until Tera cracked a little harder and then bumped against her shoe.

"What is it?" she asked, looking down at the little droid. "I know you think I should still search, but there's nothing here. I was lucky the desk even managed to not be as waterlogged as the rest of it. This whole room was reclaimed by the sea. There's nothing here."

Again Tera made the noise, and this time rolled underneath the desk. Then the little beads all turned in the same direction, almost as though they were looking at the bottom of the waterlogged wood.

"Oh, you little genius."

Standing so quickly the chair went careening out from under her, she crawled underneath the desk with her droid. As she flipped onto her back, staring up at the bottom of the drawer, she saw a tiny piece of metal imbedded there. It wasn't part of the desk build, that much was certain.

"A clue?" she muttered, grabbing onto it and moving both herself and her droid out into the light. "Or... A hologram?"

There weren't many of these left, as far as she knew. A lot more people used to use them before they went under the sea, and now it was mostly just primitive ways to keep in touch with others. At least, that was as far as she knew. But a hologram was something she'd heard about, and apparently something Tera knew what to do with. The little balls were jumping, leaping for her attention.

So she handed the disk over. Magnets connected to it and all five of Tera's pieces were rolling away with the hologram in their grasp. Right into the center of the room where they set themselves up into a circle and blue light flickered from the piece that had been hidden under the desk.

A man appeared before her. Well, not really. A holographic man who was made of blue lights and the sprinkling of flickers from where the chip had likely been damaged when it was underwater. But he was right there. A man with enough details that she could read the name on his lab coat.

Faust.

He was a small man. She wasn't sure why she'd built up the image in her mind of a tall, handsome doctor who had likely done some terrible things in his time. But this man was so far from her imagined person. He was small. Mousy, even. He had tiny spectacles on his nose and was balding only on the crown of his head. He had a thin, pointed nose that was constantly wrinkled as he stared at something in the distance.

"It's on?" he said. "Are you sure?"

Ace backed away, blindly reaching with her hand for the chair so she could sit down on it and stare at the absolute magic in front of her. A real hologram. It was like she was standing in the room with him. Even if it was a recording, it was still impressive to see.

"If you're looking through my office, I can only imagine you're here for one reason. And Jessup, if it's you, then you put this down and go back to your family. You're wasting precious time."

Doctor Faust slid his glasses back up his nose and the hologram glitched. She could see it roll up through the sparkling blue lights that made him up. One moment he was standing straight, and the next he was glitching in stages away from her. Walking through the room and then sitting down where there might have once been a chair on the opposite side of the desk for someone to sit in and visit with him.

It was odd, watching someone sit where there was no chair. But the look of hopelessness on his face made her breath catch in her throat.

"That's why I can't keep going," he muttered. "This is wrong. It's beyond wrong. What we're doing to these people, and they don't even know it? None of us should have done any of this."

"Done what?" she found herself asking. But that was the part that had been skipped. Because the doctor just sighed and ran his hands through the meager hair on top of his head.

"I don't know what to do. All I know is that the information you seek is in Tau."

"Tau?" she repeated, watching the hologram suddenly freeze and then shudder. "There's not a city named Tau."

She didn't think, at least. There were only three remaining cities that she knew of. Alpha, Beta, and Gamma. There had been a fourth, but it wasn't called Tau. And that city had long been lost to the sea. It was destroyed a long time ago. Now there was just Beta and Gamma.

There was another city? Was that what this key was meant to do? Open the doors to a city that she shouldn't even know existed?

"Tera," she said quietly. "Please replay what you can and fix whatever is damaged. I need to know more about Tau and about where the key is."

Her droid made a soft cracking sound and then she could see it working. The doctor moved all throughout the room. His image was projected everywhere, from the door to the window to suddenly right in front of her like he had just stood. And then he started talking again, even if the sound was distorted, like it was underwater.

"The key to the vault is in my private quarters. That's above the Painted Lady. But I caution you, whoever you are that found this message, to know that there are limitations to what you will find after you use the key. You don't want to know the truth of all these cities under the sea, I can promise you that. And if you do find out the truth, then I pity you for what you will find." Doctor Faust took his glasses off and rubbed his eyes. "And I hope you can find some pity for me when you find out all the things I have done."

She watched the hologram start to shift and move again, glitching forward and back. "What did you do?" she asked quietly, watching this tortured man move throughout his office, talking to himself and recording messages that had been stolen by the sea. "What did you and whoever else was helping you do?"

There was the faintest click, and suddenly she was staring right at him. He had knelt in front of the office chair as though he knew someone would sit right where she was sitting. His beady eyes stared up at her, and she felt like he was looking into her soul.

"Do not trust anyone from Tau. Don't believe them if they say their city has been destroyed. Tau is enduring. That is what it has always done and what it will always do. That city is full of villains and to underestimate them is to invite a massacre to your world. Do not trust them. Not a single person from that city."

And then the hologram dissipated. There was nothing left of him, and nothing left of the hologram either, it seemed. A little fizzle, a strange hissing noise, and then Tera dropped the small chip that was now smoking. The little coil of black made her realize that she was the only person who would ever know what was said on that hologram. No one else had found it. And somehow, she wasn't sure what to do with that information.

He had told her very little, other than where the key was. Her stomach still twisted in knots, though. She was so terrified what kind of key she was getting for Jacob. A vault could have anything in it, but the warnings about Tau were clearly meant for people to heed. This was a dangerous new city, if it even existed.

"Tera?" she asked as the droid rolled up to her feet. "What do you think?"

She'd never wished she'd given her droid a voice more than she did in this moment. It clicked, rolled, clacked, did all the things it could to communicate, but she still had no idea what it was saying.

All she wanted was for someone to tell her that she was doing the right thing. That yes, this was hard. It was never meant to be easy, but she was moving in the right direction. Of all the things she'd done in her life, she had made a good choice to be here.

Get the key. Save her sister. Go back to living in Gamma where no one cared if she was alive or dead, but at least her sister was still thriving.

Yet this whole adventure had wriggled its way into her mind. Maybe she didn't want to just exist. Maybe she deserved more than living in that clocktower, working on her droids and being covered in grease.

She touched her hair. Her fluffy hair that had been shorn so ragged at her shoulders, and she remembered that her hair had once been pretty. At the very least, she'd brushed it regularly, and it had streaks like she'd just seen the sun. She liked her hair. And she'd taken that away from herself because it was easier to forget that she was a person at all, rather than risk being seen by someone she didn't want to see her.

Tears gathering in her eyes, she sighed and placed Tera in her pocket. "It's going to be fine, Tera. We stick to the plan, right? That's the only thing we can do."

She was so caught up in her own thoughts that she didn't even think about listening to her surroundings. Ace was usually so aware of everything around her. She'd had to be. Gamma was a prison, after all, and in these moments she forgot that.

A boot hit the ground hard. The almost stomp broke through her thoughts and suddenly she looked up to see a group of people standing in the doorway to the office. The woman in front had a scar down the side of her face, right through her eye that was sunken into her skull. A faint yellow ooze seemed to smear underneath, as though she'd lost the eye recently and infection had set in.

Then she smelled the rot, and Ace knew she was in so much trouble.

"Now who do we have here?" the scarred woman said. "I don't think you belong here."

"I recently moved into the area," she said, trying to scramble to make it seem like she was exactly where she was supposed to be. "Sorry I haven't been able to introduce myself before I tried to find a bed."

"A bed?" The woman stepped into the room and nudged the broken hologram with her foot. "Seems like you are here for a different purpose than a bed."

Shit.

She reached into her pocket and palmed the scalpel in her pocket. She really had hoped she wouldn't have to use this, but her luck had been real bad lately.

"I guess you know more than I do," she ground through her teeth.

"Oh, I do. We're going to rip you apart, piece by piece, until you tell us how you got in here, where you came from, and what you were going to do." The scarred woman tilted her head to the side in a very raptor-like motion. "You're cute. It's a shame I'm going to carve stripes off of you before you talk."

"What makes you think I'm that good at withstanding torture?" Her hand was shaking in her pocket.

"Because I don't want to hear a word until I'm done carving. Then I'll allow you to speak."

Oh, she was so fucked.

Chapter 16

I don't like it that she's in there alone," he muttered, yet again. He hadn't been able to stop saying the words since she'd basically begged him to leave her alone.

"Yes, Maketes. I believe you've made that very clear."

"What are you even doing here?"

Fortis shrugged. "I am meant to be here."

"That is not very clear, and I don't appreciate the prophetic tone." Maketes spread his hip fins wide, glancing toward the building again. They were far enough away that the achromos wouldn't be too nervous or try to go to the higher window where Ace was. But that also meant that he couldn't see her.

And he wanted to watch her. He wanted to stare at her every move just so he knew she was all right.

Fortis had coiled himself around a neon light. The bright purple of the sign only made his own color seem all the more prominent. With his tail looped through one of the words and his upper half hanging down over it, he looked like a strange serpent rather than an undine.

But his hair floating around his head helped a bit to make him look more like their own kind.

Maketes couldn't stay still. He had circled that same sign more times than he wanted to admit, and was on yet another round of circling when Fortis reached out and grabbed his tail. Claws dug into his scales, and he hated the feeling so much that he lashed out. With a hiss and a swipe of his claws, he found himself face to face with the massive depthstrider.

"What?" he hissed.

"Tell me why it's her," Fortis said.

The words were confusing. "Why what is her?"

"Mira and Arges. Daios and Anya. You and this criminal who has been locked away by her own people. I wish to understand what it is that calls you to her."

"That's stupid."

"It's the truth. And the moment you admit that you have been called to her side is the moment you will stop fighting against yourself. What is it about her, Maketes?"

He wanted to swim again. He did better moving when he was angry, not staying still. But he could feel his gills fluttering just at the thought of her, and again, he couldn't help himself but talk when someone brought Ace up. "I don't know. I like her. I genuinely like her. Even when it was just a droid reading me her messages, I found her funny. She's dry, in a sarcastic kind of way, and that always made me chuckle. I like making her laugh too. Even if it's because she's annoyed with me. It's a battle to get her to show any kind of reaction and... Well."

He was rambling.

Clearing his throat, Maketes waved his hand through the water.

"I just like her. I can't explain why. It's just all there. Every time I'm around her, everything falls into place. It just feels right."

And he didn't know how to explain that in better words. There should have been a way for him to say that she meant far more to him than just a friend. That he wanted her to be with him all the time, and when they were apart, he felt strange. He wanted to listen to her talk, collect all of her smiles, and all the other things that were probably too clingy for him to ever say to her.

Fortis nodded. "You are here because you are supposed to be here, Maketes. I wish you would let the sea guide you in this."

"And what would the sea do? She is an achromo. I know that. You know that."

"The others are making it work."

"But what if they are an anomaly?" He ran his fingers through his hair, watching the strands billow around his head. "Mira and Anya wanted to leave their homes. They had people to fight for, but not like Ace. She has a sister, a young woman she would do anything to keep alive. I can't take her away from that. And she would have to leave it all behind. Her own people are not likely to allow her to stay in touch with her family when she's with someone like me."

He would not be the reason she lost her sister, and he would be if he continued down this path. He had to throw all of these thoughts and feelings to the side.

"Perhaps you have thought too long and too hard on this reasoning, and you have moved away from where the sea wishes you to go."

"Since when were you anyone's guidance?" Maketes grumbled. "I still don't understand what you're even doing here."

Again, Fortis shrugged. That stupid movement where he lifted his shoulders and held up his hands like he, too, had no idea what he was doing here. "I go where the sea bids."

"You are the most frustrating person in the sea, you know that? I wish I could throw you into the abyss and feed you to the ancients."

"Someone else has tried. They would not eat me."

Bubbles of anger erupted from his rib gills and filled his vision with gray specks of air. "Of course they wouldn't! Even the ancients wouldn't eat your fat head. They probably worry you would infect them with whatever madness it is that gives you the right to be such a... a..."

Fortis tilted his head to the side. "I don't think I've ever seen you at a loss for words."

"Algae sucker!" He was at a loss for words, though. He was so angry, so filled with rage that he couldn't control, and he didn't know what else to say. Instead, he just pointed at the depthstrider.

Amused, Fortis gave him a little nod. "I understand."

"Do you?"

"Quite well."

"Good, because I don't understand what this is supposed to mean, but at the very least, you get the threat." He took his jabbing finger away and blew out another bubble net of breath. Then he looked up at the building and grumbled, "What is taking her so long?"

"I do not pretend to understand the nattering of achromos, but I believe she was trying to find something in that room."

He couldn't stand another second with this depthstrider who said things like he was the first person to come up with the words, when in reality, he was just repeating what everyone else said.

"That's it," he muttered, flicking his tail and heading back to the building. "I'm going to check on her."

"I thought you said nothing could happen between the two of you? That Mira and Anya were just anomalies?"

"Maybe they are!" he shouted back.

"And?"

"And what, Fortis?"

"And what are you going to do about that?" The big male suddenly swept in front of him, stopping his progress with the sheer mass of his bulk. "Are you going to sit around and decide that the sea is lying to you? That you found this woman for no reason at all, and that you are unworthy of her? Or are you going to do something about it?"

"What would you have me do? I can't steal her away like in the old days. I can't take her, hide her, feed her, gift her all the things that I desperately want to give her. I can barely flutter for her, Fortis!"

The depthstrider placed a webbed hand on his chest, the massive clawed hand nearly as large as Maketes's entire pectoral muscle. Tiny, sharp points of nails dug into his skin. "Barely fluttering is still fluttering, Maketes. It may not be the display you always wished you could give someone, but it is still a display. You are showing her your need, and that is more than you ever have for anyone else."

Of course it was. Of course, he fluttered for her because she was the best person he'd ever met in his entire life. And probably was the best person he ever would meet in his entire life.

Fortis seemed as though he could tell what was happening behind Maketes's eyes. Because he gave him a little shove, letting him float a small distance away. "You're the only one holding yourself back, little brother."

Maketes hated how right he was. They had only been holding each other back in these moments. Both he and Ace. They'd looked at each other as friends for such a long time, it was hard to be anything else. But maybe, just maybe, they hadn't allowed themselves to be anything else.

"What if I ruin it?" he asked, his voice wavering with fear. "What if she doesn't want to be more and then I lose both her and my friendship with her?"

"It is a risk you have to take. What is your future without taking that risk, Maketes? You remain her friend? You watch her find someone else, because she eventually will. If you do not give her another option, then she will never know that option exists."

Even though this was terrifying, it gave him some sense of purpose. It felt right to swim down this stream. If he could just tell her how he felt, then maybe she would listen. Maybe she would understand that all he wanted was just her attention, even if that attention came from when she was angry.

"Right," he muttered. "No time like the present."

He'd never get a talk like that again, which made him actually want to tell her his feelings, so he might as well capitalize on it. Maketes pushed his fins, speeding through the water until suddenly he realized there was a bloody handprint on the window where he had left her.

His stomachs dropped. His hearts thundered in his chest. He couldn't get enough oxygen in the water because he was so terrified that he had made a mistake he could never come back from. He'd left her alone.

Leaving her alone had been a bad idea. He knew it. She knew it. And he'd still left her, anyway.

"No!" he shouted, swimming up to the window and slamming his hands upon the glass. Through it, he could see that his little kefi was still alive. But such was meager comfort when he surveyed the scene before him.

There were males and females in the room with his achromo. They surrounded her, all of them holding weapons in their hands. He'd feared the blood on the window was Ace's, but now he wasn't so sure. There was another young man holding his side where red blood oozed out from between his fingers, and Ace held a bloodied weapon in her hand. His little achromo had more bite to her than he'd thought.

At the sound of his strike to the glass, everyone in the room froze. They stared at him, the shock in their expressions only making him wish to harm them more. Did they really think she had come alone? Was it so much of a stretch to imagine he was the one protecting her?

Then he heard the words that made his blood boil.

"You have an undine for a pet?" One of the women said, the scar on her face making her stand out far more than the others. "How interesting. I've never heard that one before."

"He's here for me, and he's not going to let you get away," Ace hissed.

"Oh, what a pity that he'll have to watch you die. He's out there. You're in here." And then the woman had the audacity to draw her finger across her own throat and laugh at him.

That one would die first.

He felt the massive wave of Fortis approaching. The other male was larger and slower, but he brought a tsunami along with him as he moved through the water. On his face was an expression of glee unlike anything Maketes had seen before.

Fortis let out a booming laugh that had all the achromos covering their ears at the thunderous sound. "I know why the sea brought me here!" Fortis shouted, and then he was swimming away. Moving so quickly that Maketes marveled at his speed before he realized what the depthstrider was doing.

Casting one last look at Ace, he promised her with his gaze that she would be safe. "Get yourself in a corner, kefi."

"What?" she cried out, lashing out at one of the men who lunged for her. The scalpel was sharp, it seemed. The man flinched back with blood on his hand.

"Get to a corner now, Ace! And hold on to something!"

He could already feel Fortis coming back, this time even faster. All nineteen feet of bulk rushing through the waves. He would hit this building harder than any storm ever could. The movement of his purple tail became a blur, the undulation of his body spearing toward them, every inch of his form power and control and then...

Sound was muffled underwater. Maketes saw the glass crack and then shatter before he heard the painful crack that echoed throughout the water. In one moment, he was next to the glass, and the next, he was sucked into the building.

Maketes hit the wall hard, feeling it crumble under his weight the moment he struck it. A giant thud soon reached his ears, but he thought that was he who had made that sound. Air bubbles obscured his vision, but he could taste her in the water. All he had to do was fight against the current that ripped at him.

"Brother!" a deep voice cried out, full of glee and insane happiness. "I found this one for you!"

Suddenly an arm parted the bubbling water, fins somehow flared against the pull of the water and holding Fortis in place. In his grip was the woman who had taunted Maketes. The same woman who had likely harmed his kefi.

"I need to find my own achromo," he said, staring into the woman's frightened eyes. "So I will make this quick when I wish for you to have a long and painful death."

He didn't have to do anything. Because at the sight of him reaching for her, the woman opened her mouth and screamed. A sharp inhalation came next, one that would surely drown her. But he still took her writhing body in his arms and squeezed. Hard. He squeezed until he felt her ribs break, until she became slippery in his grip and then her torso and the bottom half of her legs drifted free. They were sucked into the rest of the building, where many of her other men had likely disappeared.

Where her remains ended up didn't matter. It only mattered that she died while he could still watch.

Maketes breathed in, trying hard to find Ace in all this mess. He'd told her to get to a corner, and she was smart enough to find one. If he could get there...

Fortis grabbed him by the back of the neck and tossed him out of the greatest current. There he found her. Huddled in the back corner, pressed there by the weight of the water.

Maketes immediately placed his hand between her breasts, seeking the sensation of her heartbeat. It was wrong, beating erratically, but it was there. So he didn't think. He just... reacted.

He grabbed her, yanked her toward him, and plunged the tentacle into her neck. He would breathe for her. Even if he had promised that he would ask any achromo permission first, Maketes did it out of necessity.

Keeping her alive was all that mattered.

Chapter 17

Everything hurt, and she feared she was dying. Maybe that was a bit of an exaggeration, but her body didn't feel right as she woke. Ace felt like she'd been hit by all the weight of a falling building, or maybe just struck hard by the body of an undine.

First, she noticed the pounding in her skull. The aching thud right between her temples, radiating up from her jaw and into the back of her head. Every heartbeat echoed in her ears until she swore she was hearing things. Even her eyes hurt, although she had a feeling there were little shards of sand grinding underneath her lids. And then there were her shoulders.

They ached beyond any pain she'd ever felt, like she'd lifted her entire bodyweight too many times. All she could feel was the overwhelming stiffness of her entire spine. It wasn't just her shoulders. It stretched down between her shoulder blades, all the way down to her hips.

A little groan escaped from her lips, making her feel foolish. Even in all this pain, she knew that staying quiet was important. She wasn't cold. Which meant she wasn't underwater and the last thing she remembered was... was...

Her eyes flew open. The burning pain of dry eyes got even worse, and they watered until she couldn't see anything. But Ace was so lost in her memories, she didn't care.

She'd been underwater. The last thing she remembered was a massive undine darting toward the windows and shattering them. She hadn't even known they could do that. They couldn't. That was always the benefit of being in one of the cities. Humans knew the undine couldn't crash through the windows like that.

She remembered the rush of icy water that had slammed her against the wall. That was why her entire body hurt. She had been struck with all the force of the sea. She'd been pinned there, unable to move because of the rushing water that was impossible to fight against. Ace remembered the terror. She'd been forced to struggle to even keep the air in her lungs because the sea had tried to crush her.

And then hands. Clawed hands that had grasped at her and a sharp sting at the side of her neck that had hurt so much she'd been shocked into... passing out? No, that had been the ocean itself. Because there'd been that ache in her throat and then she'd been dragged out into the open ocean without her suit.

She sat straight up, ignoring the way the entire world shifted to the side as she did so. The dizziness wouldn't stop no matter what she did, so she endured it. Instead, she stared down at her hands until there stopped being four of them.

Her hands returned to normal and then, only then, did she feel like she was marginally okay. The open sea, a deep voice reassuring her...

"Fuck," she muttered, closing her shaking hands into fists.

She was alive.

That's all that mattered.

She didn't have time to sit here and think about how dangerous that had been or how she had even breathed. She didn't have to touch her neck, even though it made every part of her scream to not do so. Nothing had actually happened if she just sat here and didn't move.

Something shifted in her pocket, rolling around until she opened the pocket so Tera could tumble out. Her droid rolled across the rocks that surrounded them, drawing her attention to where they were. Because now that her panic was in full force, all she could see was that they weren't, in fact, somewhere safe at all.

Rocks dug into the back of her thighs. A faint dripping sound echoed with wet plops in a rhythmic quality that already grated on her nerves. Even the smell wasn't like the cities she'd been in. She was used to smog and the scent of bodies, or at the very least, metal. The air here was… crisp. And then, as she lifted her head and waited for the slanting world to stop spinning, she realized there were stalactites surrounding her as well.

She was in a cave. Nothing here appeared to be even remotely human. The cave wasn't even that large. It was maybe the size of her living quarters in Gamma, enough to walk around and maybe take fifteen paces in one direction before she'd hit a wall. In the dead center of the room was a pool of water. Glowing with a gentle green light, there was floating algae that seemed to shimmer in the dim light. It was enough light for her to see, but that was all.

She was all alone with the soft sound of lapping water and her droid.

"How did we get here?" she whispered, the words sounding too loud in the echoing space.

Tera was quick to clack against itself and then suddenly her droid zipped toward the water. She didn't even have the energy to chase after it, hoping that her droid wouldn't launch itself past the stones and sink to wherever the bottom was.

But it didn't. Tera found itself a small patch of sand and started... writing? Was her droid writing out words? She had no idea it even knew how to do that. Ace sat there in stunned silence as her droid methodically took the time to write out words in the sand.

Undine.

So, Maketes had brought them here. With the thought came anxiety that swelled and crashed over her head. Where was he? He had brought them here, but he wasn't still here with her. Had something happened to him? Had the tower crumpled to the sea and injured him?

She crawled on her hands and knees toward the droid. A wave of nausea threatened acidic vomit at the back of her throat, but she didn't care. She wouldn't puke here, not when there were so many questions that needed to be answered.

"How?" she asked, then shook her head. "Too many words. How did I breathe?"

Wiping away the sand, she gave Tera a blank canvas to write. And her droid did. It zipped around, the letters perfectly straight and neat as it worked to write out another single word.

Neck.

"My neck?" The pain. Tera must be referencing the pain.

She lifted her hand, only to freeze as the droid clacked loudly against its pieces. It raced to write another word, then another.

Don't touch.

"Don't touch it?" Of course she was going to touch it now. She pressed her fingers to the skin, feeling the tiniest hole there that was covered with a sticky liquid.

All the blood drained out of her head. She was suddenly so dizzy, while tiny speckles dancing in front of her eyes. What had he done to her? Was that the pain? He'd done something to her neck, and she had no idea what he had done, but she wasn't dead, so he'd done something so she could breathe underwater or some other madness.

Where was he?

Swallowing hard, she put her hand back onto the sand to balance herself. "I'm going to puke."

Another word etched into the sand. Don't.

She let out a little puff of laughter. "I don't have a lot of choice, Tera. Please move."

Her droid bolted so far away from her she thought she could hear it on the rocks only moments before she threw up. There wasn't much in her stomach, but apparently there was quite a bit of salt water, which was a horrid taste on her tongue. Stomach acid and salt. She'd never be able to eat another salty thing in her life.

Expelling all that water helped settle her stomach. She could think a little more clearly and manage the terror a bit better. She was in a cave, but she wasn't a fainting damsel in distress. She would make this work for herself because she had no other choice.

"Okay," she muttered, pushing herself back until she was kneeling in the sands rather than on all fours. "Okay, you can figure this out. You're not dead yet."

But what was there to figure out? She spent the better part of what must have been an hour just staring into the water in front of her. Because she was stuck here. Swimming wasn't an option. Even though it was far warmer here than it had been in Gamma at night, she didn't want to get wet. What if it got a little colder? What if she was wet and shivering and then slowly just succumbed to hypothermia?

All the ways that she could die played in her head. And then all she could think about was that if she died, so did her sister. She was the only one who knew that the fucking key was in Doctor Faust's home, and she was the only one who knew where his home was. If she died, then no one would get the key and her sister would die too. Jacob would do it. He liked killing people.

But also if she got in that water and tried to figure out where she was, then she would definitely die. Because that was the open ocean. If a shark didn't get her, then an undine would. The depthstriders had surrounded Gamma, all she could imagine was that they would rip her apart like she'd seen happen before. Besides, it wasn't like she could swim to Gamma on a single breath of air. She was stuck.

With all of those thoughts came the fear that she was alone. Maketes should be here with her. He was ridiculously good at being where she didn't want him to be, and yet, the one moment she needed him, he wasn't here. It made something in her break.

Tears welled in her eyes. Not from the grit and the sand, but because she was terrified something had happened to him. What if the suction from the sea had injured him? What if one of those people in Gamma had fired off one last parting shot? There were so many holes in her memory, she wouldn't have the faintest idea if something had happened to him.

And then the water rippled again. It moved like there was something coming to the surface and she froze. Just kneeling there with her knees aching and her heart in her throat. What if it was a depthstrider? What if it was another undine who wanted her dead?

Then she saw that dark head of hair and the bright splash of yellow that was at the surface. A deep sigh erupted from her mouth, more of a sudden thrust of relief. It was him. It wasn't someone coming to kill her.

"Maketes," she said, before launching herself at him.

His arms came up for her as though he knew what she wanted. Those strong arms caught her with ease, only sinking back into the water a little and only with the slightest "oof" as she kneed him in the gills. But she couldn't get close enough. She couldn't hold on to him tight enough to feel like she was finally safe.

His clawed hands came around her, clasping her tighter and pressing her underneath his chin, where she was nestled against the cold chill of his gills. He exhaled through them, water spilling down over her body, but she didn't care. She only knew that in this moment, she wasn't alone anymore.

"Kefi?" he asked, his voice pitched low, as though he was afraid something was in the cave with them. "You're okay, dear one. You're all right. I'm here."

She shook her head against his throat. "I don't know what happened."

"I'm not leaving again." He flexed his tail underneath her, swimming them to the edge of the water. Then, with a sudden jerk of his tail, he propelled them out of the water enough so that he was sitting on the sand.

It took such little effort for him to wrap her up in his arms. His tail came along her back, holding her tighter against him. She was surrounded by him. The seawater scent of him was so much better than what the sea actually smelled like. He was both warm and cold, a creature who smelled like salt and the deep cold waters that had always been her home.

Every bit of her tension unraveled. His hand came up to her short hair, carding through the locks. The tiny pricks of his claws eased her tension even more until she was a puddle being held against his twin heartbeats.

"I'm sorry," she whispered against his chest.

"For what?"

"For... this."

"You don't have to apologize to me. Ever." He held her even tighter, his arms shifting around her back as he got more comfortable. "I was bringing you a fish to eat, but I'll admit, this is far more pleasant."

She huffed out a small laugh, her breath fanning across his chest and sending tiny goosebumps dancing across his skin. "Pleasant? It's nice for me to attack you the moment you show up?"

"This is the kind of attack I enjoy." Again, that big hand smoothed down her spine, and suddenly this wasn't just easing her fear.

It was more. It was so much more.

Heat flushed from the crown of her head to the bottom of her feet. All she could focus on were his hands. How his fingers spanned the entirety of her back, each claw tip just barely touching her skin. He was so warm even though some parts of him were cold. It was like everywhere he touched her, she was a furnace.

But no, it was more than that. Her heart was already beating harder and more heat burned between her legs. She wanted him. She wanted him to move that hand that was on the small of her back even lower so she could feel him grip her ass. That massive hand would have no issue grabbing onto her, rolling her over, moving her against his body as she so desperately wanted.

She wanted to grind down on him. She wanted to rock against him so those scales rubbed against her clit in a way she knew would be life changing. Ace just... wanted.

He'd saved her life more times than she could count. And as she leaned a little farther back from him, her eyes half lidded and heavy with desire, she saw the same need in him as well.

Maketes lifted his hand between them, those thick fingers brushing up her neck and gently cupping the side of her head. There was so much power in that hand. She'd seen him kill people without a thought, and yet he was shaking to remain as gentle with her as he could. "I almost lost you," he whispered, his words guttural and harsh. "I do not like this feeling, kefi."

"Yeah, me either," she replied, seeing his gills flutter against the sides of his head.

Hadn't he said that was a good thing? Proof that he wanted her?

She could even see it in the way he stared. His eyes widened. He must be able to feel them moving, and he knew as well that she could see them. If he was human, she thought, he might have blushed.

How was she supposed to stop herself? She touched those fluttering gills, feeling them undulate through her fingers. "I can't remember what you said about these moving," she whispered, the lie rolling so easily off her tongue. "Can you tell me what it means again?"

His tail shifted between her legs, slithering a bit with the movement and rubbing against her legs. "You know what it means."

"I want to hear you say it again."

A low rumble echoed through his chest, something that sounded almost like a groan. "Ace—"

"They're just words, Maketes. All you have to do is tell me why these are moving so much." They moved faster with every word she said, shifting against her fingers until they were nearly a blur.

Again he arched. As though he wanted to press himself against her, but there was still some barrier between them. Words that were left unsaid.

There were so many things between them, though. She had a lot of questions that needed answers, but first, she wanted to prove to herself that Maketes was here for the right reasons. Or maybe, just maybe, she wanted to feel wanted.

Hovering her lips just barely over his, she breathed in his shuddering exhalation against her lips. "Go ahead. Tell me."

"We're friends," he rasped. "Just friends."

She could be brave. She could be the brave one to say what they were both thinking. Or at least, what she hoped they were both thinking.

So Ace framed his face with her hands, sliding her fingers along the softness of his gills on either side of his cheeks, and felt them somehow go even faster. And then she leaned so close that her lips nearly touched his.

"What if I want to be more?"

181

Chapter 18

The question froze him. He wanted to be so much more than friends. He'd said the same things to Fortis, but the fear of what that meant for the two of them was hard to ignore.

She asked for him to let go of his own fears. He wasn't the male anyone ended up with. He was fun for a little while, but then females always wanted a male who could actually give them a family. Someone who didn't have the problem of being golden and all that came with his coloring.

But this one... This achromo had seen so much more in him. She had made him laugh. She trusted him to keep her safe, and when was the last time someone had done that? When had a female ever looked at him as anything more than just fun?

His hands clenched on her waist, and he wanted to do so much more. He looked into her pretty brown eyes, seeing the entirety of all the things he adored in them. Her bravery. Her honesty. Her loyalty.

All of those things and more made her so much more real. She wasn't just someone he shared a friendship with through messages that only the two of them saw. She was someone who meant so much more.

Breathing her scent deep into his lungs, he allowed his eyes to drift shut as she brushed her fingers over his gills again and again. He could feel her breath fanning across his lips. He heard the faint sound of her heartbeat and the little breaths that shuddered in and out of her mouth.

He slid his hands down her spine so slowly that they both stopped breathing. Pausing just before he touched anything that a friend certainly wouldn't touch.

"The gills of my people flutter when there is someone they are interested in. When they wish to create a show to entice a potential mate." His voice was deeper even to his own ears, gruff with need and desire that he still feared he shouldn't show. "Mine have never fluttered for anyone else."

"Does that mean you're interested in me, Maketes?"

"It means..." He licked his lips, watching her eyes widen at the sight of his black, ribbed tongue. Fuck, that did things to him. Already he could feel his cocks hardening, pressing against the scales that kept them hidden from her sight.

He rolled his hips, lifting his tail just slightly so he could press it against her heat. It was so hot between her legs he could feel her melting into his scales. He wanted to know what that heat was, to explore it far more than she might even let him. Everything about her called out to him. He was stuck in her siren call and there was no way for him to get out of it.

She moaned, the little sound echoing around them. Ace froze, her eyes widening a bit as though she didn't intend to make the sound.

"Again," he growled, rolling his tail between her legs a little harder this time.

The whimper she made was the prettiest sound he'd ever heard, and even then, he wanted more. It would never be enough to hear just the one little sound of her walls breaking down. Maketes wanted to swallow down every sound of pleasure she made. He wanted to press the scent of her desire into his scales so he would never forget this moment.

One of her hands slid down to his chest, bracing herself so his movements didn't knock her free from his tail.

"Do you know what a kiss is?" she asked.

"Yes." Of course he did. He'd seen both of his brothers press their lips to their mates, and though he'd thought it was rather odd, it was more than tempting. With Ace, he wanted to do everything.

He wanted to taste every inch of her body, even if these thoughts were perhaps too much. He couldn't devour her the first time she let him touch her.

"Can I kiss you?" she asked, and he could hear the vulnerability in that question.

And then he remembered what she'd shared with him. That no one else had wanted her. She was the one who everyone had overlooked. And though it was his luck that they had done so, he also understood that she might be a little nervous.

He couldn't let her do all the work. Not when she was the brave one who had initiated this.

With a deep growl under his breath, he let his hands wander where they wished. He grabbed handfuls of her ass, feeling the softness, just the right amount that he could grab onto. The plushness in his grip nearly sent him into a void of pleasure and desire from which he would never escape. That growl in his chest grew louder as he used the leverage of his grasp to thrust her even harder against him.

Her breasts flattened against him, pressing against his chest as all of her was suddenly against all of him. "Gods, there's so much of you I want to taste, kefi. But first, give me your lips."

That was all it took. She fell into him, the soft cushions of her lips pressing against his, and it unleashed an animal inside of him.

The sound he made was a moan of pure anguish. With lips and teeth and tongue, he tried to devour her. Her taste flooded into his mouth, the sweetest sunshine of her lips that only made him need her even more. He kissed her without skill or talent, only pure desire as he delved between her lips. Seeking more of that taste. Needing to touch her more.

She sucked on his tongue, the tip of her own tracing the ridges and bumps. His hands squeezed her ass, kneading it as his fingers slid along her legs. He wanted to touch more of her. Unknowingly, he drew her even closer. Drawing her legs up to his ribs and pressed her knees there, so she had slid up to his stomach.

He wanted to see her, he realized. Breathing hard, he drew back enough to stare into her eyes that were already half open. He pressed his webbed hand between her breasts, the softness of them already calling out to him even though he'd already laid his head on them. All it took was the slightest pressure to lean her back against his tail. To spread her out before his gaze so that he could look over all of her. Over the splayed legs spread around his hips, the heaving breasts that were right there, all of it hidden from his sight by clothing that shouldn't be on her.

"I want to see you," he rasped.

And there it was again. The flash of nerves that he should have guessed would come. She didn't want him to see her, but he desperately needed it. If it took him talking her through it, then he would thank all the gods a million times that he had been gifted with a voice.

She stared up at him, those brown eyes a little wider than before. But he could still see the trust in those depths.

Splaying his hand between her hips, he set his fingers against her soft belly and drew his fingers up her torso. The movement dragged her clothing up with him, revealing inch by inch of lovely skin. So much of it. So much lovely, warm-colored skin that looked like she'd been kissed by the sun even all the way down here in the ocean.

He stopped just before revealing her breasts to his gaze, waiting for her to look at him. Her eyes had been locked on his hand, watching his movement. They were both captivated by the sight of his hand on her.

And as she looked up at him, he could see she was waiting. Nervous, but waiting for him to do something and he... Gods, he needed to.

Maketes dragged his hand up and over the peak of her right breast. Just enough to reveal that there was another layer of clothing underneath her shirt. He let out a little huff of frustration, ridiculously needy, but also annoyed by the new barrier.

"What is this?" he muttered, curving his hand so he could follow the strange contraption around her ribs.

"A bra," she replied, amusement tinging her words.

"A bra? What reason is there for such a torturous thing?" It seemed to go around the back of her, and was cutting into her skin. She wasn't bloody, but there were red welts beneath the tight band of it.

"I don't actually know," she replied, arching her back and presenting him with the prettiest picture. She was so delicate and lovely like that. Spread out for his taking. It made it hard to focus for a second before he felt her fingers brushing his at her spine and suddenly there was a pop.

And oh.

Oh, he had known there was so much to worship, but he hadn't realized there was more. Just the barest hint of her breast had released from the fabric that hid her from his gaze. But the rosy tip made his mouth water.

"Kefi," he growled, the words rumbling through him before he could catch them. "I need you to trust me."

"I do."

"Because I know you think I'm an animal, perhaps capable of hurting you even after all that we have done together."

"I trust you," she repeated, her words breathless.

"Good, because for a few minutes, it's going to feel like I'm trying to consume you."

Then he descended upon her. His hands grabbed onto her sides, holding her in place as his tongue traced along her skin. He licked to the peak of her breast, drawing that rosy tip into his mouth and swirling his tongue along the sun kissed taste of her. The tip beaded against his tongue, and the more he touched her, the more she moaned.

Her hands came down into his hair as he licked her, sucking hard enough that she arched against him again. He switched to the other breast, tasting her as he had been begging to do for such a long time in his mind. And still, it wasn't enough.

Maybe the problem was his hands. He grabbed onto her ass again, yanking her against him so she could roll like she had done before. Then she did. She ground against him, rocking against his scales with her head thrown back and her throat bared. He wanted to bite that lovely column. The taste there must be even better than here. So he did. He licked his way up to her throat, looming over her so he could capture her lips again. Those hands grabbed onto his hair hard enough to sting, and still, it was perfect.

He was so caught up that he didn't notice his cocks had been released. Not, at least, until she leaned back and was pressed against them. They both gasped, eyes meeting and chests heaving to breathe.

Should they stop? He didn't want to. But he knew it had to be startling.

He knew nothing about her anatomy, but he knew that two cocks weren't what the men of her people had. And she could definitely feel them. Because as she stared into his eyes, she shifted. Her spine sliding against them, parting them so they were both pressed against her lower back.

She bit her lips, and he couldn't look away from those tiny, blunt teeth pressing into the softness of her mouth.

"How do I please you?" he asked, not sounding at all like himself. "I want to make you scream, kefi."

She opened her mouth, closed it, and then appeared lost for words. But she shifted on him, rolling those hips again until she was a little higher on his tail and his cocks were cushioned by the softness of her ass. Divinity. That was all he could think.

Her hand grabbed his and slid it down the front of her pants. His fingers were met by short hair, distracting him until he then found a soft wet heat that was so intriguing. Her head had tilted back again, pressed to his tail even as her mouth dropped open.

Sliding his fingers through the wetness to her core, he drew them back in the same path and listened to the deep groan form in the center of her body, then release from her mouth. It echoed in the cavern, the sound of her need making him wild.

She pushed her pants halfway down her thighs, giving him more room and more sights to see. His cocks kicked against her bottom, and suddenly she was grinding against him. Rocking against the heat of him from behind, while also rocking against his fingers.

He had to be careful with his claws. Vowing to bite them all clean off, he pinched his fingers together so there was more texture from his webbed fingers for her to ride. He helped her along the way, easing his fingers back and forth.

But it was her movements that captivated him. Pressing against his cocks so that they were rubbing against her. Faster, harder, rougher, until one of his cocks slid up between them. And now he was pressed against the core of her. The heat that had captivated him from the very first moment she'd been close enough for him to realize where it was coming from.

The sound he made was somewhere between a groan and a hiss. He started to shift away, not wanting to overwhelm her with the feeling of him, but she gasped out a rough, "Don't move!"

And then that wonderful, magical woman did something he never expected. She reached her hand between them and planted her palm against his cock. Pre-cum dripped out of the tip, making it so easy for him to slide against that talented little palm. Her fingers pressed him harder between her legs where his own hand was. He could feel the two of them so easily. Her heat, his hand, his cock, her hand. All of it was nearly too much.

He hissed again, knowing that he must look crazed. His gills were fluttering so hard he could feel the wind of it. A bead of sweat rolled down between her breasts even as she opened her eyes to stare up at him. And maybe she didn't think of him as a monster, because the moment their gazes met, he could see only her desire.

"Move your hand, little one. Stroke me," he rasped. "You feel so good."

Those eyes rolled back again, and then she was holding him harder, rocking her hips faster. He stayed still, shifting his fingers, moving them in a wave so he could press against every part of her that rubbed against him. He wanted to know what would happen next. His people enjoyed sex, but it was always so bloody. He wanted to know what it was like to watch her kind fall apart.

And then... Then it happened. He felt her tense against him, felt the throb against his fingers and webs even as her mouth fell open in silence. Then there was the little groan, the aching need that boiled out of her throat and he lost himself as well.

He came hard, both of his cocks twitching against her as he shot over both her belly and up her back. His cum coated her, and something deep inside of him clicked into place. Like this was right. Like she should be coated in his scent so that no other male would ever dare to come near her.

He felt a little undone as he stared down at her. The looseness of her hips, the release of tension that had been bothering her. All of it was his doing. He'd done this.

Maketes gave her a few more pets that had her twitching before he freed his fingers. Even then, he watched her as he pressed his slick hand to the glimmering cum on her stomach, smearing their pleasure together and gliding his hand up to frame her breast.

"So pretty," he murmured, running his thumb over her nipple. "But next time you'll scream for me. We both know you can be louder."

Chapter 19

She didn't know what to say or what to do. Her entire body was limp, liquid, far more relaxed than she had been since... forever. She couldn't remember a time when she was more relaxed than she was in this moment.

And for once, she wasn't worried about what she looked like. She didn't care that he was staring at her, or wondering if she looked good spread out across his lap. She didn't fear that he wouldn't like her soft belly, or that her hair must be tangled and sticking up at all angles. None of that mattered. It didn't even matter that her glasses were nearly halfway down her nose.

All that mattered was that her body felt so good.

She'd made herself come many times in her life. It was a fun pastime and necessary for a bored teenager. But no one else had ever made her come.

Ace hadn't realized just how fulfilling that would be. To have someone else that she trusted enough to actually put his hands on her, to make her feel like she was pretty. Worthy. Wanted.

He'd made her see stars in that experience. She didn't care that she was a little lost in life. It didn't matter that the key was no closer to her grasp or that her sister had no idea what threats were coming for her. All that mattered was the liquid feeling of her muscles and the sensation of his tail moving behind her back.

Or was that his cock? She realized the slight movement must be his cocks going back to wherever he hid them, because the other one slid between her legs and seemingly disappeared as well.

Two. He had two cocks, and that was a surprise she hadn't been expecting. The undines differed from humans, obviously. She'd been expecting that. But she hadn't thought they would have two massive cocks that made her want to do a lot more than just rub up against them.

But rubbing against them had been good, too. She would do that again.

Looking up at Maketes, she didn't feel fear when she noticed their differences again. His gills were flat against his face again, smooth as they usually were. They became streaking highlights of yellow that made his cheekbones look even sharper. And those dark eyes that once had made her nervous, now all she saw was the depth of emotion in them.

He was handsome. Far more handsome than she had ever given their kind credit for. From the hollows of his strong neck muscles to his incredibly sculpted chest, all the way down to the "v" muscles that narrowed into his tail which was the loveliest yellow color, all of it captivated her.

She wanted more of him. More of this. Whatever it was between them, and she was hesitant to even define what it was, that was what she wanted.

More. That's all she could think. More of everything and anything until she was glutted on him.

"You are so beautiful," he murmured, his hand ghosting up her side again. Those webs were like velvet sliding against her skin, so soft and yet somehow so wicked as he'd pressed them against her own velvety lips between her legs.

Just the mere thought of it had her wanting to press her thighs together to ease the ache between them. But they had already crossed a line that friendship usually drew. So now she just... she wasn't sure what to do with him.

"Thank you," she whispered in response. "So are you."

Which was a true statement, even if it made him laugh at her. He rolled them both, sliding into the water with her in his grip.

Immediately, she braced herself for the icy chill that would steal her breath, especially without the added layer of her shirt to protect her. But instead, she found the water to be quite pleasant. Almost warm, even.

Blowing out the breath she'd just sucked in, she looped her arms around Maketes's neck and instead looked around them. The green glow turned into sparkling green stars as he disturbed the water. They scattered around them, looking like he had lightning attached to his body.

"What is this?" she asked.

"They glow when touched."

"They?" She'd heard of bioluminescent creatures before, but this just looked like water.

"Algae. There are millions of them all throughout every wave in this place, and even more out in the sea. They feed the ocean just as the ocean takes care of them." He curled his arms under her butt, sinking them lower until the glowing waves lapped at both of their chins.

And then she just… stared. How could she not? This otherworldly creature was grinning at her, those eyes showing far too much of his emotions, and she wanted to kiss him again.

Ace had never felt this way about another person in her life. She was always the reserved one. Always the person who saw responsibility and grabbed onto it with both hands.

"I don't know what we're doing," she said. "Everything feels different, though."

"It should."

"Oh."

What was she supposed to say to that? It felt different. He agreed. And that was that. It wasn't like there was more to say, even though it terrified her that maybe there should be a lot more to say.

He leaned forward and nipped at her neck with those sharp teeth, right over the spot that still stung a bit if she focused on it.

Then the menace said, "Are you going to ask me about this?"

She waited for the original rage and fear to come bubbling up like it had when she'd first touched her neck and realized he'd done something to her. But instead, all she could feel was the smallest sense of warmth and maybe a bit of irritation. But it was irritation that also made her want to tease him.

"I guess." Ace released one hand from his shoulders and touched the soft spot on her throat. "I did notice that something was different here."

"My people have found a way to connect with yours." His hand shifted under her bottom, one broad finger slowly stroking between her legs before he retreated back to holding onto her. "Besides that, of course."

Her cheeks flamed bright red. "Stop that."

"Stop what?" This time his opposite hand moved up her side, gently brushing against her breast before retreating. "Do you not want me to touch you, kefi?"

"No." Wait — "I mean, yes. It's fine if you touch me. You're just distracting me from this conversation."

"Maybe." Those talented fingers pressed down against her ribs, hauling her a little higher in the water until her breasts were at eye level for him. She could see the heat in his eyes again, and it made something in her squirm. "Perhaps I need to distract you better."

"Maketes, we need to talk about the hole in my neck you added without my permission. What do you mean, it's a connection between our... our... species?"

Fuck, that broad tongue slipped out from between his teeth. He licked first one breast, then the other, the ridges moving over her nipples in that distracting way that had her seeing stars. Then he drew one into his mouth, sucking hard enough that she felt it all the way between her legs. The slick heat of his mouth was in sharp contrast to the body temperature of the water.

"Hm?" he murmured, the sound vibrating over her sensitive nipple before he released it with a pop. "Oh, I can breathe for you underwater."

He licked her again, somehow coiling that long tongue entirely around her breast and the sensation...

No, hang on. "You can breathe for me?"

She slapped her hands against his shoulders, shoving him until he had to move back. He licked his lips, still staring at her chest, clearly incapable of looking her in the eye when he could instead look at her breasts.

"Maketes!" She forced him to free her, wriggling out of his grip so she could duck underneath the water and cover herself with her hands. Glaring, she muttered, "Would you just look at me?"

"I am looking at you. All that wondrous, full flesh. Seeing you like this makes me want to bite you." Baring those sharp teeth, he added, "Only if you wished, I suppose. But I would like it known that I very much would like to."

Heat flooded through her at the image her mind conjured. Him looming over her, rutting into her like an animal with her neck in his teeth. And it wasn't... It should have been terrifying. It should have been an image that made her disgusted. But it didn't.

Not in the slightest.

"Explain the breathing," she ordered, although she felt like there were more words unspoken. Explain the breathing before this gets out of hand again.

He sighed, then flicked his tail and moved all the way across the pool. "I need space from you to talk."

"Is it that bad?"

"No, you're too distracting. I can't think with all..." He waved his hand up and down, dunking it into the water so he could gesture to her entire form. "All of that. It's too much. My mind can only do so much."

And that might have been the nicest thing that any man had ever said to her.

She blinked a few times, then moved through the water so she could brace herself against the lip of stone. There was something unnerving about treading water without knowing what was beneath her. Especially without Maketes to hold on to her.

There was plenty of space between them now, but she also leaned over the edge and yanked her shirt over her head as well. Just for good measure.

Dunking back into the water, she braced herself and then turned to look at him. "Better?"

Those heated eyes looked over her and groaned. "No. Now look at you. That shirt does nothing to hide and everything to somehow make you even more tantalizing."

She glanced down to see that the shirt had become entirely see through. Clinging to her breasts, the fabric creating little hills and valleys along her skin that was... pretty. Was this the first time she'd ever looked at her own body and thought it was pretty?

That thought definitely needed to be unpacked later, but not right now. Even if it took the entirety of her self control to yank herself out of the water, sit down on the lip of the stone, and cross her arms over her chest. "Talk."

"I don't want to talk right now."

"I do."

"What do I get if I tell you?"

Oh, this devious man. He looked at her with all that hunger, and she wanted to promise him everything. She wanted to tell him that there was a lot more she could do and now that they weren't only friends, she wondered if maybe she just... could tell him that.

So she tilted her head to the side and was braver than she'd ever been in her life. "If you're good, I'll show you what humans do with their mouths and cocks."

"Excuse me?" His eyes had widened.

"Cocks don't just go into pussies." Even though at the words she spread her legs a little wider, just to get his attention. "They're also good for sucking. You like what I did with my hands? It's ten times better with my mouth."

He dunked completely underwater, like he'd forgotten how to

swim. One moment he was there, staring at her with an open mouth, and the next, underwater. He came up spluttering, wiping his face clear of water before opening his eyes and gaping at her again.

"What?" he said.

"You heard me. Just tell me what I want to know, and maybe I'll entertain the idea."

Maketes swallowed so hard she could hear it. "There are two other human pairings with my kind. Both of them realized that we have a tentacle that is seemingly there for breathing purposes. We haven't used it in a very long time, but have realized we can connect with your species underwater. It is unnerving from what I've heard, but it keeps you alive. The tentacle is fairly long on its own, and seems to be a bit stretchy, so you don't have to stay in my arms at all times."

She could feel her eyes getting wider and wider with every word. She could breathe underwater if that thing was in her neck? She supposed the goo made sense now. The thick liquid likely made it so the tentacle couldn't pop out easily and also made sure that there was an air-tight seal on it.

Maketes took another deep breath and kept going. "It is a permanent reconfiguration of your body. I'm sorry I didn't ask permission. I was told that I have to ask permission before I did it. But the water was flooding the room, and you were going to die if I didn't do it. So it seemed better to ask forgiveness later after I was certain that you were alive rather than try to mime in the water what I was doing. Besides, you passed out."

"Oh," she mumbled.

"Anya and Mira were both very explicit that I was not to do anything permanent to your body without asking you if it was all right for me to do so. I fully understand that there are some limitations to what you can and cannot do, and I would very much like to have you around me at all times. The breathing is likely not going to be something you enjoy very much, but it is something that I can do to keep you safe. Which is important to me. When I thought you were harmed, I didn't know what to do with myself. That is not something I will willingly endure again, so I'm afraid I don't feel bad about changing anything in your body without your permission."

He took another deep breath, and she held up her hand to make him stop rambling. None of it made sense anymore.

When he froze, she said, "Thank you for explaining. I think I understand what it is now."

He blew out the breath. "Good. Does that mean you'll do that thing with your mouth?"

Was all of that rambling because he wanted to be extra thorough so she would give him a blow job? Maybe men really weren't all that different, no matter what species they were.

Still, a deal was a deal. And she was more than ready to get payback for the way he'd made her see stars.

Ace licked her lips, watching as his eyes followed the movement. She could see the hunger in him, the need. All of it was nearly too much and yet she wanted to keep teasing him.

"All right," she said with a laugh. "A promise is a promise."

He started moving toward her right at the same time she saw something flash in the depths. It wasn't as big as the shark, but it was something. Shrieking, she launched herself out of the water just before a tentacle reached for her foot.

Maketes coughed out a laugh, but then hissed out his own angry sound when the tentacle attached to him. "Damned squid," he muttered, batting it away before two more tentacles latched onto his waist.

He yanked it off of him, but she noticed the red circles left behind on his belly, and the scales that had been pulled up by the sheer force of the suckers.

The long, suffering sigh that he gave preceded him rolling his gaze up toward the ceiling.

"Fine," he muttered. "I'll take care of the squid and then I'll be right back."

She rolled her lips, trying hard not to laugh. "I'll be waiting."

Chapter 20

ometimes the sea worked with him, and other times, she taught him patience. The squid brought him right back to an entire shoal of them. And each individual squid seemed to have a vendetta against him.

Or maybe that was just how he felt because he knew he had something to get back to, and the squid were not happy he was in their hunting grounds. It wasn't like the People of Water and squid had ever gotten along. Those creatures were intelligent enough to know that his kind were a threat to their food, and his people just didn't like their damned beaks. Squid were far too protective over their food, and they were so quick to bite and use those suckers at every chance they could get.

He hated their species and enjoyed fighting them to get some of his pent up aggression out. Because at this rate, she wasn't going to use her mouth on him like she'd promised. Maybe sometime soon he could convince her to do so, but realistically, too much time had passed.

The moment was gone. Simmering just underneath his skin. But he didn't want to push her to do anything she wasn't excited to do as well. He'd wanted to explore her body. He'd enjoyed seeing her undone by pleasure.

They had other issues. Other problems. Soon enough, they would need to return to her city of Gamma, even though it made his stomach twist with acid. He wanted to throw up at the mere idea of bringing her back to that place where she'd almost died.

So instead of thinking about it, he tore into the squid. Ripping tentacles off gelatinous bodies made him feel a little better, even if that wasn't the healthiest way to deal with the emotion. Perhaps he was taking his feelings out too much on them. The water was rather clogged with their blood and the awful scent of their ink. He could barely see his hand in front of his face.

Ridiculous. And yet, here he was. Using violence as a way to still his mind so he could prepare something that would make her like him even more.

Which... now that he was thinking about it, he actually had quite a good plan for that.

Darting up through the water after he'd made it very clear to the squid to leave him alone, he headed up to the surface. The water lightened quickly. They weren't that far down in the depths, after all. The cave he'd brought her to was nearly at the surface itself, although he didn't want to tell her that. He'd come here many times in his life, exploring as a child while trying to get away from those who teased him.

His head broke through the surface, and he was surprised to see the sun almost setting. But the waves were calm and quiet, a calm sea that reflected an unbroken image of fluffy skies. There was a storm in the distance, but he didn't think it would affect his plan. Not yet, at least.

"Perfect," he exclaimed, before diving underneath the waves and heading back toward her cave. The plan formed in his mind just as he hit the warm vents that heated her pool.

He would show her something that no mate had yet. He would prove to her that while he was different and perhaps a little scary, he was still worthwhile to keep around.

Because if he didn't have to prove himself to her, then he didn't have to prove himself to other people. And Maketes wasn't ready to accept that just yet.

Ace was right where he'd left her. She was sitting at the edge of the water, staring down at her droid who was zipping around in strange patterns. He recognized the words from when they had been messaging with each other. But he'd always had a voice to read the messages to him. Now, he still wasn't sure what they said. But it didn't matter.

"Kefi," he said, interrupting their conversation.

And the way she looked at him, with that smile on her face... it turned his heart into molten lava. Rubbing at the sudden tension there, he nodded to the back corner of the room. "There's a small crevice there. I need you to climb through it."

"What?" Her eyebrows raised. "You want me to squeeze through a tunnel in a cave?"

"Yes. You'll fit."

She shook her head. "I'm not going to do that. What if I get stuck?"

"Then I'll come get you."

"Not if I'm halfway through the tunnel and you can't reach me! That's how I die, Maketes."

He leaned his arm against the side of the water, grinning at her.

"Remember how I made you pet a shark?"

"Shut up."

"Remember how you fought against all those people in that tower? You even held a knife and cut one of them. I smelled it." He tapped his neck gills, still looking up at her with all the adoration in his chest. "You're braver than you think, kefi."

"You keep calling me that, and it sounds like you have a cough." She crossed her arms over her chest, looking at him and shaking her head.

But he could see that spark of bravery in her. The sudden flicker of a flame that called her to adventure, even when she wanted to deny it. He could see her mind was filled with all the dangers that she would entertain by doing this, but her heart wanted to go. It wanted to dive into the unknown with him.

"If you go through that crevice, I will meet you on the other side and tell you what the name means."

That was enough of a deal for her. She narrowed her gaze on him, those laser eyes seeing everything before she nodded. "Fine. But if I get stuck and die, I'm haunting you forever."

"I wouldn't want it any other way."

The moment she started into the small crevice, turning sideways so she could fit, he dove into the water to meet her outside. Sure, she had an ass that might make this difficult for her, but it was a beautiful ass and one that he was quite fond of already. She'd fit just fine, and he never would have sent her in that way if he had thought for a second she'd get stuck and die.

Curving through the spears of dying light, he raced to the other side of this outcropping. In his mind, he played what she was doing. First, she had to reach the first bend. She'd have to slide down and crouch to get under it, like he had when he was a child. But if a small male like himself could get through, so could she. A few rocks would then be in her way. She'd have to climb up them to get to the flat portion which would lead her... here.

He broke through the water with a sharp flick of his tail that sent him flying out of the waves and up onto the flat rocks that met the sea. They were still warm from the sun's rays throughout the day, and their smooth texture let him slide almost all the way to the opening she would exit.

He waited there, listening to her panting sounds and curses that echoed just out of his reach. "You're almost here!" he called out, grinning even wider when she hissed out more curses. Some mixed with his name and were quite elaborate.

But then she reached the opening. Ace strode confidently out before freezing with her hand raised to her eyes. She blinked, squinting against the vision of the sun before her.

"What is this?" she called out.

"The sun," he replied, looking back to see the rays skittering across the water and turning the waves into diamonds. "Just like your people used to see every day."

A few more blinks, and she lowered her arm. Then he could see the expression of awe that crossed her face.

Ace took a step out, staggered, then a few more steps and reached for him. Her hands were trembling as she clutched his wrist and stared out at the blue sky and even bluer water that was just barely rolling with the tide. He tried to see it all through her eyes.

She'd been under the water her entire life. A creature who was meant to be here in the sun with the sky above her and the wind playing across her skin. There were few achromos who had ever been here, perhaps none that still lived.

"What is this place?" she asked, her voice trembling.

"This is where your people were born." He drew her into his arms, giving her something to lean against as she felt the sun on her skin for the very first time. "You were meant to stand here with the sun on your skin. Soon, perhaps you would become tanned as it sank into the very essence of your body. Every morning, you would wake and see the sun reflecting on every surface. Even tiny beads of water on leaves turn to gemstones. And in the evening, when the sun sets and all the world grows still, a symphony awakens. Insects that sing every night, birds that call out to each other, the howl of furry creatures who live beyond in the hills."

A shuddering breath blew out of her. Those trembling hands still clutched at his forearms. "We're... above?"

He pointed just over her shoulder, allowing her eyes to follow the line of his finger so she could see where he was gesturing. "There, on the horizon. You should see the faintest dark line there. That is land. We are on a small island, if you can even call it that. There isn't much here other than the small cavern and this spot we stand on. But there is land just out there. Land your people used to live on."

Tears welled in her eyes, dripping down her cheeks as she looked. "Land?" she repeated, her voice nearly impossible to understand. "You mean there's dirt there? Earth and green things growing?"

"I don't know if anything's growing. The storms have taken much from your world." He pointed to the storm that was brewing just far enough away from them. "There is one."

The thunderhead was massive, but they always were. Dark purple and raging, with lightning arcing in between the billowing heads. It went on for miles, as far as the eye could see. But, like most, it was clustered together. They would have hours before it reached them, and he was particularly good at telling when they would get too close to him.

"Oh," she whispered. "So the rumors are true, then."

"What rumors?"

"That we can't live above?" She turned her head to look at him, gazing up with those sad brown eyes. "I had hoped for a second that maybe you were showing me we could live here. That the storms and the earthquakes and the volcanic eruptions were all made up, so we had to stay down there. When I was a little girl, I used to dream that there were still people living in the sun. That if I was really good, someone would let me come and live with them."

His heart broke for her. The People of Water did not need the sun like hers did. He didn't need the air or the wind or all the things that only earth could give them. The ocean was made for him and his people, while the land was made for hers.

Everything in him screamed to hold her tighter against his chest. To let her sob out her frustrations of her life and to absorb it into the hard muscles of his chest. But he knew that's not what she needed right now.

She didn't need to sit in those terrible emotions or thoughts. What she needed was to sit in the sun and experience this for a few moments so she could hold them to her heart forever and never forget them.

So he released her and nudged her forward. "Go on. Explore your sun and all the sights you might never see again."

She looked back at him for a second and then she was off. Racing across the top of this tiny island that wasn't all that big. But it was enough for her to run. She leapt between the rocks, poked around in the pools of water that still had some crustaceans and small snails inside of them. She triumphantly held up a crab for him to see, and splashed in the warm water that she swore was almost hot.

Ace had her moment in the sun, and he encouraged every second of her child-like wonder. He named every crab. He splashed the water back at her. Even grabbed a handful of seaweed and tossed it at her head.

There were only a few hours left of sunlight, though. And soon enough, the sky turned pink as they prepared to say goodbye to the sun. Unfortunately, that also meant the storm was too close for comfort.

But he couldn't rush her. Not when she'd finally settled on the warm stones and was staring out at the sky that was filled with a rainbow of colors.

Her eyes were wet, glimmering with unshed tears that she kept dashing away so she could stare a little longer. Maketes lowered himself into the waves, swimming so he was right between her legs.

She didn't look at him, but he hadn't expected her to.

"We have to go back soon," he said, remorse filling him at even having to say the words. "I'm sorry."

"Don't be sorry. You gave me a gift that no one else could ever have dreamt of. This was so beautiful. To know that even though it's dangerous to live here, even though there is a storm at my back, right now, all I can see is a sunset." She hiccuped, the sound somewhat a cross between a gasp and a sob. "I never would have seen this if it weren't for you."

"I only gave you what you deserved to see."

"No, Maketes. You didn't. I'm a convicted criminal who has stolen from good people. I don't deserve any of this, and yet, you are the one giving it to me." She turned that teary eyed gaze down to look at him and framed his face with her hands. "Thank you for this. It was the best afternoon of my entire life."

He didn't fight against her when she leaned down to kiss him. How could he? He wanted those lips against his, and he greedily took what she offered. But only for a few moments before guilt crept in.

Maketes leaned away and tilted her chin up. "Look at the sunset, Ace. You deserve to see it for every second that I can let you."

"My name isn't Ace," she whispered, her gaze locked on the darkening sky. "It's just what I prefer people to call me. My name is Maura."

"Maura," he repeated, and then shook his head. "Ace is a wonderful name, too."

"Thank you. For everything, Maketes."

He leaned down and rested his head in her lap, wrapping his arms around her waist and holding her for a little while longer. "You're welcome."

Chapter 21

What was she supposed to do now? She sat there, watching the sunset and the sky change from pink to red to a deep purple. Small sparks of light filled the sky, and she realized she was seeing stars for the first time as well. A million stars, all laid out in front of her as a galaxy revealed itself right above her head. It was so beyond beautiful.

She knew whatever her people were trying to find was dangerous. The rumble of thunder was an ominous warning that her thoughts were correct. Whatever Jacob wanted to do with that key? It wouldn't just affect her own people.

Whether it was weapons or some other kind of terrible thing that would poison the water, it was something the undine had to consider as well. And now that she had grown ever closer to Maketes, she didn't think she could take that key and not warn him.

It all felt too real. Talking to him through a droid was so much easier and yet, this was so much more than she had expected.

Running her fingers through his hair where he rested his head in her lap, she turned her gaze from the sky to him. Maybe it was wasting precious moments. Maybe she should have stared at the sky and the stars for every second that she could. But when she looked down at him, all she could see were the stars decorating his skin. Tiny flecks of starlight, each one bright yellow and so lovely it hurt to look at him. They decorated his neck, his shoulders, dotting down the valley of his spine and the muscles in between his shoulder blades.

The sparkling lights were so pretty, it made her heart twist and her throat tighten up. He looked at her and he thought she was pretty. He told her that he was interested in her, far more than any human man ever had been. And even then, she was still searching for a key that both of them knew could change… everything.

"My sister," she whispered, trying to get the feelings out in a way that made sense.

"Your sister needs to be saved. I know. They are going to kill her, and that is not something I will just stand by and watch happen. Trust me in this, Ace. I will keep her safe."

Of course he would, because that was who he was. Maketes would protect anyone who needed it. She knew that much about him. She'd also seen how far he was willing to go to protect her.

A chill ran down her spine. An idea forming that was so wrong and yet so right at the same time. She didn't want to ask him to kill for her, but if that was what it took…

Another rumble of thunder preceded him lifting his head, and a bolt of lightning illuminated the look of determination. As though he'd already come to the same conclusion she had just thought of. As though he knew he would tear the world down for her.

The first drops of rain hit them. Heavy, thick balls that splattered on her shoulders and down into her hair. They were drenched in moments, staring at each other as an icy wind blew up as well.

"Ask me," he said, his voice low and quiet. "Ask me and it will be done."

"I'm not a murderer. I'm a thief."

"I am a murderer. You have seen me kill for less than keeping those you love safe. The burden will not be yours to bear. It will be mine."

Rain dripped down her cheeks, or maybe those were tears, because they burned hot enough to brand her cheeks. "I can't ask you to kill someone."

"You won't be asking me to do that. You're asking me to save someone's life, and how I do it is up to me." He reached up and smoothed his thumbs along her cheeks. "You have to know by now that I would do anything for you, kefi."

She did. And that terrified her because there were so many things she could ask him to do. So many paths down this road that would end in blood and violence.

Maketes drew their faces together, pressing his forehead against hers and breathing her in as the rain grew ever colder. They stayed there in the storm, letting the thunder and the lightning spark around them, until it was almost too late.

"We have to go," he murmured. "The rain turns into hail quickly. Those shards of ice are sharp enough to cut through your skin."

She nodded.

Ace slipped into the water, holding onto him as they sank beneath the waves. In the meager light, she could see him reach for something at the back of his head, and then she remembered. He was going to breathe for her. How strange that experience was going to be and yet, she didn't flinch when he drew the end of it toward her neck. The tiniest prick and then she felt her lungs inflate.

Like she was breathing. She could feel him inhale for her, drawing air through his gills and then breathing it into her lungs. Her chest rose on its own, the sensation odd but not repulsive.

Maketes sank them a little lower in the water, hail raining down from above and scattering into the water. But they slowed as soon as they were underneath the waves, and it looked like it was snowing around them. She'd only seen such things in pictures, and now, because of him, she had seen them in real life.

She reached out, her fingers just barely touching the gills on his ribs and he breathed for her and feeling the air then travel into her own body. Maketes placed his hand on her chest. Together, for a few moments, they breathed together. The silence of the dark water was filled only with the softest sound of rain above their head and the sinking hail that filled her vision with white.

Finally she looked up at him, her gaze traveling over that muscular chest and up his strong throat. The moment her eyes met his, the gills on the sides of his head flicked open, fluttering. And then... Oh, and then every single light on him glowed. She'd known he could illuminate himself, but she hadn't realized it would be like this.

Tiny freckles of light speared out into the darkness of the sea. She had seen them before, but he was so much more brilliant in this moment. Staring at her with a grin on his face. Like he knew something she didn't. Like he wanted her to see how happy he was that they were connected.

"You can talk," he said. "The others could, at least."

"I'm underwater." Bubbles floated out of her mouth, but the impossible was really happening. She was talking. Muted words, yes. Quieter than most could pick up, but he had better hearing than her.

That grin grew even wider. "Do you want to see my world? For a few moments?"

They didn't have time. She should be telling him to bring her back to the city so she could search for that key, so they could figure out what to do and how to do it. And yet... She found herself nodding.

"Hold on tight," he said, wrapping an arm around her waist.

She already knew he could swim quickly. But she hadn't realized how fast he could go. Maketes flashed her another grin, and they were speeding through the water. Racing through it so fast she could hardly keep her eyes open and her hair blew back from her face. His ribs expanded, his gills working over time to breathe for both her and him.

It was like his breathing had pumped her body full of adrenaline. She could feel every muscle twitch in his body, every flicker of his tail and the fins that carried them through the currents. He moved like a dream. Like a torpedo through the water until they slowed, and she realized where he had brought her.

There was a group of massive creatures here. Blue and speckled, they were nearly as long as the towers in Gamma. With straight up and down tails like a shark, they moved far slower. Just gliding through the ocean, a trio of them, all slicing through the waters that were now far out from the storm. As Maketes moved around them, she realized their mouths were long and flat, not at all like a shark's.

"What are they?" she asked, reaching out for the tip of a fin and gliding her hands along the smooth surface.

"Your people call them whale sharks," he said with a soft snort. "They are not whales. But they are quite friendly."

"How did you know they were here?"

"I am part of the ocean. I know where many things are." He moved them with a flick of his tail, shifting them closer to the giant whale sharks.

There were tiny fish clinging to their sides. Sucker fish, she realized. They were attached by the mouth, but didn't appear that they were eating at the sharks. In fact, it seemed like they all lived together rather symbiotically.

"Do you want to ride one?" Maketes asked.

He didn't just ask what she had heard. There was no way that he'd asked if she wanted to ride a whale shark.

"Excuse me?" she tapped her ear. "I don't think I heard you correctly."

But that grin was back. The one that said he knew what she was thinking. "Yes, you heard me right. Do you want to ride one, kefi?"

She didn't have to think hard. There were a few seconds of hesitation before she blurted out, "Yes, yes, I very much want to ride one."

The look of pride on his face made her glow. She could feel her heart thundering in her chest, and there was a strange feeling twisting in her guts. Like she wanted to kiss him again. Like she wanted to grab onto his face and let him know how much this moment meant to her.

He didn't give her the chance.

They were suddenly arcing above the whale sharks, twisting and looping until they were right above them. She had never swum like this before. With such ease and such ability.

She hadn't swum that much in her life at all, though. She wasn't an engineer, nor was she someone who had access to the water. So having him doing the swimming for her made it feel like she was flying. He had her back to the whale sharks, so she looked up at the rippling water above their heads.

The moon was just visible above their heads through the water. And somehow, it was even prettier than the sun. The silver light cast rays throughout the water, turning her skin gray and the whale sharks to look like ghostly, ethereal beings as one of them passed over her head.

Maketes held her hand in his, just like he had with the other shark, pressing their palms to the pale belly as it passed. It was so huge, and it made her feel so small to be around these creatures who had been here for ages.

Then she gasped, sucking in air through the tube as they were falling. Sinking through the water until Maketes shifted her into the crook of his arm and their backs hit something sturdy and strong beneath them.

She looked over at him, seeing the soft smile on his face. "Are we..."

"Yes, we're lying on its back."

Ace sat up as quickly as she could without pulling the tentacle out of her neck. Then she could see where they were. There was a massive creature underneath her, its head stretching so far out of her reach. So large. The blueish body beneath her was speckled with little white freckles, but she was here. Sitting on the back of a whale shark as it swam throughout the water.

She let out a sound that might have been a giggle, she wasn't sure. She'd never made that sound in her life.

Pressing her hands to her mouth, she stared wide eyed at the undine beside her.

He reclined with his hands behind his back. All those muscles were flexed, tightening the moment she looked over at him as though he wanted her to see how muscular he was. Perhaps he did. Then those fluttering gills at his neck gave him away.

"This is really happening," he said. The note of pride in his words made her feel so good. "You're welcome. Again."

She threw herself at him. And sure, it wasn't as fast of a movement underwater as it would have been in the air, but she still did it. She landed on his chest, her hands tracing every bit of him that she could reach, his ribs, petting through his gills before she grabbed onto his face and gave him a kiss that seared her right to the bones.

He let out a little groan, the sound echoing through her entire being as he held her against him. "We can't keep doing this. The beast beneath us will get angry."

"I don't care, let it." She kissed him soundly, lingering with her teeth and tongue until she had to yank herself away from him. Because she couldn't miss a moment of this.

The shark beneath them moved with such grace, it was almost like they weren't moving at all. And as she braced herself above him, lifting on her hands, she could feel her hair billowing around her head. The glasses on her face only made it a little awkward to see. The water distorted a bit beyond the lens, but there was so much here that stunned every sense.

"Wow," she whispered. "This feels like a dream."

"It's no dream. This is the real sea that you've never been able to see before. It is an honor that I was able to bring you here today."

"An honor?" she repeated, before looking down at him with an incredulous expression. "What do you mean, it's an honor? For you or me? Maketes, this is more than I ever dreamt I would do in my life. This is beautiful and wonderful, and I cannot thank you enough for what you have done. This is a dream come true to see the ocean as you do."

He reached up, tucking a strand of hair behind her ear. It immediately pulled free, but it was more the motion than what he accomplished with it. His hand lingered on her face, following the line all the way down to her chin. He stared at her like he looked through all the walls she had put up and he saw the real person inside of her.

It terrified her that he saw so much of who she was. But at the same time, it was such a relief that someone finally saw her.

"I had a feeling it would be like this," he murmured. "From the first moment Anya spoke of you, I could feel that the sea wanted to draw me to your side. But I never guessed how this would feel."

"How does it feel?"

He traced her bottom lip with his thumb. "Oh, kefi, someday I will tell you that."

"You harbor a lot of secrets, undine."

"Shh." He pressed that thumb over her mouth to silence her. "Stop talking. You're going to miss this moment, just like you might have missed the sun."

So she turned her head and watched the sea. Because he was right. This was a once in a lifetime opportunity, and she would not waste it.

Chapter 22

He glided with her through the sea, all the while reminding himself that he couldn't keep her. It wasn't right for him to force her to be underneath the sea. But then, another part of him was reminded of the other two women. There was room in their home. They were building more and more onto it, taking pieces of Alpha and making their own little town where there were individual places for people. Growing areas. Spaces where humans could thrive, even under the sea.

And if he could bring some of them above when there weren't storms, perhaps they could figure out a way to expand back onto the land where humans lived as well. All they had to do was create a home that could hold up to the sharp storms of ice and flying metal pieces that would slice their skin, the heat of the day, and sometimes tides that rose over the building.

If anyone could do it, it was Mira and the other women who had created a home for themselves where he had left them. And his dear Ace, his little kefi who had proven herself thoroughly intelligent. He was certain she could do more than he expected.

And yet, there were only a few moments for him to even consider these things before he knew their time was running out. Because though they could enjoy time on the back of a whale shark, reality was barreling toward them.

Her sister needed saving, and if she wasn't going to ask him to help her, then he would figure out a way to do it on his own.

The problem was that he didn't know where to find her sister. Maketes glided with her back toward the cave, still feeling like he was missing a piece of the puzzle. There were things he didn't know, things that he wasn't certain he would ever understand.

Ace was asleep in his arms, though. And he didn't want to wake her to answer his questions. So once they got back to the cave, he kept her relaxed in his arms with his breathing tube in her neck, and popped his head above the water.

"Droid?" he called out, hoping that he wouldn't wake the sleeping achromo in his arms.

Her droid zipped toward him from behind a rock, clacking together in excitement as though it recognized him. It should at this point, but he never knew with droids.

"Ah, good. You're still here."

It wheeled in a circle and then stood still, eerily like a pet waiting to be told what to do.

"Who is this Jacob, and how does he know about her sister?" That maybe wasn't the right question. "Actually, how does he keep track of where her sister is? His threat is very real, I'm certain, but I want to know how he's keeping track of her."

The droid started to spell out a reply on the sand, but froze when he made a tsking noise.

"I can't read your language."

It clacked together harder and then moved farther away from him. With all five of the silver balls splitting apart, it quickly worked on a picture in the sand that was eerily accurate to what he imagined it looked like in real life.

"A surveillance drone?" he murmured. "He's sending one of those out to spy on her sister?"

The droid made two sharp clacks and then started on another corner of the picture. It drew Ace out in the sand. She was so accurate, it was like he was looking at her. Right down to the bend in her glasses that was just over her right ear where she'd maybe broken them before.

"So it's Ace's drone that keeps track of her sister? And he's just watching through the same thing that Ace is using?"

Two clacks.

"One means no, two means yes?"

Two more sounds, which he could only mean that he was right. Perfect. This would make communicating with them a little easier. He was used to droids who could speak on their own. At least, Byte could. Bitsy, Anya's little interpreter, was still broken and unfortunately never had a voice of her own.

Pressing his lips together in disappointment, he hummed low under his breath. "Understood. So Jacob is using Ace's own droids against her, then. Shit. Well, that doesn't make it easy to find where this sister of hers is being kept."

The droid circled the drawing a few times and then pointedly stared up at him.

"I suppose I could have someone else follow the droid," he murmured. "I can't leave Ace's side, but there are others who may help."

Not that he wanted to ask them. The only people who seemed to lurk around him these days were Fortis and Fortis's son. Neither of the depthstriders were the people he wanted to work with. If only because they annoyed him.

However, it gave him the opportunity to annoy Fortis even more than he already did. Which was a chance he would normally take willingly.

But he hated the idea of other undine around her. And maybe that was because she hadn't gone through the correct mating rituals with him. He hadn't fed her properly. He hadn't given her all the trinkets and gifts that he could find. Ace had accepted nothing from him but his body and that didn't sit right with him.

There was only so much a man could run on hope. Hope that she liked him as much as he did, that she would stay, that she saw something more in him than just the male who was fun to pass the time with.

Logically, he knew that wasn't what he was to her. But there would always be some fraction of that fear.

He felt her stirring against his chest, and he gave the little droid a severe look. "I'll consider it. You think that's the way to find her?"

Another clack, and then they'd run out of time for their private conversation. She was already coming to the surface of the water. Not spluttering like he had expected, or even panicking. She just rose to the surface and blew some water out of her mouth.

"I fell asleep," she said, looking up at him from where he was propped against the edge of the stone.

"You did."

Maketes couldn't help himself. He reached out to palm the back of her head in his hand, stroking her temple with his thumb as he looked down at her. She was such a courageous little creature who had no idea how much she held his heart in her hands. Someday she would know. Likely someday soon. But at the moment, all he had were these finite moments when he felt like this and she still didn't know.

She grinned up at him. "That's wild. I didn't know it was possible to sleep underwater."

"The others do. I've seen them sleeping with their partners, tangled in kelp so the sea doesn't carry them away." He tugged her a little closer, lowering himself in the water until their lips almost touched. "I would like to do this with you someday. I will hold you as the sea rocks us to sleep."

Somehow, it felt like a sexual thing to say. He watched as her pupils blew out, her already dark eyes grew even darker as her breath caught in her throat. He wondered what was going through her mind.

Perhaps she, too, was stuck remembering that she'd promised to kiss him with that mouth. That she'd promised to show him that achromos were better with their tongues than any of his people could hope to be.

Maybe it was a dream, though. There was a long way for them to go before they would be alone again.

He had half a mind to encourage this moment. If he drew her even closer, kissed her as he had before, perhaps she could be convinced. They could linger here in the cave for days if they wanted to. Because now that she'd mentioned using her mouth, he wanted to taste her as well.

He should have talked with Arges or Daios more about... all of this. He knew that they had mated with their females. Both of them always smelled like their partners, no matter how long they had been gone from their sides. The scent of their women was melted into their scales at this point, and that was something he wanted as well.

How, though? He had no idea.

Maketes wasn't exactly experienced in this. He'd only ever tried to mate with a female of his own kind once, and it hadn't gotten very far. He had seen the swiping claws and the rage on the female's face as she'd swam at him. Terror was to be expected during mating but that feeling had been enough for him to call it off.

Ace seemed kinder. Softer. She was ready and willing to welcome him with open arms instead of claws and teeth.

Then Ace leaned over the stone and looked at what her droid had drawn. Her eyebrows drew down in concentration. "You were trying to figure out how I was keeping track of my sister, huh?"

It was like she'd thrown him out of the water and let him flounder on jagged rocks. "I was wondering how Jacob knew where she was."

"He's not as stupid as I thought he was, that's how. He was following my damn drone the entire time I was using it, and that gave him access to... everything." She blew out a long breath, and bumps rose all over her skin. He watched them, surprised to see them again since the only other time he'd seen them was when she was cold or in the heat of passion.

But she wasn't cold. He knew that. She wasn't shivering and her teeth weren't chattering. She certainly wasn't feeling the heated blood that had turned them toward such carnal pleasures.

So what were those bumps now?

He touched them, watching her hair raise a little more before seeming to settle at his touch. "What are these?"

She looked down at them. "Goosebumps? You don't get goosebumps?"

"Goose... bumps?" He shook his head. "I know the second word, but not the first."

It seemed he had successfully distracted her from worse thoughts, because she turned toward him and held out her arm for his inspection. "Goosebumps. I don't know why we call them that, because a goose is kind of like a chicken or a duck. It's a response from my body whenever I'm unnerved or excited or cold or... I guess maybe it's better to say whenever we're feeling some kind of heightened emotion, we get the bumps. Or if we're cold."

"Like my gills." He picked her up so he could look at these bumps. It almost appeared like they were attached to the fine hairs on her arms. "Are they your hair trying to get off your body? Perhaps you used to have spines that covered you. It would make more sense if it was a defense."

"I don't think humans used to have spines instead of hair," she said with a soft laugh.

"Is it so hard to imagine?"

"Well, we're mammals. We had fur."

He shook his head. "Your people have a name for everything. Fur or spines, I find it hard to believe you truly have no natural defenses."

Ace tapped the side of her head. "My brain is my weapon. I think that's true for most humans."

Maketes lifted her even higher, until she was standing on the rock and he was below her, holding onto her waist and staring up into her eyes. "It is a lovely brain, but it is no match for tooth or claw."

A soft laugh bubbled out of her, flowing into him with the soft sound. And then she was stroking his hair, like she seemed to always enjoy. He curved into her touch, knowing this was the last chance they'd have for a little while yet.

"Maketes?" she said.

"Yes?"

"What does kefi mean?"

"I will tell you when all of this is done. When you have your hands on that key, and when your sister is free from the man who would kill her." He turned his head and pressed a kiss to her palm. "No matter what happens, you are always my kefi, and I will help you until the very end of this."

He could see how his words hurt her. She flinched as though he'd struck her, but there was also safety in what he said. Because they were a vow. He would protect her and her kin for the rest of his life, even if that was insanity.

Haunted memories filled her gaze. It was so easy to read this achromo. She feared for her sister, for his people, for all the things that she could not explain.

"Come," he said. "It is time for us to return to your city. We have put it off long enough."

He knew deep in his bones that both of them wanted to put it off longer, though. It was easier to exist here in this bubble of a cave where he could show her the sun every day, or at the very least, the stars. Even if it was storming, he would find a way for her to enjoy herself.

But they could not do any of that with the threat of her sister's death hanging over their head. They could do nothing without giving her the chance to save her family and all those that she loved. It seemed they came to that conclusion at the same time, because she placed her droid in her pocket and wrapped her arms around his neck at the same time as he drew her in by the waist.

Together, they sank back underneath the water. She reached for the breathing tentacle herself, sliding it toward her neck with his guidance and finding the right place to put it. She inserted the end into herself, and he'd never been prouder. Breathing for her as he turned them into the darkness of the sea, Maketes told himself all would be well.

They were doing the right thing.

They were saving her sister, and who knows what would happen after that?

Still, he couldn't forget the way she'd looked at him. The way she had been so close to asking him to kill for her. This key was something that made her worried, and that in turn worried him.

Once they had it in their grasp, what were they going to open?

That thought coiled up inside of him, like an eel waiting to strike at the right moment. He couldn't give her the chance to hurt his own people. Maketes was enamored with her, but not that much. He wouldn't sacrifice his people for anyone.

And yet his claws curled tighter around her the moment he saw the glowing neon lights that offered their first glimpse of Gamma. He didn't want to let go of her. He didn't want to give her the chance to make him choose.

Because he wasn't sure that he would choose his people after all.

"There," she said, pointing to a building bathed in yellow light. "That's where we need to go."

He dove, and vowed that no matter what happened, he would at least keep her safe.

Chapter 23

The building bathed in yellow light said PAINTED LADY in the neon glow outside of the building. She'd expected the doctor to live in a much nicer area of Gamma, but this apartment building was just run down. Even before the flooding had occurred—before the undine had attacked the city—this hadn't been a great place to live. She could see it in the rickety way they had tried to make the building stand a little straighter. The rough supports were already falling apart.

Someone had gone to great lengths to make sure this building remained standing. And soon, all that effort would fail.

They had to get in and out as quickly as they possibly could. She didn't want to linger any longer than she had to. They found an opening at the bottom. Not a crack, like in some of the other buildings, but a genuine opening that was likely meant to make it easier to service the building that clearly needed far more repairs than the others.

Maketes swam them up into the air, narrowing his gaze as he made sure no one was in the room they entered. But this building looked abandoned.

Considering the way the walls were already bending in on themselves, she had a good guess why there weren't any people here. It seemed like this wasn't safe, even for the worst criminals.

The entrance appeared to be some kind of tech room. There were plenty of old servers and huge computer parts that were all rotting here. Each one was waterlogged beyond reason, but there was a small service droid in the corner that bumped against the wall repeatedly. Poor thing was stuck on something and couldn't move.

"This place isn't safe," Maketes intoned, his voice deep with worry. "We should find another way in."

"I don't know where his apartment is, though. I have to find some kind of a directory before we can do that." She wriggled in his arms, trying to get free. "I can reprogram the droid."

If she fiddled with that box on the back, the droid definitely had a map of the tower. Maybe it wasn't as rusted shut as it looked. Usually, service droids were sent all over the entire tower to fix whatever needed to be addressed. Which meant this droid knew where Doctor Faust's apartment was.

They were so close. She could taste it.

Maketes tightened his arm around her waist, holding her a little firmer against his chest. "Wait. We don't know if anyone is here."

"I can tell no one is here. And if they are, then what is the problem with getting out? They aren't in this area." She wiggled a little harder. "Let me go."

"There could be danger."

She twisted hard and then ducked underneath the water. With the added help of being very slippery, she was able to move out of his grip and kick her feet to the edge. She knew, without a doubt, he could catch her if he wanted to. But he didn't. He let her clamber out of the water, dripping wet, and plod toward the droid that was still banging itself against the wall.

The droid was little more than a square box. Someone had put wheels on the bottom, but she had a feeling this service droid had been used as a catch all for tools. It would arrive wherever it was needed with the tools of choice, and then disappear once the technician didn't need it anymore. Ace caught the back of it, gently holding it in place as it tried to move forward again.

"Damn," she muttered. "You've been here a long time, haven't you?"

Even Tera clacked in her pocket, as though the other droid could feel its pain. It had bashed itself against the wall so many times that its screen was cracked. Shattered into jagged little shards that showed the inside wiring and the motherboard panel that was somehow, miraculously, still dry.

She didn't even have to get the rusted back of it open. She just turned it around, held it in place with her foot, and then crouched down in front of the shattered glass.

"All it takes is a couple wires in different places," she muttered as she plunged her hand into the shadows. "Tera, do you mind?"

Her droid clacked and then raced down her arm. The beads attached themselves to the metal sides, running up and down on the inside until they found what she needed. The motherboard was a start, but without a screen, there wasn't a lot she could do with this droid. Unless it had a controller.

Sometimes service droids did. They broke down often, so a controller was placed on the inside. That way, someone could manually drive the little droid back to the depot, where they would get fixed. And there it was. A controller, just like she needed. Of course, it was in the farthest back of the compartment, and she hissed out a long hesitant breath as she sank her entire arm into the cavity.

"Careful," Maketes muttered, as though he was scared if he spoke too loud he'd distract her.

"I know."

"There are shards of glass all over that thing."

"I'm aware," she grunted, shifting her hand through the back pieces. There were loose bolts all throughout, and frayed wires that she was a little concerned would shock her if she got too close to them.

Then her hand closed around the controller, and she gently pulled it out. Tera guided her the entire way, clacking once for right and twice for left, until she had the piece in her hands and was free from the threat of cuts.

"You hurt yourself," Maketes grumbled.

Peering at her forearm, she shrugged. "Just a couple scrapes. Nothing broke skin."

He grumbled a bit more about irresponsible women and how she couldn't take care of herself, but he stayed in the water and that was the best she could ask for. He didn't insist that she come to him, either.

Turning the controller on, she stared down at the bare bones coding that made up the droid's features.

"Not much here, Tera," she muttered, stretching out one of her legs when her knee protested. "They must have taken all the droids with more detailed software."

But with a couple more wires placed in the right spots, the droid's controller came back online in a big way. The long tube in her hand didn't have the keypad anymore, though. So she grabbed one of Tera's pieces and attached it to the end.

"Can you get me into the database? I need to search for Doctor

Faust's apartment number."

And then it was easy. The coding flew in front of her eyes, easily read after she'd spent years figuring out how to program droids. He was on one of the lower levels, thank goodness, and she knew how to find him in just a few moments.

Turning to look at the undine behind her, she knew that was likely going to be an issue. He was already glaring at her, with his arms crossed over his massive chest. He looked like he was about to tell her to get back into the water at any second.

She was a droid lover. Her entire life had been wrapped around their creation, their feelings, how people had turned droids into something masterful and beautiful at the same time. So it broke her heart a bit to turn the droid toward the pool of water. It wouldn't survive the icy salt. But also, maybe it didn't need to. The poor thing deserved a quiet death.

"I'm going to Doctor Faust's apartment," she said. "You're going to follow me in the water because that's the safest way for us to do this. Once I get the key, you can come find me back here."

"It's dangerous, Ace."

She nodded. "Yeah, so far this entire adventure has been really dangerous. But I think that's a risk we're both going to have to take."

She released her hold on the droid and watched it go careening toward him. It worked better than she could have guessed. He didn't dodge it, because he was so surprised that there was a metal box lunging for him. So it caught him right in the chest and made him sink a bit.

Hopefully, the glass didn't cut into him. She'd hate to be the reason he had yet another scar.

Then she darted out of the room with Tera in her grip. He

wouldn't follow her into the tower, even though he had in the others. But even if he did, she was running way too fast for him to catch up. She skidded to a halt in the hallway beyond, though.

No wonder no one was here. This tower really was falling apart. Massive beams had already tumbled through the ceiling, leaving huge pillars in her wake with dust and insulation matted around them. Wires hung in sparking ends that cascaded fire onto a floor that was so cracked, she had no idea what it used to be.

"Carefully then," she muttered, picking her way through the pieces.

It took a little while to even get out of that hallway. A chunk of insulation had fallen onto her shoulders, and she'd never thanked the gods more for being the size she was. She was strong enough to take that hit, but other people might have folded under the impact. As it was, there was insulation in her hair and some of it had gotten down her shirt, so itchy she wanted to scratch her skin off.

But once she got through that terrible hallway, it opened up again. She was suddenly reminded of Beta. The narrow hallways were more tubular than square. Halogen lights, a particular kind of lighting that always brought up memories from her childhood, swung from one end of the ceiling. There were no windows on the walls, either.

When she was little, it used to make her nervous. But now, as an adult, all she could see was the city she had fallen in love with, and the one she missed.

Sighing, she followed the map that the droid had given her. In her mind she repeated the steps, four lefts, two rights, go straight through the four way and then... voila. She avoided all the chunks of insulation on the ground and a few more beams, but then she was here. Right in front of the apartment where the key was supposed to be.

"How do you think we get in?" she asked Tera, running her fingers along the box where a keycard should be installed.

Maybe if she had the right tools, she could get Tera to hack it. Doors weren't all that hard to open if one knew the right tricks, but they were a little difficult to open without the right tools. She supposed she could just hit the box off the door. That was always an option. But there might be a mechanism to lock it even worse if that happened.

But then Tera rolled out of her pocket and onto the floor, hitting the ground with a hard thud. All five pieces pressed against the bottom of the door, clacking and making all the noise that it could. Taking the hint, she pushed the bottom with her foot.

And the door swung open.

"Ominous," she muttered, before walking into the obviously abandoned room.

The whole thing had been ransacked. Every bit of it. She could tell there used to be a small living room to her right, everything in browns and beiges. A sofa had been ripped apart so much all she could see were the bones of the inside that had been under the cushions. A coffee table was little more than shards on the ground, and a hole in the ceiling had half a beam hanging out of it with water dripping onto a ripped up recliner.

To her right was a kitchen, but all the drawers had been pulled out. They were all on the floor, some of them broken beyond fixing. Even the doors were hanging off their handles.

There was a single window looking outside into the sea, and it was little more than the size of her head. But the small amount of illumination turned the entire room into a sickly yellow shade.

"No one's been here for a really long time," she said. Her feet crunched through the debris as she headed toward the back. "There has to be something in his office, right?"

But the door in the back didn't lead to an office. It led to a tiny room with the remains of a bed and an open area that looked like a closet. This doctor hadn't even had his own private bathroom in this place.

"Damn it." Now what? Was this a dead end?

She had nothing to go on. No hope. If this entire place had been stripped for parts, someone else had the key.

But then Tera attached itself to the wall, zipped up it, and then was right against what looked like a security box. Her droid fiddled with something and then...

Holograms. More holograms.

She watched as people broke the door down, muttering things she couldn't quite make out through the tinny recording. She sank down onto her haunches, watching as they destroyed the entire room. They were decorated in strange costumes, it seemed. Like they lived only during Halloween. Masks, feathered hats, and colored patterned clothing.

"The toy tower?" she muttered. "Why would they be here?"

A few of them carried bats that they used to break everything in sight. A few others had knives that they used to attack the couch and chair like it was a person they were gutting. But her eyes were on one of the men who was not partaking. He was a little older than the others, gray-haired, and his eyes were too aware of everything around him.

He was looking for something. While all the others were pure chaos in holographic form around her, he was the one who was the eye of the storm. She watched him move slowly, chatting with the others, pretending to be part of the fanfare. But then he slipped into the bedroom. He fiddled underneath a space where the bed might have once been and then slipped something into his pocket.

Without even looking like anything had happened, he joined the others, grabbed a bat, and started destroying things as well. Like he hadn't just taken something very important from this room.

"Who is he?" she muttered, narrowing her eyes on the hologram. "Because he has what we need."

She had no way of knowing other than going to the toy tower on her own. Which... wasn't entirely something she wanted to do.

But it wasn't like she had a choice. Ace had to get that key, and this was the next step in her plan.

Blowing out a breath, she held out her hand for Tera to hop into it. "All right. Looks like we're going into the mouth of hell itself."

She just had to convince Maketes to take her there.

Chapter 24

The depth of fear he felt when she wasn't in front of him was nearly paralyzing. If she were any other female, he wouldn't have been so terrified. The women of his kind were stronger than the males. He would be able to leave without fearing that someone else would kill her. He would be able to head out into the sea, hunting for her food, knowing that she would be safe.

But now, all he could think when he left her side was that someone else could kill her and he wouldn't even know until he came back and tasted her blood in the water. How did Arges and Daios do this? They were larger than him by far, significantly more capable of protecting their women.

It didn't matter that he'd already killed for her. None of those memories gave him the slightest amount of peace when he knew, without a fraction of a doubt, that time away from her was time when someone else could finish the job.

He'd just gotten enough fish to feed her before turning back to the city. There was a pit in his stomach. The fish weren't enough. They were small, not impressive, and she would see what a meager offering it was. He should have fought a giant tuna or swordfish for her. Bringing back a fish the size of his hands would only whet her appetite.

But then again, she was very small. Perhaps she wouldn't notice the difference.

He went back to the place where they were supposed to meet, finding her already waiting for him there. He could see her even before he broke the surface of the water. Her pretty brown hair puffed around her head, a little tangled now that she'd been in the sea for so long. But he liked that about her. There was a certain level of wildness in knowing that he had a part in tangling that hair.

Ace leaned against the side of the opening, staring down into the water like she'd been waiting for him for a while. He lifted his head into the air, a frown already on his face as he held the fish out to her. "I brought you food."

"We need to go to the most dangerous building in Gamma."

Well, his little kefi had never been very good at preparing him for the insane things she was about to say. He swallowed hard, trying to roll the words over in his mind.

"What?" he blurted out, setting the fish on the floor beside her. "Why would we go there?"

"They stole the key."

"I thought the key was supposed to be here."

"It was supposed to be here, but the security system picked up that another gang has it. I don't think they know what it is, or maybe they do. If they do, then that's a bigger problem neither of us is going to fix easily." She made grabbing motions with her hands. "Let's go."

He used his hip fins to nudge him out of her grabbing reach. "You need to eat."

"I need to save my sister."

"Yes, you do need to do that. But you can't save her if you work yourself to death. We will go to this..." He took a deep breath, reminding himself that whatever he said to her was a promise. He couldn't tell her they would do something and then go back on it. "Dangerous place. We will go there. But first, you need water, food, and to rest."

"I already drank some from the wells here." She pointed behind her. "That's good enough."

"It's not," he hissed. "You have to take care of yourself, Ace, or you cannot take care of anyone else."

His words seemed to sink in. Her face turned a little ashen, and it was almost as though she'd heard those words before. Because, almost too stiffly, she nodded and then gathered the fish in her arms. "Not here, then. This building is going to collapse at any moment."

"Where?"

"I don't know where is safe here."

He did. Or at least, he knew where there was enough safety that they could be alone for a few moments. Enough for her to eat. To rest without someone breathing down the back of her neck.

It was a small outpost that was part of the tower, but it had been closed off to the others for a very long time now. He suspected it was a control tower once. There were more in the other cities that floated off at a distance from the main building. He remembered that there were achromos in them, sometimes. Not often, but enough that he had seen them moving around like a small school of fish.

This one had twin bridges that connected it to the other towers, but they'd been broken long ago. So it was just a single pod, floating out in the ocean with flickering lights that sometimes turned on, and then turned off for long periods.

He swam up into it with her in his arms, breaking open what looked like an emergency hatch and then following her up into the cool room.

Maketes hadn't expected it to be quite so cold. But apparently his little kefi had. She reached for Tera, water drops splattering out of her pocket as the droid hit the ground and rolled toward the controls.

"The heat's always the first thing to go," Ace muttered, her breath fogging in front of her face. "It's all right. It'll warm up soon enough."

"We can eat in the meantime." He gestured to the fish that she still clutched in her arms. "That should be enough to sustain you, should it not?"

There were about fifteen fish in her arms, which she looked over before her jaw dropped open. "I can eat maybe two."

"Two?" he frowned. "That's not nearly enough. I have to insist that you eat more than that."

"I quite literally can't."

"You will eat more."

"Maketes, if I eat more than two, I'm just going to throw it back up." She selected her two fish and then shoved the rest toward him. "Here. These are yours."

He took them, but he wasn't happy about it. If she wanted him to feast with her, he would. But it felt like a rejection of everything he had done. Everything he was offering.

He'd already stolen her. That much was complete. But now he was giving her food, and she didn't want all of it. He'd never known that to be something that happened. What did it mean? What was he meant to do when a female accepted some of his offering, but not all of it?

A little off kilter, he picked up one of the fish and swallowed it whole. Though eating them was lackluster now that they were no longer wriggling.

And then he realized she was staring at him. Her jaw had hinged open, and he was certain that was surprise, not that she was still hungry and wanted more fish to put into her mouth.

"What?" he asked.

"You just... swallowed it."

He wiped his face, making sure there weren't any scales left on his mouth, but that wasn't why she was looking at him. Frowning, he watched her a little more closely. He hadn't surveyed her while she was eating what he'd brought her before. Mostly because he considered it rude and because they hadn't eaten in front of each other regularly.

"How do you eat it?" he asked.

She reached into her pocket and pulled out a capped scalpel. The same little blade had cut through her enemies. But this time, Ace used it to slice into the fish. She gutted it, wasting all the good parts by washing them into the open water, and then slowly... flayed the skin off as well.

He bared his teeth in horror as he watched her then slice flesh from the naked body and then put that raw piece into her mouth.

"You're ruining all the best parts," he muttered. "That's how you eat them?"

"I'm shocked you're swallowing bone."

They stared at each other in disgust for a few more moments before they both started to chuckle. He waved up and down her body with a laugh. "I forget so easily that you're..."

"And I forget you are..."

That stare turned heated. He could see the desire in her eyes right before she looked away. Like the thought of him being different had made her...

No, that wasn't possible. But wasn't that also how he'd seen it last time? It was like she found him more attractive when he was just himself. As different as that was. As strange as it must be to her.

His kefi was more interested in moments like this. Small moments where they were together. She didn't care if he was big or terrifying, nor did she care if he could provide for her. She just wanted quiet memories between the two of them, and for him to make her laugh.

Fuck. How was he supposed to deny her when she saw so much more of him than he'd ever dreamt any female could?

Sighing, he put the fish down and watched her eat. It should have made her uncomfortable, but he could see her doing the same motion she'd done before. Pressing those thick thighs against each other as though she could hold herself together just through sheer will.

By the time she'd finished eating, the heating unit had turned on. Tera was still doing something with the control panel, but he could feel the warm air billowing into the room. Perfect. Because what he had planned to do would require her to be warm.

"Ace?" he finally said, watching as she washed her hands off in the emergency hatch opening.

"Yes?"

"Come here."

A shudder danced through her, and he could see all those little bumps rise on her skin again. But she turned toward him, heat in her eyes and her breath coming quicker. "Why?"

"You know why."

"Tell me anyway." She sauntered toward him, a confidence in her hips that he hadn't seen before. Then she placed her fingers on his shoulders, dancing up to the fins on his throat.

He arched into her touch, already hard behind the scales that kept him safe from her gaze. "You made a promise, didn't you?"

"Oh, and you think you deserve to have that promise fulfilled?"

He'd saved her life multiple times, so he thought maybe he did. But he didn't want to ruin this moment. Not when he knew that it was so tenuous and he wanted this to happen so dearly. So he arched into her touch, leaning back against the equipment that dug into his spine.

He hit something that made all the lights turn out in the room. Blinking in the darkness, he watched her lean around him, set her glasses on the back of the console, and hit another button. Instead of the blinding lights overhead, the only light that came on was the red emergency light. It bathed her body in sensuous colors as she placed her feet on either side of his tail.

Gills already fluttering, he watched as she sank onto her knees. The heat of her pressed against his tail and he nearly lost his mind, but it was more than that. It was her hungry gaze on his chest, the way her hands slid down the planes of muscles and teased his abs until they flexed against her touch. It was the way she leaned down and her hot breath skated over his chilled flesh.

"Breathe," she whispered against his skin, pressing kisses down his torso in a way that made it hard to see.

Breathe? He couldn't think about breathing when her hands were everywhere. Nor when those talented little fingers brushed against his gills along his ribs and made the world go black.

"Maketes," she whispered, and he had to open his eyes at that sultry siren song. And he was treated to the best view he'd ever had in his life.

She had her belly against his tail, that glorious ass perked up in the air. All he could see was the round swells of it, the beauty of those globes that already had his mouth watering. The softness of her breasts pressed against him, and he could see how they were also pressed up higher. Her hands were stroking the scales of his tail, not quite in the right spot, but close.

"I know you have two," she murmured. "Can I please see them this time?"

See them?

Right, she wanted... Fuck.

He swallowed hard and released the tension of the muscles that held his cocks in. They extruded, already glistening with pre-cum and pure need. He'd thought maybe it would startle her, but instead, her eyes only widened. That was it.

Her hand came around the top one. He bucked against her firm grip, a low hiss escaping him as he slid into her grip. It was beyond what he had ever experienced. Her fingers were so tight. The pressure that built just from that single touch was beyond what he had ever felt by himself.

"Easy," she murmured, her breath fanning over the tip. "We're just getting started."

And then she swirled her tongue around him.

He saw stars. Back arching, hands grabbing at nothing, stars that only got even more powerful as she drew him into her mouth. That wicked tongue kept moving, swirling around him and then flattening along the base. She sucked harder than her fingers had grabbed him, drawing him deeper down her throat until he was certain this would be the death of him.

He'd never known things could feel this good. He hadn't even realized that part of his body could feel this good. The females from his kind were so incredibly rough, and this was not that.

This was delicate. Soft. The warmth of her mouth was a stark contrast to how cold he usually was and already he felt like he was going to explode. Everything in him tightened, drawing up as though he was already going to come, but it was too soon for that. He wanted to feel her on him more. He wanted to sink deeper into that heat.

Rolling his tail, he drew her up until she was balanced so that he had access to her. He could already smell her. That warm, earthy scent slicked between her thighs. With a single movement, he drew her pants off her legs, though they still dangled off one of her ankles. She braced herself with one hand against his stomach, the other now wrapped around his bottom cock as she worked them both.

Her mouth popped free from the top one, the sound echoing in the small room before she dove for the other. He wasn't even sure she was breathing, but did it matter? Did anything matter?

Her soft core clenched before him and that was all he needed as an invitation. He had to do something. He had to keep himself busy or he would end this before it even started.

Maketes turned her so her back pressed against his tail, and then plunged his tongue into her depths. He slid the ridges along her inside walls, pressed the base of those bumps against the little button that had made her cry out last time. And then he mimicked what she was doing.

The taste of her exploded on his tongue. Warm and earthy and so much her that he realized this was a terrible idea. He wouldn't last like this. Not now that she was whimpering around his cock, tiny shudders moving throughout her entire form every time he withdrew his tongue, only to sink it even deeper inside of her.

Now her hand worked faster, tighter, switching between each of his cocks as she sucked even harder. He could feel himself tightening again, and knew he was about to lose control. So he worked her harder as well. Faster. Together, they drew each other to the limit and just when he was certain he would fall first, she clenched around him.

The slight scream that echoed through her throat vibrated through his cocks as well. With a low grunt that should have been a curse, he came so hard he thought he pulled a muscle in his back, hunched over her as he was.

But she drank it all down. Swallowing every single drop he gave her. He drew away from her, leaning back against the consoles again, and stared down his glistening body to see her lick his second cock clean as well.

Her loose legs were still wrapped around him, but now he could feel how drenched he'd left her. His scales would smell like her for days after this.

She sat up slowly, rubbing herself on him, and she shifted to sit on his lap. At his look, she licked her lips and grabbed her glasses from the console beside him. "Was it everything you hoped it would be?"

Red light had turned her into a sultry witch of the sea. He reached out and traced her bottom lip, watching the movement with pure rapture in his head. "Kefi, there are no words."

"Is that a good thing?"

He tugged her against his hearts, holding her tightly against him as they both sank toward sleep. "Yes, kefi. For a male who won't shut up like myself, I think that's a very good thing."

255

Chapter 25

In her dreams, she saw her sister.

Ace was back in Beta, like she had been as a child. Only this time, she was grown. She was the same size as she was in her waking mind. An adult in all ways. And still, people walked by her and muttered behind their hands.

They always had, though. They knew what she'd done. Everyone always thought she was the odd one out in her family, but now they had proof. There was something wrong with her mind. What kind of person thought they could make a droid that would steal anything she wanted? They'd known something was off about her, and now? Now they knew they were right.

The discomfort bubbled in her chest. She'd thought she'd grown past this feeling, but it was the same as when she was a child. She didn't want them to look at her. Oh, they could think whatever they wanted. If they wanted to pretend that she was a terrible person, that she was ugly, that there was a broken thread in her mind, so be it. But she just wanted them to stop looking at her.

That pain and ache were the same as always. It made her feel like she was less than they were. Like she was the problem, when in reality, she knew it had nothing to do with her. They felt better tearing other people down. It meant they weren't at the bottom.

She was just the unlucky one who lived there.

Ducking down a familiar hallway, she felt a bubble of heat burst in her chest. False bravado melted away into comfort as she moved down the halls where she'd grown up. Her cousins had raced down these steps, and suddenly, there they were. The children she remembered them being. Pattering feet echoed as they called after each other, certain one of them had stolen a toy that wasn't theirs to have.

She spun, watching them race by her and disappear into a faint fog at the end of the hallway. Somewhere in the recesses of her mind, she knew this was a dream. But the feeling of her family being so close by... It made her want to linger.

Ace trailed her fingers along the wall. She knew this smooth, cool texture with the pattern of rivets that bumped against her fingers every five heartbeats. She could count them in her sleep and use them to find her room, even in the dark.

"One, two, three, four, five," she whispered. Over and over, until the numbers brought her to the room, she wanted to see the most.

Already she could smell it. The heat of growing lights and the loam that surrounded countless vegetables. Their garden was the best producing in the entirety of Beta, all because of her sister.

"Laura," she whispered as the door appeared in front of her. Immediately, her chest squeezed in pain and tears built in her eyes. Not because she was upset or feared what was on the other side, but because even in her dreams, she missed her sister so much, it ached.

Pushing open the door, she walked into the sanctuary her sister had built herself.

Plants grew in abundance here. They toppled over the tall tables, spilled out onto the floor where their father had built structures to keep the dirt in. Giant monstera leaves butted up against the glass over their heads, reaching for the grow lights that lined the ceiling. It smelled so good. Like greenery and food and life that nowhere else on Beta could replicate.

And there, in the center of the garden, was her sister.

Beautiful, beautiful Laura. The best of both their parents. She was lean, like their father, with glorious dark hair that spilled over her shoulders in a cloud of waves just like their mother. She wasn't the kind of pretty most people noticed. Sometimes she faded into the background along with Ace, but there was something delicate about her. Maybe not in her body or form, but in the soft way she saw right through a person to the soul underneath that they hid from everyone else.

Maura and Laura. Her parents had thought it was hilarious at the time, only to realize how frustrating it was to try to scold Maura when Laura was also in the room.

Tears in her eyes, she walked toward her sister and tried to tell herself that this was just a dream. She shouldn't get too attached. She shouldn't feel like the world was ending just because her mind had conjured up an image of the sister she missed so much.

Laura was wearing the same brown smock she always wore, dirt smudged across the front and her hands. There was dirt under her nails, and a smear of yellow pollen across her cheek. When she looked up, her soft brown eyes lit up with happiness.

"Maura!" she said, wiping her hands off on her thighs. "I didn't know you were coming today!"

It was the same thing she'd said the last time Ace had seen her. The same moment, too. This was where she was supposed to tell her sister that they were taking her away to Gamma, and that they'd never see each other again. But she'd keep Laura safe. She always did.

Instead, Ace took a step closer to her sister, then another. Then yanked Laura into her arms and hugged her hard.

They stayed like that for a while. Just the two of them. Breathing each other in because that was all she wanted to do.

"Maura?" her sister said quietly. "Is everything okay?"

"No," she whispered. "It's just that I miss you so much."

"But I'm right here."

"You won't be. Soon enough, I won't remember what color your eyes are, or where your ticklish spots really were. All I'll remember is the need to keep moving forward. To slog through life so that I can make sure you're safe."

"Maura, you're scaring me." Her sister leaned back, staring into her eyes with a frown on her face. "Everything's going to be fine. The garden has plenty of food this year, and everyone has been working together wonderfully. I don't think we should worry about much."

"I'm going to..." Ace choked on the words. For a moment, she was thrown right back into this moment. The moment when she had known she was going to disappoint the only person who mattered in her life. "They're taking me away, Laura. For a long time."

"What did you do?"

And there it was. The end of this memory that was still seared into her entire being. As Laura reeled away from her, bumping into a table full of tomatoes as the red fruit fell from their stems and plummeted to the floor. A few of them burst on impact, red seeping into the drainage grates on the floor.

"I didn't do anything, it's just—"

"Maura! I thought we had talked about this. I thought you were giving all that up because you know how dangerous it is? You're my only family. We are each other's only family and for you to risk that..." Laura turned, gripping the table hard.

What her sister hadn't known then, and likely still didn't know, was that Ace had seen her reflection. She'd seen the terror in her sister's eyes as she realized she would now be alone. They'd been together their entire lives. Maura and Laura, the sisters who were inseparable even in grade school. And now? Now they had to walk their own paths, even though it scared them both.

"Listen to me," Ace said, placing her hand on her sister's back. "I put the money aside for you. It's in a bank vault. I already wrote down the numbers and slid the paper into your pillow. They can't find that money, and they never will. Spend it wisely, and they won't know what you're spending is the money I stole."

"I don't want the money, Maura!" Her sister spat the words, but then spun and held Ace tightly in her arms. "I just want you."

Even as she hugged her sister back, she knew it wasn't the truth. They needed the money more than they needed each other. That was why she'd done it.

Sure, part of that had been because she'd wanted to see if she could do it. There was a level of thrill that came with fooling all those rich people. But another part of her wanted to make sure her sister was safe.

Even after she was gone.

"I need you to know that I love you," she whispered into Laura's hair. "I love you more than the morning rays of the sun that filter into our room. I love you more than the shadows of rays on the floor or the songs of the whales in the distance. And I will love you for as long as there is a drop of seawater on this planet."

"Ace—" Her sister had never called her by that name. "Don't do this to us."

She had to. Because she didn't have another choice.

"I have to go," she whispered. "They won't give me another chance."

But it was more than that. It wasn't that anyone was giving up on her, it was that unfortunately, she'd given up on herself. And she remembered it now. She remembered feeling so lost and knowing that nothing she did would ever make her feel like herself again. This place, these people, they saw her as an animal.

Laura's eyes filled with tears. "Don't."

There was so much in that word. Her sister begging her to stay, yes, but also the fear of what she would do on her own.

"You're going to be fine," she whispered. "I'm going to make sure you're fine."

"You can't promise that. Ace—"

Again, the name that her sister never called her. No matter how many times she had corrected Laura, her sister never called her by her chosen name. She was the only one who still called her Maura.

Then she was yanked out of the dream, watching her sister fall onto her knees and tears streak down her cheeks. Just like it had really happened. Because people had barged into the garden, guards who stepped on her sister's plants and knocked over two standing planters as they dragged her out.

Even saying goodbye, all she'd done was destroy. From her sister's garden to her sister's life. She just wasn't any good if she was there. The best she could offer Laura was help from afar, and that was exactly what she'd done.

She lunged upright, awake as though she'd blinked her eyes and now she was back. Back in the control center, draped over a warm man who had wrapped his arms around her in her sleep and now released her, letting her sit straight up and breathe through the memory.

"Ace?" he said again, and this time she recognized the voice. He'd been trying to get her to come out of the dream for a while, she guessed.

Brushing her fingers through her hair, she released a shaky breath. "Yeah. Yeah, I'm awake now."

Maketes shifted her on his lap, turning her to look at him. And then he wiped away the tears on her cheeks with his thumbs. Carefully. As though he was afraid she was very breakable right now.

Maybe he was right. She felt like a single kind touch might shatter her into a thousand pieces.

Closing her eyes, she leaned into his touch.

"Bad dreams?" he asked. It was the most real question she'd ever heard from him. Not like he was pretending or annoying her or doing anything at all other than being here in the dark with her.

Breathing in the seawater scent of him, she sighed, "Terrible dream."

"I can banish it with you, if you'd like."

"How do I do that?"

His thumb moved along her cheek again, so gentle that it made her feel fragile in his grip. "You share the dream, kefi. You tell me what it means, where it came from, and then I take it into the sea. The next time I am in the abyss, I will leave it there for you."

Ace opened her eyes, smiling at him even though it hurt to do so. "I don't think I want to talk about it."

"Then that's all right too." He tried to smile, but she could see the pain in his eyes. "You don't have to share anything you don't want to."

Damn it, those tears burned her eyes again. She couldn't be weak like this. This was why she'd never gotten attached to anyone. If she was weak, then she would cry, and nothing would get done. She had to bury it all deep inside herself, even if it meant that she constantly had stomach aches and felt like her chest was on fire.

"No," he murmured, using both hands to frame her face and make her look at him. "We do not hide from hard feelings. You are brave. A courageous woman who pet a shark, rode a whale, and who touches one of my kind without fear. Memories have no power over you."

"What if they do?" she replied. "What if they are all I can see? My own failure. My own wish to keep my sister safe and yet all I have ever done is put her in harm's way?"

"That is how your mind wishes to remember your last moments with her. But you need to tell it you did everything you could to keep her safe. And you still fight to keep her safe. That is honorable."

Nodding, she tried to let the words sink in. Honorable. Brave. She was more than just the thief that the world threw away. She was Ace, the destroyer of Alpha and... lover of an undine. If she could let herself believe that.

Nodding, she framed his face with her hands as well. Dropping her head until their foreheads touched, she let her eyes drift shut. "I don't know what god smiled upon me when they sent you to my side, but I am grateful for it."

"I am the lucky one, kefi."

"No, I don't think you understand. You've been so kind to me. You've worked to make me a stronger person in such a short amount of time and I don't know what I give back, or what I even could. I owe you so much more than just my life, Maketes."

His breath fanned over her collarbone, and he dragged her closer to his hearts. "No. You owe me nothing."

"You make me feel seen," she said, then kissed his shoulder as she let him coax her back down. "I don't think you realize how long I've felt invisible. No one ever saw me. No ever cared to."

"I have long felt the same way." His lips pressed to her hair. "Sleep, my achromo. I will guard your dreams for the rest of the night."

"But who will guard yours?" she murmured, already falling back into that dreaming realm.

So she wasn't sure if she dreamt up what he replied, or if he had actually said the words. But what she thought she heard was, "You, kefi. All my dreams are of you."

Chapter 26

The toy tower was the last place she wanted to go. So many rumors tainted this place as a madhouse, and she didn't want to find out why everyone said that. After all, everywhere in Gamma wasn't "normal". For so many people to fear this area of the city? There had to be a good reason.

Holding onto Maketes's shoulder, she bit her lip as they approached the building. They couldn't stay in the water for very long now that her suit was gone. And though they'd tried to find another one in the control tower, apparently those were hard to come by these days. They had to move fast and get her into another building, even if it was the toy tower.

Lights flickered around it. A rainbow of colors that lured any and all toward what was meant to be a fun and childlike area to be in. She knew this building used to be a store for children until it had flooded after the undine attack. Then it was just... taken over by gang members. Supposedly, the most insane ones were the only people who lived here.

The closer they got, the more her stomach twisted. All the windows were covered up. Every single one of them.

Whoever lived inside had plastered flyers and posters onto the windows, making it almost impossible to see inside. There was the faintest hint of shadows moving beyond, so the lights were still on, but that was all she could see.

"I don't like this," Maketes muttered, even as he looked for entrance.

"Neither do I."

"We should find somewhere else to go."

"There isn't anywhere else to go. Everything I could find leads us here, and if this is where I find the key, then this is the only place we can go." She rubbed her hand on his chest, trying to soothe the fears from him, even though she knew that there was no way for her to fully do that. "I have to do this, Maketes. You know that."

She knew he did, but it broke her heart to realize that she was going to make him even more afraid. Everything she'd done so far made him worried, and that didn't settle right with her. She wanted him to believe in her. To trust her. All the things that she'd always wanted from other people. But she didn't want to put him in a position like this.

"There," he said, and then they were darting through the water. Past all the plastered up windows. Beyond the looming shadows that looked like people holding knives with severely blighted bodies.

He swam with her past all those horrors and then tilted her head to his shoulder. He made her look away from the nightmarish shadows. At least until they got to their destination. There was a small crack at the base of the tower. Not much of one, but enough that she could slip through on her own.

Ace reached out and grabbed onto the shards of metal that were bent back into the ocean, pausing only when Maketes's hands grabbed onto her waist. Gently, he turned her to face him. And then he framed her face with his webbed hands, making her look at him.

"Be careful," he said, his deep voice echoing through the sea. "If they lay a finger on you, I will rip their arms off their bodies. I will tear them apart, kefi, and I will feel no mercy."

She'd seen him do that exact thing already. It should have terrified her that he was capable of it, but instead, now all she felt was the warmth of reassurance.

Touching her hand to the side of his neck, she trailed her fingers through the pretty gills there. "When are you going to tell me what kefi means?"

"Soon. If you come back to me."

If.

A burst of fear flooded through her. His gills flared even wider, and she could see in his eyes that he knew what she was feeling.

"Ace," he said, his words belaying that he was ready to call this off. Soon, he would gather her back up in his arms and dart through the ocean. He would take her so far away from here that she would forget about her sister or all the terrible things she'd done to keep Laura alive.

So she propelled herself backward, into the small opening where he could not follow her. She pressed a kiss to her fingertips and sent it out into the ocean for him, before she turned and yanked herself through the twisted metal.

There weren't a lot of floating objects here. It made a warning bell flash in her mind. Because if there wasn't anything floating here, then that meant someone had been looking for items in the water. This exit wasn't a secret one. People had been here.

And if people had been here, then that meant wherever she was going to exit wasn't all that secret either.

She still had her scalpel. It was in her pocket, and Tera was there too. If she had to get herself out of a situation, she could. Even if that meant finding a way out that wasn't the same as the one she'd exited.

Unlike the other humans in this tower, she had someone in the sea who would help her if she had to flood the place.

A twisted spike of metal caught on her shirt. She turned to yank it free, only to get caught up by her icy fingers. She couldn't open and close her hands all that easily, and that made her clumsy. The twisted metal freed her shirt with the tug, but it also sliced through her hand. Blood plumed in the water, tendrils of it reaching out in the stillness that was odd to swim in.

She'd gotten used to the rolling waves of the sea. The building stopped all those waves, though, and now it was just still.

Her lungs screamed for air, and she turned. Kicking against the metal, she swam toward the shimmering light at the surface. Every inch of her prayed that it was an empty room that she would swim up to.

She didn't gasp as she crested the surface. Instead, she kept her head low and wiped her nose free before taking in a deep inhalation. At least that was quieter than the gasp that would have told everyone where she was.

The base of this tower was flooded, it seemed. The foundation had cracked long ago, leaving fissures like veins spreading throughout the base of this room. Some fissures were hidden underneath beams that had fallen from the ceiling and created small grottos she could hide in. And she'd need to.

Groups of men and women clustered around fires that were on the ground. But the people weren't right. Just one glance and all she saw were scars and wounds and strange faces. It looked like they had purposefully scarred their faces. Everyone seemed to have some form of mark on their face, right down their eyes, all the way down their cheeks. Some had scars that made a permanent smile stretch beyond their lips.

As she watched the nearest group, a woman stood with a doll in her hands. A baby doll, wearing a bright blue dress. She reached behind it, cranked the small pull tab on the back, and giggled as the baby laughed. Then she tossed it into the fire and danced around it.

This was beyond odd. This was a dangerous, mad place with people burning toys to stay warm.

She reached for the beam above her head and used it to push herself back underwater. Swimming to the next beam and the next hiding place made it a little easier to survey them all. She didn't even know what she was looking for, but she hoped the key itself would be rather obvious.

Until she noticed that the nearest group next to her was eating. Their boisterous laughter filled the room with a cacophony of sound. One of them gestured with a long bone that had gristle hanging off of it.

"You caught him first?"

"Yeah, he came over the bridge at the switch. Didn't have any idea that I was still standing there." The second man who spoke had a greasy lump of hair hanging off of his chin. Bald other than that greasy beard, he looked like a villain in a fairytale. "Too easy to pick off."

"How'd you kill him?" asked the first man, ripping a huge bite of meat off the bone. "Gun?"

"Nah. I like to do things with my hands."

The flash of silver caught her attention as the second man pulled out a hunting knife that was longer than her forearm. "I gutted him to make sure the meat stayed sweet."

The meat?

Her eyes tilted to the side, even though she knew she didn't want to see the truth of what they were saying. Next to the fire, she had thought it was a third man. His booted feet were set up like he was sitting with them. But as she moved just slightly in the water, she could see that he was missing an arm. Intestines hung out of his belly, and his head lolled forward.

Dead. So dead. And that arm was hanging over the fire beside the men.

The first man had been eating... By all the gods, that was an elbow in his hands. The gristly meat hanging off of it was the man's biceps.

She pressed her hand to her mouth so she wouldn't make any noise. The fish she'd eaten last night rose in the back of her throat, pressing against her tongue and begging to be released.

They were eating people here.

Oh, fuck.

Fuck, they were eating people, and she was in the middle of everything. Her heart thundered in her chest. Even though she was in icy water, she felt flushed and hot. This was wrong. It was so fucking wrong. She'd always heard they weren't right in the toy tower, but she hadn't realized...

Ace ducked under the water again, making sure any whimpers were little more than bubbles that could easily be misconstrued as something dropping from the ceiling into the water. Because she couldn't do this. She couldn't be surrounded by cannibals while she was looking for some stupid key that probably didn't exist anymore.

She couldn't.

She had to go back out to the ocean. Fuck Jacob. He could get the key on his own. She'd tell him where it was and everything she knew about it, but she would not stay when these people would eat her if they found her.

But then the thoughts fluttered through her mind again. She could hear her sister's voice in her head. Laura had begged her to stay back then. And if she failed in this, wasn't she failing her sister again?

So she turned under the water and told herself she was everything Maketes had said. She was brave. She was capable. She was a courageous woman who knew how to take care of herself and if that meant facing a group of cannibals?

Oh, she was going to puke in the water. They were eating that man.

Grinding her teeth, she forced herself to swim past all the people. She tried hard to not look at all the other bits of meat they were eating. Meat she was now certain didn't come from rats, like her own people had been eating. But it was so hard to not look at the absolute madness unfurling around her.

No wonder people didn't come here. No wonder everyone warned the others to stay as far away from this cursed place as possible.

The farther into the tower she got, the more insane things she saw. People here wore the children's masks on their faces. But they were too small for adults, so they were just tiny masks with scarred faces spread out on either side of them. Every time she ducked behind a beam or underneath the water and watched them stagger by.

They were all so oblivious. They bumped into each other, laughing or drawing weapons afterward. There was no in between. Like their emotions were too intense for any of them to react predictably.

Until she saw one walking by, pouring a white powder onto their hand and then snorting it. So they were also the ones who had the most drugs at their disposal as well. She hadn't realized there were drugs even left in this city, especially if these people were using them so rapidly.

Finally, she reached the end of this fissure of water that ran all the way into the heart of the tower. There were fewer people here, most of them seemed to gather together in the main room. It made getting around them easier. But her feet felt like they were going to fall off and her hands were so numb she couldn't feel her fingers, so she had to get out of the water.

Placing her hands on the floor, she glanced around to make sure no one else was here before sliding out of the water. Shivers wracked her body.

Get warm first, then she could keep searching. But she needed to get out of these clothes and into something far more manageable if she was going to do quite literally anything here.

Shivering with her arms wrapped around herself, she opened the first door she could find. There were countless people in there, all of them ripping apart toys. Some of them were on their hands and knees, knives poised at the throats of stuffed animals and blades digging into the soft bellies.

The next room was empty of anything useful. There were no people, but it seemed to be a room filled with the remains of old rocking chairs. The eerie stillness sent her rushing away.

It was hard to find a room where she could be alone, but eventually she managed. There was a single door that almost felt like it was locked until she pushed her way into it. Someone had placed a wall of giant bean filled bags in front of it. But as she stumbled inside, she could see it was actually a bedroom.

A bed in the corner was cozy, and the windows didn't have all the coverings like the rest of this place. Instead, it was cozy and warm, with a fire crackling in the center and light filtering into the shadows.

A blanket in the back caught her attention, along with what looked like a pile of used clothes. That was good enough for her. Ace descended upon the clothes, stripping out of the sopping wet fabric that clung to her and putting on a black shirt that had seen better days and pants that were nearly serviceable. Tossing the blanket over her shoulders, she took a deep breath and tried to get her bearings.

"Oh," a voice said, interrupting her quiet solitude. "I didn't think to see a young lady in here."

She turned to see the same old man who had been in the security system hologram. Although now he was even older. The gray on his hair had turned snow white, the wrinkles on his face were even deeper. But the smile on his face was tender as he looked her over.

"Don't worry," he added. "You're safe here with me."

"Somehow I doubt that."

"I wish I could convince you, but..." He opened his hands. "I am just an old man. And I have lived here before all this became... all this."

Frowning, she looked him over before sitting down on one of the many bean filled chairs. "Prove it to me."

"Are you really in the place to be saying that?"

She grabbed her wet pants and pulled out the scalpel, along with Tera. The droid zipped throughout the room, moving until it was behind the man. It tapped against his heels, and he involuntarily took a step toward Ace.

He chuckled, as though none of this was scary to him in the slightest. "All right, I take the hint. I'll prove it to you."

Chapter 27

Maketes did not find it natural to trust any achromo. They all made decisions for their own betterment, not because they thought it was the right choice. He'd seen them choose themselves over and over again. Even when it came to their own families. Their friends. All the people who should have mattered.

But this man? He wasn't sure how he felt about this man.

He watched through the window as the old achromo settled himself down on the strange circular chair across from Ace. There was a calmness to the achromo that belayed a strength beyond the madness in this tower.

Maketes wasn't certain if that was good or bad. He'd seen strength like this in warriors his entire life. Males and females who knew the value of hard labor, but who were capable of so much more than just using their bodies like a weapon. This was a man who was used to using his mind as well as his strength.

Laying his tail down on the rubble of what might have once been a bridge between towers, he watched the two of them speak. At least for a while. Then curiosity got the better of him and he moved ever closer. They weren't looking at the windows, anyway. They had leaned into each other, listening intently as the other achromo spoke.

What were they speaking of? Ace seemed to be controlling the conversation, for which he was grateful, but he wondered just how much this man would convince her to do.

Finally, he was close enough to hear them. If either of them looked up, they would see him looming outside of the window.

"And that is how I came to be here," the old man said. "Many of these cities have secrets that none of us could have guessed. And all of those secrets, just knowing even one, is enough to get you killed."

"So you're hiding?"

"As well as I can. But realistically, there is nowhere to hide from these people. At least now, I have leverage. I can keep the secrets from others if I must."

Secrets? What secrets? Maketes frowned and drew closer to the glass, if only so that he could overhear them easier.

Ace slumped back in her chair, the scalpel forgotten in her lap. "There's really another city down there? You grew up there?"

"Tau," he said quietly, as though even the word itself was poison. "A city of terror and nightmares. The things I have seen and heard, those are things you will never forget. It is a place for the lawless and the unworthy."

"That's Gamma."

"You have no idea what they are doing down there. All the cities, every single one of them, are run by Tau. There is someone powerful in each city that has a direct connection to them. Every single person takes their orders from the depths of this sea."

He watched Ace's face go pale, and he knew this was when

everything changed. Even he hadn't realized there was another city, but it made sense. There were far more cities down here than anyone knew about, but wouldn't his people have found it? If there was another city in the depths...

Fortis, he thought. Damn Fortis and all his secrets.

Blowing out a long breath, he stared through the bubbles of the smoke screen for a few moments until he focused on what they were saying again.

The man had leaned forward, something in his hands. It looked like a strange little rectangle. Nothing all that important until he realized Ace was staring at it as though it was worth more than all the treasure in the sea.

"This key has unlocked more horrors for me than it has helped," he said. "But I do think that it will answer many of your questions."

"I was sent here to get the key to unlock something. I never knew what it unlocked, only that the person who sent me said it was the key to unimaginable power. I thought it was a weapon storage."

The man shook his head. "It's far more than that. Whoever has this key has the ability to speak with Tau. That person is the only one who can be informed by Tau itself about what to do, who to work with, and all the other terrible things that city can provide."

Ace's face turned bloodless, and Maketes felt all of his fins flare wide.

That key... It was host to unimaginable things, absolutely, but it was also the secret his people had been searching for. A way to control the cities was right within his reach. It was the end of the age of the achromo. If he got that key, found out where they were hiding, then he could lead the force that would destroy the achromos at their root.

Could he pick her over that? Knowing that this key would be the end of both of their peoples?

Watching her through the window, that inner turmoil ate him up. She deserved so much more than someone who would have to betray her. She had never been chosen first in her entire life, and this was his moment to do that. But he didn't know if he could.

Ace's expression hardened. "If that's the truth, then Jacob cannot get his hands on any of this."

Thank all the gods of the sea. He wouldn't have to choose between her and his people.

But it did mean… Her sister. Everything she'd ever done in her life was for her sister, and now what was the choice? Where did they go from here?

Breathing hard, he watched her move and couldn't believe how lucky he was to find her. This achromo, this woman who had burned through every hesitation he'd ever had with their kind. She was beautiful, remarkable, a terrifying creature who was willing to give up so much for him and his people, even though she wasn't part of their lives.

He would dedicate himself to her wellbeing. Even though he already had done so. She deserved everything he had to give her.

But then there was a knock on the door and both achromos in the room stiffened.

"Expecting someone?" Ace asked, her voice hardened with fear.

"No," the man replied. He stood, holding a hand onto his lower back as though there was pain there. "I am not."

Maketes bared his teeth in anger the moment the door burst open. He didn't need to see who was on the other side or who dared to attack his woman. With a flick of his tail, he darted away from the window and toward the opening he'd already found nearby. He didn't care who stood between him and Ace.

They would fall under his claws. Each and every one of them.

Breathing hard, he slammed against the opening. The sharp pieces of metal tore at his scales, ripping them from his flesh and darkening the water with black. But he didn't stop. He didn't hesitate. Deep furrows etched into his scales all the way down his sides. And still, he did not stop until the blinding pain turned white hot and then the building released him from its tomb of metal.

He burst out into the water and tumbled out onto the smooth metal floor. With a hiss that echoed throughout the room, all the fins and spines down his back and forearms stood out as he faced the people who stood in his way.

There were more of them than he'd anticipated. Terrifying examples of what the achromos could become if they were allowed out into the wilds on their own. Masks covered their faces, and all of them had long, wicked knives in their hands.

He bared his teeth, showing them his own weapons that were far greater than their own. If they wanted to threaten him with those tiny knives, they deserved to know what beast they faced.

The first person rushed toward him. It was a female, and she screamed as she ran. There were two knives in her hands, both of them flailing with her anger. He turned away from the sight, flexing his arm spines as she got close. They caught her in the chest and just underneath her jaw, spearing through the soft flesh and bursting out of her mouth. She let out a little gurgling noise, her eyes widening. But she didn't stop trying to stick him with those knives.

"Pity," he muttered as he retracted the spines and let her drop onto the ground. "There is some bravery in you. Or perhaps it is foolishness."

They all converged on him, then. Everything became a blur of flashing scales and sharp objects. His claws bit into every flesh that he could find, while his jaws continued to rend flesh from bone. All he could hear were the screams of the dying and those who continued to fight him as though there was no choice for them to stop. Some of them should have run. Some of them could have.

A knife plunged through the fluke of his tail, then another. Five of them that all pinned him to the floor, lest he rip them through the delicate membrane. He wouldn't be able to swim right if he tore his damn fluke in half, and he was fucking proud of how pretty it was.

Hissing, he spun around on the people who were there, but they danced out of his reach. More leapt onto his back, and he knew they thought this was the end. They would pin him down, slice through more of his fins, force him to bend to their madness.

All of his spines stood up straight again. Shorter spines than the ones on his forearms, though just as sharp. They all lifted at once, piercing through the flesh of these achromos almost too easily. Blood dripped down his sides, but this time, he did not retract the spines. He used their bodies as shields, stuck as they were on the spines that held them against his sides. A few of them were still alive, moaning or shrieking in their pain.

He must look like a nightmare. At least four corpses were stuck on him as he pulled out the blades in his fluke, one by one. He glared at them all, hatred seeping out of his pores along with the black blood that spread around them.

"I am going to kill you all," he said. "I will watch you die. Hold you close as the life flees from your body so that I can consume your souls. One by one. I will devour them and bring them into the abyss where you will be plagued by the souls of the drowned for an eternity."

They couldn't understand him, but perhaps there was some sense of reason in their minds still. A few of them stepped away from him. Doubt flashed in their gazes as they had a moment of hesitation. Others tightened their grip on their weapons.

The sound of more footsteps approached, and Maketes knew he had to leave. This was not where he should be. Enough achromos could kill him, after all. He was only one warrior against many. Even if they weren't all that talented at fighting, even if they had weak weapons, eventually they would overwhelm him.

Baring his teeth, he planted his hands against the floor and launched himself forward. Now that he'd been inside these buildings a few times, he knew how to move. His slithering tail was muscular enough to propel him forward with ease, even weighed down by the corpses. His arms were strong from years of swimming, and he dragged himself through the halls without having to stop. Even as he dripped blood. Even as he left a dark trail for anyone to follow, it did not matter.

Because he knew Ace was in trouble. If he died, then he died. It was an honorable death for one such as him and he would not mourn dying for the woman he... he...

Bursting through the hall in the direction where he knew she was, he could see that there were only a few people left outside of the room. A shriek of anger echoed around him, and he recognized the voice.

She fought. His kefi, with her heart of a shark and her bravery of all the sea itself, fought back against those who would hurt her. He'd never been so unworthy of a mate.

Maketes lunged for the two men lingering outside of the room. The first he grabbed at the shoulder and waist, ripping into the man with his claws until he'd nearly torn the achromo in half. Letting him drop, he loomed over the second man, his tail coiled beneath him to give him even more height.

The achromo stared up at him, his jaw loose as his gaze danced over all the dead bodies still clinging to Maketes's form. The knife in his hand flashed, lunging forward, but all he managed to do was catch his blade on one of the bodies.

Maketes grinned as he sliced through that man's throat and left him staggering down the hallway in seek of help. It was hard to fit through the door with all the bodies attached to him, so he had to retract his spines to get through. The bodies hit the ground with hard, wet thuds, and that was enough for everyone in the room to look back at him.

The old man laid in a corner. His hands clutched his throat where red fountained between his fingers. Wild eyes watched him, and Maketes wondered if the elderly man thought he was looking at his doom.

In a way, he could be. If there was anything that he'd done to Ace that was even questionable, Maketes planned to kill him too.

There were only three people left in the room. Two cackling females who paced back and forth in front of him like he should be intimidated by their show, and a man who held Ace by the hair.

In a flash, he used his tail to whip the two women's legs out from under them, slamming his tail down upon them so hard that he felt their ribs break on impact. Then it was just him and the man. And the crowds of people trying to get into the door that he currently held closed.

"This what you want?" the man said. He wore a strange white mask with long, tall ears. Then he ran his blade along Ace's throat, leaving a faint red line behind, but not breaking the skin. "This little bitch?"

He didn't hesitate. He lunged forward, leaving the door unguarded as he reached for the man. It took such little effort to grab onto his hand, using it to reel the achromo in. Ace dropped like a stone, falling onto her hands and knees and crawling away from the two of them with the slightest whimper in her throat.

He'd deal with her fear later. Right now, he held the man up by his throat and kept a grip on the hand that held the knife.

"This doesn't deserve to touch her," he snarled, before taking the knife from the man's grip with his teeth. Then he drew the hand closer, watching the man's eyes widen beneath the mask as those fingers came ever closer to the sharp teeth filling Maketes's mouth.

Those fingers slotted between his teeth too easily. Three of them came off with the first crunch. Blood spurted into his mouth and the sound of the man's screams was music to his ears. He wanted to hear those screams for the rest of his days, enjoying the sound of bone snapping. Biting another mouthful of fingers, he finally spit them all out onto the floor and dragged the man closer to him.

"I will bite pieces off of you now," he growled, his fins standing straight out. "I want you to stay awake for all of it. Every bite. Knowing you are being consumed by the very thing you fear."

Chapter 28

She dropped the moment Maketes grabbed onto the man. Considering the last time he'd attacked people for touching her, she knew not to look. She didn't even glance up at the noises that were being made or the way the man was screaming. She didn't want to know what was happening.

Instead, she crawled toward the man who had been telling her every secret he'd kept.

His name was Martin. He grew up in Beta just like her. And then he'd become a rather well-known coder, someone who was particularly skilled enough to catch the attention of people with power. While he hadn't known Doctor Faust himself, he had been the person sent to collect the key nearly a hundred years after the doctor had died.

Gamma had been flooded before that. The key wasn't a threat. But now? Now the key was a threat, and he was the only one who knew how to protect it.

Ace slipped in the blood pooling on the floor. Her hands were coated in it now, all the way up to her wrists. But she couldn't stop. Not when she knew there was a chance for her to get to him.

Poor Martin. She slid behind him the moment she could, leaning him against her chest more comfortably than where he was leaning against the wall. She'd known the moment that insane man had barged through the door that they were in trouble. Martin had stood in front of her, taking the slice that likely would have killed her.

Unfortunately, that act of heroism was now going to kill him.

His bloody hand found hers, clutching her in a grip that was stronger than she'd expected for a man currently dying. "The key," he muttered, his voice almost impossible to understand. "You have to take it."

"Martin, where is a med kit?"

"The key—"

"I don't care about the key right now. There has to be a med kit in here. You aren't going to last much longer and I need you to tell me where it is."

But she could already see the answer in his eyes. There was no med kit. He wasn't going to point her in any direction because this tower had already used all of them. Some part of her recognized that was the likelihood, considering the people who lived here.

He shakily held up the key that he'd worn for years around his neck. "Take it."

"Fucking hell, old man," she whispered, tears streaming down her cheeks now. "Just tell me how to save you."

He didn't. Martin grabbed her hand and slid the keycard into it. He wrapped her fingers around it hard, firmly holding the key with her. "Take care of it," he garbled, even as his eyes turned glassy.

A spray of blood soaked her feet and his pant legs. But she still tried not to look as she kept her gaze on the man who had given her everything she was looking for and also proved that the world was much larger than she'd thought.

"I'm so sorry," she whispered. "I'm so sorry I couldn't save you."

Martin squeezed her hand one more time and then he was just... gone. Like the lights had gone out inside of him. One moment he was looking at her, and the next, he wasn't there anymore. It was just a husk of a person lying across her legs, staring up at her with empty eyes.

"Fuck." The stuttered word was more of an exhale than it was speaking.

She stared down at him and everything felt so wrong. He was a good man. He had been a good man. No one deserved to die like this, choking in a pool of his own blood because some madman had followed her. It was her fault. Somehow, yet another person had gotten caught up in her shitty luck.

He'd listened when she'd told him about her sister. He'd known there was a reason behind her being here, and it was far more than someone who just wanted control.

This was a man who had tried. He'd been put in Gamma for reasons that were so far beyond him, and he didn't deserve to be here. This was a place for criminals like her. This was a place for people to go who deserved to be punished.

Not... not this.

A webbed hand broke through her stare. She recognized the yellow scales hidden beneath the blood, but everything was so cold. It felt like she'd peeled her skin off and now everything was a live electrical wire against her nerves.

This wasn't how any of this was supposed to go. She was meant to get into a tower that was largely abandoned. She'd go into a man's apartment, get the key, and leave. She'd head back to Jacob and all the people that she hated with every fiber of her being. The key would change hands. Her sister would be safe. It was such an easy plan, and now she was shaking, holding onto the hand of a dead man.

"Kefi," Maketes said, his voice breaking through the thoughts that plagued her. "We have to go."

"He didn't deserve to die like this," she mumbled through freezing lips. "He was trying to help."

"No one deserves to die, but we all do. He died honorably, protecting someone else. Come with me, Ace."

She didn't know if she could let go of Martin's hand. What happened to his soul? Had it already fled from his body, or should she stay a little while longer? Just to make sure he didn't linger in this awful place where they ate anyone who annoyed them.

"Maura," the sharp tones that wrapped around a name she hadn't heard in ages made her head jerk up.

He looked at her with those black eyes, completely coated in blood. Red and black. Human and undine. It all coated him from head to toe, like some kind of avenging god who had come for her very soul. Along with the soul of the limp man who rested against her.

"It's all gone so wrong," she breathed, staring up at him like maybe he had the answer. "I don't know what happened."

"Come here. We have to go now."

His hand was right there. All she had to do was reach out and take it. But when she reached for it, Martin's hand slid from her own. The limp fall caught her attention. She couldn't... He'd be alone...

She couldn't breathe. Deep gasps filled her lungs and still, it wasn't enough. Not nearly. She couldn't get her lungs to expand the way they had her entire life, and she thought maybe she was dying too. Maybe she already had. This place was cursed, clearly, and if she couldn't breathe, then she was going to end up here with Martin forever. She didn't want to do that. She wanted to make it out of here.

That webbed hand closed on her wrist and dragged her up into him. She slipped on the blood coating his chest, the metallic scent of it filling her lungs. She should have known that he was some kind of avenging angel himself. A creature who brought death wherever he went, but even in her state of panic, she knew that was her fault.

He killed for her. Everyone who had died at the tips of his claws had been her fault, too.

"Hold on to me," he growled, wrapping her legs around his hips. "This isn't going to be fun."

None of this had been fun. What did he mean? What could be worse?

But then she realized, yes. It could get worse. Because Maketes wasn't going to fight anything as they raced out of the toy tower. Instead, he was going to use his body like a battering ram.

Anyone who stood in their way was thrown to the side as he thrust himself between them and her. Forward they went, rushing through the halls as he used his tail to throw them into the air. They came down hard every time, so hard that her teeth rattled and her jaw clenched harder while she gripped him. There were plenty of weapons. So many shouts that her ears rang. But even worse, she knew he was taking even more injuries for her.

She could feel the blood dripping down him. Not just the blood of those he had killed, but more wounds that split open along his back and ribs as he ran from a fight. Every muscle in him tensed as they raced away from danger, and she couldn't help but wonder if he had ever run from a fight before. Or if this was the first time he'd ever done so, and if it was because of her.

They struck the water hard. The same water she'd come in through, even though she knew it wasn't a wide enough gap for him to escape out of. If they weren't careful, he was going to tear himself apart even more than he already had. She watched over his shoulder as knives were thrown into the water after them. A few of the crazies even leapt into the water as well, but they weren't fast enough swimmers to keep up with an undine.

"Ace," she heard him say. "Breathe."

She couldn't breathe underwater. Her lungs had been screaming for air for such a long amount of time, she almost felt light-headed with all the gasping she'd been doing.

But then a bell rang in her mind. He wanted to breathe for her. He wanted her to plunge that strange tentacle into her neck so that he could take some of the weight.

Some of the pain.

When she didn't move, he attached the tentacle for her. She almost didn't feel the cold water that turned her fingers and toes numb. She couldn't feel anything anymore. So she snuggled in tighter to him, letting Maketes gather her closer to the heat of his gills and keep her safe. Because he would. He always did.

Right now, all she could do was stare at the rapidly darkening water and the black blood that surrounded them as he ripped and tore himself apart just to get her to safety.

They burst free from the building as a groan of metal filled the ocean. She could see the plume of dust from where they'd come. The building started to crack, the foundation getting even worse as the gap they had come through caved in. Then the sound. The echoing cry of a building that had long been standing falling to ruin.

Ace felt nothing other than a small sense of victory at that. She hoped the entire bottom floor had just flooded. She hoped the sea would cleanse that place of all the evil that had spread within those walls.

Maketes's hands came to her bottom, holding her even tighter to him. "Put your feet in my gills."

That sounded like it would hurt him, and she was done hurting people. So Ace didn't move.

He didn't give her the choice. With a grunt, he used first one hand, then the other to guide her feet into the slots of his gills. She could feel how it made it slightly more difficult for him to breathe. And still, he did not stop. He swam them fast away from the city, but she could still see it.

The room they had been in before was splattered with blood. Martin had taken all the posters down so he could see the sea, and now his body rested in a room that came out of a nightmare. She feared the blood on the glass would dry and his spirit would never see the sea again.

She didn't know how long they swam. All she knew was that she blinked and suddenly the city was gone from her vision. Swallowing hard, she took a deep breath in through the tube and felt a little better. Maybe she just needed to shake off the terror of what had happened. Maybe she had just needed a few minutes to come back to herself.

Then she realized there was another undine swimming next to them. This one was massive. So big she thought for a moment that Maketes had brought her to another whale shark. But no, this was an undine.

He looked to the side, meeting her gaze with black eyes that seemed to swirl with too many colors to count. Colors that made her want to stare into his gaze a little longer, drawing her into the net of his eyes that were equally pretty as they were terrifying.

He was purple, she realized. Purple with little yellow lights at the ends of his fins that made her want to reach out and touch them. Even though she knew that was dangerous. Even though she knew she shouldn't touch an undine without knowing who or what they were.

"Your achromo is awake," the undine said, and that deep, booming voice hurt.

Bubbles obscured her vision as she hissed out a pained breath and clapped both her hands over her ears. As if that would help. They were underwater, and that only seemed to amplify his voice even more than if they were out of the water.

Maketes cupped the back of her head, drawing her face in toward his neck. "Lower your voice, Fortis."

"The achromo is in our world."

"And you are too loud. Lower your voice."

Ace pressed her lips against Maketes neck, mouthing the word "Thank you," so that only he would know she had said anything.

His fingers carded through her tangled hair before he drew his hand away. "The blood has washed free, Fortis. If you and your people wish to hunt in that tower, it is a feeding ground."

"I have already told them to destroy it. You did a good portion of that, ripping through the foundation. You have the strength of a much larger male."

Maketes's gills brushed against her thighs, as though they were standing up in pride for a moment before he flattened them again. "I'm taking her away. We need to figure out what to do with this key before we return to the ocean."

"Figure it out soon. I do not think you have as much time as you believe." Fortis turned, and she got to see the entirety of him as they swam past.

That was a massive creature. A male undine that was so beyond her reckoning. She had known they were big, but she hadn't realized they were... monstrous.

Nerves churned in her belly as she watched him just floating there, watching them as they moved away from him. As though he saw straight into her soul and saw something far more than she did.

The farther they got, the more she realized she'd seen him before. This was the undine who had broken through the glass, an impossible feat he should not have been able to do.

Swallowing hard, she held onto Maketes a little tighter and tried to keep easing her mind. Anxiety had no place here in the deep, where there was no up and down. Maketes could let her go and then what? She would be floating in nothing, not knowing that she was only sinking farther and farther away from the sun.

So she held onto him harder. Clinging to the cool softness of his flesh, as she prayed that someday she would see the sun again.

Chapter 29

He could feel the tiny tremors going through her body. She's terrified of what she saw in that tower, and frankly, so was he. He didn't need more of a reason to hate her kind, but if he had seen that before he'd ever met her or Mira or Anya? He would never have been able to see them as anything other than animals.

There were varying degrees of every person. He knew that. Even his own people had those who grew too mad with power or all the other issues that he had seen in his own kind. Some people were born wrong. The only difference was that the People of Water took care of those with fractured minds.

The achromos clearly did not. They put all those people together, only compounding the issues, and giving them free rein to get even worse.

He hugged her closer to his chest, his hearts bleeding for her. She'd seen too much. Ace was strong. Stronger than most people he had met, but he understood that there was something rotten in that building. Something that could easily bleed into a soul and make it hard to focus on anything else. He was still thinking about it, too.

He'd seen them eating each other. He'd seen the bodies that were still on the floor, half chewed and half cooked. Even worse, on their way out, he had seen the countless bones with teeth marks on them. No creature was meant to eat its own kind, no matter the opportunity that arose.

So he took her to the only place that he knew would distract her. The only place that would give them both a bit of peace after the awful things that had happened.

He would bring her above.

The journey to the place he was thinking of was rather short. But the entire time he prayed to every god of the sea that he could name that there would be no storm above them. He wanted her to see the sun again. He wanted her to tilt her head up to the sky, watching the shadows of the clouds play across her features as she finally relaxed again. Just as she had the first time.

She deserved to feel the heat of the sun melt into her very bones so that maybe, just maybe, she could forget what they had just seen. Even just for a few moments. He wanted her to find peace.

So when he popped his head above the waves and saw the sun was shining, he felt every muscle in him sag with relief. Thank all the gods that they had listened to him. Because they both needed this.

Rotating his body, he tilted until he was on his back and she was stretched out across his belly. She could feel the sun on her back while he drew them ever closer to shore.

"Where are we going?" she asked sleepily.

"Once, a long time ago, the achromos moved to the very edge of the sea. The storms had drawn them here. It was where they would make their last stand against all the world that moved against them. For a while, they thought their new homes could withstand the power of the ocean and the storms that threatened their lives." He felt his second set of lungs expand, holding themselves full of air so he remained buoyant as she braced herself on his chest and watched where they were headed. "But they were wrong. The homes were safe enough, but they still flooded. It was not a place where they could live forever. But it was here that the dream of living in the sea was built."

He knew what she was seeing. He'd come here many times in his life. There were small buildings that were crumbling after the storms had ripped off their roofs. About twelve of them all clustered near the ocean. What she might not notice is there were at least twelve more under the water as well. The sea levels had risen so high that the houses had been swallowed whole. But that wasn't what he wanted her to see, anyway.

This achromo settlement had a dock system that had somehow survived. It was a floating dock, and he wasn't sure what they used it for, but there was a suggestion that many boats had once surrounded it. And as they approached, he was pleased to see it was still in use.

Breathing out a small sigh of relief, he headed in that direction.

"There used to be massive creatures who laid on top of these," he told her, tilting to use his arm and webbed fingers to paddle them closer. "They weighed more than even one of my own kind. They were loud and constantly jostling to get on the floats."

"What happened to them?"

"The same thing as the rest of the warm-blooded creatures who couldn't live in the sea." He grabbed onto the edge, helping her to the float and then palming her bottom to throw her up onto it. "They died. The storms made it impossible for them to find places to rest. I used to find their bones as a child."

"Morbid." She rolled onto her back, staring up at the bright blue sky and breathing a long sigh of relief. "I understand their need for rest, though. This is nice."

"Your body is not built for swimming as long as mine is."

Ace tilted her head to the side, watching him where he also rested. But his version of resting was letting the sea hold on to him and coiling his tail underneath the float. It was so easy for him to wrap himself around the worn wood and not move. For her? It was taxing on her body just to hold on to anything and not float away.

Still, she smiled at him. A soft expression that barely reached her eyes, but it was a start. "No, I don't think my body will ever be as good as yours at swimming."

Some soft emotion passed between them. She turned her face back to the sun, and he cushioned his head on his arm. Just watching her.

The sun played across her features, giving her natural warm glow a more earthy tone. The soft rounded edges of her cheeks made her look a little happier than she was. He could tell there was still stress straining her mind. The tightness at the edges of her eyes gave that away. But as he watched, the wrinkles on her forehead eased and her breathing evened out.

They were all good signs, but still not perfect. He was struggling to come up with a way to help her, a way to make it so that he could prove how much he wanted her to be happy.

Then she spoke.

"I still can't believe that you don't have someone waiting for you back at home," she said quietly. "You have taken better care of me than anyone else in my life ever has. You give a shit about people. You make it seem so easy to just... do it."

"Do what?"

"Take care of others."

He breathed out a long sigh. "You don't think you're good at taking care of others?"

"It seems like everywhere I go, people die."

Ah. That was the problem. Not that those people had lost their lives, or that he had killed them. She was afraid because she had been in the room, and everyone constantly seemed to die around her.

He reached out with one hand, catching hers in his. He held onto her, trying to thread his fingers through hers and only stopping when the pinch of his webs hurt. "You did not kill them."

"If I didn't walk into that room—"

"He had the key, Ace. He was the person you were looking for, and you would have had to find him no matter what. If you hadn't walked into that room, perhaps you would have found him elsewhere. He might have been surrounded by other people and forced to blend in again. He might never have gotten the opportunity for you to see how kind he was, and that he wasn't the monster the others had become. There are so many other outcomes you are ignoring."

A tear escaped her eye and trailed down the smoothness of that cheek he so adored.

"I know that," she croaked. "Logically, I do. But it feels like everywhere I go, no matter what I do, I mess everything up."

"I know that feeling." He drew himself out of the water, enough so that he could look at her and not just her profile. "I have spent my entire life hiding who I really am. I have been the loudmouth. The male who goes out of his way to annoy everyone around him, because while they still like me for it, it keeps them all at arm's length."

She opened those gorgeous brown eyes again. Their gazes met, locked, and then she asked the question that nearly shattered him. "Why? Why do you think we do that?"

"Because we're afraid if anyone sees who we really are, that they won't like us. And what greater wound is there than to show someone who you really are and have them like you even less than the person you made up?"

She squeezed her eyes shut even harder. "Yeah. That would be terrible."

No, that wasn't the answer he wanted. He didn't want her to retreat into her mind like this. Not when there was so much more he wanted to say.

With a flick of his tail, he landed on the float next to her. The entire thing tilted toward him, rolling her in his direction until he crawled up higher and slammed the whole thing back down into the water. A giant splash covered them with icy seawater, and she let out a little shriek of anger while sitting up.

Good enough. He'd wanted her full attention, and now he definitely had that.

Glaring at him, she crossed her arms over her chest that was once again covered in clinging fabric and far more distracting than she had any right to be. "Maketes!"

Prowling over to her, he forced her back down onto her back. With his forearms on either side of her, he caged her in with his body. There was nothing she could do now. She couldn't look away from him, nor could she hide from the difficult feelings.

"I like you," he said. Perhaps she needed him to be more direct. "I have seen much of who you really are. I have seen you in the face of bravery and fear. Every ounce of who you are only made me like you more, kefi. You have no need to fear that I will ever see something about you that I do not like, because even if I dislike it, it will only make me adore you more. Your flaws are just as beautiful as your perfections."

Her eyes had rounded, widening with every single word. "Why would you say that?"

"Because I cannot imagine a life without an adventure by your side. The thought of you disliking anything about yourself makes me want to fight those thoughts. But I cannot fight you." He leaned down and bumped her nose with his. "You are a beautiful creature, inside and out. You should hold no guilt for being who you really are, Ace. None in the slightest."

She took a deep, shuddering breath. He could see the turmoil inside of her. Felt the way her body tensed as though the words she was going to say next were so difficult. They wound up stuck inside of her rather than releasing the way they needed to.

"I..." She swallowed. "I have spent a lot of my life pushing people away. Men, especially. When I was young, I didn't like the way they teased me and made me feel lesser because I wasn't as pretty as they wanted me to be. And then, as I got older, I was angry that they didn't think I could do the same things they could do. I have spent my entire life trying to prove myself worthy to those who didn't deserve it. And you are the first person I've found that it really matters what you think of me."

He opened his mouth to reply, but she pressed those tiny fingers to his lips. He held his tongue as she continued.

"I am so honored that you have given me time to become braver. You have shown me what it is to not fear what someone will think of me, but just to trust that you believe in me and that you have my best interest at heart. I cannot tell you how healing it has been to be in your presence and to know that you're going to stay. Even if I make a mistake."

His hearts warmed in his chest. He wanted her to feel like that. He wanted her to know that he would see her mistakes, and he would swim through them with her.

Her hand curled around the back of his neck, drawing him ever closer. "But when are you going to tell me what kefi means?"

Rolling them so she could at least feel the sun on her back while they were here, he ran his hands up her thighs and relented. Perhaps she would think him too forward once he told her what it meant. Maybe she would think that he was too much for having called her this for such a long time, even before he had known she would stay.

"Kefi is a spirit of joy," he murmured. "It is the feeling in your chest when you experience a passion for life and new things. The sensation of excitement, but even more than that. It is the true joy of adventure."

He watched her eyes grow wider and grew ever more uncomfortable with her silence. He'd expected many reactions, but he hadn't anticipated her remaining quiet. Anything would be better than this. Any word, any reaction, any look.

But then she blew out a long sigh and all the tension that had been riding her shoulders finally eased. "That suggests you see a lot when you look at me."

He reached up and tucked a strand of her short hair behind her ear. "I see joy, Ace. That's all I see when I look at you."

She swallowed and then grinned down at him. The happiness in that smile was almost blinding.

"Oh, Maketes. I don't know how I could ever live without you now. You wondrous, terrifying beast of a murderous creature. You have turned my world upside down."

And then she leaned down to kiss him, lingering long and quiet as they sought peace in each other's lips. He'd never been happier.

Because he was finding that he was right. She was his joy.

Chapter 30

She asked Maketes to leave her in the sun on her own for a while. He'd made sure she ate, and besides, after the evening they'd spent counting stars, she needed a moment.

He thought she was his joy. No one had ever looked at her and seen anything but a strange girl who tried a little too hard to push people away. And now, she had this creature who had come out of the depths of the sea who looked at her like she'd hung the very moon itself. The same moon he had brought her to see, when likely no other human alive had the opportunity to do so.

They'd woken to the rumble of thunder in the distance. She forgot how quick he was to wake, and how ready he was to protect her. He'd immediately snarled, his voice waking her more than the thunder did as he curved his body over hers. Ready to take whatever hit might be coming for either of them.

As for Ace, she'd just stared up at the wall of golden muscle that protected her. How the hollows between his pectorals cast shadows over his entire body. The multiple wounds closed after the sea had dried them, scabs forming as they dried on the dock. Fangs descended from his mouth, but those sharp teeth were never rough with her. He'd kissed her and never broken skin. Not once.

But she'd also seen him rip out a man's throat with just his teeth. What a strange combination that was. To know he was capable of such violence and yet to also be confident that he would never harm her. No matter what befell either of them.

When he'd been certain the threat was just a storm in the distance, he'd slipped into the water to find her something to eat. Apparently, he wanted to make sure she was somewhere safe and with a full belly before he would take her anywhere else.

Now that left her alone.

Ace sat on the dock, dry and warm enough for now. But already there was an icy chill in the air as the storm barreled toward her. Soon enough, she knew that would be a problem.

The world above was so beautiful until it wasn't. Until she was forcibly reminded of how terrible it was to be in this place while knowing that at any moment, a storm will blow her back into the sea. She hugged her legs a little tighter, making herself small on the float in the middle of the ocean.

Worse, she knew there was a city behind her. She could almost feel the lives of those who had once walked through there. They must have been desperate. The last of their kind, if Maketes was right.

They probably came here hoping if they were going to die, at least they could see the sunsets over the ocean. Just like she was looking out at now.

It was the perfect place to think, and Ace had a lot to think about.

Drawing out Tera from her pocket, she let the droid settle on the dock. "Careful, there's water everywhere. And I think it's too deep for me to dive in after you."

A resounding clack from her droid was the only response she got. Which she knew meant that the droid would be extra careful.

Turning her attention back to the sea, she settled her arms around her legs and blew out a long breath. "What am I going to do?"

The droid settled in its careful rolling and seemed to look up at her.

"The key, Tera. It opens something dangerous and horrible and no one should have access to such a thing." She said the words all on a sigh that came from deep within her belly. "Definitely not Jacob. He doesn't deserve this power."

And therein lay the problem. She didn't know what this key would unlock. Martin made it seem like it was just the knowledge of Tau, but then he'd said a few other things that made her stomach churn in her belly. Like it was also a connection to that city deep in the sea. A direct connection. So she was hesitant to give this key to anyone at all.

She picked it up from where it dangled on a chain around her neck, smoothing her fingers over the metal plate. The dim sunlight caught on a few letters that had long ago been worn away. But she thought it said a name. Like there was someone else who had originally worn it, and now it was in her hands.

Had they also felt the same level of responsibility? Because this wasn't something she even wanted, now. She didn't want to choose who got it.

"I should throw it into the sea," she mumbled. "Maybe that's where it belongs."

A fish slapped the dock next to her right foot, and Maketes

heaved himself up onto the dock with her. His bulk made the water roll over the edge, and she just barely caught Tera in her hand before it was swept right off.

"Sorry," he said with a slight grin, before settling the dock. "What belongs in the sea?"

She flashed the card at him. "This."

"Ah." A troubled expression crossed his usually jovial face before he wiped it away. Maketes never liked to look too serious for too long, and she wondered if that had to do with people not liking him.

What he'd said yesterday still didn't settle well. But she supposed that wasn't something she could control. He had to love himself for who he was, and she couldn't make him do that.

But she could love him hard. She could love him hard enough for the both of them.

And fuck, that thought terrified her. It was the first time she'd thought the words that maybe, just maybe, she was in love with him. An undine. A creature who might not even be compatible with her in the long run.

They couldn't even live in the same world. They didn't breathe the same air, not for long at least. And there would always be that barrier. No matter what they did with each other. She would always need to leave the water and he would always need to leave the air.

He brushed his soaking wet hair away from his face, biceps and pecs bunching with the movement. "Why are you looking at me like that?"

"Like what?"

He gestured over his own face. "I don't know. There's an odd expression all over you."

Fix your face, she thought to herself. The last thing she wanted was for him to realize that she was stupidly in love with him. She wasn't all that sure how to deal with that realization herself, if she was being honest.

Instead, she shook her head hard to clear out the thoughts. "I just don't know what to do with the key. I don't think Jacob should have it, but I don't know who should. I'm afraid of what this opens. Perhaps it would be better to give it to you and have you cast it into the very deepest part of the sea. Then no one can have it."

He seemed troubled by the thought. "If it is that important, should we leave it up to chance that someone else might find it?"

"Who would find it at the bottom of the sea?"

But then Tera clacked against her leg, getting her attention. She lowered the key down to the droid, who circled around it, making a move almost like it wanted her to flip it over...

Right.

Looking at the back, she could see there was a tiny tracker implanted on the back of it. "Shit," she muttered.

"What is it?"

"There's a tracker on the keycard. Whoever keeps track of these things—I'm going to guess that person is alive and well in Tau— knows that the key has been taken."

All of a sudden, she felt rather exposed. Like she was out in the open, which she was, and anyone could find her. All Tau had to do was hit a button and they would know everything about her whereabouts. Her skin scrawled at the mere thought of some stranger watching her every move.

"We have to throw it away," she hissed.

"Then someone else will find it." He reached forward and wrapped her hand in his, curling his fingers around the card until the metal edges pressed almost too hard into her hand. "This is our responsibility. We have to make sure that everyone stays safe, Ace."

But at what cost? She looked up at him, indecision filling every inch of her body. She didn't want to know what it would mean if she got rid of this keycard. But she also didn't want to risk everyone's life again.

What she saw in his eyes, though, steadied her. She took a deep breath, blew it out with him, and then nodded. "You're right. Someone has to do something about it. Maybe we can destroy it."

"And all the secrets it keeps? This could be the answer to all of my people's problems. We don't know what is on the card until we use it."

Her hands were shaking as he gripped them. "What if the secret on this card is far worse than we could ever have imagined?"

"Then we will use that information to our benefit."

"How is that possible?"

"We have to trust each other. The information you have in your hands could contain what my people have been searching for. I need a way to save my people. If this Tau is the reason why achromos have attacked our kind for centuries, then I need to know. Perhaps there is only the one city we need to attack to end all of this. A sea without war, Ace."

Her heart thudded hard in her chest. "Were you going to attack other cities?"

"Beta is already rumbling again. The weapons are online, and they are pointed toward any of my kind that swim by. Alpha was destroyed, and that is something that we will always have as a success. But the reality is that your people are continuing to create more weapons. Gamma clearly has intent to do worse, if your Jacob is seeking something like this."

"Perhaps he knows it's a direct link to Tau."

"Or perhaps he merely seeks more power."

She blew out a long breath. "You're afraid."

"I do not know what your people will do with this information, but I have every right to fear their choices." He cupped her cheek in his hand, the cold webs chilling her even further. "Our kinds have hunted each other for as long as your people have been in the sea. I fear what it means for our future."

She didn't know if he meant their future together, or for both of their kinds as a whole. But did it matter?

"My sister," she whispered. "I need to know she'll be safe if I do this."

His hand slid into the back of her hair, drawing her closer so their foreheads touched. "I promise you, I will do everything in my power to make sure your sister is safe. I have friends who can find her. If Jacob was able to find her by following that drone, then so can we. If you promise to help us, then the People of Water will do everything in our power to help you."

She had to take that as the truth. He'd not lied to her yet, though her stomach was already cramped at the idea of keeping this keycard. She couldn't give it to Jacob. That mass murderer would only kill more people with whatever opportunity she gave him. There wasn't a chance she could do that. So there wasn't really a choice here.

She had to help the undine. She had to do it.

Because even if she saved her sister by giving it to Jacob, she knew Laura would disown her the moment they saw each other again.

If they ever did.

"Giving the key to Jacob means I will never see my sister again," she quietly said. "It will keep her alive, but I know without a doubt he'll use her again as a threat. Over and over again. So many times that I won't know what to do about it. Eventually, I will be locked in the same trap that he's caught me in now."

"I fear the same thing."

She ducked her head to stare down at her hands, trying her best to stay in this moment and not let her own fears and insecurities blind her. "If I give it to you and your people, Laura might not make it out alive. He might kill her on the spot after he finds out what I've done. But there's a chance you find her, keep her safe, and maybe..." She took a deep breath. "Maybe I'll get to see her again."

The faintest rattle reached her ears, as though his gills had all flipped out to stand straight. When she looked up at him again, she could see she'd been right. Every gill on his body was straight out, even down his back and down his arms, where the deadly spikes had impaled people only yesterday. The ferocity in his expression sent chills down her spine.

But he was gentle, ever so gentle, as he reached out and cupped her jaw. "I promise you, I will make sure you see your sister again. I know it is not an easy ask for you to choose my people over your own. I know that it is difficult to imagine what might happen if you do. But others have done the same, with less reassurance that everything will be all right."

"Mira and Anya," she whispered. "I've heard you talk about them. And Anya... I talked to her for years. I know it wasn't an easy choice for her to destroy the city she grew up in."

"They are both brave women." He leaned down until his lips almost ghosted against hers. So close, and yet so far. "Just like you."

She felt nauseous at the thought. Could she deny everything she was? Who she was? It wouldn't be easy to just decide to say fuck it and she would live with the undine. There were a lot of things that could go wrong, and even more things that she didn't know.

Where was she going to live? How would she eat? Would she ever be able to truly live?

Did it even matter? Because she stared into his black eyes and knew it didn't. If she got to be with him, then it was worth the risk. Especially if she wasn't also risking her sister's life.

"Okay," she whispered. "The keycard is yours. Whatever comes after that, I don't know."

His hand clenched on the back of her neck and a relieved sigh breathed across her lips. She hadn't realized how much tension he was holding in his body until he released it.

"We'll bring it to Mira, then," he said. "You brave, wonderful woman. My kefi. I promise you won't regret this."

Chapter 31

He feared she would, in fact, regret this. There was no way he could know for certain that he or his people could do anything he'd promised her. But the moment he gathered her up in his arms and sank beneath the waves, he knew he would do everything in his power to ensure it wasn't a lie.

If she wanted to see her sister, then he would make that happen. It was an easy request, after all, and one that he likely should have offered long ago.

The People of Water knew the ocean better than the achromos ever could. It only took a little while for him to be found by a few depthstriders. He scented them deep in the water, watching as Maketes carried his new female through the sea toward a home where a few of her kind were considered safe.

It took even less time for one of those depthstriders to get close enough where they could hear him speak.

"Brother," he called out, then correcting himself when the scent of the undine came closer. "Sister, I apologize."

The massive female rose from the depths, her chest bound in tight fibers. Her hair was twisted back from her features in tight coils that drew her skin into a tight frown.

"Brother is more accurate," the female said. And Maketes corrected himself.

"Two soul?" He paused in their swim, tucking Ace a little tighter to his side and giving him a nod. "It is an honor."

Such people were honored among his kind. To have two sides of the same shell was both a blessing and a curse. Both male and female, they were quite literally special. He'd heard that the achromo had similar creatures, but the two souled people of his kind were capable of self reproduction. The creature before him was, in fact, both male and female. Though this one wished to be seen as the masculine version of who he was.

The new male inclined his head, accepting the honor Maketes bestowed. "You carry an achromo through our waters."

"We journey to the home where the People of Water and achromos live together."

The other male flinched back, disgust filling the water with its scent. "Why go there? Such a cursed place should not exist. The achromos should stay in their towers and confinement."

"We seek a better future."

The depthstrider was confused by the subject. Most of his kind were, though. They were all bred to hate the achromos, and very few of them saw any reason to find goodness in her kind. But then he pried Ace's face away from his neck, turning her to see the giant dark blue depthstrider who loomed before them.

Ace smelled afraid, but she still managed an awkward smile and a half wave. "Hello."

The word was so quiet, no one could have heard it but him, and he only heard it because he was right next to her. But still, he smoothed her hair back from her face and petted the top of her head.

"She says hello," he told the depthstrider. "They are capable of much more than we gave them credit for."

"You treat her as a treasured pet."

"Perhaps." He felt Ace stiffen in his grip, and it took everything in him not to laugh at the depthstrider's statement. "But she is a good pet. One who speaks to me about many things. You would be surprised at how quick-witted their kind are."

He had a point to this conversation, although he could see Ace was getting more and more angry. He also realized there was a time limit to this. They had to keep moving, because the ocean here was too cool for her skin. He could only keep her warm for so long before he needed to find more temperate waters.

"Are you curious about them at all?" he asked the depthstrider, watching for any kind of reaction.

There was the faintest flickering along his shoulders. Just the slightest hint of color that was nearly impossible to even see. But it was there. It flickered, and that meant this male was interested.

But the depthstrider flared his light tipped fins and hissed. Through bared teeth, he snarled, "I have no interest in the achromos. You speak of ill thoughts from a poisoned mind."

"Certainly. But I need someone to help me find this one's sister." He gestured with his hip fin, almost as though he was just keeping himself upright, but it sent Ace's sweet scent toward the other creature. "There is a drone that goes from Gamma to Beta. And with it, information. I need to know where that drone goes, and if the woman it goes to can be taken from that city."

Again the flared gills, the bright fins that glowed. "Why are you asking me?"

"Because I need someone trustworthy. Someone who won't murder the achromo if we get her out. I need someone... Interested."

Ace struggled in his arms now, clearly not happy that he would suggest an unknown person of his own kind seek out her sister. But this was the way of their people. If he could, he would choose to trust any of the People of Water who wanted new knowledge of her kind.

"Maketes," Ace snarled in his ear. "That is my sister you're sending a random undine to track down."

He ignored her and inclined his head to the depthstrider. "I would be in your debt if you find this one."

The depthstrider nodded. "I'm interested, certainly. I will find you at the nesting site where you head."

"Thank you."

The depth strider swamAce slapped his chest as hard as she could underwater. "That undine doesn't even know what my sister looks like! How is it going to find where she is if it has no other information? And the drone? It doesn't know what drone is going to Beta. There could be countless drones for all you know."

He tucked her a little more firmly against his chest, holding her even through her struggles. "My people do not hunt like achromos. They will find your sister by scent alone. It is easy to do, considering you all smell quite... strongly."

She stiffened even further, and he wondered if that was an insult to her people. He liked her smell, but he could also track her for many miles. "Maketes. I need you to at least tell that undine what Laura looks like."

"I don't know what Laura looks like."

"Then we need to turn around and tell them, and you can translate for me!" She let out a little shriek of rage. "Are you swimming away from them right now? I said turn around!"

"They know it is a drone that travels to Beta, which means there are only so many that they will need to follow. Our kind were made for hunting. This is a challenging hunt, and therefore, that undine will have every reason to devote their entire attention to it." He turned her in his arms, making her look up at him. "This is the best option. A depthstrider hunts until their last breath. They are all gifted in more ways than most. If he must, he will look into the future to find your sister and then bring her home."

"The future?"

He relished the wide-eyed stare that looked back at him. At least now he had her attention.

"The future." Maketes waved at his own eyes. "You didn't notice Fortis is a little different?"

"I was a little preoccupied by all the death and the people who were trying to murder us," she muttered, but then she stiffened again. "Wait, I do remember something off about his eyes. They were a lot of colors! And the depthstriders in the first building as well."

He snorted softly, his gills flaring against her thighs with the movement. "Kind of. The more colors that are in their eyes, the more they are looking through your future. I told you that. They see the past, the present, and the future. It is not a pleasant experience, at least in my opinion."

"You don't like them looking into your future?"

"I like to be surprised," he replied. "Like with you. I was so surprised to find out you were not who I thought you were. You were so much more than I ever expected."

She tucked herself a little tighter against his side, her breathing settling as she drew air through the tentacle. "I'm glad I was a surprise. You were a surprise for me, too."

"Was I?" He pretended like he was shocked. "And here I thought I was exactly as you thought I was. I told you what I looked like."

"No you didn't! You said you were an undine like all the others. That doesn't mean I had any idea you would be this… this…"

"Strong?" he supplied, flexing a little in her grip.

"That wasn't what I was thinking."

"Ruggedly handsome?" He tilted her back so she could more easily see his sharp jaw.

"No, not that either." A small smile cracked across her face.

"Ah. You thought I would be larger."

"No!"

She was laughing now, the bubbling sound filling him with so much joy that he felt the reasoning for her name again. Everything in him breathed out a sigh of relief. At least she wasn't angry with him for sending out the depthstrider anymore. He needed all the reassurance he could get now that he was bringing her back to the others.

Ace shook her head at him, trying hard to not fall under his antics. But then she reached up and traced the jaw he'd just flaunted at her. "Beautiful," she said. "I didn't know you would be so beautiful."

It wasn't a word he'd ever used to describe himself. Beautiful was a word for pretty things, delicate or soft creatures who were created more for their aesthetics than their use. But then the word settled into him. Beautiful meant she looked at him like she'd looked at the sunset last night. With those wide eyes taking in all the splendor that was stretched out in front of her. She'd looked at that sunset like it was her reason for being, and if that's what it meant to be beautiful…

Well, he didn't mind that at all.

He tucked her a little more firmly into his grip and zipped through the sea. He curved around Gamma with her, letting her see the neon lights in the distance and all the fish that swarmed around that place. Her breathing caught as they swam by, but he didn't think that was because she wanted to go there.

Instead, it was just her moment of saying goodbye to the version of herself she left behind in those walls. He swam higher through the towers, passing just overhead until they were off into the distance where she had likely never been. There were no human cities here. Why would there be? They all clustered deeper in the waters where the storms couldn't reach them.

But he and his people had found a haven. Just deep enough for the storms to only make the waters a little rougher, but not so shallow that the waves would easily touch them.

With a grin, he spun with her in his arms. A spiral in the water that sent them both careening through a current that they could ride for hours on end.

Neither of them talked much. They just rode the sea current that drew them closer and closer to the home he hoped she liked. Because soon enough, she would live here. With him, he hoped. Although he knew perhaps that was a stretch.

They reached the home where his pod had grown even larger. Arges had been the greatest warrior their people had ever seen. They followed him wherever he would let them, and many of them had come here.

The first thing he noticed was that many of the new pod members had already decorated. From far and wide, they found round stones they then embedded into the sand. Each one had a meaning and a perfect place that created a spiral in the sand. The spirals led to the bed where his people slept, sometimes in a pile with their families, other times floating there, just letting the sea hold them in place.

As they sped overhead, he looked down to see a few families had joined them now. There was a mother and father, the massive female lucky enough to still have the male she'd mated with. She held onto the fin of a tiny female who was struggling hard against her mother's grip to get to her father's waiting open arms.

A pang of jealousy struck him. It was the life he'd always wanted, and the one he would forever be denied.

But then he felt a warm hand on his chest, smoothing away the ache that burned there where his hearts pounded. He remembered that while it hurt to see other people so happy, he was also blissfully happy on his own. Because he'd found his joy, and she was right here in his arms.

Holding Ace a little tighter, he zipped past the nests and all the stone beds, heading to what was quickly becoming an expanding city. Once Mira started building something, it appeared it was rather hard for her to stop.

"What is that?" Ace asked, her voice dropped low in awe.

He knew she could see the small village that Mira had built. She was beyond just an engineer, because the genius it had taken to weave all of these pieces together was remarkable. What had just been a single pod that was created for life support of a single person became so much more. They'd expanded into Mira and Anya's bedrooms, then a garden building. But now that they had so many pieces and parts from Alpha, it was even larger.

Mira had created a kitchen, a dining room, then a living area for everyone to gather. A research pod that stood off from the side of the others, then a storage unit as well. Countless other buildings were ready to be attached just in case they were needed. Or perhaps, in the hopes that they were.

Anya was particularly happy to be on her own, or only spend her time with Daios. But Mira needed people. She enjoyed the company of others, and he'd seen the toll it had taken on her recently. She wanted to be surrounded by her own people.

And Anya? Well. Anya wasn't particularly good company. The two of them didn't quite like each other all that much.

Now he feared if either of them would like his achromo.

"Are you ready?" he asked, nodding at a few of the others who had swum up to their side.

"Not really," she replied with a small laugh. "But I'd like to be dry."

"I can promise you that."

Anything else? He wasn't sure how much he could promise.

Chapter 32

Holding onto Maketes felt like the only grasp she still had on her sanity. She'd gone from the frying pan into the fire. They were surrounded by undines, and she hadn't realized their kind came in so many colors. No wonder they called humans achromos, a name which meant colorless in Latin.

Humans really were colorless in comparison. They came in tones of beige, but these creatures were in a rainbow of colors. Everywhere she looked, there was another color. Blues and violets, bright greens and yellows, even a few flashes of red that were so distracting, she craned her neck to stare at them as they headed off into the distance.

They were so beyond beautiful. All different kinds of flukes and fins decorated their sides. The gills that framed their faces were all different, too. Maketes's were smaller than some, and there were a few who had massive fins on each side of their face. Rib gills seemed to have the same treatment. There was no way to know how large they were going to be or how thin the filaments were.

It was almost mind bending to see them all. To her people, the undine were monsters. She'd never given it much thought to what they did when they weren't hunting humans. In a way, she'd assumed they were all holed up in some cavern in the middle of the ocean, clawed hands stretching out of the darkness when they scented prey. Or perhaps that they just floated there, waiting for the next attack.

They were silly thoughts. She knew that now. Because there was a mother here with her child, tugging on its tail and laughing as the little one got more and more angry. Then there was a young couple, each of them twining around the other as they swam toward the surface. Their tails were so graceful and long, looping in a spiral that looked like DNA as the sun's rays grew stronger and highlighted the female's lovely dark blue scales and the male's pretty green.

This entire place was like a dream. And as they approached the building that she never would have guessed was here, she realized she had thought so low of the undines, but clearly they were far more than she'd ever imagined.

Maketes held her a little tighter as they approached. She could feel his claws digging into her sides, pressing her to his skin like someone was going to take her from him.

But no one even swam toward them. It seemed like some of the other undines were looking at her with rather odd expressions, but no one spoke to them. She supposed that was likely because they already knew other humans. She could only guess that this was where Mira and Anya lived, considering the home was filled with greenery that she could already see through the windows.

Ace couldn't wait to get out of the water. She loved experiencing all of this with Maketes too, but having a bit more of a civilized place to rest her head would also be very welcome.

Still, she placed her hands on his shoulders and squeezed hard enough to get his attention. "You seem nervous."

"I am."

"Why?"

His forearm flexed against her back, the hard muscles there bouncing with emotion. "I just... I want them to treat you kindly."

Was that what he was worried about? This sweet, wonderful man feared that she wouldn't get along with the others?

Ace chuckled, the sound causing bubbles to erupt from her mouth. "I've been around humans my entire life, Maketes. Some of them don't like me, others do. It's okay if they don't like me."

"It's not."

"Why?"

He paused near the building, his gaze dancing over her features. "Because you are the most wonderful person I have ever met. The idea of them disappointing you, or seeing less of you than you deserve? It kills me."

She bumped her nose against his. "I promise, if they are mean, I will tell you."

"You will tell me."

She nodded, and then for good measure, pressed a kiss to his lips. Because it seemed natural to do so. They were here, they had been... whatever they were. And now it only felt right that she kiss him and linger when...

Well, fuck. She didn't know if it was the right thing to do in front of what was essentially his family. But he reacted like she'd stuck him with a brand. Maketes became a live wire in her arms, all of his gills fluttering like mad and his arms dragging her even closer. It was so nice to have someone be this obsessed with her.

Then he sighed against her lips, bubbles obscuring her vision of him for a few moments before he swam her closer to the building again.

"Be safe, kefi," he said, before holding her up to the opening of the moon pool. "I will return for you."

"Where are you going?"

"To find my brothers. They need to know who I have brought back to our home, and what our plan is." His gaze lingered on her face, as though just looking at her eased his anxiety. "You can hold your own against them. Yes?"

"I don't think there will be any issues."

Although now he was making her nervous.

He flicked his tail and headed away from the building, so she turned toward the surface at the same moment his tentacle disconnected with her neck. Nowhere to go now but up, she supposed.

Kicking her feet, she headed up and grabbed onto the edge of the moon pool. With a sharp gasp, she drew air into her lungs all on her own and heard the sound of footsteps approaching.

Ace had only just managed to ungracefully crawl her way out of the water and roll wet and soaking onto the floor when a door burst open. It hit the wall hard, and Ace caught a glimpse of the interior. It was rather bare in this room, with a table set up on a raised platform in the back and glass windows everywhere. There was an opening to her right that looked like it might go into a garden area which had recently been expanded, guessing by the old bolts sitting next to the new ones she could see glinting in the light.

But then she could only look at the beautiful woman standing in the doorway. Not a single golden lock out of place. She was a stunning example of near perfection. Her blue eyes were so lovely, the curves of her body carefully hugged by a rather lovely looking dress that was in the peak of fashion. The blue gown tucked in at the waist, hugged her breasts, and showed off the ring of pearls around her throat.

Surreal, Ace had the momentary thought. It was surreal to see someone so put together in a building that had clearly recently been built.

"A-Ace?" the woman said, her voice stuttering over the word.

She blanked for a moment before realizing this had to be Anya. "Well, damn. I always heard the Songbird of Alpha was beautiful, but I didn't realize you would look like this."

Like a model had stepped off a magazine. That's how she looked. So beautiful it was blinding a bit, except then Anya burst into laughter that was so incredibly off key and grating to listen to, and Ace realized it was her friend after all.

Anya rushed into the room, reaching for Ace and dragging her into her arms. It was like this beautiful version of the person she knew didn't care in the slightest if her dress got wet or if she smelled like the sea. Anya just held her tightly and rocked back and forth.

"I'm okay," Ace said with a chuckle, but then remembered that Anya was hard of hearing. And she wasn't wearing Bitsy.

So she drew back, holding onto Anya's forearms and making sure her friend could see her lips. "Anya?"

Anya nodded frantically. "Yes, it's me!"

Tears burned in her friend's eyes, turning them red and glossy, as though she was fighting hard to not let them fall. Had Ace earned this emotional reaction? They'd been talking for years, after all. But some small part of her had been afraid their relationship was entirely online. They had felled Alpha together, but did that mean they were friends?

Obviously, her fears were unfounded. Because Anya yanked her in for another rocking hug that nearly sent them both to the floor as they stumbled in the water.

Glancing up, she saw another woman leaning against the door Anya had just come out of. The redhead had hair like fire billowing around her. A sensible pair of pants and a tight black tank covered her body in stark contrast to Anya. The redhead grinned at her and then waved a single hand.

"Mira."

"It's nice to meet you," Ace gasped out before extracting herself from Anya's grip. She tried to stay facing Anya so that her friend wouldn't miss the words. "I've heard a lot about you two. Though, obviously, we've talked before."

Anya shook her head with a wry grin. "I feel like we've known each other for ages."

She was right. They'd been talking for nearly six years, long before she'd been tossed into Gamma, trying hard to overthrow the people who deserved to be overthrown. She'd just... Ace wasn't used to people wanting to be friends with her. Even back in Beta, no one had wanted to talk to her that much.

Clearing her throat, she looked over to Mira, who hadn't moved yet. "I don't think we've spoken yet."

"Not much, but enough. It's good to see you. When Maketes was heading toward us with someone in his arms, I had a feeling he might have caved and brought you here."

Right, this was an awkward conversation. So Ace changed the subject swiftly. "You're from Beta as well, right?"

"As well?" Mira arched her brow. "Engineering department."

"Droid research."

They stared at each other for a few long minutes, and she could feel Anya's worried stare going back and forth between them until both Beta explants started laughing.

Mira shook her head. "Another Beta reject. Were you working in the droid depot when... Fuck, what was his name? Billy? When Billy ran the place?"

A cold shudder ran between her shoulder blades. "That fucking asshole? Yeah, I did. He tried to grab my ass more times than I could count and then got mad at me when I did my job better than he could."

"He was bad. I heard whoever replaced him was better."

"Not by much."

And just like that, everything softened. Anya threaded her arm through Ace's and drew her into the village they had made.

The room with the moon pool was, she could only assume, a meeting room. Because as she walked into the next room that was filled with color and stuffed cushions, she imagined this was the room the two of them spent their time in.

Plants hung from the ceiling, their tendrils reaching down for everyone who passed. She almost couldn't even see the glass, there was so much greenery in here. The floors were covered with layers and layers of carpet in every color and texture possible. Giant cushions were plumped everywhere, likely for seating. The walls were mostly glass as well, and there were small reading nooks with stacks of books.

"I make sure Mira keeps all her metal pieces and parts out of this room," Anya said, her voice turning slightly scolding. "I've stepped on far too many screws already."

"She's a bit pushy," Mira replied from behind her. "You'll have to be aware of that if you're staying here with us."

But when Ace looked at Anya, certain her friend would be angry, Anya was just grinning.

"I can't hear her," Anya said. "I'm sure she said something mildly nasty."

"Not at all." Ace looked over Anya's shoulder and caught Mira's wink.

She thought she would quite like being here with the two of them. But, realistically, she couldn't stay here. Could she?

Anya grabbed her hand, threading their fingers together. "You can stay. I recognize that look, and I'm sure it's the same look I gave Mira. Oh, please stay with us! I would love nothing more than someone else to talk with, and I'm sure Mira is quite tired of me by now."

Again, Mira nodded frantically over her shoulder before shrugging. "I'm used to people from Beta. We're a little harder around the edges."

"I grew up in Beta and have lived in Gamma for too long to be considered soft," Ace replied. Although then she looked down at her clothes and shrugged. "At least not in personality."

With a soft sound, Anya whipped around to look at Mira. "Clothes! She's soaking wet."

Mira nodded before heading past both of them to get clothing for her. In that moment, Ace saw the three of them in the reflection of the glass. Anya, petite and willowy thin. Mira, tall and broad shouldered with strength radiating through all of her body. And then Ace, curvy and equally just as strong.

Equally as pretty.

It was the very first moment in her life where she had seen her own reflection and thought herself attractive. But there it was. Looking into her own reflection, seeing beauty.

Her breath caught, and she didn't know how long she stood there, staring at herself until Mira came back and threw some clothes into her arms. "These should fit you. If they don't, we'll get to making new pieces for you. Should be comfortable enough for now, though."

She glanced down to see a worker's uniform in her hands. The man's large hoodie and soft pants should fit her just fine. And they were far more comfortable than any clothes she'd put on in years. So she headed into the room where Anya drew her and changed into the dry clothes. It was all still rather surreal.

Until she got back into the room and looked at Anya and Mira talking. They both looked back at her and all she could think to say was, "Anya, why aren't you wearing Bitsy?"

There was a low quiet, and then Anya replied, "Bitsy was crushed in Alpha when I set off the bomb. Mira has been trying to fix her, but she's never been the same."

With a small quirk in her lips, Ace shrugged. "That's why you never ask an engineer to touch anything in the droid depot."

It would keep her hands busy to help. She didn't want to think about anything right now. It was all so overwhelming, but it seemed like the other two women didn't anticipate leaving her alone.

Mira stood first, rolling her eyes at the two of them. "An engineer does a fine job. But if you want to take a crack at it, follow me."

Anya grabbed onto Ace's arm again and dragged her with them, whether Ace wanted to go or not. "Come on. If you can fix Bitsy, that would be the second best thing to happen today!"

Pulling her friend to a stop, she made sure Anya could see her lips as she said, "What's the first?"

"You, silly."

A warmth bloomed in her chest as her two friends pulled her into Mira's domain, which was filled with the scent of oil and so many pieces and parts of metal that it was shocking it could all fit in here. For the first time in what might have been years, Ace felt like she was... home.

Chapter 33

He hated leaving her behind, but he also knew that it was necessary. The other women weren't as terrible as he made them sound, and he wasn't even sure why he had said it. Maketes adored both Mira and Anya for who they were. Strong women with hearts of gold, who had chosen their mates over everyone else.

He could only pray that his chosen mate would do the same. But he also had a duty to his people, and that was a hard realization to work through. His people needed him to provide information, and he needed... her. Every inch of her.

Even now, he still burned after she'd kissed him so easily in front of his people. Ace had just grabbed onto each side of his face and kissed him like it might be the last time they ever saw each other again. He should have laughed at her, told her not to worry, and that everything would work out the way it was meant to work out.

Instead, all he'd been able to think was that she was kissing him and that he wanted her to be kissing elsewhere. He wanted her everywhere.

On him. Around him. With him inside of her. Just that single kiss had made it difficult for him to think about anything other than her taste, her touch, and all the beauty that made up who she was.

It had him on edge. He'd admit that. Even going to see his brothers made him angry. He wanted to turn right back around and go to her. What if she was being mistreated? What if the other two women made her feel unwelcome?

Just the thought had all the lights in his body flickering to life. His spines were standing out straighter, harsher. He was ready to fight on her behalf again. He'd even fight his own kind if that was what it took.

"Maketes!" a voice called out. Arges, most likely, his blue shaded brother's voice was easier to pick out. It was always kinder than the others.

Still, he flared all his fins and turned toward the sound like it was a direct attack. Arges paused where he swam, a frown on his face as he surveyed the anger in Maketes's gaze.

A grin spread across his features, like he had discovered something incredible. "Brother," Arges said. "I heard you brought back an achromo, but I didn't think it was this bad."

"This bad?"

He waved a hand up and down, gesturing to all of Maketes's body. "Look at you. All vibrant and showing off. You haven't mated her then, I suppose?"

A much deeper male voice answered from behind Maketes, and he felt the hard slap of a fluke across his back. "This small one has found a mate already? Was it the one he brought back with him? She scented pretty in the water."

That was it.

He turned with a small flick of his hip fin and raced for Daios.

Catching his brother hard in the chest, they both tumbled through the water until Daios hit the sand on his back. But as much as he tried to claw at the big, red finned devil, Daios blocked him at every turn. All the while, the massive male was chuckling.

"Look at him! All caught up in the mating rage, I can tell. This one is already done for, Arges."

"Don't tease him so much. You were just as delicate when you first found Anya," Arges replied. But there was laughter in his voice as well and it made Maketes see red.

Snarling, he turned toward Arges. "You both are a waste of my time."

"And yet, you're fighting us." Arges spread out his arms wide. "Come on, little brother. You need to get some of this energy out."

They were right. He did. And there was no better way to do so than to take a pound of each of their flesh. Baring his teeth, he raced for his blue brother, only to be caught around the tail by the red. They all struggled, tooth and claw flashing in the sands until there was black blood in the water. And that was enough for him. He didn't care who was bleeding, only that there was blood.

It was more frustrating than either of his siblings could know. The two brothers had gotten their women easily in comparison to him. They didn't have to worry about a friendship breaking down, because they hadn't been friends before they fell prey to the feelings that now boiled inside of him.

It was frustrating. She frequently denied his offerings. He'd yet to kidnap her and take her away from everyone, because that cave had arguably been part of the job. Then there was the gift portion of it. He should have gotten her some trinket by now, but he hadn't had time to do so. All because they were swimming around because he was trying to be a good male who kept his people safe.

Snarling, he swam up toward the sun, where he intended to spin around and use all the force of his momentum to pin his brothers into the dirt. One by one, he would beat them.

But then he was caught by a dark purple webbed hand around the neck and then he was hanging from the depthstrider's grip like a child. He writhed against the hold, his tail flailing and all of his body coiling around the thick arm that now drew him back down toward the sands. But nothing and no one could fight against something this large.

Fortis held him in his grip, bringing him right back to his two brothers, who were both breathing hard and had a few claw marks down their chests, but were no worse for wear than he was.

Frustration burned in his chest. He wanted them to be hurting. He wanted them to wear the scars of this moment.

At least, until Fortis gave him a hard shake. "Snap out of it. I recognize the mating need has you in its grip, but that doesn't make you a mindless beast."

The words sank through the anger that raged through him and Maketes let the anger go. Fortis's hands on him didn't hurt, after all. The big male was just forcing him to stay in place. His gills flattened, his spines drew back down, and then his tail became loose beneath him.

He swore the sea toyed with the ends of his tail, whispering that he needed to relax or he would never keep her safe. If he wasn't thinking with a rational mind, then he needed to force himself to do so.

Breathing in and out for a long moment, he nodded. "I am better."

"Good." Fortis released him and then shook his hand off as though he were clearing the scent from his fingers. "Disgusting. I'll never understand such anger and need for an achromo."

Daios snorted. "Just for that, I hope you find the most difficult one out of us all."

The glare that Fortis leveled him with should have turned him into chum, but then Fortis leveled the rest of them with that same look, and Maketes slunk back to his brothers. There was such disappointment in that gaze. More than that, though, were the eyes of a male who saw too much.

"The three of you are just the beginning," Fortis said, his voice deep and low. It was the same tone he used when he saw into the future, and it was the tone that Maketes hated to hear. "If we continue to fight, the future becomes foggy with fear and more blood. We must focus on the gift that is now in our hands. The one that Maketes has brought us is far more useful than a singular weapon."

"A gift?"

Fortis heaved a sigh and stared up at the sun beams above them. "Give me strength," he murmured, clearly calling out to the gods.

Ah, right. Now that he was thinking a little clearer, he knew what the big male was talking about. "Right, the keycard. Ace has it."

"The key?" Arges asked, clearly not following.

"She was sent to find a key from Gamma. They were going to trade us meager weapons if we got it. I thought you'd already have been briefed on this?"

Arges still appeared lost, but Daios nodded and replied, "We were. He was busy with Mira at the time, if I remember correctly. I had my concerns about what the key would open."

"It seems it's not a key for a vault, like the people from Gamma thought. It is a key to knowledge itself. Especially about a city called Tau."

Daios looked confused by that name, but Fortis and Arges

stiffened. He'd never seen the depthstrider turn that color either. It spread from his dark tail all the way up his chest, turning him not only a strange shade of dark purple, but sinking him into the background of the sea. Almost as though he was invisible to the naked eye.

Argeş hissed long and low. "I have heard that name before. A soldier uttered it before I tore him in half."

"Did you say... Tau?" Fortis asked, his voice so low it was little more than a growl.

"I did." Maketes tilted his head to the side, confused by the reaction in front of him. "I didn't know it existed, neither did the achromo I brought home. Why do you know the name?"

Suddenly, all three of them were looking at the colossal beast, but Fortis wasn't looking back. His gaze was out beyond them, toward the sea and the depths that sank so far into the abyss no light could survive. It was there that Maketes had never explored, but it was there that Fortis lived.

"It is a name that is spoken only rarely amongst the depthstriders. A whispered echo of a place that once existed. Few of our kind have ever found it, and those who have only remain in memories and in the souls that visit us." His eyes swirled with colors, as though he were already speaking with the dead. "Those who linger in the sea, in the place between life and death. Those are the ones who have seen this city."

All the scales on his tail lifted, sudden fear lancing through his entire body. "Ace said the key holds all the knowledge of this place, and perhaps a direct connect to those who rule it. Apparently, there are quite a few people in each city who have a direct connection with them. The man who held this key believed that someone in Tau controlled every achromo city under the sea."

"That cannot be," Fortis snarled.

His two brothers turned to him as well, their brows furrowed in concentration. But it was Arges who spoke first into the angry silence.

"Maketes, do you believe her?"

"I don't have to believe her." He thudded his hand on his chest. "I know it to be true. The man was not lying. I was there when he spoke, and I traversed through Gamma to get her back. The people in that tower were wrong. Corrupted. They ate each other and all those who threatened them. But this man spoke true, and his voice rang with purpose."

"Then it is true that Tau exists." Arges shook his head. "This place should not be in the ocean."

"I say we use the key." Maketes needed them all to listen, because he knew his purpose was to tell them. "Use the key. Find this controlling city. If we can figure out where it is, then we can destroy it. With that knowledge, we could force all the other cities to run on their own. Perhaps if Beta no longer gets orders from someone more powerful than them, then they will have to work with us."

Daios shook his head. "That is why we destroyed Alpha. It has only made tensions worse between us and the achromos. It is a failing mission, brother."

"Perhaps. But if Tau controls as much as they say..." He didn't know how to tell his brothers that this was important.

The sea swirled around him, kicking up sand so that it misted around his body. He could feel the ocean urging him on, telling him to continue arguing with them. It was his job to convince them that this was the right path to swim.

Yet, he didn't know the words. He couldn't find them. Because in the end, he didn't know what this key would open or what it would unlock.

So instead, he pressed his closed fist over his hearts. "I know this is the right path. I know this is the only choice for us."

All three of them stared at him, and he could feel the currents change in his direction. One moment, they looked confused, and the next, understanding passed over them like a wave had crested over their heads.

"It's the right thing to do," he repeated.

Fortis nodded. "Keep me informed. I was told that you are seeking out your achromo's sister as well. Would you like me to get involved?"

His hip fins flared in surprise. "You know of that?"

"I know of everything that happens with my people. Especially when there is a yellow finned bastard who asks one of my hunters to find an achromo without killing it." Fortis's jaw clenched before he continued. "I will help them find this woman if you wish. There has been no news of her that I have heard."

"I would be in your debt."

Surprise lifted Fortis's brows before he nodded. "Consider it done."

Then the purple beast swam off. Gone, with just a flick of his tail, like the conversation was over just because he'd decided it to be so.

Daios frowned, then bared his teeth in a nasty snarl. "I don't like that one."

Arges snorted. "No one does. That's his charm, don't you know? I pity the achromo he finds who will break him."

All three of them burst into laughter. Maybe part of the hilarity was of anyone liking Fortis at all.

"Fortis and an achromo," Maketes stammered through his laughter.

"Can you imagine? He'd eat her in her sleep before he'd admit to wanting to keep her."

"Eat her just so that he doesn't have to admit maybe the achromos are prettier than he thinks?" Daios shook his head. "Maketes, what's yours look like?"

Just like that, all the need was back. It burrowed into him like a knife and he groaned at the thought of her. "Soft. Everything about her is so soft."

"They are awfully soft," Arges replied. "Too easy to cut."

"No, no..." He lifted his hands as though envisioning her ass already cupped in his palms. "There's so much to grab. So much to spread out like a banquet before me."

Daios made a disgusted expression and then slapped at Maketes's hands. "Stop that."

"What? There's plenty of her to please me."

"Stop... doing that." Daios slapped his hands again. "Let's get you back to your achromo before you tell us too many personal details."

Chapter 34

There we go," Ace said, tapping the top of Bitsy's head to send her back to sleep. "That should do it. Her hard drive was completely fried in the explosion, but droids like these usually have some form of backup. I think I found the right one."

Anya sat in front of her, leaning forward with her head in her hands. It was very much like a family member would look when a loved one was in surgery. Which was sweet. There weren't a lot of people who looked at droids like she did. Sure, Bitsy was a very important function of Anya's life. But she was also a friend, and Ace knew what that felt like to need someone to be there with her.

Tera whirled in a circle on the table before them, very pleased with what had occurred. Ace's own droid had been necessary to make sure that Bitsy was fixed right. But her droid had seen a lot of injured creations, just like Bitsy.

Together, they were unstoppable. Ace tapped her finger on top of one of Tera's balls. "Nice job. I think that's all we needed."

Finally, Anya stirred. "Do you think she's going to be okay?"

"Yeah, she'll be fine. That personality of hers will come back in no time. We just have to wait for it to re-download, and that can sometimes take a while."

Anya lifted her head, those terrified and lost eyes finding Ace's. "What did you do to her just now?"

"I put her into rest mode. She'll be... essentially sleeping while she downloads everything that she lost. It's better for their processing core, and makes it a little easier on them to just wake up the way they previously were, rather than have to deal with the download while they're awake. It's sometimes a little stressful to try to accommodate the changes and new programming."

What she didn't want to admit was that it was also a little shocking for people to see. She'd only seen a droid get a new personality once while it was awake, and it had been careening about the room trying to figure out what it was supposed to be doing.

At the time, her professor had said some people likened the change to a seizure. She'd never forget seeing the poor thing like that. It had seemed so eerily in pain.

Mira knocked on the door and stepped into the room. "There's an undine here to see you," she said with a smile. "A yellow one."

"Maketes is back already?" She frowned and stood. "I thought he had to go debrief his brothers."

"It doesn't usually take long. From my understanding, there's something you're supposed to give me?"

Shit. He'd already told them she would just hand over the keycard? Ace felt her stomach twisting and a rolling vomit rise the back of her throat. Again, her mind screamed in fear that this wasn't the right thing to do.

Yet, her soul screamed that it was. She knew what was going to happen to them if she didn't. She knew that the key in the wrong hands would only cause chaos unlike anything this world had seen.

Jacob didn't deserve orders from the very best, but she had a feeling those in Tau might very well enjoy giving him those orders. He was an intelligent man, conniving and cruel. But they would know how to control a man like that and promise him all the things that he shouldn't have.

So she reached underneath her shirt and pulled out the keycard. It dangled from her grip, right there for everyone in the room to see. And finally she murmured, "I think this is what he means."

Mira's gaze had lit up with curiosity. "Now, what is that?"

"The key to Tau," she replied. "Apparently, there is another city. One that makes the decisions for all the others. I'm uncertain if this will open up a tracking beacon, though. It has a tracker on it."

Mira snatched it out of her grip and frowned down at the card. "Well, we can't hack into it here then. I refuse to risk this home, no matter what treasures we might find on this. Anya?"

"I'll tell Daios to get ready." The blonde had jumped up, although Ace felt bad that her back had been to her. Anya didn't know half of what was said.

And still, she was ready to leap into the fray. Both of these women were so sure of themselves, but even more sure of their partners. It made her feel a little strange.

Those thoughts must be all over her face. Mira took one look at her and then pocketed the keycard. "What's that expression?"

"What expression?"

"The one on your face right now." Mira pointed at her features and then waved her hand up and down. "Something is wrong."

"Nothing is wrong."

"You didn't look like that when you handed this card of world destruction over to me. But the moment Anya brought up Daios, you looked like the world ended. Did that big bastard say anything to you?"

Anya slapped Mira's hand out of the air. "Stop picking on him!"

"He almost killed me! Multiple times!"

"Get over it."

Ace held up her hand for silence as her mind swirled with what they were saying. "Daios almost killed you?"

"It was a long time ago, but yes. The red one doesn't like humans." Then Mira frowned at her. "You don't seem like you've met him yet, if that's confusing for you."

"I haven't met anyone yet. Maketes brought me right here."

The two other women looked at each other, and something seemed to pass between their gazes. Then they were both laser focused on Ace again, and that was the last thing she wanted.

She didn't like the looks in their eyes as they advanced on her. Both of them grabbed an arm each, and then they were dragging her from the mechanical room.

"Where are we going?" Ace asked, more than a little uncomfortable.

"First, I want to know why you look like that, and then we're going to introduce you to the rest of the people who live here. Because you should have been introduced the moment you swam up to our home." Mira tugged on her arm, and all three of them walked over to the living area where there were countless cushions to plop down onto.

With a little shove, Mira pushed until Ace was sitting down in the largest one and the two other women sat down right in front of her.

"Spill," Mira said.

"We just want to help if we can," Anya added, softening what she hadn't heard Mira say.

"If you aren't mad at Daios, then what is wrong with Anya bringing him up?" Mira pushed a little harder, and something snapped inside of her.

She was with friends. They weren't going to make fun of her. If anyone could understand her problem, then it was the women in front of her.

"I just don't know what Maketes and I are," she started, and then the words were a flood she couldn't contain. She went from wanting to hide her feelings, to needing to purge them right here and right now. "I know he wants me. I want him too. There's a strange connection between the two of us that I can't deny, even though it feels wrong that there's any connection at all. He's... what he is and I'm a human. I can't even promise him that we'll stay together for a long time, because we're from two different worlds. Even then, I don't know if he wants me to stick around. I have that keycard and I have information that you all need, but that means nothing when it comes to us."

Mira blinked a few times and then muttered under her breath, "Maketes, I thought you'd be better at this."

"Excuse me?"

Anya glanced over at Mira and firmly said, "Repeat."

Mira did, and then Anya looked back at Ace and nodded. "I also thought he'd be better at this. Of all the males here, he's the one who seems the most grounded. He's kind hearted, and he has never looked down on our people. He's been more intrigued by our differences than feeling as though he has to point them out."

Mira snorted, "Or be afraid of them. You'd be surprised how many undine are against having humans around just because of what they think we stand for."

"I met a purple one who seemed to not like me," Ace muttered.

Mira nodded. "Fortis. He's around often, but... Yeah. Not the best."

"Not at all. That one is terrifying." Ace shook her head and then shuddered. "I just don't know how Maketes feels."

Though she knew the words were hard, and that neither of the women could speak for him, she had hope that they could shed some light on this situation. And maybe it was her own insecurities holding her back. The last thread to snap before she tumbled headlong into...

Love, she realized. She might love him.

Mira leaned forward, braced on her elbows with her fingers linked. "Maketes has always been the one who seemed fine. He hides everything with humor, and while I find that entertaining, I see it for what it is. He's hiding something. Lately, he's seemed a lot worse. There's been more pranks, more antics, more jokes. Almost to the point where it feels like I can't talk to him at all. No one can have a real conversation with him because he takes nothing seriously."

That all made sense.

"I think he was sad," Ace replied. "He was watching everyone he loved find people to love, and he was alone in fearing that the things he saw in himself would only make people think less of him. He was sad and hiding and watching everyone else find the loves of their lives when he was convinced it would never happen to him."

Mira leaned back in her chair and shared a look with Anya. Then she shook her head, lips pressed into a straight, flat line. "That moron. He never sees himself as a catch. I look at him and I see the best person in the world, and all any of us have ever wanted was for him to be happy."

Ace sighed. "He knows that, in a sense. But he also knows that there are pieces of himself that some people wouldn't accept." She looked down at her hands, seeing her thighs beneath them. Larger thighs than most people found attractive. "I have a unique understanding of that."

There was a slight pause, and then Mira's hand covered hers. "Just tell him. Undine are remarkably stupid when it comes to relationships, because they don't do it themselves. Oh, and let him get you something. Even tell him to do it, if that makes you feel better. Gift giving is a huge part of this. If he hasn't already been hunting items for you."

She shook her head. "Nope."

"Well, he's doing it all wrong then, and that's probably why he's been feeling a little off. Undine have a very particular way of finding a mate. They hunt them, they feed them, and then they bring them treasures from the sea." Mira sat back and slapped her thighs. "That's all you have to do. Get him to give you a gift. I assume he's already hunted for you?"

"Yes, but I'm not particularly a fan of fish."

"Ah, well, that would make him feel a little odd too. Feeding their mates is a big deal."

She'd been doing this all wrong, obviously. Sighing, she pinched the bridge of her nose and tried hard to keep her mind from rambling through all the options ahead of her. "So, we've both been idiots not realizing that the other is trying to... whatever."

"You have to say the words if you want them to be real," Anya quietly replied.

So she did. She just let the words out. "I think I'm in love with him."

The ear piercing shrieks that came out of their mouths had her slamming her hands down over her ears. Narrowing her gaze, she stared at the two women who had just grabbed each other and were hysterically shouting. But still, it made her feel good, too.

Because it was exciting. These emotions made her feel... special.

She was in love with him. No one else. And maybe it was high time that she tell him.

Mira stood, patted her pocket in an obvious movement to make sure the keycard was still in her pocket, and then gestured for Ace to get up. "Come on. You go tell him that, and I'll figure out with Arges and Daios where we are going to plug this keycard in. There has to be some abandoned research facility that's still functional enough for me to do my work without someone coming and attacking us."

"Well," Anya replied, standing too. "Not attacking you until you crack into the keycard."

"Something like that." Mira was still grinning, though. "Nothing we can't handle or haven't handled before. You, however, are going to go get your man."

Yes. She was. She was going to tell him everything that had been plaguing her, and he was going to sit there and listen. Because one of them had to do this, and one of them had to be the person who made the leap.

If that had to be her, then fine. If he didn't return her feelings, which she hoped he did, then she would stay here with the other women. It wasn't like she had anywhere else to go. Her sister might even join them.

Maybe. If that's what Laura wanted.

She squared her shoulders, set her jaw, and nodded. "Right. If he's waiting, then I have a plan."

"What's the plan?"

"Tell him everything."

It wasn't really a plan, but an action that she needed to do. But as they strode through the hallways into the main chamber, she found her heart beating harder and sweat staining underneath her arms. Was she going to do this?

Adrenaline pumped through her veins, her breath nearly wheezing in her lungs. Then she saw him.

He was leaning against the edge of the moon pool, and the moment he saw her, all the lights on his body flashed bright and hot. She could have counted each glowing star on his form if she wanted to. But all she could see was the happiness in his expression and the relief in his gaze.

"There you are," he breathed. "When I heard all of you shrieking, I thought something was wrong."

No, nothing wrong, just a bunch of women having a moment. She shook her head, vowing to not let those words come out of her mouth before she tucked a short strand of hair behind her ear. "Can we talk? Somewhere private?"

She realized how bad those words sounded. She would have been terrified if he'd said that to her.

But he just grinned in that easy going way. "I was going to say the same thing. Care for an adventure before we crack the world in half, kefi?"

It was the only thing she wanted. So she reached out a hand and jumped into the water with him. No hesitations. No anxiety. No fear.

Just like he'd taught her.

Chapter 35

He had so much he wanted to say to her. But first, he had to do what his brothers had advised. The mating needs were riding him too hard, and right now, he needed to focus on fulfilling all the parts of himself that he had been denying.

He'd already stolen her. Brought her to the peak of desire. He'd fed her, made sure that she was well and safe and whole, but he had yet to find her a treasure that would show her just how much of a provider he was. What he needed was proof that he was better than all the others. Proof that he was the only one she should consider as her mate.

Such a task would make him feel better. Then he could know that he had done all that he could. After that, it was her choice to measure him and to decide if he was a valuable enough male or if she would choose another.

He hoped she would choose him. Forever. Even his people stayed mates if the male had survived the coupling. He'd never wanted to know what that was like, but now? Now he did. Now he had found a soft place to rest, and he wanted to dive so far into her body that neither of them knew where the other began.

"Maketes?" Ace asked, affixing his tentacle to her neck. "Where are you taking me?"

He'd already zipped away from the pod, just now realizing that he hadn't made sure she could breathe before he was carrying her off into the sea.

"Sorry," he muttered, running his finger over the gooey seal where his tentacle now pierced her skin. "I should have thought to do this first."

She smiled up at him. "It's all right. I know where it goes."

By all the gods, she was just the prettiest thing he'd ever seen. With those lovely round cheeks and a face that lit up his entire world, she was the sun in his entire world. She was his guiding light, and as he swam her through the sea and toward the surface, he hoped to show her the sun once more.

But as they got closer, he could see that a storm had already reached them. White foam sprayed even underneath the surface, the waves inverting on themselves and churning air into the water. There was nowhere above he could bring her that would be safe for them to talk, which was a shame.

If he was going to give her a gift, he wanted her to see it in the light of the sun.

"I'd thought to bring you to the surface," he muttered. "But I think that's going to be hard to do today."

"That's all right." She rested her hand against his chest, her fingers spreading over his hearts. "Would you take me to a cave again? I'd like to just talk."

Right, a cave. She'd said she wanted to talk before, and he hadn't thought much of it. Fine. If she wanted to talk, then he would give her the conversation of her life. After finding her a gift. After begging her to tell him that she wanted something, anything, in the ocean. He would spend months of his life finding it if she would just tell him a single thing that she actually wanted.

He knew a cave nearby. It was very close to the surface, but he didn't think the storm would affect it too much. The waves might be a little higher, but there should be plenty of room for her to sit. Plus, the entire thing was coated in glow worms.

Zipping through the sea, he brought her to the entrance and wiggled his way in. Ace wrapped herself around him like they'd done this a thousand times. When in reality, he supposed it was only a few times in her own towers.

Strange how long ago that felt.

Once inside, he popped up to the surface and expelled all the water through his gills. Sealing them, he took a deep breath for her to make sure that the air wasn't stagnant. But this close to the surface, the air was always much cleaner than some of the other caverns. Satisfied, he brought her to the edge and lifted her up onto the edge of the rock.

"Cold?" he asked, when he saw those goosebumps pop up on her arms.

She shrugged. "A little. But it's not too bad in here."

He could offer her something to warm her. Perhaps that would be a good gift. But the only things that would warm her would get wet on the way into this cave. A wet blanket wouldn't warm her...

Her hand reached out and curved around his jaw. "Maketes, I'm fine."

"I just want you to be comfortable."

And happy.

He wanted her to feel the joy he had named her after. She deserved that more than anyone else he'd ever met.

"I'm comfortable," she said with a laugh, drawing him closer to her.

And then he really looked. Just stared at all the golden light haloing around her head from the glow worms attached to the ceiling. The glimmering green from the water around him turned her skin paler than normal, an unusual shade that only made those brown eyes of hers look even more stunning. She was smiling down at him, her gaze softened with an emotion he couldn't name but one that echoed deep inside of him.

He couldn't stop himself. He circled her hips with his arms, staring up at her like she'd hung the sun.

"You're so beautiful," he said quietly. "Beyond what I ever expected when we first started talking."

That smile turned even brighter. "You say the sweetest things."

"I mean every word."

"I can tell." Her fingers toyed with the gills at the side of his face, watching them fan out and flutter for her. "I think... No, that's not the way to start it. I don't think. I am nervous that what we're doing is going to change our lives, and I want to make sure that nothing changes between us."

He wasn't following. "Why would anything change between us?" Then he held up his finger for her silence. "Wait, unless you mean because you'll be living here now and your things aren't here yet? I'll figure that out. We have our ways to get into the cities, obviously. You just tell me where you used to live."

"That's not what I meant."

"Ah, it's probably because there are other males of my kind here.

The People of Water are very welcoming, and you are unmated. There will be many males vying for your attention." All his gills snapped back against his face and he glared at some imagined male behind her. "You are not to entice them with your curves or your smiles."

"Maketes."

"What? I am allowed to request that you not look at other males. You're too pretty and they are too stupid for you." He nodded. "That's exactly the reason. The People of Water are good at many things, but I do not think there are any males that are a good match for you."

Other than him. Which was where he was trying to go with this, but now he'd made it sound like none of them would be a worthy match for her beauty. Had he talked himself into a corner?

"Maketes," she said with a laugh, gripping his head and making him look at her. "I don't want anyone but you."

She was squeezing his cheeks, so his words were garbled as he said, "That's good news."

"I don't think you understand what I'm saying. I want you. Only you. The idea of being with anyone else drives me crazy, and I know that no one will ever compare." She drew him even closer, her breath fanning over his lips. "I think I'm in love with you, you crazy undine."

She was still holding him a little too tightly, but that didn't matter. Because the moment she said she might love him, all of his lights flared brighter in the room. Everything inside him felt lighter. Better.

"You think?" he asked.

Her hands slid from his cheeks down to the gills on his neck. A bright red stained her cheeks as she replied, "I'm pretty sure."

"That's good, because I know I'm madly in love with you. I have been since that first moment I saw you jump into the water with me. From the moment I saw you face your fears and challenge the world head on. I was in love with you before we even said a single word to each other, and now having you beside me is my reason for breath. I didn't know I could need someone the way I need you, but now my need is endless."

"Stop talking," she whispered.

"I don't want to stop talking. I want to tell you a thousand more ways of how I love you. I only said it once so far, Ace. There are many more ways I could tell you. For example—"

She kissed him, and all the thoughts fled out of his head.

Those lips against his were the softest things he'd ever touched. He loved it when she did this. He loved kissing her and feeling her little inhalations when he surged forward so their chests were pressed against each other. He loved holding her, feeling her tiny hands pressing against both of his hearts that beat only for her.

He loved it even more when she made those little noises in the back of her throat. The little moans that filled the entire cave with the sound of her pleasure. The sounds that made him see stars and want to feast upon every part of her body. All of it and more was what he loved about her.

She was a fantasy come to life. Better than any dream he could have dreamt up with his own mind.

"I meant every word," he said against her lips, urging her backward until she was leaning against a stone. "I do love you."

"I know you do, Maketes. Because I love you, too."

"Fuck," he groaned, tilting his head back slightly before looking back at her.

By the gods, she was perfect. Those blush stained cheeks. Her lips were already red and swollen from his sharp teeth and little nips he couldn't stop giving her. She was breathing hard, those perfect breasts heaving with every single breath.

Spread out in front of him like this, she was a feast for the senses. Just the scent of her, that sunshine touched skin, drove him wild. But hearing her? Seeing her like this? All it made him want was to know what she tasted like right now. He wanted her desire to coat his tongue, and then he wanted to never leave that taste behind. He wanted her with him forever, every moment he dove into the water and every moment he was parted from her.

"Maketes?" she whispered.

"Yes, kefi?"

"I don't want to stop this time. I want to know what it feels like to have you inside me. I know that maybe that's rushing things, but..." Those cheeks burned even darker. "I want this to be forever, you know? Why not now?"

He blinked a few times, the words sinking in before he blurted out, "But I haven't brought you a gift yet."

Fuck, he hadn't. He was so stupid! He should have found one before bringing her here, because he was going about this all wrong. She needed a treasure. That was how it worked.

Kidnap, feed, treasures. It was always the same for every male and every pairing. If he didn't do all that, then would the sea even bless their union? He might bring about an age of storms underneath the sea if he did all of it wrong.

And he wanted this to be real. So badly. He wanted every ounce of her need and desire and want to be for him because he'd earned it. She deserved that much from him.

But she was looking up at him with a grin on her face that was so wicked it gave him pause.

She didn't usually look like that.

At least... Not without good reason. She'd looked at him like that when she'd sucked on his cocks and just the memory made him harder than he'd ever been in his life.

"What?" he finally asked. "What is that look for?"

"What look?"

"That look on your face that you usually only get right before you're about to do something mischievous." He leaned closer to her, nipping at her chin in the hopes to get her to talk. "What is on that beautiful mind of yours? Quickly, because I need to go find you a treasure that will convince you to say with me forever."

"I have a treasure in mind," she said, those talented fingers dancing down his chest. "And it's one that you don't have to leave to give me."

That... wasn't possible. Treasures had to be found. That was why they were treasures. A simple rock wouldn't do. If it was that easy to just grab whatever was nearby, then people would be mated all the time. But it wasn't that easy. It wasn't meant to be that easy.

But he couldn't focus all that well when her fingers were now at his stomach, toying with the grooves between his abs. "The treasure I'm thinking of is something only you have."

His breathing grew ragged. He was trying his best to remember he knew how to talk, but her fingers were at the edges of his scales now. "Do you want one of my gold scales? I can rip them off for you, but they grow back. I don't think they're worth all that much, either. It's not a treasure."

She waited for him to stop babbling before her fingers played over the largest scale that hid his cocks. She knew exactly where they were now, it seemed. Clever girl.

"No, Maketes. These. I want these as my gift."

These?

What were these?

He stared down at her, hoping his expression wasn't one of pure panic. He didn't know what she wanted and he could only pray that she would tell him soon, because he felt like he was falling apart at the seams.

A soft laugh escaped her, and then her fingers were toying with the seam that held him away from her.

She wrapped an arm around his neck and jerked him closer to her. Then she whispered in his ear, "Give me your cocks as a gift, undine. I want to feel them both inside of me."

By the sea, she always made him see stars.

Chapter 36

She could see the hesitation on his face. And then she realized that while she knew a lot about her own style of sex, she didn't know what undines even... did? She knew that he liked her mouth on him, and that he had cocks, but everything else was a mystery. He was an entirely different species, so she could only assume that meant he had different erogenous zones and other things that he preferred to happen during sex.

The hesitation at even initiating sex made her wonder if maybe those differences were more than she'd thought. Sure, she'd seen his cocks. She knew he had two of them and that gave her ideas for all sorts of possibilities. She'd even sucked him off, so she knew he wasn't poisonous to her—although she really should have thought of that before licking him.

So she had to imagine that there were just differences in sexual practices that made him nervous. Or things she didn't know.

What if he expected her to lay eggs?

She could feel her face pale at the thought. Oh god. What if he didn't know what sex even was?

No, that was a silly thought. He'd come in her mouth already and she knew that he didn't expect her to lay eggs. Unless maybe that had just been a precursor to the egg laying.

Better to just answer it all up front.

Swallowing hard, she motioned to draw him out of the water. "Is there anything I should know about... uh... sex with your kind?"

The stunned expression on his face hadn't moved. "No?"

"That sounded like a question."

"It is, I suppose. How does your kind mate?"

"With..." Her face was already bright red. Did she really have to have this conversation like this? "Well, you've already had your tongue in it, Maketes. Do I have to spell it out for you?"

"Oh." He nodded a little too vigorously. "Right. I remember."

Okay, he was far too distracted for her to ask questions. Because his eyes were on her tits and nowhere else, which she could only imagine meant conversing was out the window. At least until after the act.

She pulled on his arm, encouraging yet again for him to get out of the water because he was so stunned with everything she was suggesting that there wasn't much brainpower left for him.

Sighing, she watched as he stretched his body out on the stones. It didn't escape her notice that he chose to lay out on the sharpest ones, the ones that would likely have cut her skin if she was the one stretched out on their surface. Instead, he took the brunt of that pain. If he even felt it at all.

But it lay his body out for her to play with, and she would not complain about that. Because... well, look at him.

All those muscles were flexed, primed, and ready for whatever she planned to do. Those slabs of muscles called to her. Maybe she'd drag her tongue between the grooves of his belly. Or dig her nails into the flat planes of his pecs that bounced just at the mere suggestion of her gaze. She supposed she could tease him, tempt him, make him moan with every bit of what she did to him.

She hadn't felt like this ever in her life. This sexual dominance had never been who she was, but with his gaze on her like that, as though she was the most beautiful woman on the planet, she felt like she could do anything.

Ace pulled her shirt off, up and over her head. She could feel his gaze trailing along her body and, for the first time in her life, she didn't want to hide. She didn't care if he saw the softness of her belly, or the rolls on the sides when she sat a certain way. All she cared about was that he burned for her. His gaze devoured every bit. He didn't hesitate or skip over certain parts. He just looked at her and she could see the need in his eyes.

Those giant hands came up to cup her ribs, lifting her breasts and holding them together. "Look at you."

Yes, she wanted him to look at her. She wanted him to luxuriate in everything she was, because right now, she felt powerful.

Leaning down, she kissed him. Their tongues tangled, the ridges on his giving her all kinds of ideas of how to use them. Because she already had before. She'd felt those ridges sliding through her folds and knew how incredible it felt for him to be between her thighs. But right now, she just wanted to enjoy the power.

So she leaned down and indulged her senses in every part of his body. She grabbed onto his flexing shoulders, feeling the sheer power in them as he held himself back. She slid down his body, writhing over the ridges of scales that pressed against her in all the right places. She did exactly as she'd wanted to, dragging her tongue between the hollows of his abs and tasting the brine of the sea on his skin.

Then she slid even farther down, finding the scales that hid his cocks from her sight. He was doing such a good job hiding them, but up close, she could see the slightest parting of the scales where they pressed from deep inside.

"Are you going to let them out?" she rasped, her mouth already watering for them.

"I had planned on enjoying you for a little while first," he growled, but then his hips bucked as though he couldn't stop himself.

Her fingers toyed with the slight opening, sliding against the delicate flesh that was revealed beneath the scales. "What would happen if I licked you here? Would that feel good?"

He stared down the muscles of his body at her, already panting. Every breath flexed the gills at his ribs and still, he looked at her like he was starving. "I honestly don't know," he growled before they popped right out of those scales.

She'd forgotten how glorious his cocks were. Of course, she'd only seen them up close the once, but really she wasn't sure how she'd forgotten the massive length of them. The gray skin glistened in the light, the slickness looking like oil in the sunlight. The sheen of them was even more captivating because she could only guess at how they would feel.

She wanted him to drown in her, just like she was drowning in him. So she wiggled higher up his tail and cupped her breasts on either side of his cocks. The soft slide of him past her skin was tantalizing, but she was more interested in the sound he made when he did so.

He arched his back, those hips almost trying to get away from her as his eyes screwed up tight. All of his gills flared wide again, fluttering so hard she worried they might break. He was such a picture of desire.

With his head thrown back, the tendons of his neck tight as she worked him with her breasts. Up and down, slowly. Both of his cocks pressed against each other so they were both enveloped in slick heat.

There was that feeling of power again. She was more than in control. She played his body like she was a musician and he was her instrument. The groans and moans that escaped from his mouth were the song she made.

His webbed hands grabbed at the rocks, holding on for dear life as she showed him a pleasure she was damn well certain no undine had ever shown him. Then he was reaching down, grabbing onto her and hauling her up his body. Every inch of her slid against his cocks, though, certainly something he hadn't thought about because he let out a little whimper before kissing her harder than he had before.

"You have to stop," he panted, pleading with her. "I want to enjoy you and every moment of this."

"Are you not enjoying yourself?" she asked, leaning back to pull off her pants. When she was bare against him, she pressed herself against the warmth of his belly.

He arched underneath her, spreading her slickness over his skin as though he couldn't get enough of her. "Too much. Enjoying myself too much, kefi."

"Isn't that a good thing?"

Those webbed fingers speared through her folds, pressing against her clit and rubbing there almost frantically. Like he needed her to enjoy herself. Like he wanted to feel her pleasure just as much as she had given him.

He grabbed onto her waist, lifting her easily as he turned her around. Flat on her belly, she stared down at his cocks while her pussy was presented to his gaze. She only had a second to feel slightly uncomfortable being so spread before he made that sound of pleasure again.

"Suck, kefi, I'm done behaving."

Crack.

His hand smacked first one side of her ass, then the other. Again, another round of smacks until she reached for his cocks and sucked the first one into her mouth. She ran her tongue along the head, moaning as he dove for her pussy and feasted.

His tongue was everywhere. No skill. No finesse. Just pure, unadulterated need for the taste of her all over him. She groaned again, feeling those ridges on his tongue rub over her clit, back and forth, flicking so many times she felt like she was going to lose her mind.

He speared her. His tongue sinking deep inside of her, sliding in and out, the thickness of it and those ridges doing something that she'd only thought toys could do. She hadn't realized... she didn't think...

She leaned off of his cocks, breathing hard as she whimpered, "So good. You're so good at that."

The vibration of his answering growl nearly sent her into oblivion. But she didn't want to fall first. She wanted him to come so hard that he would never forget this moment.

Until she remembered that she was in control here. That while he might want to be in control, he wasn't.

Drawing away from him, she felt a shiver of need trail down her spine when he made a sound in the back of his throat, like she had taken away something precious. Something... She turned around on him and suddenly couldn't think as she saw that long, black tongue dart out. He licked at his lips like he had just drank the finest of creams.

Her eyes rolled back in her head, but she could not let him distract her like this. She had a purpose. She had a plan. So she turned around on him, planted her hand on his chest, and then reached between them.

"I have always wanted to try this," she said with a soft gasp as the head of him brushed against her pussy. The heat that poured from him seared her to the bone.

"Try what?" he asked, bucking up against her like he couldn't control himself.

"Two at once."

She breathed the words out like a prayer, and then notched him in both places. She'd dreamt about this before. Never with a human man, but always with some dark, shadowy figure that filled her dreams with broad shoulders and heated words.

Maketes's hands came down on her hips, his breathing ragged and his eyes a little wild. "Wait, hang on."

Even though it was strange to hear those words, she froze and waited for him to continue. The look in his eyes was more than just passion now. There was the slightest hint of panic.

"What is it?"

"I've never..." He swallowed hard, his throat bobbing. "I've never done this before."

The words came to a screeching halt in her mind. He'd never...

Did he mean he'd never done this?

She opened her mouth and the words that fell out were, "What do you mean you've never done this before?"

"My people are violent in mating, and few males survive afterward. I am a smaller male, very attractive to the opposite sex because of my size and the ease with which they would beat me. But I wanted to live. I knew I likely wouldn't come out of such a battle without..." He swallowed again, and she thought maybe this time it seemed more like a gulp. "I don't know what I'm doing."

There it was. The truth of his anxiety. Because he didn't know what he was doing, and suddenly this was all so overwhelming. Before, he'd been the one playing her body. But right now, he just needed reassurance that this wasn't going to be like with the others.

She leaned down, brushing her lips against his. "I promise I will be gentle. Nothing about this has to be violent, not unless you want it to be."

"I really don't want it to be," he murmured.

"Then I will be soft. I will be gentle."

"Soft," he groaned, his head hitting the stone behind him. "You really are so soft."

"Can I keep going?"

At his jerking nod, she slid down. Working herself over him. The first inch of him stretched her near to bursting, but she was a determined woman and she'd never been a quitter. The second inch slid a little easier, and then the third was almost too wide. She was panting now, a sweat breaking out as she lifted herself and plummeted, each time taking more and more of him.

She was so full. Stuffed beyond thinking, beyond existing. All she could feel was the sensation of him, the fullness, the slick slide as he plunged deeper and deeper into her body. Her mind fractured, her breathing becoming even faster, her heart thundering in her chest.

Then she was there. Her clit pressed against the scales of his tail and she could breathe again. Taking in a deep lungful, she finally looked up at him to see that wide-eyed gaze.

"You take me so well," he said, his voice tinged with wonderment. "You've never been more beautiful."

Maketes reached out a hand and pressed it against her belly. She looked down to see a bulge there. A bulge that was him inside of her.

She could feel him throbbing in both her pussy and her ass, feel the heat of him as he pulsed again and again.

She lifted, and he hissed out a long, disappointed sound. Freezing, Ace looked at him with a question in her eyes.

"I just..." He hesitated before blurting. "I thought it would be longer than that."

"Maketes," she said with a slight laugh before nearly lifting herself off of him. "It's only just begun."

She let herself fall. Dropping down on him with all the force of her weight, and watched as his eyes widened. She lifted herself again, the slow slide that had both of them moaning before falling. Again and again. Landing harder and harder each time.

He'd never done this. She didn't even know if his kind did this at all. But now, she got to watch his eyes roll back in his head as pleasure overtook him. She pounded down on him, feeling every inch of him sliding deeper and deeper.

Her muscles clenched. She could feel an orgasm grinding through her, ripping through her entire body and throwing her into oblivion. Ace stopped breathing. Stopped thinking. She was pretty sure she stopped being for a huge portion of it. Time slowed and stopped as she bent over him, taking him as deep as he could go.

She moaned, the sound echoing around them, and then suddenly, she felt him pulsing inside her as well. She could feel the thick ropes of his cum as he painted her insides, the deep, guttural sound he made echoing along with her moan.

It was the most sublime and beautiful moment she'd ever endured. Feeling him seeking out his pleasure, feeling the kick of his hips as he ground himself just a tiny bit deeper, as deep as he could go.

Panting, she stared down at him in amazement. She hadn't known it could ever be that good. Ace had come plenty of times in her life, but that? That wasn't just an orgasm. That was two souls intertwining.

He cupped her jaw, clearly feeling the same way. He drew her down until their foreheads were pressed together, both of them breathing hard enough that the air between them fogged.

"I was supposed to give you a gift," he whispered. "But you are a gift from the sea itself, kefi. My joy. You make me so happy."

Some broken part of her that had never felt wanted or needed clicked back into place. And oh, Ace's soul *glowed*.

Chapter 37

Somehow, that perfect, beautiful woman had stolen his soul. He knew perhaps it was a silly thing to say, but he'd felt that way after leaving her in that warm cavern, heated by the mess of their pleasure. He had to find his brothers. They would meet somewhere. He could only assume that was the plan, and he wanted Ace to be with them when they finally unlocked what that keycard hid.

But first he wanted to get her warm. Fed. Pampered as she deserved.

The heated feeling in his chest had only exploded after what she had done. What they had done.

And even more than that, she'd said she loved him. Him. The male who no one wanted because he couldn't give them children. He couldn't give her children either, although he didn't know if his people and hers were even compatible in that way. All he knew was that she didn't care.

Some part of her had looked into his soul, seen all the things he despised, and she did not care. He loved her beyond reason, but he'd never dared to hope that she would ever feel the same way. Now that he knew she did? He felt as though he could lift the entire world on his shoulders.

Before he could make it back to their pod, a dark shape approached him. He thought for a moment it was Fortis, but quickly realized it was Fortis's son instead. The boy rushed toward him, tail flicking and powering him through the water.

"What is it?" Maketes asked, his voice lowering into a growl. "Has something happened?"

"No. They are preparing to use the key." The young male paused before him, fins flaring wide to keep him still. "They did not want to do so without you and your female."

"They sent you to find me?"

"They did. I was the one who sought out her sister as well. My father requested that the task be transferred to me after the original depthstrider found your achromo's blood."

His stomach twisted, and he felt like he may vomit. "What news?"

"We moved her. They were already tracking her through the city, and your achromo's criminals grew tired of waiting for her to return. I took her before they could kill her in her sleep, but it has made Beta mad at us again." Fortis's son shuddered. "It is a shame. That city was once safer to be around, but now it is dangerous again."

"Because of you?"

With a slightly arched brow and an arrogant flick of his tail, the male started away from him. "No, because of you and your achromo. I placed her sister in the village near our pod, but the others are waiting for you in the abandoned research facility at the edge of the abyss. It is the closest one to depthstrider territory. My father wished to be there to see what this key holds secret."

Of course he did. The depthstrider would stop at nothing to know every detail that anyone else knew. Fortis had to have his fins coiled around everything.

But if they were opening the keycard soon, then they wouldn't have time for him to pamper Ace. He'd wanted to shower her with gifts this morning, more than just the gift of his cocks.

Fuck, already he was getting hard again just thinking about her saying that. He needed to get himself under control.

Turning, he swam through the sea and caught a current back to her side. They had no equipment, nothing to keep her warm in the depths where they were going.

So he would have to be fast. Faster than he'd ever swam before.

What a welcome challenge it would be. No one was faster than him, after all. Now, he got the opportunity to prove that.

She was waiting for him when he swam back up into the cave. Sitting on the edge of the water, with her arms wrapped around her legs as she usually did. A soft smile appeared when she saw him, and he didn't have to say anything at all.

"They're opening it now?" she guessed.

"They are."

"So we need to go."

"We do." He reached for her even as disappointment tinged his words with slight sadness. But this was no place for them to linger, anyway. No matter how magical the sparkling glow worms made her skin.

Gathering her up, he spoke as she affixed the breathing tube to her neck. "We are going somewhere very, very cold. I will try to get you into the facility fast enough, but tuck your feet into my gills for now. I will keep you as warm as I can, kefi, but I don't think it's going to be very comfortable for you."

"That's all right." She snuggled in tighter. "You're always warm enough for me."

His hearts glowed ever brighter at her words. It was blazing hope that they would be fine no matter what happened. As he sank with her into the depths of the sea, holding her tightly so the currents didn't rip her away from him, he swore he could feel the sea itself helping. The goddess that he worshipped pushed him forward, moving him ever faster until even he felt like just a blur. No one could keep up with him if they tried, and soon enough, the facility bloomed out of the darkness before him.

He'd been here as a child with Arges. They used to play in these waters, flirting with the idea that they would fight a depthstrider. Not that any of the creatures had risen to their challenges, but he assumed they had been watching. All they would have seen were two young males, flaring their fins wide and bursting with pops of color as though they had any muscles on them yet.

Now, they were two beasts who fought anything in the sea that wished to battle them. He and his brothers were more terrifying than any in the pod, and yet, he wasn't sure how proud he was of that.

Holding the achromo in his arms that meant more to him than life itself, he had to wonder how wrong he'd been. At that time, he'd wanted nothing more than to hunt her people. Now? He would do anything to keep her happy.

Darting to the moon pool, he practically threw her out of the water and into the room beyond. Mira was waiting. She caught Ace, who stumbled across the slick floor and wrapped her up in a blanket.

"I got you," Mira said when Ace started to struggle. "I got you.

Let's get you warm, droid builder, yeah? Get some of that ice out of your veins. That'll help."

He stayed in the water, watching with concern as his achromo's teeth began to chatter. How hadn't he noticed that her lips had turned blue? Or that her skin was even paler than normal?

He'd been so focused on swimming, and swimming fast, that he hadn't realized she'd gone so still. So quiet. Or maybe he had realized it, but he was so caught up in his own thoughts that he hadn't... realized.

Mira gave him a curt nod, waving at him with her hand. "It's too small of a facility. We set up in front of a window so everyone could hear. Your brothers are out there."

"But she's—"

"She's fine, Maketes. This is what we sign up for when we stay with you." Mira gave him a small, tight smile and then waved at him again. "We'll get her warm."

He hated to leave her, especially when he felt like he'd done something wrong, but he still sank back into the water and headed out to find this window. It didn't take long. Three large males were clustered around it, each of them jostling to get closer. But he refused to be stuck in the back. Wriggling up between them, he made sure he was the closest to the window.

"It's about time you got here," Daios grumbled. "I'm tired of being in these depths. Too close to the sulfur smelling bastards."

"You like us well enough," Fortis replied. "We got you where you are today."

He could feel the tension building in the water. If he wasn't careful, these two were going to tear each other to pieces. "Stop it. I want to hear what the women are saying."

It was Arges's hand on his shoulder that calmed him, though. His brother had always been good at doing that. With just a touch, Arges spread that calm throughout the body of anyone who was near.

"She's fine, brother," Arges said, that deep voice sinking through his anxiety. "They are hardier than they look."

"I remember you told Daios that they are more delicate than we could imagine."

"Because Daios needed to hear that. They are fragile creatures. Easily broken if one doesn't watch them carefully. But you watch yours too carefully, little brother. Now I am telling you that they are stronger than we give them credit for."

He had to take it to heart. He knew how strong Ace was. He'd seen it with his own eyes. Her muscles, her ability to take whatever was thrown at her and continue forward happily. All of it was far beyond what he had thought she could do.

And still. He feared for his mate.

He didn't settle until Ace wandered into view. She had different clothes on, and a crinkly metallic material covering her shoulders. But her lips were no longer blue, and she clutched a cup in her hand that was steaming.

"What did they give her?" he asked, a low growl rumbling through his chest.

"It's just hot water. They found it when we got here. Apparently, one of the replicators is still functioning." Arges squeezed his shoulder. "Calm yourself. No one is hurting her."

It felt like he was the one hurting her. But then he had to focus, because Mira sat down in front of the window and held the keycard up. "Everyone ready?"

No. He wasn't. He wouldn't ever be ready for this.

But he could feel the energy from behind him as all the males gathered themselves, ready for whatever would come from it.

Mira lifted a small device and then picked up Byte. The little droid backed right up to the window and then reached out its metal claw for the keycard. He'd forgotten that Byte was capable of that.

"Wait," Anya said. She pulled Bitsy off her head. "She said she has a protocol that should keep anyone from knowing where we are. I'm not sure if Tau has better technology than Alpha did, but it's worth a try."

Bitsy clambered over to Byte, then wrapped herself around the other droid. Even from here, he could see the little hearts floating on the lens that Bitsy held. She really adored Byte, and he was sure it was no task for her to plug herself into him.

Then Ace stepped forward too, pulling Tera from her pocket where she always kept the little bead droid. "There's a few protocols on Tera that might be helpful as well. They can't block anything from coming through, but they can scatter any messages. So... can't hurt."

Tera joined the other two droids, and then Mira plugged the keycard into a slot in the front of Byte's belly.

They all held their breath. Waiting to see what happened.

Nothing.

Nothing happened for long heartbeats and Maketes was sure he'd gathered them all for a stupid reason. This wasn't useful at all. It was a key to nothing. And then a chirp from Byte. A rumble of noise, and a sudden projection up onto the glass.

Words. So many words. Mira reached up and scrolled through some of them, her fingers touching the glass as though it were a screen.

"Schematics," she said, her voice filled with awe. "All the cities they... they have deeper portions. They weren't just built on top of the ground, they have roots that stretch deep into the stones. They blasted into the base of the stone that surrounds each city. There are hidden bases in every city."

Anya stepped up to another portion, her gaze narrowed in concentration as she pulled a separate square over to her side of the glass. "It's worse than that. Look at this."

She tapped the glass, and suddenly there were pictures thrown up on the wall. Photographs of his own people, torn apart with their guts hanging out of their bellies and notes all along the sides. Dead People of Water. Murdered in cold blood with far too much knowledge about their species spread out on metal tables.

Fortis hissed and a faint sickly yellow illuminated the images in front of them.

"It wasn't just my father experimenting on the undine," Anya said. "These documents are from a much more advanced facility. See the tools? I haven't seen tools like that ever, and I lived in Alpha."

But then Ace spoke, and he felt his hearts leap into his throat. Because she had pulled a square over to her side and tapped on it. All the other projections disappeared, and in their wake was the image of two achromos.

A man and a woman. A man with a sharp jaw and a hard expression, with a scar on his cheek that looked like a knife wound. The woman had her dark hair severely pulled back, but even her gaze was cruel. Suddenly, the image of them moved.

"Anyone who is in possession of this keycard needs to be aware of two things," the man said. "First, you are now in service to the city of Tau. If you deny being in service to us, then we will find you. We will replace whoever owns that keycard and we will dispose of your body. Second, we already know where you are, who you are, and every detail about you. Third, we will give you unimaginable power if you work with us."

The woman leaned a little closer, her hand coming up and tossing markings out from their projection to hover before them. "These are our coordinates. Don't think for a second you can attack this city. We have weapons unlike any you have ever seen before. We are the originators. We are those who built this city. Defy us, and we will come down on you with all the knowledge of more than two hundred years of life."

The projection disappeared, leaving only the strange squares again.

"The originators?" Mira repeated. "What the fuck does that mean?"

Ace clicked the next square that was beside her and pulled up a document. The women read it together, their faces growing paler and paler the longer they took.

"What?" Arges snarled. "What is it?"

"The originators," Ace finally replied. "They're the original people who created... all of this."

"That's not possible," Anya argued.

"You're looking at it, Anya. You're looking at it!" Ace yelled the last piece, her hands shaking as she set the cup in her hands down. "They cloned themselves. They replaced their broken bits with the fucking remains of those clones. They've been here the whole time, because they never let themselves die."

The words hung before them, and he couldn't fathom what that meant.

Tapping on the glass, he had all the women look at him. Then he asked, "What does that mean? They didn't let themselves die?"

Chapter 38

She stayed in that hidden research facility for hours with the other two women. The undines were quick to get them food and Arges apparently had some idea of transporting blankets to them so they could continue working. Fortis was the only one who remained behind, and she swore he was reading through the glass even though the others assured her that none of the undine could read their language.

Not that it mattered. The documents that were on this keycard were so horrific, it was hard to think straight.

The undine deserved to know what was here. They deserved to know who their real enemy was and that their battle wasn't over yet. But she thought the rest of her people deserved to know, too.

So while Anya and Mira gathered all the useful information they could, Ace took her droid aside and worked with Byte. Together, the three of them ripped apart all the documentation and historical information that would sink the people who were tied with Tau.

At least, she hoped it would.

Anya staggered over to her, Bitsy now affixed to her face. "What are you up to over here?"

"Making a video. Just like we had planned to do for your father," Ace muttered, making a few tweaks to what Byte had already suggested.

"Do you really think that's going to work?"

"It has to." She warped a bit more of the video, using more of the images that were attached to the keycard. Ripped up undine. Torn apart human bodies. All the terrifying things that no one should ever do and yet, somehow, these people thought it was okay that they had done so. They'd even recorded it.

Anya's hand came down over hers, stilling her fingers as she worked on the projection. "Ace. I don't know if this is going to work."

"You don't understand. If this doesn't work, then it means there are no good people left. If anyone can look at this video, this massacre of the human and undine form, and still feel like it was the right choice, then what monsters have we become?"

Ace felt the weight of everything they had discovered sink onto her shoulders. Because there was so much of it.

She threw up the video that she'd put together. Big. The entire glass wall was suddenly taken up with the sights and images.

"Byte, record my voice," she said.

Mira walked up to them, her arms crossed over her chest. And as a trio, they watched the images of carnage unfold before them.

"This is Tau," Ace said. "This is the city that has survived longer than any of us realized. A city deep in the sea, making decisions for you. Not in your best interest, not for your life to be easier. This city only has one thing in mind."

The images changed to the vision of the founders of each city. Beta, Alpha, Gamma, even the ruins of Omega. Faces that they'd all grown up with, worshipping the ingenuity of the people who had brought humanity under the sea. The faces warped into ones that looked eerily similar but were laid out in stasis pods, each one filled with seemingly the same person.

"These people used us as fodder for their experiments. Their clones exist in captivity. The originators, as they call themselves, have been ripping people apart. These are not just broken little toys for them to tear out hearts and lungs and plasma to keep them alive for longer than any human should have any right to. They are killing people. Actual people." Ace's voice broke.

Again, the images changed. This time, they showed all the research facilities that had been hidden by Tau. All the tubes filled with the bodies of the undine, not just torn apart, but laid out on research tables with their organs floating in beakers beside them.

"What you see here exists right underneath your feet. In every city, there is another city beneath it. Teeming with people and research teams who have hunted the People of Water and torn them apart. Tau wants more than just immortality in the form of replacing pieces of their broken bodies. They want the longevity of the undine. They have been researching this species for over a hundred years and soon, they will make a hybrid that they will use to their own advantage."

She swallowed hard. Looking at the images made her stomach turn, because they could so easily be Maketes.

Slowly, she zoomed in on the face of a bright green undine. His eyes were closed, and to the unsharp eye, he might even look peaceful. Until one looked a little closer. A smear of blood on his cheek marred that handsome face that was so eerily human.

With her voice thick, she finished her speech. "If you can look at this person and not feel anything, then how far have you fallen under

Tau's spell? These are not animals. They look like us. They feel like us. They have families and hopes and dreams. We have been taking those away from them. So the question I ask you all is, can you live with yourself now that you know the truth?"

A small click echoed in the room as Byte stopped recording.

His head popped out of the box, the binocular eyes looking at all three of the women before him. "Mira? Shall I transmit to all the cities?"

"They'll never play it," Mira replied.

Tera rolled around Byte and clacked a few times. Ace picked her droid up and gently deposited it back into her pocket. "My droid can hack into anything, and already did. You say the word, and all of this will be broadcasted onto every single screen in the remaining two cities. They won't be able to stop it until it's played three times. Then the message will disappear, even from their records."

Anya shook her head. "You think Tau will let us do that?"

Ace shrugged. "I don't think they've discovered where we're coming from yet. If they knew where the message was being transmitted from? Yes. They could stop it. But they don't know we're in this facility. Not yet, at least."

She could see there was only one person she needed to convince, though. Because Mira wasn't looking at her. Mira was looking out the door at Fortis. The massive undine hovered in front of the window, his arms crossed over his chest, and she was certain he was looking into her soul.

There were three lights approaching behind him. Blue, red, and yellow. She only had a little time before the overprotective brigade ruined everything.

Stepping up to the glass to make sure he heard her, she looked him right in the eye. "You know this is the right thing to do."

Those dark eyes swirled with too many colors to count. "You risk letting Tau know where we are. Once that transmission is sent, they will send the full weight of their power upon this facility. Your message may not even make it to the cities."

She narrowed her eyes, knowing those colors were coming from the place Maketes had talked about. Where the sea itself gave him a vision of the future. "What if I encode it? What if I send it through a droid, not a building?"

Mira hissed out a long breath. "Ace."

"What if a droid was the one sending the message?" she asked again, her fingers creeping into her pocket.

Those colors swirled again, and he just nodded. "If you do that for us, I will keep your sister safe. She is with our people now, but I will ensure she is even safer than that."

Everything in her twisted. "You have my sister?"

Ace reached for the console in front of her, bracing herself against it in shock. Because if he had her sister, that meant that Laura was alive. Jacob hadn't killed her. Laura wasn't even in Beta anymore.

She could see her sister again. She could hug her. She could hear someone call her Maura again, even though she hated the name.

But if a droid was sending the message, then it would have to be a sacrifice. She pulled Tera out, tears building in her gaze as she looked down at the beads that all turned their faces to look at her.

Breathing in a ragged breath, she whispered, "It was always going to end like this, wasn't it? My oldest friend. I cannot make this decision for you."

Tera clacked a few times and then seemed to head toward Byte. The other droid reached out its arm and gently slotted Tera against his side. The glass cleared in front of them, and then words replaced the video she had made as Tera spelled out words.

I love you.

Let me do this for you.

A sob broke free, and Ace slapped her hand over her mouth. She stared at the words, imprinting them on her memory so that she would never forget the bravery of this droid. The one and only thing that would save her people for good.

Mira reached out and took her hand, squeezing it. "Your droid is remarkable."

"Yes," she whispered. "They really are."

The other undines joined them, and she could see the troubled expression on Maketes's face through the glass. Something had happened. They were rushing toward them too fast, and all of them looked angry in some measure.

"I think we've run out of time," Anya said, placing her hand on the glass for a second before turning. "We have to decide what to do now."

"We send the message," Ace said, determination hardening every muscle in her body. "We must have faith that there are still good people out there. That even with all the struggles they've been through, there are enough people in the cities who will look at this tragedy and see it for what it really is."

She made eye contact again with Fortis through the glass. All those swirling colors had stilled, and finally, he nodded. It was all the reassurance she needed.

This was the path forward. She would stride down it with confidence, even if it meant she had to lose something she dearly loved.

Grabbing Tera from Byte, she placed the droid in her pocket. Instantly, the entire room flooded with movement. Bitsy held onto

Anya's head as her owner stripped down and started shoving her limbs into a wetsuit. It was the first time Ace noticed there were three laid out by the moon pool, just waiting for them.

Mira started boxing Byte up, closing all his compartments with rushed movements. "Go ahead of me, Ace. I'll get this place all set up."

"Why?"

"I think we've been found out."

She raced for the wetsuit, setting Tera on the ground while she shoved her limbs into the stretchy fabric. Daios was already in the moon pool, reaching for Anya the moment she was ready.

It brought more tears to Ace's eyes, seeing how gentle the big man was with Anya. Yeah, he was kind of an ass. He'd been gruff and hard to deal with, but he loved Anya. That much was so obvious.

Maketes's head appeared next to his brother, right before he lunged out of the water. He propped himself up next to her, the sea splashing up and over her knees as he reached for the wetsuit to help.

"Quickly now," he muttered, forcing one side up and over her shoulder and nearly lifting her off the ground. "They're coming."

"Who?"

Mira blasted past her, handing Byte over to Arges, who tucked the droid under his arm. She was faster at putting the wetsuit on, but she'd had a lot more practice than everyone else. "Tau," Mira grumbled. "I wasn't as good at hiding us as I thought."

"How do you know it's Tau?" Ace asked, but then she turned and saw what was coming for them.

Lights in the distance. So many of them they looked like a giant band of white. So many lights that all she could think was that those were the people who were going to... Fuck.

"Oh, we're so screwed," she muttered, yanking the last bit over her shoulder and zipping the suit up to her chin. Tera clacked at her feet, and she gripped the droid in her fist.

"You're with the fastest male you could find. We'll be fine." Maketes's hands landed on her waist. "The others, though? I pray they learn how to swim."

Arges gave his brother a dirty look and yanked Mira into the water. It was rather strange to watch someone else put a tube in their throat. Ace watched Mira's throat bulge with the tentacle in it and wondered if that's what her own looked like. It was a surreal thought as Byte poked his head out one last time. He threatened ruining his functions with water, all to toss out a few words of wisdom.

"I transferred all information from the keycard to a secret location. Your droid absorbed the tracking of the keycard, but all information is now maintained within Bitsy and myself."

Those tears burned again. "Thank you, Byte."

Arges and Mira sank underneath the churning waves and then Maketes dove in with her as well. She could feel the cold sinking over her head, and everything inside of her burned.

He held her close to his hearts, closer than she'd ever thought possible. She curled into him, needing to be held and reassured that they were going to be okay.

"What's the matter?" he asked. "They aren't going to catch up to us."

She pointed toward the dark abyss. "I need you to bring me to the deepest part of the ocean. There's one last thing we need to do."

He didn't question her. He just drew her deeper and deeper into the sea. All the lights went out, and that made her feel even worse. Tera moved in her palm, though she could barely feel it through the wetsuit, and she wished that her hands were free. She wanted to hold her friend, knowing that the loss of them would forever mark her soul.

When Maketes finally paused, she lifted Tera up to her face so she could look at the little droid in the faint light glow of Maketes's scales. "You have been my best friend since I was a child. Every step of the way, you were here for me. Letting you go is the hardest thing I've ever had to do."

"What?" Maketes asked. "What are you doing?"

"Tera has the tracking on it. The signal for the video to be transmitted to all the cities. If we want to promote even the promise of an uprising against Tau, Tera has to do it. And we can't keep running." Already the lights of Tau were so much larger. They only had a few moments for this goodbye. "We're dropping them in the sea, Maketes. The abyss will keep them safe until Tau can find them, but it won't be easy to find something smaller than a thumb print. It's the best chance we have. Each bead will fall separately, and the message will be sent with each bead."

Tera rolled in her fingers, looking at Maketes and then her. Two of the magnetic balls detached and snuggled up to her thumb, almost as though the droid was hugging her.

Maketes's hand came down on top of hers, trapping the droid between them. "We'll never get them back, Ace. If you drop them... they're gone."

"I know," she whispered. If she had been above water, tears would have streamed down her cheeks. Instead, all she could feel were her eyes growing painfully hot.

"You don't have to do this. We will find another way. You do not have to sacrifice any more than you already have."

She hiccuped, drawing water into her mouth before expelling it roughly when she remembered he was breathing for her. "I know."

He peeled his hand away from hers, and she looked down to see that Tera had gathered all of its pieces together in a small cluster. As though the five pieces wanted to see each other one last time before an eternity alone at the bottom of the sea. All by themselves. Without anyone to talk to them or joke with them or bring them on adventures.

Another sob wracked through her chest. "I can't do it," she said, staring at her dearest friend. "I can't do it."

Tera bumped against her thumb one last time, and then all five pieces rolled off her palm. Ace tried to catch it, but the weight of the droid dropped through the water faster than she could move. They disappeared out of sight, and she felt like she'd left a piece of her soul behind.

Another sob. Another cry that echoed through the water as she screamed out her loss. Because even though it was the right thing to do, she had never felt such pain.

Maketes scooped her against his hearts and then swam. Faster and faster. Behind him, she could see the lights of Tau were even brighter. Then the little zips of lasers firing at them, but Maketes was too fast. He swam like the sea itself guided him, and all she could think was that her entire life had been about sacrifice. She just wanted, for a few moments more, to not have to sacrifice *everything*.

Chapter 39

Ace didn't know how long they traveled through the ocean, only that they eventually shook the soldiers of Tau. The lights disappeared in the distance, just like the shattered feeling of her heart. Eventually, she became just as numb as her body. The cold of the sea settled in her chest, sinking through her very flesh and bone until she felt like she didn't care about anything anymore.

It was nice to exist in that place for a little while. It didn't feel like she was doing anything wrong, and she wasn't hurting anyone but herself. Because she knew it wasn't healthy.

Logically, she could look at what she'd done as the right choice. She needed to let Tera do the job that they had always wanted. Her droid only had one function, and that was to be of use. The fact that it could save not just her, but so many other people? Of course it was going to take that role happily.

But then her mind would scatter into the darker thoughts. Tera was just going to be alone down there. In the icy cold, knowing that time was passing, but that it was on its own. Worst-case scenario, Tau found her droid. And if they did, they would tear her droid apart for whatever it hadn't wiped from its own memory yet.

Because she knew that's what Tera would do. It wouldn't give any information up about her, and that meant it had to start destroying itself on the way down.

Maketes's arm tightened around her, and she could feel the ache in him as well. He wanted to fix what was broken, but he didn't know how.

Neither did she.

After all they had been through together, this was the most broken that she'd ever felt. Her droid. Her best friend. All of it had been traded to save a sister who she wasn't even sure wanted to be saved. What if Laura was happy down there? What if she had wanted to stay in Beta?

"Kefi?" Maketes asked, his voice pitched low and gentle.

She nodded against his neck, then buried her face in his gills. The thought of facing anyone or anything right now stung.

"We're here."

"Where is here?" she breathed against his skin.

Hopefully, somewhere she could pretend the world didn't exist for a little while. If she could take some time to herself, she could piece all of these shattered bits back together. All she needed was a few minutes to herself and then she would crawl out of this dark hole.

"This is where Fortis had his son bring your sister," Maketes said. "I thought, perhaps, you would like to see her now."

One half of her soul screamed "Yes!" and the other half wasn't so sure. What if Laura was disappointed to see her? The 'what ifs' could swallow her whole if she let them.

He had taught her to be brave, though. Maketes had always believed she was braver than she'd ever been, and she wanted to prove him right.

So she peeled her face off his side and looked around them. They were in a much calmer sea now. The water above their head was so close she could almost touch it. The sun shone brightly with a blue sky that was so vivid it turned the water around them into a sapphire pool.

Another pod was in front of them. Or what remained of one. This one looked mobile. It had clearly once been intended to send out into the depths of the water, perhaps to anchor itself somewhere as a home. But it had gotten stuck on this shoal. Half of the pod was out of the water, half of it in the water. Tipped onto its side like this, she could only imagine half of it was even useable.

But somewhere in that wreckage was her sister. Somewhere, Laura waited for her.

Squeezing his shoulders, she asked, "Can you come with me?"

"Your sister has not reacted well to my kind, apparently." Maketes held her out away from him, the breathing tentacle loose between them. "I think it would be best to not scare her any more than she already has been. And there's... other surprises, as well."

"Other surprises?"

He shrugged. "Fortis and his son work in mysterious ways. The depthstriders see more than any of us."

"That's not an answer to my question."

The soft smile on his face was the only response she would get, apparently. "It's not a bad surprise, Ace. Just go inside and see your sister. You'll feel better."

She wasn't so sure about that, but if her only option was to go inside and face the music, then... well, she supposed she had to do just that.

Sighing, she detached from the breathing tentacle and nodded.

She could do this. It wasn't the end of the world, even if her sister didn't want to see her. She had faced a shark, rode a whale, weathered storms above the sea, and even fought against Tau. She'd survived cannibals! She could survive her own sister's disdain, if that's what it came to.

There was a small opening in the bottom of the pod, likely what had once been a moon pool. She slipped through that opening and pulled herself into the pod.

The interior was eerily similar to the one Mira and Anya lived in. Even with the podium in the back, now at a severe angle, where a bed had once been. Now the mattress had slid off the frame and a broken pot with dirt smeared across the floor was beside it.

The first thing she noticed, however, was the sound of voices. Not just one voice. Not just her sister talking to herself, but a man's voice. Listening intently, she realized there were at least two men and then... another woman? Not her sister.

"Hello?" she called out. "Anyone home?"

The voices stopped, and then a man stuck his head through the opening to the next room. He had tousled brown hair, a mousy face, and freckles dusted across his nose. Glasses perched in front of his eyes, very similar to her own, although his magnified his eyes considerably.

"Hello?" he replied, although it sounded more like a question. "Who are you?"

"Ace."

"We weren't expecting any... humans."

"Well, the undine thought maybe you'd been terrified enough for one day." Standing on the slanted floor, she shook herself free from water and reached out a hand. "Nice to meet you. I'll be honest, I thought I was only going to see my sister in here."

"Your sister?" His mouth dropped open before he took a step back from her. "Are you... Are you Laura's sister?"

Oh shit. "Yes."

"The criminal?"

There it was. Sighing, she rolled her gaze up to the ceiling before sighing. "Yes, the criminal."

The sound he made was a cross between a squeak and a gasp before he darted out of sight. So that's how this was going to go. Somehow, Fortis and his son had brought a whole gaggle of humans to this place, and that was going to make all of this harder for her. The bastards.

She froze at the sound of running. Was she going to have to jump back into the water? Were they going to attack her?

But all she saw was the faint blur of a familiar form and an amazon running toward her. Without hesitation, Laura flung herself into Ace's arms. They both staggered backward until Ace's back hit the wall and still, her sister hugged her so hard she couldn't breathe. Ace had a moment of stunned shock. Was her sister really hugging her? Was this actually Laura?

Then the smell hit her. Basil and herbs, the scent of loam that always clung to Laura no matter where she was. Green things and pottery. All the scents that had always made her think of her sister, even after the years it had been since they'd seen each other.

Squeezing her eyes shut, she finally hugged her sister back. Years of sacrifice. Years of pain. Years of torment and fear and sleepless nights. They all flowed away as her sister held her and she held her sister back.

"It's you," Laura whispered. "I never gave up hope. I knew you'd come back."

Tears burned in her eyes and then fell. But this time, they weren't sad tears. They weren't tears that were born of frustration and anger. They were happy tears.

Finally, everything that she had done mattered.

Squeezing Laura even harder, she then leaned back so she could look at her sister for the first time in years.

"Look at you," Ace whispered, running her fingers underneath Laura's eyes. "You have wrinkles now."

"You should talk. You look even more like a criminal than the first day you left."

"I can tell you aren't sleeping enough. You've got dark circles under your eyes."

Laura laughed. "So do you."

She wasn't taking care of herself, but Ace was here now. Ace would take care of her, just like she always had.

"Come here," she whispered, tugging her back into her arms.

All was right in the world. All of it.

"I'm not as brave as you," Laura murmured. "The undine are terrifying. They brought us here, and I was certain it was because of everything we'd been doing. But I remembered that you always were different. So no matter what the others said, I held out hope."

"The undine are the reason we are together." Ace made eye contact with the second man and woman that also joined them. The two looked like brother and sister, with dark hair and dark eyes that had seen too much. "They are the ones who listened. They are the ones who fought for us. And now, I will do everything I can to fight for them as well."

The other humans looked at each other in doubt, but Laura pulled back and grinned. "Look at you, always breaking the mold."

Ace shook her head, trying to clear it of all the questions that were there. "What do you mean you thought the undine were taking you because of what you were doing? You're a gardener?"

Laura's expression turned sheepish. Her sister held out her hand

and then drew Ace into the other room. There were countless droids that had come with them, apparently. Ones that fit in pockets, ones that were similar to Byte. Even a few gliders that were currently out of the water and being worked on. The room smelled musky and metallic, just as her old workroom had. For a moment, Ace was right back there.

Working in the droid depot with her shitty boss, but her fantastic coworkers. The two siblings she almost recognized. They must have worked there as well when she was in the depot, just not in her department. And the other man…

"You used to program droids," she muttered, then shook her head. "Laura what—"

"You were right," Laura interrupted. "Beta was corrupt from the top down. There were too many rich people and not enough shared wealth. After they locked you up, there were a lot of folks who felt just like I did. We all got together and realized this was far too important to ignore. We had to keep going. We had to keep doing what you were doing. Steal from those who wouldn't even notice the loss of money, and then redistribute that wealth where it needed to go."

Ace could hardly keep up with what her sister was saying. "You were always too afraid to leave the garden because the plants might die."

"They did." Laura's expression hardened. "And everyone who killed them suffered."

Where had her baby sister gone? In her place was a woman who had seen the problems in her own city and she had taken every step to fix them. Whereas Ace had just wanted to see if she could do it, Laura had done so much more than that.

Stunned, she looked between all the people before her and coughed out a little laugh. "Well, aren't you all the bravest people I've ever met?"

Laura shook her head and then gestured for Ace to sit down at a table next to the glass. "Tell me everything. I want to know what happened in Gamma. Why are the undine working with you? How did you start working with the undine at all?"

She sat and blurted everything out. All the hardship, all the terrors. She kept her relationship with Maketes at a minimum, but it was rather hard to do because halfway through her storytelling, he appeared behind her. The glass was the only thing that separated them, and though she could see her sister and her friends get nervous, they relaxed once they realized he wasn't going to bust through the glass.

She ended the story by putting her hand against the glass where Maketes was. "The undine are a beautiful people. They are more similar to us than I ever gave them credit for."

Laura grinned. "I know. We saw your message."

"What message?"

The man with glasses shoved them up the bridge of his nose and said, "The one you sent to all the cities. It was broadcasted in here as well."

"I know that was you," Laura added, her eyes glittering with pride. "No one else would be so ballsy as to take on a city like Tau through a droid."

"How do you know I used a droid to do it?" she asked.

The woman behind Laura turned a screen for her to look at. And there, still hovering on the screen, was the last image of the video she'd put together. But it wasn't the gory picture of a dead undine who looked far too similar to a human. No, it was a picture of her.

No one would know that it was Ace. It was a photograph of her standing in front of the circular window of her clock tower in Gamma, her back to Tera as she was silhouetted by the neon lights in the sea.

And then there were the words that broke her heart in two.

Human compassion is the greatest power you can wield.

Use it.

"Tera," she whispered, pressing her hand against her mouth as tears welled in her eyes again. "That droid was one of the best."

"And you made that droid," Laura said, sinking on her knees in front of her. She held their hands together, squeezing Ace's fingers tightly in her own. "Now we're here to ask you to build a lot more with us. Droids that can watch all the people who said they were going to do the right things, and then didn't. We're here to help, Ace. Just tell us what to do."

She looked over her shoulder at Maketes, a plan already forming in her mind. "Are you willing to do anything?"

"Yes."

The other three echoed the word.

So Ace grinned at Maketes and said, "Do we have room for them?"

Maketes rolled his eyes, but then nodded and tapped his ear.

"Right," she turned to the others. "How would you like a new home? And a translation upgrade, so you can understand the undines?"

Chapter 40

Maketes set the final stone on top of the tall pillar he had helped create. It wasn't a massive pillar, not like he'd seen for the markers of his own people's deaths. But it was still visible from very far away. Each individual stone was stacked with a memory, starting with the strongest memories at the base with the widest stones.

Tall pillars surrounded it, along with short stacks that had already been tilted by the waves. For his people, they were allowed to mourn as long as the stones still stood. The sea was gentle with the stones of those who needed more time to heal. But once the waves and the currents tipped the rocks over, it was time to move on.

As they placed each stone, they spoke aloud a memory of the droid who had given its life to ensure that they all lived. Tera had succeeded. Every city that was still standing had seen the message that Ace had sent. Even Tau, most likely. He couldn't imagine there was much of an uprising in that city, but he wouldn't be surprised if a few people had been uncomfortable facing the truth of what they were doing.

Ace floated next to him, her hand on his shoulder as she kicked to keep herself in place. Drawing her in close, he pressed her against his hearts and listened to the soft sounds of her sadness.

They'd forgone the tentacle this time. Instead, she wore a rebreather from Mira so that she could swim on her own and sob in her grief. At least she could feel her emotions more clearly now without his breath forcing her body into confusion. At least, that's what both Anya and Mira had said.

They wore their own rebreathers as well. Both of them holding onto their own mates. Sadness tainted the surrounding waters, turning the sea blue with a bitter taste that coated his gills.

"They were unlike any droid I ever built," Ace said quietly, staring at the pile of stones.

He could taste her tears in the water, and hated that there was nothing he could do. Not right now. Not when she had lost her friend and there was no way for them to get it back.

Her sister was not here, neither were the other humans. But those four still didn't like being in the water. Especially not with so many People of Water around them now that there were even more joining their pod. He wasn't sure what Arges was doing to get so many of their kind here, but he had a feeling it was just their people's natural curiosity.

Even Fortis's son had been hanging around far more than normal. He'd caught the young man's gaze on Ace's sister more times than he could count.

His mate breathed out a long sigh. "Thank you all for coming. You don't have to stay any longer."

Shaking his head, he drew Ace even tighter and squeezed her hard. "We can stay as long as you'd like."

The others came quickly to their sides, the women pushed by their mates through the water so they each could hug Ace. He noticed the differences in the way they did so. Anya came first, shoving Mira out of the way to scoop Ace up in her arms. There was so much love squeezed into her with that movement. Mira waited her turn, and then gently took Ace into her arms. She hugged her as though she was lifting her up into her arms, scooping her like one would someone who had just broken.

Both were individual in the way they handled things. And while Anya and Mira might not get along with each other, they both enjoyed Ace's company.

His mate was a woman who could be with quite literally anyone. She fit in with every crowd. Those who were rougher around the edges, and those who were kind and quiet.

He was never not impressed with Ace. But right now, he knew his job. And that was to distract her.

The others left a cloud of sand dust in their wake as they disappeared back to the rest of the pod. Maketes squeezed Ace a little tighter. "Are you ready to go?"

She nodded a few times, staring at the small pile of stones one last time. With a darting movement of his tail, he launched them away from that sad place. The stones would remain. She would mourn for as long as the sea saw fit, but for now, he wanted to make sure that she saw life the way she deserved.

He had just the perfect idea for it.

Zipping through the water, he took hours just swimming with her. Letting her mind wander and her heart settle. It had been nearly two weeks since they'd first say goodbye to Tera, but he knew how it plagued her.

That droid was part of her soul. Now, he needed to fill her soul with more than just that memory.

Maketes had spent these past two weeks trying to find the perfect spot for this moment. After searching, he'd spent hours each day praying to the sea goddess for a clear day when they built the stones for the droid. The gods had heard him, and already he'd checked to make sure that this place would remain full of sun and bright sky. There were no storms even close to them today, which meant he could thoroughly indulge her in all the things that he'd prepared.

Circling back to the area, which was much closer to their pod than she would likely realize, he drew her up to the surface.

"What are we doing?" she asked, her voice a little warped by the rebreather.

He helped her keep her head above water and slowly pulled her rebreather off himself. "Look behind you, kefi. I thought, if anyone deserved a day for yourself, it was you."

She turned and he could see the shock in her gaze. He'd been shocked to see it, too.

Even the People of Water had thought the sea had taken back all the sand it had once deposited on the land to soften its crashing waves. But this tiny cove had weathered every storm and still had much of the white sand that sparkled in the sunlight. He wasn't sure if it had merely been shoved here by the last storm, but they were safe for now. It was surrounded by impressive white cliffs, sheared and softened by the crashing hurricanes that had occurred for centuries now.

It was beautiful. It was ragged and raw. There were no trees at the tops of those cliffs, nothing green in the slightest. But this white sand cove sparkled like the prettiest of gems he could have gifted her.

He now knew that gifts for his kefi did not come in the form of physical objects. She preferred memories. Time spent with him that she would never forget. Those were the greatest gifts he could give her.

"Oh my god," she whispered, swimming toward the shore and then pausing when her feet hit the ground.

He'd brought her to an island before. She'd been on the dock as well. But he knew that this was the first time his achromo was stepping foot on land. Real land that was solid and firm beneath her feet so she could exist where her people had once conquered.

She walked out of the waves and for a moment, he saw her as the goddess he'd always compared her to. White wave caps lapped at her thighs, breaking and cresting and crashing against her sides. Then she was walking straight out of the sea and onto the sand.

A small bubble of laughter escaped her as she fell onto her knees, knocked by a particularly large wave that then picked her up and carried her all the way onto the beach. He joined her, allowing the sea to toss him out of the water as well. Even if it would be difficult to get back in, he wanted to see this joy on her face.

Her hands dug into the sand, taking fistfuls of it and tossing it back down with wet plops. She kept murmuring little sounds of shock.

"Sand," she whispered. "Just like in the books they gave us."

"You have seen this before?"

"Only in pictures. We were told there weren't any beaches left. That the storms had taken those until there was only rough rock. But to see this now..." Her hands sank into it again, and then she looked up at him in that way that always made him feel like a god himself. "Thank you."

"You don't have to thank me for bringing you here."

"I do."

She crawled toward him, and all he could focus on was the

seductive sway of her hips. The way she crawled made all those curves stand out even more, so pretty, so tempting, so much that he could not have right now, because she was supposed to be in mourning.

Yet, he was a weak man. He allowed her to push him onto his back, and remained right where he was, without complaint, as she straddled him. Those tiny hands braced her up on his chest.

Her dark eyes were filled with something he hadn't hoped to see, though. A softness. A relaxation. She had let go of the guilt and the mourning for a few moments to look at him lying beneath her on a rare beach.

"You look so pretty in the sunlight," she murmured, tracing her fingers over the peaks of his cheekbones. "Your scales are always yellow, but in the sunlight they're almost blinding."

"I don't want to blind you."

"You always do. No matter where you are, even in the darkest parts of the sea, you blind me."

The words filled him with more love and hope than he believed she could imagine. He filled his lungs with the emotions, as though he was sucking up every single ounce of attention she gave him and drawing it into his body so that he would never forget the feeling.

His hands found the spots just above her hips. It was like those curves called to him, compelling him to hold on to her and never let her go. "I am lucky to have found you," he murmured. "Truly."

"Oh, I think we found each other."

She leaned down and kissed him, those lips gentle and toying as she played with him. He loved her most when she was like this. Not worried about what might come, and no lingering thoughts of the outside world plaguing either of them.

It was just him and her.

His mate. His love. His joy.

The sun seemed to turn even brighter as they indulged themselves. He relearned the softness of her lips, the way she made little soft sighs when he rasped his nails down her back. Everything about her turned him into a puddle because he just wanted her. Only her. There had never been another who made him feel like this.

Then she leaned back out of his reach. A little whimper escaped him before he could catch it, but he hated to lose her, even if he was panting with need at this point. He could keep himself away from her, though. He had enough self control to let her do whatever she wanted.

Her grief was more important than his desire, that much he was certain.

Until she pulled her shirt over her head and suddenly he was greeted with an even better sight. He took in a long, deep breath, telling himself that perhaps she was only overheated with the sun at her back. If she wanted to stretch out over his cool scales, so that her breasts were flattened against his chest, he could still hold himself together. Even when she propped her head on her hands and looked at him with that gaze that he knew meant she was hungry for him.

He would let her set the pace. This wasn't the time to be thinking with anything other than the brain he had in his skull.

But when she was looking at him like that, it was hard to think of anything but that grin on her face. "I don't want to push you," he said.

"You're not pushing me." She spread herself a little closer, rubbing against him in a way that was almost impossible to ignore. "I'm asking."

"Ace—"

"Maketes. I know this might seem like the wrong time to be asking you to do this, but I know what I want." Her gaze turned a little serious, her tone sharper than before. "I understand your hesitation.

I really do. But right now, I just want to forget everything. I want to forget the world, what happened, and even that we're here. I just want it to be you and me, together. Can we do that?"

A distraction. Of course that's what she wanted.

He wasn't sure it was the smartest thing to do, considering the circumstances. She likely needed to sit in her feelings for a little while longer, but... he'd never been very good at denying her anything.

Nodding, he palmed the softness of her thighs and jerked her even higher up his body.

The sun framed her face, turning some strands of her hair to liquid gold. But it was her eyes that he stared into the most, the eyes that he so adored. It was difficult for her to even ask this of him, he knew. She didn't want him to think less of her for distracting herself.

He drew her down until her forehead was pressed against his. The webs of his fingers smoothed through her hair, holding her tightly where he wanted her to be.

"Ah, kefi," he breathed. "You never have to ask me for anything twice."

He drew her to him with soft hands and quiet sounds. When she wanted him to roll her beneath him, he didn't. He merely turned her to face the sun and ran his hands over her in that way. It was important that even while he pleasured her and drew out those sounds that always made him hard, that she still look at the world around her.

Because this was only a moment in time. A memory for her to come back to when the world was dark and the rains wouldn't stop. He wanted her to always remember the pleasure they brought each other on a white sand beach where the sun was still overhead.

Even as he could hear the storms in the distance. Even as the world felt like it could tumble down around their ears at any point.

He wanted her to know that they had loved each other in the stillness of peace. And oh, they loved each other well.

Epilogue

They'd received a message. The logo on the sealed message that Byte had been transmitted was just a giant "T".

Mira had her fist pressed to her lips, a scowl wrinkling her brow as she stared at the projection on the wall. "It's a trap," she said. "The moment we open that, they'll know where we are."

"Why would they have sent a message?" Anya asked. "That doesn't make any sense at all. If they knew how to get in touch with Byte, then they already know how to track us."

That was a sobering thought.

"If I may?" Ace asked as she walked up to Byte.

The little droid was always so kind, even when she was asking to open him up from the back. But Maketes had found a tablet to give her, one that would allow her to access the coding more easily. She had a feeling "found" meant that he'd stolen it from somewhere, but who was she to ask? She'd stolen plenty in her life.

But he'd also returned with an entire case of items for her sister and the other three humans, who now had their own section of the pod where they all lived. He had been more than kind in providing for all of them. Just as she expected, choosing to stay with him had been the best choice she'd ever made.

Plugging into the back of Byte's unit, she scanned through the coding to see if there was a location that it was tracking. But there wasn't one.

"Huh," she muttered, furrowing her brow as she looked through the long scrolling nonsense of code. "That's strange."

"What's strange?" Mira asked.

"The code doesn't have a location, but it looks like..." She glanced over at Anya. "Hey Bitsy, come here for a second."

The droid hopped off Anya's head and let Ace plug into her back. And there it was. The same code. It was just that Bitsy's unit didn't have a projection capability, so the droid likely didn't know what to do with it. She could have put the transmission on Anya's glass, but that wasn't really the function of the droid.

"It's in both droids," she muttered.

Ace leapt into movement. She raced for her sister's room with all the droids they had saved, bursting through the door just as her sister was already standing. "Maura," Laura was already saying.

"Don't open the message."

"We weren't planning to."

The small glider droid in Laura's hands already had the back of it open, connected to a very similar tablet by a handful of wires. "Every single one of them has the same message, though."

"Yeah, I was worried about that." She slumped against the wall. "This is bad."

Her mind raced, trying to figure out what it could even mean. Tau hadn't sent the message to them directly. They had sent it to every single droid that was operational. That, somehow, was even worse.

Mira cleared her throat from outside of the room. "Want to fill us in, Ace?"

"Right." She dragged a hand down her face. "Tau sent that message to every functional droid in the region, which means they have some kind of technology that tracks every droid that's been made. Which is... insane to even consider. I hesitate to open the message. Whatever droid opens it is going to be completely under Tau's control, is my guess. That will override any function that any droid has. I wouldn't... I don't know if I would open it."

Because part of her wanted to know what the city had to say. Clearly, they knew that the undine had humans working with them.

"What if another person opens the message in the cities?" Anya asked, her face screwed up in confusion. "They won't know who we are if they're having people opening it everywhere."

The young man with the glasses—whose name was Eddie—muttered, "They don't care about other people."

"What?" Ace asked.

"They know that people are going to open it in the other two cities. They don't have to look at those pings, and likely already moved them out of the pool of locations they're looking at. As far as we know, and they know, we're the only ones who would have access to opening it who don't live in a city." He gulped. "It's all laid out for them."

"Shit," Ace muttered. "Call the undine in. We need to talk to them."

Anya had already turned, but then called out, "Already here!"

Of course they were. The longer she was with Maketes, the more it felt like he knew she was nervous before she even realized she was. Darting toward the moon pool, she practically ran into the room where the undine were waiting for them.

It was just Maketes at least, which made it easier to blurt out the words. "We got a message from Tau, but I don't think it's safe to open here."

Bless the man she'd chosen, he didn't even question her. "Okay. Where do you want us to open it?"

"You think we should open it?"

He hesitated. "I think they sent us a message for a reason, and we all deserve to know what it is. What do you think?"

"I think it's a trap." She glanced over at Mira, who looked far paler than her skin usually was. The freckles dusting her nose stood out in stark relief as the engineer gulped.

"I agree," Mira replied. "I think it's a trap. I think they're going to send every bit of weaponry they have the moment that message is opened. Our own curiosity could be the death of us."

That was all she could think, too.

But then a second head popped up through the water. This one larger. So much larger. The massive purple undine stretched up through the water, his hand landing on the floor as he pulled himself a little higher through the water.

She'd known Fortis was big. She'd seen him in the water plenty of times, and even talked with him just in casual conversation. So Ace had believed she was comfortable with the big guy until this moment.

He was massive out of the water. His hand was the size of her head, and for a second, she didn't feel like she was safe.

"Fortis," she said with a soft sound at the end of the word. Damn it, she needed to get ahold of herself. Clearing her throat, she tried again. "Do you know what's going on?"

He reached out that massive hand and hovered it palm up before her face. "Give me a droid. I will open it somewhere safe."

"I don't know that there is somewhere safe."

He grinned, the flashing of those sharp-edged teeth enough to send terror skittering throughout her body. "It has been a long time since I've been invited to a hunt, little achromo. Give me the droid. Tau has been my destiny for many years."

She handed him the glider and then pointed to the side. "That button. Hit that and the message will play. You'll need a solid surface to project the message onto."

"I care little for the message," Fortis said, his eyes already swirling with those terrible colors.

He sank beneath the water and Maketes made a strangely high-pitched noise, almost like a whistle. "That big beast scares me."

"Is he going to be okay?"

"If anyone could manage Tau's warriors, it's him." He met her gaze with those pitch black eyes that reflected her terrified expression. "He's killed more than all of us combined. Fortis is unbeatable."

"We'll see," Mira muttered. "I have a feeling he's about to be tested."

426

Follow me on socials or Amazon to keep your eye out for the next book!

427

Acknowledgements

No book is the same without all the people who help work on it. From my beta team, to my editors, to my dear friends who worked with me through every nonsense question - I adore you.

About the Author

Emma Hamm is a small town girl on a blueberry field in Maine. She writes stories that remind her of home, of fairytales, and of myths and legends that make her mind wander.

She can be found by the fireplace with a cup of tea and her two Maine Coon cats dipping their paws into the water without her knowing.

For more updates, join my newsletter!

www.emmahamm.com

www.ingramcontent.com/pod-product-compliance
Lightning Source LLC
Chambersburg PA
CBHW031627310726
48974CB00003B/852